Butter and Whiskey:
The Ballad of Maggie Doyle

A novel by Judith S Glover

© 2021 by Judith S Glover

Excerpts from "The Lady of Shalott"
by Alfred, Lord Tennyson. (1832).

All characters and events in this publication, other than those in the public domain, are fictitious and any resemblance to real persons, living or deceased, is purely coincidental.

Cover design Judith S Glover

For Claire.

What Butter and Whiskey cannot cure, there is no cure for.
(An Old Irish saying).

Prelude

Another rainy Monday morning. Maggie Doyle is sorting the weekly wash. She examines the yellowed tide marks and grimy cuffs of her husband's work shirt and wrinkles her freckled nose in vexation. *Is this truly what her life has come to?* She spies a greasy stain on the shirt-front and sighs. *Out damned spot!* Reaching for the stain-remover soap that she bought on offer in the supermarket, she lathers up her little scrubbing-brush and attacks the stubborn mark with grim determination. *Eliminates everyday stains,* the packet had said. "Well, we'll soon see about that," mutters Maggie out loud. Yet, even as she scrubs, her mind wanders to bigger questions.

The Lamb of God washes away our sins, Father John had said, yet can we truly start afresh, free from stain, free from sin? Will all the water in the Liffey suffice to wash away the stain of the fruit from the Tree of The Knowledge of Good and Evil?

Maggie Doyle worries about these things; worries that the little brush will wear away the very fabric of the shirt, like the nun who washes raw her sinful flesh, in order to be pure. Clothes wear thin and so do souls, frayed ragged by the grind of daily life and the weekly bleaching of purification. How can the soul that is constantly cleansed be whole and vital? Wash with care, says the label. *That's about right,* thinks Maggie as she sets the brush to one side and bundles the shirt into her top loader.

In the afternoon, Mrs Kelly drops by for tea. She speaks of Mrs Murphy's influenza and the price of shin of lamb at O'Rourke's this week. Maggie's attention flutters away and hovers somewhere just behind the netted curtains of the parlour windows. Mrs Kelly feels the slight. She clinks the silver teaspoon impatiently against the delicate rosebuds on Maggie's best porcelain teacup, but Maggie's errant thoughts are not so easily called to heel.

Mrs Kelly's eyes follow Maggie's gaze into the street outside. Over the road at number thirty-four, Father John is making his parish rounds, stepping courteously around the edge of the neatly mown lawn and up the gravel drive to the front door. No crossed corners for the Holy Roman Church. Even without her glasses, Maggie's vision is still sharp enough to make out the greying temples and handsome features of his face.

He raps the door-knocker and steps back with patient anticipation but the occupant seems in no hurry to answer the door. He shifts from one foot to the other, then he turns to look across the road towards her own house. Maggie's heart all but stops a moment. She flushes and plucks unconsciously at the crucifix around her neck, but now old Ma McGinty is opening the door, pulling her crocheted shawl around her to keep out the cold. He turns back, then nods and steps inside. Maggie can breathe again. Mrs Kelly makes a small coughing noise. Aware, all at once, of the other woman's gaze upon her, Maggie suffers the mortification of blood rising to her cheeks. "Sure, but we're all going to burn in Hell over that one," says Mrs Kelly in a low voice.

Maggie Doyle is all aquiver. It has been seven years since Mr Doyle last laid his hands upon her, and even longer since she had felt anything like the itch of even the most pedestrian desire for his pallid body. Every night they sleep like strangers in their barren marital bed, conjugal duty abandoned, the scornful reproach of her empty womb as effective an inhibitor to her husband's feeble libido, as any bromide. But here, right now, in the Catholic Women's Union meeting in the draughty parish hall, she is all on fire, and fire such as no demon in Hell could contrive for her torment. Maggie swallows and gasps for breath when Father

John's fingers brush against her own, as he helps himself to tea and ginger snaps. *She is wicked, shameful, wanton,* she tells herself and digs her fingernails into her palm in penitence. But she wants him all the same, and the conviction of her contrition is as empty as the church's poor box.

Father John can hardly be immune to such passion and feels the spark. He has a gentle way with him, with that wistful smile and deep blue eyes that penetrate a woman's very soul. Brought up on the Beatles and sixties' liberalism, he is a modern Catholic - all love and no condemnation. He sees how the flowers of a woman's middle years blossom unappreciated, like lilies growing by the side of a busy highway. It cannot but touch his heart. He has so much love to give, and Mrs Doyle wants so much to take it. *If God is love, then how can love be sin?*

Sheltered in the rosy bower of the faded bedroom wallpaper, Maggie holds her holy lover between her legs and groans. Yet even as she approaches the climax of her ecstasy, her mind is on the sinful sheets that she will have to wash anew, though there are still another five days till washing day. Every Wednesday afternoon, when he has dressed and gone, and the bed is cold, she cannot help but shed a tear of grief. It never fails to break her heart to see the stains of wasted life that mar the white perfection of her immaculately laundered linen. Maggie wants to be filled with love. She wants a child. His child. It is not too late. So, this afternoon, when he groans then starts to pull away from her, she clasps him all the more closely to her arching body and he cannot break free.

Three Mondays later, Maggie Doyle sorts through the weekly wash with a secret smile. She dreams of matinee coats and bibs with yellow ducks. There are some things that cannot be washed away and lost. Things that grow and thrive inside, long after the moment of passion is over. Maggie knew long before she missed the familiar bloody stain upon her sensible Marks and Spencer's cotton briefs, knew, that her prayers had been answered.

Father John does not visit anymore. Angry over the seed she stole from him and frightened for his reputation and career, he keeps his profile low and faces God and Father O'Brien's wrath in the confessional one Friday morning just before Pentecost. His desertion had stung her deeply at first, but Maggie, seated beside her frigid husband in the wooden pew on Sunday morning, is a study in impassivity. She does not need him now. "The wages of Sin," Father O'Brien reminds the congregation, "are death". Yet, *she* knows that the wages of love are life, new, miraculous life. She feels it throbbing through her veins and surging throughout her organs like aqua vitae. Her soul is whole and bright. No more will she run it thin through the mangle of repentance. She gazes into the Blessed Virgin Mother's face and for the first time in her life, understands the secret rapture in those lowered eyes.

For six months Declan Doyle wears his cuckold's horns with sullen rage. *Those whom God has joined together, let no man put asunder.* But God had the sense never to get himself married. He bites his lip and eats his joyless dinner as usual, yet his eyes follow his wife with stifled loathing. Maggie rises above it on her cloud of bliss, yet his hatred seeps out, filling up the house; a subtle poison that makes her unborn child stiffen and writhe inside her. When Maggie starts to show, vows or no vows, he can take no more. He packs his bag and calls a taxi. Then clutching a bottle of whiskey, he heads home to Mammy, cowering on the back seat of the cab to avoid the gossiping eyes.

Father John can't look at Maggie Doyle. Can't bear to see the fruit of his loins as it swells and burgeons inside the softness of that body, which had so recently been his exclusive domain. He busies himself with parish business and avoids her whenever he ventures out to tender to the needs of his sick and ailing flock. But it is Father John who is sick at heart and sick of soul, and even as his former lover blooms, his handsome looks and manly graces seem to fade, like tall grasses in the summer's drought.

On Friday 13th, at ten-fifteen in the damp October morning and six whole weeks before her time, Maggie's waters break. She packs an overnight bag. Her turn now to call a taxi. The back seat of the shabby Ford Escort reeks of curry, beer and stale tobacco. Struggling not to gag, she doubles up in a sudden spasm of agony. The waves of pain from her first contractions crash down upon her, like the Red Sea upon the Pharaoh's men. She fixes her eyes on the Saint Christopher's medallion which dangles from the rear-view mirror. She prays that the kindly man who bore the little Lord to safety so long ago will bear *her unborn* child to safety now.

Arriving, at last, at St Jude's Hospital for Women, she hobbles down the echoing corridor to the maternity suite, alone and for the first time, afraid. It is too soon, far too soon, but the child is coming now and nothing can stop it.

The labour room is sanitized of germs and comfort, save for a wooden crucifix hanging on the wall. Maggie pants and moans, and calls upon Our Lady to deliver her, but the Virgin has closed her ears and closed her heart. *Perhaps the wages of sin are Hell, after all,* ponders Maggie wretchedly, as lost in her own private Purgatory, she strains and burns.

At last, just as she fears she must surely die, the infant tears free of her sullied flesh, pure and new, and ready to scream. Maggie falls back upon the sweat-soaked pillows. She smiles and sighs then holds out her waiting arms. But the midwife and the doctor hesitate, huddling together around the child and whispering in hushed voices.

"My child, my darling babby," pleads Maggie, arms still outstretched. The midwife turns, exchanges an anxious glance with her colleague, then places the hopelessly tiny infant on his mother's breast. Maggie stares into his unfocused eyes then holds him aloft for inspection, half with fear and half with admiration. From his back protrudes a pair of tiny wings, perfectly formed and covered in the purest white down.

"It's a miracle," gasps Maggie Doyle, clutching him to her swelling heart, "God has granted me a miracle!"

"Abomination!" cries Father O'Brien and almost flings himself out of the pulpit with the force of his rancour, the following Sunday. Tongues, even the most Christian, will wag and by this time the news has reached all but the most isolated hermit in the tiny town of Ennisgowan. Filled with zealous piety, he spits out Hellfire and Damnation upon his trembling congregation and shakes his fist in the face of Satan. He will be damned himself before he sees such a creature baptized. Such an affront to decency and Our Lady's Holy Church. It simply shall not be countenanced.

Father John sits cowed within the chancel, beset by demons of his own. He prays to the Virgin Mother for guidance, but his path has never seemed so unclear. *If the Father Almighty, in His wisdom, can forgive him because he makes his confession, then how can He see outcast for all eternity, his little son?* "The sins of the fathers are visited upon the children!" roars Father O'Brien, as if in answer to his thoughts. *But how can a father obey his duty to his church by forsaking the soul of his child,* wonders Father John. And, in the end, it is John Lennon's words, which lighten his darkness: "All You Need is Love."

Word travels far and fast. Outside the hospital, in defiance of the ugliness of such unfettered hatred, a small but growing throng of parishioners gather together in the evening drizzle to hold a candlelight vigil for the infant angel within. Maggie cannot see them, but she hears their hymns of faith and hope and for a moment at least, her spirits soar on the wings of their song.

But her hope cannot be sustained. Another Monday morning dawns. Back in the maternity ward, Maggie Doyle's child lies struggling for its very life, the weight of mortal flesh all too onerous a burden for so delicate a soul. The doctors, recognizing only near unviable prematurity and congenital defect, can offer no hope for salvation in medical intervention. It had been tacitly agreed; they must let nature take its course. He is in God's hands now.

A thousand miles away, the Roman dawn steals stealthily across St. Peters Square and in through the leaded windows of the Vatican. High up among the stucco rafters of the great hall, Michelangelo's Adam exchanges glances with his creator once again, as the miracle of the new day unfolds.

In a gloomy side office, the ageing pontiff and his advisors have been deep in discussion since the early hours of the morning. The rosy finger of light that reaches around the corner of the curtains and prods them gently on the shoulders reminds them that time is marching forward. The weary pontiff sighs and buries his face in his ancient hands. A storm is brewing and the Holy Church must move quickly and surely. *How could a miracle spring forth out of sin; good proceed from evil? Yet, Christ himself consorted with the harlot Magdalene and made saints out of tax collectors. By his works shall ye know him.* The world seems so complicated now, and his flock so desperate to seek a sign. The Holy Father looks up and meets the eye of his special advisor, who bends to whisper in the papal ear. "We must use this child, one way or another," hisses Cardinal Salvatore. One thing is for sure; *they must lose no time in viewing this infant and making a full and thorough assessment.*

In the early hours of the next day, in her lonely side room, an anguished Maggie lays her fading infant in the cot beside her bed. Another feeble feed. She would drain the last drop of life-blood from her very arteries if that is what it would take to sustain him, but all she can do is sit in helpless watch. Time drags by. She tries to read a magazine, but she cannot wrest her attention from her sleeping child. How peaceful he seems. How blissfully unaware of the mortal danger that lies in wait to prey upon his little soul.

At eight o'clock, as Maggie pushes away an untouched breakfast tray, Father John appears, as if in answer to her most desperate prayer. He wears his cassock, but as soon as he is done, he will discard his priestly garb forever and take the next boat to the mainland. Finding only hate and fear where he had hoped to find love, he has cast himself adrift in a sea of doubt. But first, he has one last priestly office to perform. No words are exchanged, as Father John takes out the precious flask of holy water from his cassock pocket and anoints the diminutive head of his child. *In Nomine Patris et Filii et Spiritus Sancti.* His eyes are lit by tenderness as the infant wakens, stretches wide its perfect wings, and smiles. For all that he had hardened his heart, Father John cannot but feel it soften and swell within his breast. "We must call him Gabriel," he says, squeezing Maggie's hand, "Our little angel".

At peace, at last, Maggie Doyle slips gratefully into sleep, her anxious face smooth and young again in repose. Father John watches over mother and child for a moment, then dropping a kiss upon her brow with a "God Bless you, Margaret," takes leave from Ennisgowan forever.

Late in the afternoon, Cardinal Salvatore, straight off the earliest Rome-to-Dublin flight, arrives at the hospital and wastes no time in idle conversation. "Get him out of here!", screams Maggie, as he descends upon her infant, with all the dark menace of the Spanish Inquisition. And the doctor is obliged to prescribe sedation before she is herself again. But fear is set bone-deep in Maggie Doyle's Catholic being and to stand against the Holy Roman Father, friendless and alone, demands more courage than she can muster.

By early evening she concedes to the inspection, on condition that she remain present and that the infant is not physically touched. Cardinal Salvatore assumes his most pious smile. Maggie takes a deep breath, picks up her sleeping baby, then gently folds back his blanket to reveal the downy protrusions between his little shoulders. The Holy Father's right-hand man all but gasps. *This child could certainly pose a threat to the moral order.* He stares deep into Maggie's eyes, hoping to see a sign of Satan's touch. Maggie shudders and hastily re-wrapping her infant, holds him tightly to her as if he were already slipping out of her grasp. But the inquisition is over. For now. The Cardinal bows and leaves without a word. There is much to ponder, and supper awaits him back in the rectory with Father O'Brien. He crosses himself and makes a silent supplication. God spare him from Irish spaghetti Bolognese.

The following day, barely the sixth of his short and precious life, the little angel takes a deep sigh and expires. Maggie cradles the tiny, lifeless body in her arms and rocks, moaning softly to herself. She knows that Cardinal Salvatore is waiting, rubbing his hands. Waiting to dissect her beautiful child, to lay it out like a biology specimen and pick over his remains like a great black carrion crow. To label and name, judge and condemn. She can't let it happen. *But what can one woman do against the might of the Holy Roman Church?*

And she is right. On receiving the news, The Cardinal places a long-distance call direct to The Holy Father. The truth must be established. The myth of a *deceased* angel, the offspring of the most sinful of unions, could prove even more dangerous than the reality of a living one. Had it survived, in time, its flawed humanity would surely have betrayed its freakishness. Dead – well, there is no end to the power of such a symbol, should word of it spread. "It is imperative that we undertake the post-mortem, Your Holiness," he whispers into the receiver, "it is imperative that we take control."

Sister Angela wears a grey wimple in place of a nurse's cap and exemplifies that rare and simple faith, which is fast disappearing in this complicated world. Orderly, yet kind, she nods sympathetically when Maggie begs for one final hour more alone with her baby, her darling child. She closes the blinds on the door on the way out. Sure, if ever a soul needed privacy, it would be now.

Alone in the shadowed silence, Maggie Doyle knows what she has to do. She only prays she has the strength to do it.

When Sister Angela returns and softly opens the door the promised half-hour later, she screams and faints dead away to the whirling linoleum floor. Maggie sits, mute and unresponsive, amid the blood-soaked sheets, red-stained down sticking to her mouth and chin. Like a feral cat that eats her offspring, she has devoured her lifeless infant, blood and bone, flesh and feather.

For twelve long hours, Maggie remains cocooned within her catatonia, silent and as unmoving as the statue of the Virgin in the deserted hospital chapel. The doctors shake their heads and sigh, they must simply bide their time, but the prognosis seems bleak.

The next morning, as dawn breaks, Maggie Doyle sits suddenly upright in her bed. Staring blankly ahead of her, she swings her feet mechanically onto the floor then walks the somnambulist's walk to the sink, where she takes the bar of hospital soap and crams it into her mouth. She gags and splutters, foams and spits, and works the soap until all that remains is suds and lather. But, all the soap in the Emerald Isle will not suffice to wash away the stain of her infant's blood from her mouth or the salty tang of his flesh from her tongue.

Verse 1

October 13th 1979, Liverpool, England.

Night drapes itself over Liverpool like a great black tarpaulin. The Liver Birds on the Royal Liver Building long to tuck their great bronze necks beneath their wings but are condemned to stand watch over the restless Mersey in sleepless perpetuity.
Father Frank O'Leary sits forward in his favourite armchair, in his little terraced house near the city centre, and stares at the two empty cut-glass tumblers and half-consumed bottle of single malt on the coffee table in front of him. Yet he is hardly conscious of the glasses or even the lingering taste of the fine oak matured whiskey, for that matter. His thoughts are away up the stairs in the spare bedroom with an old friend who has taken to his bed in the wee hours of the morning, exhausted and a little the worse for wear from the amber spirit. Father Frank scratches his head, as though that will somehow make his understanding clearer.
He is having trouble believing - no, that is not quite right -coming to terms with the story that has just unfolded. Frank has known John, or Jack, as he prefers to be called these days, since his days as a novice at St Kieran's seminary. Their mutual love of boxing and the racing form had bought them together, despite the difference in ages, and in an environment where close relationships were actively discouraged, they had nevertheless forged a friendship based on an openness and loyalty that was rare amongst peers, let alone ordained priests and trainees. Perhaps Frank had seen in John the son he would never have, whilst John had seen in Frank a father-figure who might fill the gap that his natural father had left. A gap that only an alcoholic parent can leave, a gap that festers like an abscess beneath the surface, a buried source of nagging puzzlement and

chronic pain. Frank had heard that hurt in John's childhood recollections and he could see the same hurt in his eyes again, that day he had turned up on his doorstep, just under a year ago, fresh off the ferry from Dublin and intractable in his decision to leave the church.

Back then John had not been ready to give any explanations but had pleaded for sanctuary and absolute secrecy regarding his whereabouts, gambling on his trust in Father Frank and Frank's own trust in him. And Frank had not let him down. Offering him accommodation and whatever support was needed whilst he found his feet, Frank had encouraged John to build a new life. Thus, without judgement and with endless patience, John's former mentor became his mentor once again. Six months on, Father John, his clerical title long forsaken and known to all simply as Jack, had acted on his determination to try a new vocation and is currently enrolled in a one-year post-graduate diploma in teacher-training. And earlier this evening, on the anniversary of his infant son's birth, he had been ready to tell his story. The story Frank is struggling with right now.

Oh, he knows John, or rather Jack, (he *must try* to remember), has his failings, failings which at last seem to have caught up with him; But he had always been a handsome young man, whose easy charm and manner attracted women like a magnet, and surrounded by such temptation it was perhaps inevitable that he would lose the battle with that gnawing need inside of him. So, yes, he had his faults, but embellishment of the truth had never been one of them. And besides, Frank had heard the rumours, everybody had. The talk of the miraculous birth and horrific fate of an infant angel in County Clare had floated across the Irish Sea, like toxic jetsam, to wash up on the shores of Liverpool, right enough. He just had never put two and two together. Or perhaps had never wanted to.

Frank looks at his watch. Long past time to be abed. He has Mass first thing in the morning. But he holds out small hope of sleep. Jack's words resonate through his brain like echoes in the cloisters of a cathedral. Jack had asked for his forgiveness and Frank had given it, not that he felt it was truly his to bestow. Nonetheless, it had been in every real sense a confession and if Frank could forgive Jack, then perhaps God could too. Frank wonders, however, whether Jack can ever truly forgive himself, for in his shame he had taken the coward's way out and left his lover, a woman alone and friendless, to her fate. Yet in fairness, he had only learned of the terrible events that followed his leaving, once he had arrived in Liverpool and how could he ever have imagined the horror of that fate or the bizarre manner in which her sanity would unravel?

Still, what was done was done. Jack had lived in silence with the tortures of his conscience for nigh on twelve months, and perhaps that was atonement enough. Father Frank rises at last from his chair and sighs. He feels old tonight, old and weighed down by the grief of the years. He looks down at the empty glasses and whiskey bottle and scowls.

Why is it that it is always the children who must pay for the sins of their fathers?

October 1979 Hackney, London.

The rain is streaming down the square panes of the decrepit metal-grilled windows and Claire can see the trees swaying and shivering along the high road that skirts the corner of Hackney Marshes below. She watches windswept figures struggle up the hill, battling with inside-outed umbrellas, as though in a silent movie. Others hold their collars up to their ears with hunched shoulders and seem to shy away from any shelter that the high wall of the former work-house might offer, as though in unconscious aversion.

Claire wonders about the people who may have gazed out from this very spot before her and shudders despite the warmth from the great shit-brown steel radiator. She has read accounts of the despair and degradation awaiting the "undeserving poor" who entered this fortress of charity. Indeed, she would hardly be surprised if the ails that plagued its current occupants did not find their roots in the cruelly enforced separation of children from mothers, and segregation between husbands and wives, whose only crime it was, was to find themselves destitute and without the means to keep body and soul together.

Claire recalls hearing that the reputation of the Victorian institution did not fare much better when the work-house system was finally abandoned and it became a hospital. Even today the locals still referred to it as 'The Butchers' and in truth, its surgical theatres and wards are well past their sell date, not to mention the nurses' home and doctor's accommodation which leave much to be desired, to say the least. There are plans in the pipeline for a bright new shiny hospital to be erected on the other side of Homerton High Street, on the site of the former skin hospital, but it is rumoured that psychiatry, as ever the poor relative, is likely to be part of the later and final stage of redevelopment. Consequently, the mentally ill seem destined to remain marooned in one wing of the otherwise abandoned site, long after medical and surgical services have been relocated. It makes Claire wonder whether the "powers that be" have any real understanding of the plight of those afflicted by mental illness, at all. Or perhaps they just don't care.

She sighs, turns from the window casement and gathers the papers on her desk before her. Glancing anxiously at her watch she closes the swollen case file she has been studying and heads for the board room.

"So, what scintillating insights do you have to offer for our edification this afternoon, Dr Carter? Hope it won't take long we have the mental health tribunal at three o'clock, and you know what they are like regarding punctuality," simpers Professor Kent. He pinches the crease of his plaid trousers, pushes his glasses back onto the bridge of his nose then eyes Claire with a look of disdain she tries her hardest to ignore.

"Case review Sir," she pushes the file towards him, "and possible discharge planning." This phrased partly as question, partly as information.

"Margaret Doyle, Currently Informal patient. Admitted to The Central Mental Hospital in Dublin on 19th October 1978, following committal under section 207 of the Irish Mental Treatment Act, (although no charges were ever pressed). Transferred here as a voluntary patient one month later due to strong reaction in the local community, and the fact she has some family ties in the London area. So, she has been with us," (she pauses to double-check), "yes, eleven months almost to the day."

"Ah, yes," muses Kent running his fingertips along the name on the cover of the well-thumbed cardboard case file. "Interesting case, our Maggie. I rather thought about writing it up for the British Journal of Psychiatry, but as I recall, the whole idea rather terrified the good lady and she point blank refused consent." There is a faint tone of annoyance in his voice, he is not used to refusal and Claire reflects momentarily that there might be unsuspected strengths to Margaret Doyle.

"And how did this transfer come about Dr Carter? Can you tell me *that*? It is hardly standard practice is it?"

Claire panics. How could she have overlooked such an obvious peculiarity of the case? She fumbles with her notes, but there is no clue to help her. She shrugs her shoulders helplessly. Professor Kent hardly bothers to disguise a sneer.

"Anyone care to enlighten us?"

The little group of trainees exchange baffled glances then turn their eyes to the floor in unison.

Professor Kent turns to a matronly West Indian woman who is sitting quietly near the door. She wears a sister's uniform and has a no-nonsense but kindly face.

"Care to help us out, Sister Alexander?"

"Why sure t'ing, Professor Kent. We done did us a swap." (She grins) "Your old colleague Professor Cranston, who work over there in Dublin, he done take back Bridie O'Callaghan in exchange for us taking Maggie. They had al' kind of problems with journalists and the like, you know, trying to get to see her and al'. And poor Maggie herself, no trouble to anyone!"

"And was that a good deal for us, Sister?" Professor Kent's voice has an unusual hint of mischief in it.

Sister Alexander sucks her teeth noisily then replies: "It surely was, Sir. We had half the nursing staff threatening to leave 'cos of old Bridie, and dat the truth. She done give' me a black eye more than once, and many get a whole lot worse. I never see anything like she, in all my long years of nursing".

"Ah yes, the unfortunate Bridget Callaghan. I wonder how she is doing now? And whether they have anyone left on the nursing staff!" He winks at the Sister conspiratorially. She rewards this intimacy with a girlish giggle.

But now he is turning the searchlight of his attention back onto Claire.

"So, paint me the picture Dr Carter. But just a sketch, after all, we don't have all day". He crosses his legs rather pleased with the joke.

"Well, in line with DSM III we are looking at an initial presentation of post-partum psychosis, with features of intermittent catatonia and severe Obsessive-Compulsive Disorder on axis I. The florid symptoms appeared to abate within the first six weeks, possibly in response to Thioridazine and Diazepam. On recent examination presenting with some residual mild delusional ideas, encapsulated around the catholic Church, although I had to dig around to find them, and moderate OCD, which fluctuates in severity, but has diminished considerably."

Kent nods.

"However…" starts Claire with an as firm a voice as she can muster, determined not to be silenced by the inevitable look of withering contempt Kent will pass her way, "However, given the circumstances around the birth and death of her child, and the fact that her symptoms appear to increase in response to certain triggers, I do not think we can rule out Post Traumatic Stress Syndrome, as an alternative diagnosis…"

Kent is eyeing her through squinting eyes. She decides to continue before he can comment.

"…possibly following an episode of what Magnan and Legrain refer to as a *Bouffée délirante*, a transient psychotic state, triggered by acute stress or trauma. This would account for the unusually speedy remission of the more severe symptoms, which we would not generally expect to see in a puerperal psychosis of such severity."

Professor Kent strokes his chin and stares at Claire for a moment as though in deliberation with himself. She braces herself for the tongue lashing, but it does not eventuate.

"Pray, continue, Dr Carter," he says waving a hand in a gesture of invitation.

"Axis II. Hmmm, a provisional diagnosis of Borderline Personality Disorder was initially suggested, but on examination, I could not find any evidence to support this and the patient has not presented any on the ward to my knowledge". (She looks towards Sister Alexander who meets her eye with a nod of encouraging concurrence).

"There has been little change in the last four months. No axis III elements. She recovered quickly from giving birth. That was 13th October 1978. No medical history of note. Axis IV. There are a number of significant factors. Loss of the same child on 18th October 1978, breakdown of marital relationship; strict religious upbringing; possible alienation from normal family and social networks. As I mentioned, Margaret was brought over to the U.K, as the reaction in the local community was so strong, to the point where it was judged that it would be entirely unfeasible, and possibly unsafe, for her ever to return home."

Kent rubs his lips. "Current medication?" He lays a particular emphasis on the letter 'M'.

"Currently none, although she is still written up for PRN Diazepam. She seemed to be very sensitive to extrapyramidal side effects, despite an increase in Procyclidine. Her medication was subsequently withdrawn three months ago with no subsequent signs of relapse. She is an informal patient, and did not want to take any more - so..."

Claire feels her heartrate increase. She does not want another battle about medication, and today, luckily for her, Kent seems in no mood for a fight. She begins to suspect that he really might have a soft spot for Margaret Doyle. But it seems more likely he just wants the case conference done and dusted so that he will have time for a cup of tea before the trials of the Tribunal.

"How is she on the ward, Sister?"

"As I say, no trouble, Sir. Good as gold that one is. She keep herself to herself, but we have seen no hint of psychosis. She jus' shy. She keep regular hours. Good self-care. We have been making good progress with the hand and mouth washing. But she still have the odd bad day. Can be triggered by any association with the trauma memory - sometin' on the TV bout little babies. Dat kind of t'ing, you know. It was awful bad on the anniversary of the baby's death an' al', but she came through it quicker than we were expectin'. She a resilient one, that one."

She smiles at Claire and Claire feels a lift in her spirits; a little empathy really does go a long way in a place like this.

"Well, what about Risk?" Kent is going through the motions, playing it by the book for the benefit of the trainees.

"Non identified," chimes in Claire. "No hint of aggression to others. No self-harm, unless you count the ablutions, but no serious damage there either. I am not at all sure she is gaining any benefit...."

Kent holds up a hand as if to stay her.

"When I want your opinion, you will know," he remarks. "Let us finish the um - sketch first, shall we? Get a fuller picture. A little more detail, I think. What about risk from others? Exploitation, financial, sexual?"

Claire flushes. As small as she feels, she knows he is right.

"I-I am not aware..." she shoots a plea of help towards Sister Alexander.

"Maggie, she can take care of herself, you know. I seen she stand her ground when pestered for cigarettes an' al'. She get a lot of respec' from the other patients. Men an' al'. She got this quiet authority ting goin' on. She be al' right."

Claire smiles. She wonders how Sister Alexander can be so informal, so relaxed around Professor Kent, but then she had reportedly worked with him for many years, and there was not another member of the nursing staff, let alone the multidisciplinary team whose opinion he valued half so highly as hers. In turn, she would never hear a bad word said against him, as his underlings quickly discovered, Claire amongst them. Her ears still burned from the dressing down Sister Alexander had given her, when she had unguardedly referred to Kent as "up himself," one afternoon when she was on the ward. It was not a mistake she would make again.

Kent looks around the small circle of professionals who make up the multi-disciplinary team.

"Has anyone else anything they wish to add to our portrait of this lady?"

Claire groans inwardly. Annette, the Occupational Therapist, takes an anxious breath and starts:

"Maggie attends a full Occupational Therapy programme, does not have much to say for herself. Seems very able. No problems with Activities of Daily Living. A little reluctant to go to local shops, but quite capable. Always helpful to others in a background way. Particularly enjoys art and pottery - and indeed demonstrates a lot of talent…" She stops. Professor Kent's eyes are beginning to glass over. He smiles tightly.

"Shall we see her then?" He nods to Sister Alexander, who exits the room. Professor Kent squints at his watch and knits his eyebrows. The cup of tea is looking less likely.

"One last thing Dr Carter. Would you enlighten us with some information about the index offence?"

Claire stammers, "She- she…it was alleged that she consumed the remains of her infant…"

"And this would make it an offence in law because?" he is directing the question to one of the horrified looking trainees, most of whom shake their heads in dismay. A hand goes up.

"Because it is a breach of common law to dispose of the remains of the deceased and thus prevent autopsy…?" offers a young man with mousy hair and a plum the size of Surry in his mouth, his hand still raised.

Kent is impressed.

"Indeed, it is. Well done, Dr Stopford-Harding. Revulsion and the outrage of ordinary decency are not in themselves grounds for the exercise of a criminal committal, there must be a legal case to answer, even though the offender may not be deemed fit to appear in court to face charges, as was the case for poor Margaret Doyle. Although it is questionable whether any …" He is interrupted by a noise outside in the corridor.

Sister Alexander re-enters the room and holds open the door. A slight woman of middle-aged appearance shuffles in, the sliding-sound of her slippers made incongruously loud by the sudden hush that befalls the little room. She sits in the moulded-plastic chair next to Professor Kent at his invitation. A hush falls on the room. Eyes cast downward she massages the fingers of one hand with the other. Claire notices the hands remain chapped and red, made all the more ghastly by deep yellow nicotine stains. She studies the face for a moment and marvels that anyone could seem so much older than their years. There is still a loveliness about the green eyes and auburn hair, but the woman's skin and hair have acquired a dullness, as though from lack of fresh air, and a marked lack of animation in her features renders them plainer than they really are. Her face is completely devoid of make-up and her long hair appears slightly unkempt, though not unwashed. The frumpiness of her 'A' line skirt and acrylic round-necked sweater along with the slippers suggest drudgery and lack of self-esteem. Claire almost itches to give her the kind of make-over they are so fond of on day time television and reflects on the transformation that just a little mascara might achieve. But her daydream is broken by Professor Kent, who has decided to put Margaret out of her misery and initiate a conversation.

"So, Maggie - Dr Carter and the team tell me you are going along very well. Is that what you think?"

"That would be right, Sir."

"And you are attending O.T?"

Maggie looks up and catches Annette's eye. Annette cannot read the look but feels somehow culpable of some kind of betrayal.

"That's right Sir...That I am, Sir."

"And what have you been doing in O.T. now, I wonder could you tell us?" To give him credit, Claire feels that Kent is trying not to sound patronising; trying and failing. There are times she questions the tradition of interviewing patients in front of a room full of strangers in this way, with the hope for any real understanding. But she is not the one in charge and her opinions are of little account.

"Cooking and knitting. Art and craft." Margaret Doyle shrugs her shoulders. What interest could it be to anyone else?

"Community Visits?" continues Professor Kent, unabashed. "Your notes suggest that you do not show any keenness to go out. Is this correct?"

Maggie becomes a little fidgety.

"Sure, but I have been to the supermarket, Sir..." Her voice trails away.

"But we gave you unlimited community leave Maggie, and you are not using it. After all Maggie, you are just about the only patient on this unit who is free to come and go as you wish. You do understand that, don't you?"

"Sir, I don't have anywhere I want to go". Her tone is subdued and suffused with a hint of sadness.

Professor Kent eyes her with a thoughtful look.

"Never mind for now Maggie, we will come back to that presently. You are not taking any medication now?"

"Just sometimes to sleep, Sir. I would rather do without."

"Mmmmm. Commendable. Dependency on Diazepam is the last thing you need. Do you ever have thoughts of harming anyone?"

"No never, Sir, I never would -no, to be sure, no". She appears mortified at the very idea.

"And yourself?"

"How do you mean, Sir?" Maggie looks baffled.

"Do ever think about harming yourself, Maggie?" Professor Kent tries to make it a casual enquiry.

"No never, Sir! Sure 'tis a terrible sin, Sir..." She crosses herself unconsciously as though tainted by the thought alone.

"I am glad to hear that Maggie, we wouldn't want any harm to come to you either." Professor Kent sounds almost tender, but the inquisition continues. "Are you experiencing any *odd* ideas these days?"

"No Sir. I - I try not to think at all." She looks imploringly around the room. But no one is coming to her rescue, so she stares at her slippered feet.

"This idea about your baby…" Professor Kent notices a fleeting look of terror on his patient's face but is not to be deterred and Claire feels herself squirm involuntarily in silent empathy.

"Do you still believe he was an angel, Maggie?" Maggie's voice is low.

"I don't know what to believe anymore, Sir. I know I was very unwell - they told me I was…" She takes out a handkerchief from her sleeve and she starts to wipe her mouth.

"Okay Maggie, thank you." Professor Kent exchanges a look with Claire. Claire is beginning to wonder whether he does indeed have a heart after all.

"How is the OCD?" He frowns as he notices her hands.

"Oh, much better, thank you, Sir…"

And here Sister Alexander interposes.

"You have your good days and your bad days, don't you Maggie, but better overall, by far."

Maggie shoots her a grateful smile. And it is a face momentarily transformed. Claire can feel tears pricking at her eyes, though she would be hard-pressed to say why.

"You had quite a few sessions of Art Therapy in the past with, let me see, um, Marion. Is she in today?" Kent directs the question to Claire, who shakes her head.

"She is on annual leave. She did send a report." Claire takes the case file and starts flicking through the pages, but Kent holds up his hand, he has heard enough.

"Oh Sir, I found the sessions very helpful. I felt Marion really understood - I don't know what I would have done without - without someone who - who…"

Professor Kent pauses for a minute, picking something from his teeth while thinking. At last, he speaks.

"To be honest Maggie, I think it is high time we thought about moving you on. We cannot have you staying in a Medium Secure environment forever, especially since you have been an informal patient for so long."

He exchanges a nod with Christine Pargetter, the team social worker. Maggie glances up and meets his eyes in horror.

"But Sir. Where should I go?"

"It's Okay Maggie, we will work something out, and we will take it slowly - but you *need* to use your community leave. You have to get used to being out in the community again."

"But Sir, I can't, I can't go back - there. I just can't." Maggie is becoming distressed.

Professor places a hand over hers.

"It is okay Maggie, we understand that. No one is going to make you go back home, or even to Ireland, if that is not what you want."

Professor Kent looks towards Christine again, a question in his eyes. She scans her notes.

"There is a sister here in London, a Kathleen O'Reagon, quite a bit older and a senior nurse by all accounts. She took a bit of tracking down but she seems to want to help. She has visited a few times, has not had much to do with Maggie for many years, but very keen to support her now. I have spoken to her quite a bit on the telephone, she seems a very pleasant, down to earth woman. Lives in the Peabody Trust buildings in Covent Gardens."

"Very nice too, handy for the opera," observes Kent with raised eyebrows. "Please arrange a meeting, we will look at a move to a local supported living or hostel near the sister and have a final discharge meeting in, say, two months. If that is alright with you Maggie?"

Maggie smiles weakly. There does not seem to be a great deal of choice in the matter.

"Is there anything you want to ask us, Maggie?" Professor Kent looks earnestly into her face, but Maggie has sunk into her thoughts, a tear running down her cheek. Kent nods to Sister Alexander, who places a motherly arm around her shoulders to usher her out. Maggie rises silently and drifts past without a backward glance. It is a movement so devoid of expectation that, for a moment, Claire feels her own heart close to breaking. No wonder staff become inured to so much emotional pain over the years. She wonders if she has what it takes to continue in psychiatry after all.

"Well?" Professor Kent leans back in his chair and runs his hands through his silvering hair, then addresses the ceiling. "She is bed-blocking, to put it bluntly. She is no danger to herself, due to her beliefs, and I would judge was probably only ever a risk to her own child, and even that is very debatable since there was no evidence of any harm to the child while it lived."

A hand shoots up. It is the same keen trainee as before.

"Sir," he suggests cautiously, "it is my opinion that she maintains the belief that the child was an angel, but is saying what she thinks we want to hear."

"Well, that is not so strange and nothing to worry about, if you think about it, Dr Stopford-Harding. The child did bear some form of deformity by all accounts, so if in her psychotic state she interpreted this as him being an angel, then that is how she remembers it. The memory is therefore unlikely to change, regardless of her current mental state. There are no other indications of psychosis, so we are looking at supported discharge." He smiles smugly then continues, directing his comments to Claire now. "Do try to get her to use those community visits - and keep an eye on the OCD. She has become a little institutionalised and I fear she is going to find the idea of re-entering the outside world rather stressful."

Claire thumbs through Marion's report.

"It's a pity Marion is on annual leave," she mutters, almost to herself.

"Oh, I doubt she could tell us much more..." concludes Professor Kent checking his watch and rising from his chair. Still time for a very quick cup of tea after all.

"But you may be right about the PTSD, Dr Carter. I am beginning to believe that we may make a psychiatrist out of you yet!"

Early April 1980, Central London

It is one of those fine spring afternoons when the daffodils in Russell Square turn their yellow faces towards the sun in delight and the cock-pigeons strut their preening court to the fluttering hens, with all the swagger and show of Beau Brummel and his dandies. Maggie Doyle has just finished a morning of bedmaking and toilet cleaning at the Russell Hotel and turns her steps towards home, or what passes for home in this land of tarmac, concrete and steel. She is mindful that her sister will be in bed, after a night shift on Intensive Care, and wrinkles her nose in displeasure at the prospect of another afternoon tiptoeing around the silent Peabody Buildings flat until Kathleen awakens.

Not that she is ungrateful. Far from it. Whilst she is by no means unmoved by the unexpected love and support this sister-stranger has shown her, she simply has no memory of her. The years between their births numbered over fourteen, and Kathleen had left the family home and the Old Country to train as a nurse in London when Maggie was still a wee thing. This being the case Maggie had found herself somewhat in awe of the dynamo of a woman who swept into her life, so unexpectedly after so many years of estrangement, and who had so rapidly taken control.

Still, reminiscent as she may be of the formidable matron popular in Ealing comedies, beneath that severe efficiency, beats an Irish heart of unalloyed compassion. Right from the start, Kathleen had made it clear that she would have no truck with hostels or half-way homes, no matter how highly recommended they might come and, having made it her business to see that her sister made the best possible new start in life, she offered Maggie a home with her in her little flat in Covent garden. Then only a couple of weeks later, Kathleen had secured a position as a domestic for her sister, in the hospital where she worked. Before she knew it, Maggie had found herself among the ranks of orange overalls who roam the wards and corridors of University Hospital, in the fight against unhealthy bacteria, armed only with a mop and bucket of disinfectant. And in essence, the plan was appropriate and well-intentioned. But good intentions all too often pave the road to hellish places, so whilst Kathleen's aim had been to keep her sister close, and therefore safe, she had overlooked a major flaw in her strategy.

At first, Maggie had been glad for the occupation and independence, to say nothing of the female company. Cleanliness being somewhat of a forté, the work came easily to her despite the long weary hours. But by and by, she realised that most of the other cleaners, at least those who did not hail from the West Indies, had crossed the Irish Sea and were from towns and villages that lay uncomfortably close to her former home. Try as she might to keep herself to herself, her workmates *would* ask questions. *Where exactly did she hail from? Did she know old Mrs O'Malley from Tipperary, or Patrick Duncan, or the old priest at St Kildare's who had died last week? Such a shock it was to everyone.*

Maggie had tried hard to be evasive, or to feign recollection of something she had overlooked in her duties, and rush away; still day by day her anxiety grew and painful memories of the past began to stir. And it was her poor red hands that paid the price. Each pang of guilt would need to be scrubbed away, each horrific image, nauseating odour and taste in her mouth expunged from her consciousness with soap and water until at last her mind was clear again. And so, when Maggie saw an advertisement in the Evening Standard for housekeeping staff at the Russell Hotel, and though Kathleen was loath to let her out of her sight, they came to an agreement that it might indeed be for the best. And it had been the right decision. The chambermaids at the Russell were, for the most part, fairly recent arrivals from The Mediterranean. They wasted little curiosity on a dowdy Irish woman in her thirties and spent their tea breaks in tightly packed gaggles, swapping cigarettes and chattering loudly in languages strange and extravagant to Maggie's Irish ears. Maggie could not have minded the social isolation less and began to feel for the first time, that she was free to breathe the London air.

Maggie pauses and looks up and down the street. Perhaps she would not go straight home today. She could visit the British Museum; it was just over the way. She follows a diagonal course across the square, but as the great monolithic structure looms into view she falters, feeling all at once conspicuous in her work clothes, and loses her nerve. Casting around she continues past the museum and into Bloomsbury Square, which lies in full sunshine at this time of the day. At the far end, she spies a vacant park bench and makes her way towards it. She cannot help but notice that most of the other benches are occupied by down and outs, bottles in brown paper bags, huddled in pairs like conspiratorial scarecrows. Yet strangely she has no fear. Like every daughter of Ireland, she has had her share of dealing with drunken men, they do not worry her. Sure, if they are not to be pitied. Or even envied. For they drink from the waters of forgetfulness and isn't that a desire she understands all too well herself?

She takes a seat and feeling the warmth of the sun on her face, reaches for the tin and lighter in her handbag and slowly rolls a cigarette, lulled into tranquillity by the familiarity of the delicate routine. She lights up, inhales, then slowly releases the comforting wisps of smoke through pursed lips. She watches the red Route-master buses and black taxi cabs make their halting diesel-belching progress through the city traffic. So many people. She had never dreamt there could be so many people in the world, living lives so completely beyond her comprehension. But perhaps life is always different from all that we could have imagined or hoped. She feels the hot prick of a tear in her eye and reminds herself how useful sunglasses can be. She takes another drag on her roll-up and notices the smear of lipstick on the end of the Rizla paper. That particular shade of crimson is probably too deep for someone of her age. She makes a mental note to look for something more suitable when she gets her weekly pay packet.

She thinks about Kathleen, who rarely wears any make-up at all, except for an occasional night out at the cinema, when she might dab on a spot of rouge and a smear of lip gloss, though it would go unseen once the lights were dimmed. Maggie had wondered why she had never married, never had babbies of her own. But Kathleen did not seem to show any interest in men and she had mentioned that before Maggie had taken occupancy of the spare bedroom in her tiny flat in Covent Garden, a friend had stayed there. Maggie frowns. Even after three months of living together in such intimate proximity, her sister's life is still a mystery. No, a closed door.

As kind and generous as Kathleen had been with her support, it is as though she is keeping Maggie at arm's length. "Am I really such a monster?" wonders Maggie. In the fairy stories of her childhood, it had been easy enough to tell; even if monsters started out as deceivers, their wickedness was quickly exposed. But fairy stories belong to a world where the difference between right and wrong, good and evil, is clear and unambiguous. She knows she has sinned, has committed an act so heinous most people would recoil from her if they ever learned of it, yet could it truly have been evil that drove her actions when it felt so much like love?

The eager sun is moving across the London sky and the shadow of the museum is starting to encroach on her oasis of light. She shivers and makes to move. Yet she is still not ready to return to the oppressive silence of the little flat she must now call home. She could wander around Covent Garden. She has ventured into the refashioned market place on previous occasions but had felt overwhelmed by the sheer variety of wares and goods displayed in the windows of its bijoux boutiques, not to mention the astronomical price-tags that came with them.

She is startled by a loud guffaw from the neighbouring bench. Its occupants are clearly sharing a joke, and for all the direness of their circumstances, there is genuine humour in the alcohol suffused merriment. The pull of the waters of forgetfulness is infectious. Maggie thinks about the few occasions she had got a bit squiffy at weddings and family parties. The comforting numbness of mild inebriation. She thinks about her husband, wherever he might be, God Bless his soul, and his retreat into the bottle. *But had she not given him cause enough?* She has to admit she had, and for all his failings, she may have gotten a lot worse from any other man; especially when the drink unleashes the beast within. Yet somehow her husband's self-pitying inebriation had seemed the inevitable extension of his habitually cold hands and passionless martyrdom to the demands of Catholic piety: a piety that negated any responsibility for his own infertility and would have condemned his wife to childlessness.

Maggie rises from her seat and brushes off her skirt. She notices an ache in her feet and back. She is feeling older lately, older and worn. Her life has slipped away before she could even live it. Perhaps she will go straight home after all and take an afternoon nap until Kathleen stirs.

She heads along Southampton Place and emerges just opposite the Princess Louise. She has passed the old pub many times and something about the old place always beckons. She pauses and frowns then crosses the busy road to find herself right outside one of the decoratively tiled entrances that frame the great bowed front window.

She looks around her, as though fearing she might be observed. She has never been in a pub alone before, for to be sure single women, or at least nice single women, do not go unaccompanied into public houses. At least, not where she is from. But this is not small-town Ireland and come to that, is she truly single? She inspects the now scarcely visible mark on her ring finger, the ghost of her discarded wedding band. *Till death do us part.* The mere putting aside of the symbol cannot untie God's sacred knot. She had not really thought of it before and now she rather wishes she might not have to think about it again.

She stands in the doorway and sniffs the welcoming mix of beer and cigarette smoke. She hears the hum of lively conversation and peers in through the half glazed, brass-handled wooden doors. Can this truly be a pub? So unlike the stripped back and unadorned premises in her home town, where the only attraction is the whiskey, Murphy's stout and the serious business of drinking, dominoes and arguing politics. The Princess Louise is a Victorian Palace of pleasure, a feast for the eyes, with her stucco ceilings and art nouveau light fittings, ostentatious wooden clad walls and colourful decadence of the ceramic wall tiles. Her etched glass-panelled mahogany booths and red leather upholstered wall seating contrive to promise comfort, good cheer and lively company: A formula so winning she has survived the make-over mania of the sixties and seventies unscathed to nurture a nostalgia for a world that we fondly imagined existed, before our own. To Maggie's relief, she can see at least a couple of lone females, who sit at little cast-iron and wooden topped round tables, reading a book or simply enjoying a cigarette, as bold as you like.

Maggie steels herself, pushes open the door and walks in. Not a head turns, not a remark is passed. She walks gingerly to the long wooden bar which stands like an island in the centre of the saloon. She soon catches the eye of the barman, who gives her a friendly wink of welcome. She feels a momentary thumping of her heart and feels an impulse to turn and run out of the building, but already he is asking her what her pleasure will be? She stammers out the name of the only whiskey she knows. There is no judgement. No disapproving raising of an eyebrow. He nods, takes a glass from the shelf below the bar, polishes it carefully with a well-used bar-towel, then holds it up to the optics whistling softly. *Would she like ice*, he asks, waving a pair of tongs above an ice bucket. Maggie grimaces. Then smiles. *Yes, yes, she would very much enjoy that*. The barman takes the pound note she is holding out and winks once more as he hands her the change. Maggie is trying to think of something sociable to say, but he has already moved on, crossing over to the other side of the bar when a young man with a ring through one nostril and another through his eyebrow leans across, his money in his hand. Maggie flinches in unconscious empathy at the idea of the puncturing of such delicate skin.

She moves to the end of the room to a plump and dimpled leather corner bench. The seat has seen better days, but its comfort is not diminished for all that. She places her drink on a cardboard coaster in front of her, dives into her handbag and ferrets about for her tobacco. She takes out the tin and starts to roll up, feeling her body relax and soften with the soothing familiarity of the ritual. Laying the pungent dried leaf along the gossamer-thin paper, she caresses the delicate tube first between her thumb and fingertips, moistens the edge with the tip of her tongue and finally lights up. Then, and only then, can she take a peep around and indulge in a timid luxuriation of the sensual feast of colours and shapes that surround her. She closes her eyes for a moment and breathes in the wafted scents of tobacco, beer and spirits that envelop her being. She exhales a long, slow breath, as though for the first time in many long months.

Maggie holds her glass up to the light and stares into the rich amber liquid then takes a sip. The peaty warmth of the whiskey catches the top of her mouth and throat and evokes an unexpected recollection of her Daddy. A fleeting remembrance of the heady whiff of single malt on his lips on a Friday night, when she would kiss him goodnight. Is it possible still to miss him after so many years?

Maggie picks up the coaster and examines the advertisement on it; an ale she has never heard of, brewed here in the city she scarcely knows. Her glass is empty already. She trots back over to the bar and orders a second. On the way back to her seat, she notices that the table next to hers has been occupied whilst she was afoot. Maggie studies her neighbours out of the corner of her eye. Lounging across the padded bench and chairs, there sits a group of four young men and women, hardly old enough, in her opinion, to be of legal drinking age, and dressed almost like vagabonds with scruffy paint-splattered clothes and multiple earrings in their ears. One of the young women, a pretty girl, has hair that is dyed blue at the tips, whilst the other sports a workman's boiler suit and has vivid ginger corkscrew curls, with freckles to match.

Maggie finds her attention drawn to one of the young men in particular who sits huddled in a duffle coat and open-toed Jesus Creepers. A thick wedge of hair hangs over his face almost obscuring his eyes, which she could swear are rimmed in eyeliner. He too wears a small hoop of gold in his ear and several studs along the top of the lobe. The other young man is good looking, he wears a donkey jacket and winklepickers and reminds Maggie of the lads of her youth, mad to be cool, yet trying too hard.

Maggie averts her eyes before they notice her staring. She wonders if they could be tinkers or travellers, yet their self-assurance and ease appeal to her and she feels her gaze tugged back to the scene. By and by an older gentleman joins them, hands full of drinks, and the girls shift along the bench, shyly inviting him to join them. He wears faded jeans and a navy fisherman's jersey. Locks of thick grey hair curl around his collar. The light from the window dances in his eyes as he leans across the table and they flash green. *Now if he isn't Irish, sure I'm a Dutchman* thinks Maggie.

The little gathering falls into animated conversation. Their voices resound with a passion usually reserved for politics where she is from, yet she can make no sense of the snippets of conversation she is able to catch. They might as well be speaking in a foreign tongue. Maggie stares into the bottom of her glass watching the transparent chunks of ice melt into the dregs of the whiskey.

Her thoughts wander back to the afternoons on the ward, where she would sit quietly in the lounge or smoking room, listening to the conversations between the poor lost souls around her. Poor young Jo, barely out of childhood. Bundled, already unwell, onto a plane by his parents in Nigeria. He had arrived at Heathrow, completely psychotic, raving about stones in his head, village witch doctors and evil spells. And Trevor, a quiet giant of man, who kept asking whether the staff and patients had been replaced by robots, and warning of the plot of the machines to overthrow humankind. Yet at other times they could laugh and joke about the soccer or complain about the unit food as though everything was perfectly normal. There were generally only a couple of women on the ward at any one time and the men, even those who could be frighteningly aggressive and abusive to the staff, seemed gentle around Maggie and the other female inmates who drifted around the ward in search of a kind look or word.

She had soon learned that cigarettes were the social currency and smoking, the glue to any hope of social cohesion. In the past, she had been only a rare and social smoker but found herself joining the ranks of chain smokers in the designated smoking area, where the trading of roll-ups or dog-eared butt ends offered some merciful punctuation to the monotony of the endless days and nights. And she had become a watcher of people, both of the inmates who remained, their routines unchanging, and of the staff who came and went; tacit reminders that there must indeed exist a world outside the walls within which she had found herself. Many a time she did truly wonder whether she had died and was in Purgatory, yet how unfathomable that such a place had become a safe haven, a place she did not wish to leave.

Maggie sighs. She is free now, yet the world seems no less alien to her. How will she ever find her way back into one that she understands? And where can she ever hope to feels she belongs? Maggie is musing on this, gently swirling the melted ice water around the bottom of her glass when she senses a pair of eyes fixed upon her. She flushes then warily raises her gaze. At the end of the table, the young man in the duffle coat has produced a small black leather-bound book and appears to be making a drawing of her, his eyes flicking rapidly between his pencil and her face. Maggie's response is a mingling of fear and anger. But it is anger that takes the upper hand.

"Now what is the meaning of this, may I ask?" she hears herself demand and scarcely knows it is she who has spoken.

The young man's face colours in mortification. But it is the girl with the red hair who speaks.

"We are so sorry. He didn't mean any harm. It is just that Roger fancies himself a Raphael..." there is genuine warmth in her voice, yet she is suppressing a laugh. The other girl stifles a giggle. But Maggie's face is a blank and it is clear that the words have no meaning for her.

So now, Roger, signalling the others to shush, finds his voice.

"Do forgive me - it's just that, well we tend to sketch all kinds of people we see and, well you looked just like a Madonna sitting there. I just could not resist. Please don't be angry. Here, let me show you the sketch..."

He is holding up the open notebook. Even without her glasses, Maggie can see a sketch of a woman. She leans forward to see more clearly. To be sure he has caught her likeness, and yet it could be a picture of the Blessed Virgin herself. Maggie's mouth falls open.

"How can you be after saying such a thing?" she exclaims softly and before she can help herself, she is weeping into her hands and is obliged to hunt around in her handbag for a handkerchief.

Now, Roger is moved to genuine remorse.

"Please, don't be upset, I beg you! I can tell from your accent now that you are Irish, so probably catholic, right? But believe me, I meant no blasphemy, it is just that well it is true, about Raphael. He is my idol and..."

But Maggie has composed herself now.

"'Tis not that, to be sure. Tis simply that no one has ever said such a beautiful thing to me before - and tis such a beautiful drawing," and with this, she is obliged to dab her eyes anew.

The older gentleman is speaking now. His voice is as mellow and English as Maggie's favourite Old Holborn tobacco.

"Look, I am sure Roger never meant to cause you any distress either way. I tell you what, why don't you come and join us and let us stand you a drink, to make up for it? My name is Peter..." He beckons her over to their table with a welcoming movement of his head. For a long moment,

Maggie does not respond. She seems to struggle with something inside. Then at last;

"T'anks. I don't mind if I do. A drop of Irish whiskey would go down very well, just now, if you would be so kind. My name is Maggie. Pleased to meet you," and moving across to a vacant chair next to Roger, she shakes hands with each of the group in turn whilst Peter heads off to the bar to buy the promised drink. The girls are called Sarah and Summer, and Maggie can see from the way their eyes follow Peter, that they both have a bit of a crush on him. The other lad introduces himself as Tony.

They are first-year students of art at the Central School of Art and design, just over the road further up and along Southampton Row, she must have seen it. And Peter is their tutor.

Maggie shakes her head and shrugs apologetically. She has to admit that she had not noticed such a place. When Peter returns, he hands the glass to Maggie and raises his own to her in a silent toast. Maggie smiles, lifts her glass and lilts;

"What butter and whiskey cannot cure...."

"There is no cure for!" interjects Peter with a wink.

Maggie's face lights up.

"Go on with yez, I knew you had the Irish blood in you, so I did." But all at once, she realises what she has said and her pulse quickens with the familiar sense of alarm that proximity to her own countrymen always raises.

"Well, I believe my old grandmother came from Waterford, a very long time since. I've no family or connections there now, that I know of. And I believe that what was left of her family were long since settled in America when they had the opportunity. But I remember her way of talking, and her love of the whiskey, and am proud of the Irish in me, *so I am*".

Maggie is more pleased and relieved than seems sensible to her, and looks away aware of the pink heat rising to her cheeks.

"You know, you really do look like a Madonna...", whispers Roger laying a gentle hand on her arm and looking into her face. "The Madonna of Southampton Row."

"Ah, get away with you," smiles Maggie patting his hand with her own, until she notices with horror the redness of her mercilessly over-washed skin and withdraws it before anyone else does.

"Now show me that drawing of yours, so I can see it properly this time, and I might be forgiving you."

Roger opens the book and hands it to Maggie. She lets out a small gasp.

"Sure, but it's beautiful, so it is." And yet it is a good and true likeness. Maggie really does blush now.

"Have you ever thought of being a model?" asked Peter now, who has been watching the interaction intently.

"Well, now you are just being plain daft, so you are. I am too old for strutting down those catwalk thingies - and far too fat, and that's a fact!"

"Well, any real woman is too fat to be a catwalk model," exclaims the girl called Summer, "though to be honest I would die for a waist as slender as yours..."

She looks Maggie up and down with apparent admiration.

"But, well, Peter meant a life drawing model, someone who poses nude, you know, for art students like us."

Maggie frowns and flares her nostrils, then shakes her head.

"You don't mean - you can't mean," she lowers her voice which trembles a little, "stark naked, in the altogether? Sure, I would die for the shame of it, so I would!"

But seeing their good-natured merriment at her prudery, she laughs along with them and somehow, there in the Princess Louise, the words sound foolishly parochial to her own ears, too.

Later in the afternoon Maggie arrives home and finds Kathleen already up and bustling around the small flat, in her blue and white-piped sister's uniform. Maggie calls a soft hello and goes to the bathroom and washes her hands then repeats the process. One. Two. Maggie counts. It will only need to be two this afternoon. She can manage with just two. She stops and carefully dries her hands on a clean towel, feeling a glow of pride. Then opening the bathroom door with her elbow trots into her room and nudges close the door behind her.

She sits on her meticulously made bed and listens to the clinking together of the dish, mug and plate from her sister's afternoon breakfasting as Kathleen does the washing up, creating a whirlpool of activity in the silence of the kitchen-dining area. Maggie's heart rate begins to increase. She can hear the agitation in that activity. She feels the pull to wash her hands again, make absolutely sure, but she knows this is not what she wants. The pull becomes tighter as the noises in the next room continue. Maggie takes a breath, collects herself and steps towards the bedroom door, then exhaling with a hard breath places her hand on the door handle and steps into the living area. Her sister is standing with her back turned to her, sorting noisily through her handbag, now.

"You are angry with me," states Maggie as calmly as she can. "You are angry with me for not coming straight home, so you are."

Kathleen spins around but it is not annoyance Maggie reads on her face.

"Oh God Bless You, Maggie, not at all. Oh, don't be thinking that, please Darlin'. I never could be. I was just, well - worried. I just didn't know where you could have got to. Aren't you always here when I wake up, and I..."

"Really?"

"Honest to God. I just feel like your mammy or something sometimes, so I do. I am sorry. You are an adult. I know you are. You don't have to tell me where you are every minute of the day and night. It's just..."

Kathleen looks at Maggie with tears trickling from her eyes. Maggie puts her hand to her own face and realises that she is weeping too. Kathleen moves towards her and takes her in her arms and holds her close. Can this be the same Kathleen she knows? Maggie feels herself soften and wants to ask her not to go, to stay, to miss her shift. But Kathleen is already drawing away, one eye on the clock.

"Kathleen, there is so much I wanted to tell you today..."

"Ah, that's grand Maggie", replies Kathleen with business-like tenderness. "And I'm thinking meself that there are things we need to talk about. Things I think you need to understand. I think it might help you. Could we sit down together over a cuppa, tomorrow morning after my shift, and make some time?"

"Sure, if you wish. I'd like that, so I would."

Kathleen looks at the little stainless-steel watch that hangs from a pin on her tunic with a grimace, places a gentle hand on the smoothness of Maggie's cheek and with a –

"Now you be sure and take care of yourself. I left some of your favourite chocolate digestives in the biscuit tin"- is gone.

Maggie sits down at the kitchen table and listens to the ticking of the clock from the bedroom. The day has not turned out at all the way she had expected.

Maggie stands at the washbasin, staring at the face in the mirror. She has felt an anxious tightening in her gut all night. Her sleep has been fitful and her dreams have been unsparing. She had risen at dawn with the sun, even though she has no shift at the hotel this morning. She has washed and dried her hands three times already and is locked in the daily battle not to succumb to the compulsion to wash them one more time. But four is such a good square number.

> *And moving through a mirror clear*
> *That hangs before her all the year,*
> *Shadows of the world appear.*

Maggie's lips move silently as she wills her brain to focus on remembering the words of the poem. She feels the beating of her heart quicken and flinches as a score of bloody images crowd into her mind. It fast becomes a battle but she holds fast, coaxing her concentration back to lines she knows so well. The images and heartbeat fight for centre stage. She acknowledges they are there, but hones the spotlight of her attention back onto the poem. For a while, it is doubtful whether she will triumph, until:

> *As often through the purple night,*
> *Below the starry clusters bright,*
> *Some bearded meteor, trailing light,*
> *Moves over still Shalott.*

Maggie relaxes. She feels the threat passing. *Not bad*, she tells herself, *the middle of part III*. Only three months ago she would have had to struggle on until well into part IV before the anxiety peaked, then finally started to abate.

A battered old bookcase on the secure ward of a run-down psychiatric hospital may not seem the most likely place to discover a love of poetry and some degree of salvation, but that is where Maggie had come across a dog-eared anthology of poetry and Alfred Lord Tennyson. Flicking through the pages in her sleeping cubicle, she had happened upon the Lady of Shalott and had been at once impressed and intimidated by its length. As she had begun to scan through it, she came to the line

"Tirra Lirra," by the river, sang Sir Lancelot.

The words sounded oddly familiar. She read on. All at once, the memories from her long-forgotten school days came flooding back. Of course, they had been made to memorise poems by rote in those days. There had been no pleasure, no literary appreciation in the exercise, just pure unthinking parroting, and woe betide anyone who missed a line, or verse. Maggie had flinched at the memory of the ruler across her knuckles. How she had hated poetry then and ever since. Even now, as an adult who might know better, she half-believed it could only have been designed for the sole purpose of tormenting school children. And yet, as she re-read the vaguely remembered lines, the imagery filled her head, and the lilting rhythm of the verse had made her smile. For a while, she felt herself transported to another sad yet beautiful world; a world so different to her own. And each time she re-visited the poem, finding fresh images and emotional nuances with each re-reading, she was struck by how her thoughts and pre-occupations would recede into the background.

And that is when she got the idea. She would learn the poem by heart again. And this time because she wanted to. And she would carry it in her head as a refuge from the treachery of her own thoughts, a life raft on a sea of mental turmoil.

At first, she had used it as a means of clearing her head before going to sleep. She would rarely make it to the end of the poem, drifting off in dreams of Sir Lancelot on his charger, or the beautiful Lady, entangled in the web of her loom. Then, one morning, when she was being particularly plagued by the compulsion to wash her hands for the tenth time and it was crashing around her mind like an enormous torrent of water, she had started to recite the poem, to funnel every mite of mental effort into recalling the words. A strange thing happened, as soon as she stopped fighting the compulsion, it seemed to lose its force. The thoughts were there and so was the anxiety, but now the waves rolled over and around her, seeping away to find their level, until all returned to relative calm.

Maggie makes some toast but cannot eat it. She sits and waits for Kathleen's return, battling with the compulsion to return to the washbasin. She thinks about her poem, but this morning it is beginning to get on her nerves. And there is not exactly a happy ending. Perhaps she should find a new one? Finally, she puts the radio on to the familiar sound of Terry Wogan and the reassuring lilt of his Irish intonation begins to soothe her. There is something about the balm of his voice that prompts her to reach for the hand cream, and soon she is gently rubbing the lotion into her poor red hands. She caresses the back of her hand with her thumb. How much better that feels.

When she finally hears the key in the door, Maggie jumps to her feet. Kathleen enters, looking washed out and exhausted. She meets Maggie's look of expectation with a wan smile and sinks into an armchair with a sigh.

"You look all done in, Kathleen..." Comments Maggie rushing to get the kettle on. "Tea will be just a jiffy. Can I get you anything else?"

"Just let me take the weight off me poor feet for a minute."

She kicks off her flat shoes and curls and wriggles her stockinged toes.

Despite the agony of the last endless hours, Maggie's eagerness to put the discomfort of anticipation behind her seems selfish. She feels suddenly ashamed. She draws back a chair from the little dining- table and sits facing Kathleen, her head bowed in contrition.

"Look, I know we said we would talk, but you get yourself off to bed. We can talk later, for it is not as though it cannot wait, now is it?"

"Indeed, tis not," concurred Kathleen "But I think t'would be better now, as we agreed. Sure, there is nothing like striking whilst the iron is hot, now is there? Put the kettle on and you can tell me about your afternoon, yesterday, while we wait. I'll be right as rain once the tea is in my system and then we can have that talk."

Maggie feels her stomach knot but scanning Kathleen's tired face, sees there is nothing to fear and smiles. She fills the kettle and places it on the hob, then promptly forgets to light it in her eagerness.

"Oh, Kathleen. I had such a lovely afternoon. I met these people - young people in a pub. Yes, a pub, I just had a little drink, or two, I suppose. Anyway, they were art students, would you believe? And they were so interesting and alive and wanted to know *me*, and I felt..."

Maggie pauses. She is not even sure what it was she did feel. Kathleen is looking at her with a quizzical expression, or is it disapproval? She falls silent.

"You felt what? Sure, don't be keeping me in suspense now," Kathleen chides in a smiling voice.

"I felt - I felt hope." Tears spring into Maggie's eyes. "I felt excitement about life. Their excitement was infectious, so it was. I wanted to - I just..."

But Kathleen's face has fallen. Maggie experiences a moment of panic. She stares down at her hands which lie clasped like lumps of liver upon the starchy whiteness of the tablecloth. The rawness of the over-washed skin screeches its silent rebuke, a constant reminder that she deserves no happiness in this life or the next; a relentless bully on her shoulders. She keeps her head bowed, she is trying so hard to stand up to the bully, but it is so hard, and she is not sure she can do it alone.

"You'll be thinking I made a proper fool of meself, I suppose," she whispers sadly. "And I probably did..."

She senses Kathleen rise from the armchair and move over to join her at the table.

"No, it's not that, I promise you. I just don't want to see you get hurt, me darlin' girl, you have been hurt enough."

A sympathy as deep as the Irish Sea glistens in Kathleen's eyes. She takes her sister's hand and looks into her face, urging her to continue. Maggie feels her heart buoyed up, and with it her courage.

"I can't explain it Kath, but I just have a good feeling about this."

Kathleen closes her other hand over Maggie's.

"Then I am pleased. And I will try my hardest not to play the over-protective mother hen, but in some ways that is exactly what I wanted to talk to you about, meself, …"

Maggie knits her brow and tilts her head to one side questioningly.

"Well, Maggie you were such a small wee thing, so you were, when I had to - when I left home, so I'm thinking you will hardly remember, but the truth is I was pretty much a mother to you for the first three or four years of your little life. You see Mammy, well she fell into a terrible bad way after you were born, so she did. She suffered from a condition known as post-partum pre-eclampsia, you have probably heard of women developing it before they give birth, and it is pretty rare for it to occur after the birth, but in her case, it did. Her blood pressure became very high and she suffered a stroke which left her left side weak and her one eye virtually useless. It was a terrible blow of course and for a few years, she really struggled to manage.

And there was I, fourteen and a sensible sort of girl, so I just took over, feeding and changing you. And I could not have loved you more if you had been my own, and that's God's own truth, so it is."

Kath pauses, places her hand over her eyes and squeezes her greying temples. Maggie reaches out to comfort her.

"No, let me finish…" Kath clasps her hands in front of her, takes a breath and swallows. "The thing is, you never knew Mammy, the Mammy we knew, before - before it happened, I mean. Maggie, she was so full of fun, so full of life. I can still remember her wonderful laugh. It was like music. You remind me of her a lot sometimes, so you do. But after the stroke, well, it was as though Daddy and me, we lost her. The stroke seemed to change her personality as well. She became embittered and spiteful. She seemed to blame you for what had happened to her as if it could be the fault of a poor wee babby. I wasn't able to talk to her anymore and I'm thinking she made poor Daddy's life a misery.

"Well, when I was getting on for eighteen, I realised that I was, well that is to say, that I could never marry, that I - Well to state it plainly, I fell in love with a lass, and she with me. Her name was Eileen. I can still see her beautiful face, like a princess she was. Well, it seems that she spoke to her priest about it in confession and he terrified the life out of her with threats of all kinds of eternal damnation and the like. And the bastard did not let up. Eileen was such a gentle girl and had been bought up very devout. I could see her falling apart before me very eyes, so torn up with it she was. In the end, she took the veil in a closed order and I never saw her again, at least not in my waking life, for God knows she haunted my dreams."

Kath pauses. The tears glisten on Maggie's cheeks. She wonders how many more must fall this week.

"What about you? What did you do?" asks Maggie her voice soft with kindness.

"To be sure I did think about joining the Holy Sisters. But I would have been living a lie. I wanted to live, I wanted to love and I could not accept a church, a God that denied the truth in the love I felt, that made love a sin. I had to go, though it broke my poor heart all over again to leave you. But Mammy was getting some strength and feeling back at least, though God knows it was never a full recovery, and you were going to be starting school soon enough, so I went, while I had the anger and strength enough to do it. I know that when Daddy died, it left you and mammy alone, and yourself only eleven, 'twas terrible early. God only knows what it must have been like for you in that house, and I'm thinking that is why you married the first man who asked you..."

Maggie startles, momentarily taken aback by her sister's insight, but Kathleen continues.

"The Lord knows Declan Doyle was a good enough sort of a man, compared to some, but he was never meant for you, Maggie. My little Maggie so bright, so alive and don't you be gain-saying me. I know you did not do as well at school as you should have. You had a curious creative mind, but the sisters would have made sure they stifled any real spark in you..."

Maggie gazes at her hands, the remembrance of the sisters in their severe habits, rulers at the ready to curb the spirit of any child who showed any defiance, any independence of thought, fills her mind. She feels a rush of anger then realises that Kathleen is still speaking. But there is a sadness in her voice now.

"Oh Maggie, I left you to save myself. I could not see it then, but tis true - and how can you ever forgive me?"

Maggie seizes Kathleen's hand and putting it to her lips, kisses it.

"Kathleen, please! There is nothing to forgive. I am only sorry that I never knew, never understood. In all those years Mammy never mentioned your name right up until the day she died, God bless her soul." Maggie crosses herself swiftly.

"God? How can you speak so? I stopped believing..."

"But Kath - I can't, even if I wanted to. Not after all that I've seen - been through. Oh, Kathleen was there ever such proof of his love? Even if I cannot fathom the meaning of it, I cannot doubt Him."

For an instant, Maggie's face seems lit from within. Kathleen wants to say that while she believes it to be real for Maggie, it was never-the-less a reality wrought by illness.

But she knows this will not do. She falls silent, a gulf has opened up between them. Even now God is wrenching them apart. Threatening to destroy, once again, all she holds dear. She squeezes Maggie's hands and wipes away the teardrops that are puddling in the corners of her eyes.

Maggie meanwhile struggles with her own thoughts. Long buried memories have been flooding back into her mind. She chews her lips then raises her eyes to Kathleen's.

" D'you know, Kath, when I was a little girl, I used to believe that I had a guardian angel that watched over me. I used to tell everyone about it until the nuns put a stop to it. Sister Mary Agnes took me aside one day and told me that fancifulness was a sin and that I was opening the door to Satan. But I could picture her face so clearly, so I could. It was so young and beautiful. I couldn't believe it was just my imagination or that there could be any wickedness in it. Still, her words frightened me and I never mentioned it to anyone again and, over time, the vividness of the idea faded. But it was you, wasn't it? It was your dear face, I remembered."

Kathleen nods her head and weeps again.

"Oh, my little Maggie. I think it was. I'm so sorry that I couldn't have been there longer for you but I want you to know that whatever you need - I am here for you, now."

Maggie bows her head. She had not meant to make her sister feel worse. She looks up with a smile and a wink.

"Believe you me, just that feeling that someone, somewhere, was looking out for me, made all the difference, sometimes. But what about you Kathleen? Did you find your love and happiness?"

"Oh, Maggie, I did right enough." Kathleen's eyes twinkle. "And I have photographs to prove it - hundreds of them, so I do, for my Vonnie and me, we had some fine old times, travelling all over the world in our holidays. Sure, haven't I a dozen photo albums on the bookshelves there," she gestures proudly, "and you are more than welcome to look through them at any time - but right now, I need my bed."

Maggie can see that Kath is exhausted, and not just from her shift. She lays her hand on Kathleen's arm once again as she starts to rise from her seat.

"Kathleen, where *is* Vonnie? She was staying here before me, wasn't she? I hope, I mean…"

"Don't you be worrying about that, me darling girl. Vonnie has had to go and look after her mother up in St Albans, for a while, and in any case, she has her own flat, so you don't need to be worrying about us," with a wink, "we are just fine. And now I don't have to hide her from you - so now it is *better* than fine!"

And with that she takes herself off to the bedroom soon falls into the first truly peaceful sleep, she has known in months, leaving Maggie to ponder on all she had learned and smile wistfully at the still waiting teapot and the tea that had gone unmade.

Late April 1980

Maggie steps up to the white hardboard plinth, holding her satin dressing-gown around her. She looks towards Peter with a quick glance and he responds with a nod of encouragement and a blink of his eyes. The gaggle of students that have filled the high-ceilinged studio are sitting at wooden donkeys with boards before them or standing at easels, clipping up pads of paper or sharpening charcoal pencils with Stanley knives. They lean towards each other in playful chatter and take no more notice of her than if she were standing at a bus stop. Peter clears his throat and nods again to Maggie. The room falls into a silent readiness and its attention falls suddenly upon her. She takes a deep breath then slips off her robe and stands naked as the day she was born. Peter looks at his watch and then up at the big classroom clock on the wall above her head and suggests some five-minute warm-up poses. He inclines his head almost imperceptibly again towards Maggie, as a signal to her, and remembering the drill she stands hands on hips with her feet slightly apart finding her balance. Then selecting a spot on the window at the opposite end of the room, she fixes her gaze and concentrates as hard as she can on keeping still. She can feel her body shaking and the rapid drumming of her heart in her ribcage, but she keeps her eyes and her thoughts on the position she is holding with her whole body. The awareness that every eye in the room is now fixed on her nakedness, presses into her mind and her head hums, as for a moment she worries she will faint, but the moment passes and she is still on her feet. *She can do this. She can.*

The steady tick-tock of the studio clocks rises audibly above the rhythmic swish of charcoal strokes on paper. It seems to tick for an eternity, and Maggie fights the desire to lick her lips as her mouth is becoming so dry. The spot on the window pane seems to dance and blur, but at last Peter's soft voice announces "time'. Maggie sighs and rubs her face, but Peter is giving her a wink of approbation and gestures with his hand for her to assume a new pose. Feeling a little more confident, Maggie turns to the left and clasps her elbows with her hands above her head arching her back a little. There is a murmur of appreciation from the students who busy themselves with sketching, and the world seems to stand still.

Maggie keeps her eyes upon a new point of focus, a splash of paint on the expanse of the white-washed brickwork, and tries to envision herself in the students' shoes. Peter and The Gang, as she now privately refers to them, had bought up the idea of her modelling again, when she had met up with them for another drink in The Princess Louise, a week after their first encounter. They had at first enjoyed her scandalised protests at such an idea, but beneath her very Irish indignation Maggie's questions and gentle demand for further details betrayed a curiosity and desire for something new. In the end, Peter suggested she attend a life class herself, so she could see what it was all about. Maggie had felt flattered, not only by their protestations that she would be so wonderful to draw, but by the insistence of their invitation into their world. Though grateful for the money, she was beginning to find the work at the Russell Hotel a chore, so if she could drop a couple of shifts and supplement her income with a different kind of work, well so much the better. And there was something else. As outrageous as it seemed to her to stand before a room of people in nothing but a smile to cover your modesty, there was nevertheless something about it that appealed; something as yet only half thought through, though nonetheless compelling.

The following Tuesday evening she had met with Summer at The Louise, who had then escorted her over to the somewhat unprepossessing building that housed the School of Art. Maggie, all atremble, had needed a moment to loiter outside and smoke a quick roll-up before going in. But Summer's patient coaxing and enthusiasm had proved the gentle antidote to all her qualms.

Maggie had felt a visceral thrill through her body that was more than mere nervousness, as they entered through the impressive wooden doors and into a lofty foyer. On either side of the foyer, she could see great stone pillars and marbled floors stretching off down arched-roofed corridors, punctuated by impressive-looking staircases with black wrought iron balustrades that swept heavenwards in rectangular spirals. Directly ahead, through bevelled glass panelled doors set between two massive stone columns, there seemed to be a great hall. Whilst Summer chatted chirpily to the doorman, Maggie had tiptoed towards it and peered in. To her surprise, the high ceiling appeared to be a glass dome some stories high; a sparkling jewel hidden at the building's heart. She had been looking upwards in wonder when she felt Summer by her side. *It was the exhibition hall, empty at present, but most weeks there was something on. Maggie must come and see next time it is in use. But now they were to head up to the fourth floor, was she okay with lifts, or would she prefer the stairs?* Summer would recommend the stairs if she was up to it, as there was nothing to be seen in an elevator. Maggie had assented, despite wondering momentarily about her physical fitness. She might have been almost old enough to be Summer's mother, but hopefully was not on the scrapheap just yet.

The stairs wound upwards and were the broadest Maggie had ever seen. Summer hurried on, bounding up two stairs at a time, young and used to the exertion. Maggie trailed a little behind, puffing and panting and longing for a fag. Summer would pause and wait for her at the top of each flight of stairs, which gave way to a landing and a set of swinging glass doors, each bearing the name of a different department.

When they reached the top landing, Summer gestured to the entrance bearing a sign which said 'Fine Art' with a dramatic flourish and, holding open the door, ushered a breathless Maggie inside. Maggie could see that the corridor led off on both the right and left of her. She bent over briefly to catch her breath. Summer, however, skipped ahead towards a row of windows, beckoning Maggie to come and see! Maggie straightened up with a grimace and, doing her best to ignore the voice screaming for a nicotine fix, moved forward to join her. The vista alone was worth the effort. From the window, Maggie found she was looking down upon the glass-domed roof of the hall below, with the rest of the building forming a sort of quadrangle around it, so that if you had walked along the corridor to the right, and continued along, you would end up where you had started. She noticed a figure standing across looking through the windows opposite them, and when the figure waved, realised it was Peter. She waved back with all the excitement of a schoolkid, and following Summer around the corridor soon came face to face with the man himself. She felt enchanted by the unexpected playfulness of the building, which had appeared so austere and dreary from without; like finding a delightful poem hiding in the middle of a chapter of tedious prose.

Peter smiled warmly at Maggie and could not have escorted her to the life drawing studio with any greater deference, had she been a member of the royal family. The studio was already filling with an assortment of students and members of the public who could enrol for this class as part of an adult education programme, so at least there was no need to feel particularly conscious of her age. Peter had thoughtfully reserved a donkey for her, (*yes seriously,* he said, *it is called donkey*), a small all-in-one stool and easel and had thoughtfully placed on it a board with paper and charcoal. *The best way*, he had said, *to understand how artists look at and think about you in life drawing, is to try it yourself.* Summer had grinned when he used the word artist, as though she was still only just getting used to the idea of being one herself.

Maggie had placed herself on the wooden seat of the donkey, wishing she had bought a cushion, as she notices some of the older students indeed had had the foresight to do. Then Summer settled herself beside her, unpacking her artists' materials from her bag, making nods and smiles of acknowledgement to other students she knew, as she did so. Minutes later the model for the evening, an unexpectedly corpulent woman in her fifties stepped out from behind the changing screen and Peter called for the class to begin.

Well now, perhaps the idea of being a model was not so far- fetched after all.

Maggie startles, Peter has signalled that the time is up, but realising that his hand gesture had gone unobserved by the model, had broken the silence with a loud exclamation of

"Time's up". She had quite lost herself in her reminiscence and had had no sense of time passing. She experiences a momentary flashback to her time of catatonic stupor barely eighteen months ago, although standing here right now it seems a lifetime. She would certainly have made good life-modelling material then, she jokes to herself. The memory makes her shudder for all that. But now she needs to concentrate on the next pose.

Peter says quietly that she is doing really well and asks whether she thinks she can manage thirty minutes. He is being careful with her, taking it slowly. He invites her to try a sitting posture, then makes sure that she is comfortable. Maybe place the right hand there, so it is supported. Perhaps a footstall beneath the left foot, so that the blood is not blocked in the back of her thigh. What may seem fine now, may feel like torture in ten minutes time. Maggie nods, she is just an apprentice, with plenty to learn. She shrugs her shoulders to loosen the muscles in her back then finds her new point of focus and stillness.

Sure, but wasn't it funny really? The look on Peter's face. A look of genuine surprise battling with a look of trying not to seem impolite by being so surprised. "Why Maggie, this is remarkably good. You never mentioned that you had such talent yourself!" Peter was examining the sketches she had done of the Rubenesque matron in reclining pose, his head held to one side. "It has such sensitivity of line and is pretty accurate at the same time. Why, you're a bit of dark horse, aren't you? Where did you learn to draw like this?"

Maggie had suddenly felt more exposed than the model. What had she done? She had picked up the charcoal and lost herself in the task. She had not meant to expose her life to curiosity. She was not ready to have to explain herself. To tell a story so damning, so shameful. But Peter had sensed her discomfort. He was sorry, had not meant to put her on the spot, he was just really impressed. *Had she ever thought of studying formally?* Now that *was* funny. Her? Margaret Doyle

an art student. Sure, that would be the day! But Peter was serious, and it wasn't kindness or mealy-mouthed flattery. *Had she any other work she could show him? He would be genuinely interested to see.* And none of her "Go on, away with yez," would throw him off the scent. *As it happens, she might have a few paintings, but they were, well a bit wild, you might say.*
Well, now she well and truly had him interested.

Maggie comes back to the room. Her nose is itching, and her legs are feeling heavy and a bit numb. She fights the urge to scratch the itch, which renders it all the more urgent. She shifts her eyes to the clock. Can there really be only a few more minutes to go? She squeezes the muscles in her buttocks to pump the blood, then focuses on her breathing.

"Right, I think we will take a break there." Maggie is struck by the quiet authority in Peter's voice. *Here is a rare thing,* she thinks, *a man who is comfortable in his own skin. A man she would like to have met when she was still fancy free, all those years ago.*

During the break, Maggie clasps her robe securely about her and takes a tour of the class. Some of the sketches are clumsy and unpromising, this is an evening class she reminds herself, so some of these will be beginners, but is her head truly that big? And does her leg twist around like that? Maggie has to smother a giggle at one of the easels, where she has to tilt her head almost horizontally even to make out any recognizable body parts. But one or two of the drawings touch her with their beauty; can that really be the way they see her? She had become so used to feeling irrelevant, another one of those invisible Irish women, past the flowering of youth, who change beds and replace towels, then trudge home in their sensible flat shoes to Marks and Spencer's ready meals for one.

"How are you coping?" Peter looks into her face with earnest solicitation.

"Fine. Just fine," smiles Maggie.

"You seemed like an old hand," then colouring, "Sorry, God! I - didn't mean old, I…"

Maggie rescues him with a smile. A fleeting thought that he might be developing a little crush on her passes through her mind, but it is chased away by Summer bounding up, full of enthusiastic praise for her modelling. Maggie places a maternal arm around the younger woman's shoulder and squeezes her. "Maybe there is hope for me yet!"

The second half of the class starts punctually. Peter is nothing if not a strict timekeeper. He checks with Maggie that she is warm enough, then arranges her in a reclining pose which shows off her long back and narrow waist. He makes sure that she will be comfortable for thirty minutes then gives the word to start. With her face turned away from most of the class, Maggie feels more at ease to let her focus roam. She is aware of Peter moving around the room, spending a few minutes here and there with each student, offering guidance or encouragement in that soft lilting voice of his. She lets the sense of hushed concentration in the room wash over her. Now that the novelty of her situation is subsiding, she has the luxury to examine her feelings. She is surprised to identify a glow of pride with herself; and not just for the achievement of meeting the challenge of overcoming embarrassment. A pride that goes deeper. Sure, isn't it a bit like Adam and Eve, when they were still ranging happily through the garden of Eden, before that business with the serpent and the apple and the Tree of knowledge of Good and Evil? Free from the taint of Original Sin and innocent in their bodies of flesh, flesh which had not yet been sexualised or thought of as something that needed to be covered and hidden away. Living embodiments of God's grace.

It takes her by surprise, this unexpected joy, for hadn't she honestly half expected to experience something very different. And if she is being honest with herself, had she not seized this opportunity for just the purpose? Penitence through self-abasement, now isn't that what she truly had in mind? For hadn't she, Margaret Doyle, succumbed to the serpent and used her flesh in the service of temptation and sin, the devil's work? She had fallen, and grasping on to another who fell along with her, they and their child had paid the price. She needs this; this mortification of the flesh, this chance for atonement. But it seems there is to be none. She feels no shame, no humiliation. *Is this God's mercy, then? Yet God does not seem merciful by nature, for He made the serpent, and He gave us curiosity and desire, so why does He choose to punish us so?*

Maggie feels the scalding track of a tear sear the coolness of her face. She cannot wipe her eyes. She must not move. She sniffs as quietly as she can and wonders if this then is to be her penance, to suffer in silence; the secrets of her heart forever unspoken, her pain untold.

"Thank you, Maggie," calls Peter, "we'll take five minutes." But, for a little while, Maggie does not move, and when she does, she pulls on her robe and rushes out to find the ladies cloakroom, where she turns on the hot water taps and soaps her hands mercilessly:

> *Four grey walls, and four grey towers,*
> *Overlook a space of flowers,*
> *And the silent isle imbowers*
> *The Lady of Shalott.*

Summer and Peter see her go. They exchange puzzled looks of concern, then tacitly agree to give her some time. When she returns five minutes later, roll-up between her finger and thumb, she is smiling, but Peter can see her hands are even redder than usual.

"You okay, Kid?" He tries to keep the tone playful, free from anxiety. She likes this. No one has referred to her as a kid for a very long time. She nods her head and gestures with her hand. She had a bit of a wobble, but she is fine now.

The last pose seems to pass very quickly. Maggie calls to mind the images in Kathleen's photo albums. Her big sister and her friend, Yvonne, smiling on a Venetian gondola, before the Taj Mahal, half tumbling off skis in some Alpine resort. Photographic records of more than twenty years of happiness and mutual devotion. More than most of the happiest marriages can boast. Maggie cannot help a little smile when she thinks about how her sister has managed it. The courageous rebel behind an oh-so-conventional spinster's manner and appearance, who gave up her motherland, family and God, to find herself. *And of course, she gave up me*! thinks Maggie suddenly saddened, but she cannot begrudge Kathleen her act of freedom, and especially not her happiness. And now they have found each other again, Kathleen's courage will be Maggie's strength. Here, now, how fitting to be in her birthday suit at the beginning of the real-life of Maggie Doyle.

"I thought you were terrific," says Peter handing Maggie a glass of whiskey at their usual table in the Princess Louise, after the class is over.

"No one would ever have guessed it was your first time," gushes Summer, "how on Earth did you manage to hold so still? I would have been dying of self-consciousness and would have started fidgeting around terribly."

"Well, I think it helped enormously having been on the other side, you know, thinking about what you are really looking at when you draw someone, and it isn't the size of their boobs or backside, now is it?"

Summer flushes scarlet at this remark and Peter chuckles. These young kids are so easily embarrassed. He had forgotten how refreshing it is to be around more mature women. He raises his glass.

"Well, here's to our new muse," he smiles. "What butter and whiskey cannot cure, eh, Maggie?"

"I'll drink to that, so I will".

A little later they are joined by an excited Tony, Roger and Sarah. They are impatient to hear how the life class went and demand blow by blow details until Peter intervenes and sends them off to the bar for another round. When all has gone quiet, he turns to Maggie. *He was serious, didn't she know, the other day. He was truly impressed by her drawings and sincerely hopes she will continue to attend the evening class herself. He can offer her regular work in the day time, modelling for the full-time students, and she can sign up for the remainder of the term for the Tuesday evenings, and see how she gets on.*

There is no mistaking Maggie's enthusiasm. She had not enjoyed anything so much for ages. Peter is pleased to hear this and reminds her that he had been serious about her showing him her work. *It was not only kids who go to Art School, but she must also realise they take mature students, in fact, are always keen to do so! Everyone has to complete at least one year of a Foundation course before applying for a degree, so she could give it a year and then see how she goes. What does she have to lose?*

Maggie is dismissive. She makes light of his suggestion. *Sure, but she has to earn a living, she can't be galavanting around college at her time of life, with no means of paying for it, or keeping body and soul together.* But Peter seems to have all the answers. She lives in London so she would be eligible for a grant from the ILEA. *It's not much, but he imagines she does not earn a great deal changing beds at the hotel. What with some evening modelling sessions and some occasional chambermaiding to supplement the grant, she might find she is better off than she is at the moment. What does she think?*

"I think that we may be getting a little ahead of ourselves, so I do," replies Maggie sagely. *But if Peter would be interested in seeing some of her work, she would value his opinion. But he had better be warned, he may not like what he sees, and it is not empty platitudes that she is after.*

May 1980

It had been agreed that she would meet Peter after the main teaching day had ended at five o'clock. A light drizzle spots the Holborn pavements making Maggie glad she had thought to wrap her battered cardboard art folder in polythene. At four forty-five she is standing outside the entrance of the Art School pulling franticly on a poorly made roll-up and getting seriously cold feet.

What in Heaven's name can she be thinking? Peter is such a lovely man, (there! she admits it, well to be sure he does remind her of her dear Daddy at times, so he does), and he is going to be horrified. Or disgusted. Or both. Oh, to be sure, he will be far too kind to show it, but it will be there. That look; the look she had caught in the eyes of the doctors and nurses when they had read her notes. A kind of appalled disbelief that could not be masked by any amount of professionalism. An instinctive desire to avoid the taint of our most basic taboo. Maybe she should just turn around right now and head back to the flat and wash her hands of the whole ridiculous situation. And now isn't that a joke? She has had it with the handwashing, (she inspects her poor raw skin), she is sick of this relentless harpy on her back. She knows what she did, and maybe only she and God will ever understand the reasons, so why must she keep punishing herself? Surely, these past weeks cannot have been for nothing. What if this is meant to be? What if it is God's way of offering her redemption, a new life after all?

Her thoughts are interrupted by a cough. She glances up and sees Peter. She smiles and, brushing the ash from her coat, stubs out the roll-up against the wall.

"You ready?" he smiles, "I thought we could have a drink in the staff bar, it won't be busy just now and we can find a quiet corner." Maggie nods, picks up her portfolio and follows Peter in through the entrance and along the ground floor corridor to a pair of double white doors. Inside, he directs her to a large old leather sofa and low table at the far end of the room and goes over to the bar. Maggie lays the folder on the table, unties the fastenings and takes a deep breath.

"How did you get on, my Maggie May?" calls Kathleen, when she hears Maggie's key in the lock later the same evening. Kathleen is a bit of a Rod Stewart fan and had taken to calling her sister by the name of his song as a form of endearment. "Oh, Kathleen," breathes Maggie, "I am not saying he liked them, I am not sure anybody could, but Kathleen, he thinks they are really good. He thinks that they are enough to get me onto the Foundation course at any rate".

"And is that what you truly want, Maggie dear?" Kathleen enquires with sudden gravity.

"To be sure, Kathleen," Maggie nods "I really think it is."

"Then we had better get your application filled in and sent off," declares Kathleen holding up a form and waving it at her momentarily bewildered sister.

"Oh, Kathleen, God Bless you," cries Maggie taking the form and nearly sweeping Kathleen off her feet in a bear hug.

"Would you believe it now, Margaret Doyle applying for art school?"

"I would believe you could walk on water Maggie, if you set your heart on it".

"Kathleen! Shame on you, for such blasphemy," but she carries on hugging her anyway.

After tea, during which the two sisters chat happily about their respective days, Maggie settles down to complete the application for the one-year Foundation course in Art and Design, and then to plan which pieces of work she will take along to an interview, should she be lucky enough to be offered one.

As it happens, the portfolio of work she had shown to Peter, was not nearly as full as it had been when she had brought it home with her to the little flat, for Maggie had spent the evening before, sorting through the collection of painting and drawings, weeding out those she judged unsuitable for public scrutiny. And it had been at no little emotional cost. How sharply her chest had constricted, as she had pulled the carboard folder out from its place under her bed and looked inside it for the first time since her discharge from the hospital.

The first image she came across had proved no less confronting than she had anticipated and she had found herself transported back to the little art therapy room with Marion, the Art Therapist, sitting quietly to her side, as had been her custom. The paper had been soaked in red paint and almost scrubbed through with the agitation of her paintbrush. Maggie recalled how she had glanced towards Marion and almost laughed. Normally at this point, the paper would tear and she would scrobble it up into a ball and throw it into the bin, sometimes rushing to the sink to scrub the paint from her hands, until Marion would gently remind her that it was only paint and she was safe in the art therapy room. But on this day - on this day she had felt she could bear to stop and simply let it lie there. Let it be. Laying down her brush, she had pushed it away from her, and Marion had simply nodded in acknowledgement. It had been a turning point.

After that, the images had become more obviously and conventionally depictive, though often distorted and confused. Angels and Madonnas, demons and saints; suffused with menace and grief, countless fragments of familiar catholic iconography burst out of her unconscious, jostling for domination across sheet after sheet of pristine cartridge paper.

Maggie had leafed through the folder, examining each painting in turn. Some seemed fresh still in her mind, others on the hand, had taken her almost by surprise, consigned perhaps to temporary and blessed forgetfulness. It had not been an easy task.

She recalled how, little by little, she had begun to trust in Marion as a quiet and unjudging witness to this out-pouring of her internal turmoil until at last, she had felt ready to speak. To give words to her grief and guilt, her fear and horror. To feel the relief of a soul unburdened. The comfort of a trouble shared.

Then Maggie had turned to the shadowy image of the Cardinal. Just seeing it again, all these months later, had caused her breath to catch in her throat.

"It is the Cardinal," she had whispered back then, searching Marion's face for recognition. "He would have denied my baby a baptism, would have barred his soul from heaven for all eternity. Would have …." But she had been unable to carry on.

"You fear him, even now?" Marion had asked, reading the terror in Maggie's eyes.

"I am not sure he will ever really let me go…"

And even as Maggie remembered she had shuddered. She had still been unwell then, she knew that. Yet, all the same…

Still, looking back, and despite the pain and confusion they evoked, Maggie could recognize a growing aesthetic, even in these early attempts. Fortunately, the number of images she had made in the actual therapy sessions, had been balanced by a good selection of studies and experimental projects she had tried, when the art therapy room had been open for studio-time. The content of these studies had been emotionally neutral, yet while they demonstrated a development in her technical skill, Maggie could not help but feel they lacked the creative flair of the other more personal images. She knew enough of Peter by now, to know that he would want to see some genuine aspect of herself, in her work. She would need to strike the right balance, even if it meant going out on a bit of a limb.

She had thus selected out those which she felt to be too revealing or disturbing, and had placed them safely at the back of her wardrobe. She did not care to have to look at them again in a hurry, if ever, yet she could no more bring herself to destroy or discard these tormented souvenirs of that other life than she could disavow that part of herself that had been forged in the darkest hours of her suffering. Yet, even as she stowed the painting safely away, she was struck by a strong feeling of relief; relief that she had escaped being entirely sucked back into that place of such savage pain and despair. It had not been without good reason, that Marion had hesitated to allow Maggie to take the folder home with her when she had asked. Technically, they were considered part of a patient's records, although photographing them all would satisfy that function. Part of her felt that it would be better for Maggie to leave the images behind, as though in safe-keeping, and yet the making of them had become so big a part of Maggie's recovery that it would seem a deprivation to refuse her them. In the end, therefore, Marion had trusted in Maggie's instinctive sense of what was right for her, and relented.

When the selection had finally been completed, Maggie had slumped exhausted on the floor next to her bed and had stared at her hands. They were grimy from the dust and tiny flakes of dried paint, yet it was no visible stain that caused them to throb with the demand for purification. Maggie had sighed, she was too emotionally spent to fight it. So once, just this once, she would give in. But she had done well, and she would not deny herself this recognition. It had been difficult, but it had been worth it. Such self-compassion may do much, for even as she had picked herself off the carpet and headed for the bathroom, the grip of the compulsion loosened its hold a little. *Three times,* she had congratulated herself afterwards, *just three times. Not bad, not bad at all.*

All the same, and try as he might to disguise it, Maggie had been able to read it on Peter's face, that he had been taken aback by the raw and undisguised anguish that exuded from one or two of the pieces. This said, Maggie had been all the more impressed by the sensitivity with which he navigated away from focusing on its origin, commenting only and hesitantly that they put him in mind of Bacon, or perhaps Goya at his darkest. Maggie had responded with a blank question mark. She had no idea what or who he could mean, and Peter realised at once that here was a talent uninfluenced by education or example, which made the imagery all the more remarkable.

He went on to discuss the formal qualities of the paintings, which had been made only with acrylic paints and school quality water-colours, drawing attention to Maggie's use of colour and composition, and what he called "painterliness." Maggie had listened, her eyes wide and lips parted, hanging on his every word. Through Peter's eyes, she began to see beyond the discomforting content and appreciate the more formal aspects of her own efforts. *Not that emotion was not important*, added Peter, *of course it was, but learning to harness it in service of the artistic endeavour, now that was the key to great art.* Maggie's skin had prickled as he spoke. As he continued, she had marvelled at the animation and passion in his voice and looks, and it was a passion that seemed contagious. Maggie's creativity seemed to have erupted as a brute outpouring, driven more by a psychological necessity than any aesthetic intention, the force of it had taken her by surprise. Yet, as time had gone on, she had taken increasing satisfaction and even pleasure in the execution of the images. Listening to Peter, it was as though, for the first time in her life, somebody else was speaking her language and she found herself impatient to learn more.

Peter, perhaps not entirely oblivious to the impact he was making, had smiled that gentle smile of his and pointed out a series of the images that he felt displayed a development in her style. These, he suggested, should be among those she should take to her interview. (He did not seem to doubt she would be offered one). And it might be a good idea to include a good selection of life drawings, so as to demonstrate the less, well, primitive side of her talent. *And she should probably catch up on some art history,* he had concluded with a smile.

The Angel, Islington.

"I'll be late back tonight. I am going to see that new play at the Royal Court. So, can you give Annie a call and check she is okay with the design for the wedding invitations?"

There is a mumbled half response from behind the Guardian. It has the ring of anything-you-say-dear-without-having-heard-a-word-of- it about it.

"Peter, are you paying attention?" Wendy's voice jars with a shrillness that has become all too familiar over the last twelve months.

"Yes, what Dear?" Peter folds down the broadsheet and looks at his wife over the rim of his half-moon glasses. Then spying a black shape on the kitchen counter shouts hoarsely, "Stanley, get off the worktops, how many times must I tell you!" The black cat stares as him with an expression of imperial disdain, then slopes off down and away to his favourite spot on the windowsill. Peter shakes his paper with irritation. Wendy ignores him, fondling the head of a second, tabby-coloured cat, who sensitive to the angry vibes, is rubbing against her shins for reassurance.

"It's alright Ollie, Daddy isn't cross with you, *you* are a good boy".

Peter rolls his eyes. He thinks about saying something about how she spoils the cats, but he can feel her waiting for the argument that will inevitably ensue and decides it is just not worth it this morning. Wendy looks back up in his direction and continues tightly:

"The invitations, I just asked you to call Annie this evening..." but her husband's eyes have already flicked back to the columns on the folded broadsheet.

"Oh, what's the point! I might as well do it myself, I'll end up doing it anyway, just forget it and read your paper," Wendy snaps.

"Oh, for Christ's sake, Love. Must we have this every morning? I get it. You think I am a waste of space, but c'mon Love we been married nearly twenty-five years, surely you know by now that I am not very with it, first thing in the morning."

"First thing in the morning?" snorts Wendy "When else do I ever see you? You spend more time drinking in that damn pub with your little fan club than you do with me. Peter Pan and his gang of lost fucking children".

"Don't call me that!" Peter is raising his voice now. She had called him Peter Pan since the night they had first met, back in the heady days of all night jazz gigs at The Flamingo Club in Soho and dancing till the small hours at The Humphrey Littleton Club in Oxford Street. He was eight years her senior, but it had been Love at First Sight, and to her eyes, he was eternally young and handsome; a worldly Peter Pan to her naïve and homely Wendy. But now the name is mocking, a rebuke.

"Well, maybe it is just nice to feel appreciated."

"Appreciated! I worshipped you, and you lapped it up. You had such a gift, Peter, you were going do such great things, you made Piper and Freud and the rest of that crew seem so pedestrian, and then..."

"And then what?" There is a chill of anger in Peter's voice.

"You got lazy, Peter. You started that teaching and somewhere along the line you just gave it away, lost the drive…"

"Your idea - we had no money, remember? You were studying and someone had to pay the bills…"

"Oh, so now it was my fault. The truth of the matter is, you couldn't bear it when it turned out that I was the one who was successful."

"That's right. Wendy Carmichael PhD, chair of English Literature, respected academic, published author, loyal wife and mother and all-round superwoman. Have I missed something? Sorry, I was forgetting. Why don't I just cut off my balls and wrap them up for you with a big red ribbon?"

Wendy crumbles suddenly. She slumps into the chair opposite Peter, face in hands. Peter becomes aware that he is shaking. A mark has been overstepped. He knows it, yet is somehow unable or unwilling to own it or pull back.

Presently, Wendy raises her head and smooths back her hair, the same hair he had loved to run his fingers through, was it really so long ago?

"I can't do this anymore Peter…" she says with sadness. "We'll maintain this pretence until after the wedding, I am not having us ruin her day, then I'll move out to the house in Aldburgh. The Dean has offered me a one-year sabbatical to write this book, I can go there, work in peace and quiet. We can sort out the legal stuff as and when."

"You never mentioned a new book, what is this one about?"

"Beckett. The later stuff…"

"Ah, yes Beckett. How apt. The Absurd. You fucking hate Beckett, you fell asleep in the last play we went to!"

They both laugh.

"Do you remember Wendy, we never missed a new play before Annie came along and God, we saw some rubbish?"

"Good stuff too though…"

Peter nods, then shakes his head with the smallest of laughs.

"We had a good run, Peter. Let's end this now whilst we can still be friends, for Annie's sake and for all those wonderful years". Wendy's voice is low and soft, as though the bitterness and anger have drained away like the passing years.

Peter chews his lip, pinches the bridge of his nose to hold back the tears and nods. He has seen this moment coming for months, maybe years even, like realising too late you have boarded the wrong non-stop train and having to sit it out until you reach the final destination. Now the moment of arrival is here he feels sadness. And bored. Why do marital arguments always have to sound the same? Shit, they cannot even stretch to a note of originality in the dying throes. This one has cliché stamped all over it. And why? Because it always comes down to the same old issue. The thing that you found most attractive about your partner when you first met, is the very same thing that drives you nuts ten years later. Wendy had loved his lack of ego and hunger for success and fame when they had first hooked up. She had fallen for the old overlooked and misunderstood genius thing and the prospect that she could be the one to give him the self-belief he needed. The woman behind the great man. By the time she realised that all the devotion and dedication of her love was not sufficient to defeat his inner demons, Annie had come along; but the less he thinks about that, the better. Then later, her consolation for her disappointment with Peter was to seek the accolades of academia for herself.

And now here she is, a world authority on twentieth-century English Literature, with two, no it was three books under her belt, not to mention the three moderately successfully novels she had had published in the last four years. If he had not been such a coward, he would have had an affair and put them both out of their misery years ago, but even though he had lived through the sixties, his ideas about marriage and fidelity were forged in the fifties, when divorce still left a nasty taste in the mouth and was the reserve of film stars and the aristocracy.

Peter realises Wendy is waiting, patient, but expecting a reply. He reaches across the table and taking her hand in his, strokes the wedding ring they had found in an antique shop just up the road on Islington Green, long before they had made the Angel their home.

A tear rolls down Wendy's cheek. Peter nods his head thoughtfully and meets her eye.

"I know you are right. I'll move into the spare room tonight. I think we can manage not to kill each other until Annie is married."

Wendy kisses his hand.

"My Peter Pan," she whispers wistfully, and this time Peter smiles.

5th May 1980. Liverpool.

Jack is sitting in front of the little T.V in Father Frank's sitting room watching the BBC news. He knows he should be working on his end of teaching-practice assignment, yet cannot tear himself away. Some two hundred miles away in London's South Kensington, a drama is being played out in the Iranian embassy. The news cameras have been trained upon the grand building for the last six days. Inside twenty-six men and women have been held hostage at gunpoint. Jack tries to picture what that must be like. One day you are going about your business as usual and then the world turns upside down. But for all his imagining he cannot find it in himself to honestly care, and wonders when his heart had become so hardened. He searches again to find some pity or warmth in his heart but finds only a morbid voyeurism that feeds upon the titillation of round the clock media coverage, like carrion on roadkill.

At least it is not the Irish for a change, he thinks, and there is perhaps a small comfort in that. Few Irishmen had escaped the anti-Irish sentiment that had swept the mainland since the IRA bombing campaign had swung into force since 1973, and it had not been twelve months since Airy Neave had been blown to pieces in the car park of the House of Commons. It was bad enough that the Irish had been the butt of English jokes for the last hundred years, but now it was not unusual to be viewed with aversion and suspicion, never mind which side of the border you came from. Jack shakes his head sadly, how can there be so much hatred in the world? And how can people kill each other over the minor doctrinal differences that separate their faiths. He knows full well that there is more to it than that, yet isn't that how it all started? He supposes that he ought to understand, but indeed he cannot.

Back in rural Southern Ireland, it all seemed so clear cut, and as a boy he never questioned it. But if he had been bought up in another family, in another place, or another time, wouldn't he have felt exactly the same about whatever set of beliefs he had been born into? He has thought about such things a great deal since he arrived in Liverpool, almost as if there had been a domino effect, and the first domino to tumble had been caused by the prohibition of the baptism of his dying baby son. This had not been Love. This had been Power. People always say God is Love, but the threat of the loss of his love, the threat of damnation is about control. Why hadn't he seen it before?

He had had a good life in the church, he supposes. There was comfort, a career and certainty, and no need to struggle with the bigger questions. But surely, he had done so as a younger man? Try as he might, he can't remember. His own past seems screened off to him by an impenetrable fog. He wants to talk to Frank, who is unwavering in his faith, despite his impressive scholarism. Frank whom he reveres and to whom he can always turn. Yet, still he feels afraid. Of what? He wonders. Of upsetting him, or incurring his disapproval, or worse, his disappointment. Jack feels adrift. Frank has been his lifeboat, but even lifeboats can capsize when the swell is great enough.

The scenes on the flickering T.V are shifting quickly now. There has been the sound of gunshots and there is smoke rising from a shattered window. The siege is coming to its inevitable and bloody end.

Jack wonders about the application he has only this morning sent off for his probationary year's teaching at a school in London. Perhaps he is crazy. He has a sudden thought that London might swallow him up, and maybe, maybe spit him out again. He thinks of Jonah and the whale. Perhaps, exactly such a transformative experience would be the antidote to his ills. Ever the pragmatist Frank had advised him to - "Just get on with it" and perhaps he is right. Life is not a dress rehearsal, no matter what the afterlife might hold in store.

That evening Maggie breezes into the life drawing studio a little earlier than usual and finds it empty apart from Peter who is sitting on the dais smoking and staring at the floor. Maggie coughs to let him know she is there. He smiles a sad smile, then greets her and says he has something for her. Maggie grins. Peter delves inside his leather satchel and produces a battered paperback tome. *Gombrich's The Story of Art*. Maggie raises her eyebrows. Peter suggests she will be needing this is she is going to pursue a place on the foundation course. Understanding how painting has developed over the centuries and how art reflects history is fundamental to any good painter's education. Maggie grins again, then covers her mouth with her hands, suddenly self-conscious of her tobacco-stained teeth. As soon as she gets the better of the hand-washing she will tackle smoking. But not yet, please God, not just yet. A woman needs her crutches, so she does.

She reaches out and takes the book with a cautious hand. Peter cannot but notice the stains that discolour her long fingers as she turns the pages with rapt attention. By and by Maggie becomes aware that he is watching her and flicks a glance towards his face, but cannot read his looks, any more than she is now able to concentrate on the pictures and writing on the pages in front of her eyes. Finally, she lowers the volume and looks directly at Peter.

"What? Is it something on my face you can be looking at? As I am thinking it cannot be that you have never seen a woman read a book before!"

"Please forgive my manners, Maggie," blurts Peter in a tone of genuine apology. "I was just wondering if, well, if you have ever been to an art gallery?"

Maggie laughs.

"Sure, what business would I have had doing anything of the kind?" Then, realising how odd this sounds coming from someone who is going to apply for art school, adds - "That is to say, I had thought about taking meself off to that big fancy one, you know, down the way with all the pillars and steps, Trafalgar Square, is it now?"

"You mean The National gallery?"

"Sure now, that would be the one. Only, to tell the truth, I have been just lacking the courage. It seems an awful grand place, so it does."

"Maggie," asks Peter softly "would you do me the honour of allowing me to act as your guide and show you around one afternoon, perhaps this weekend if you are not working?"

Maggie blushes.

"I would absolutely love to, and I am not working Sunday afternoon, but I am sure you must have plans yourself…"

Peter closes his eyes and imagines the silent frostiness of his flat.

"Believe you me Maggie, you will be doing me a huge favour right now."

Sunday afternoon arrives with all the pleasantness that one might reasonably expect from an early English summer's day. Maggie is waiting, seated on the stone steps of the National Gallery, watching the pigeons and tourists go about their respective business around Trafalgar Square. She eyes her watch and notices that the hour has not yet struck, but knowing Peter will not be late, throws down her roll-up and crushes it beneath her shoe. She follows a couple of straw-hatted ice-cream-lapping day-trippers with her eyes and feels for all the world as though she too is on holiday. And here is Peter, on the dot, making his way across from the underground station, the breeze catching his quiff of greying wavy hair, and making his shirt sleeves flutter.

She rises to her feet, raising her eyes, to greet him. There is a moment of awkward formality. Do they exchange kisses to the cheek, like the little groups of friends she notices passing before them into the gallery, or shake hands or what? Peter, a seasoned cheek kisser feels the awkwardness of the moment too, but shrugs it off with a purposeful clapping together of his hands and a - "Well now Maggie, was there anything you particularly wanted to see, or are you happy to put yourself in my hands?"

Sure now, if only all hands were as gentle, thinks Maggie to herself and nods happily. Peter, taking the part of the perfect gallery guide ushers her towards the imposing entrance of the gallery with a smile. Maggie clutches her handbag for reassurance, takes a breath and steps in, head bowed, as though entering a cathedral.

Inside, the lobby throngs with eager culture-vultures. Maggie has seldom seen so many people in one space. Where she comes from the town and his wife head to church on a Sunday. Londoners, it seems, head to the galleries for their glimpse of the Divine. Peter struggles through the crowd to find Maggie a paper-guide to the layout of the gallery. Handing it to her, however, he explains that rather than just wandering aimlessly, he had taken the liberty of selecting a limited number of pieces from around the gallery for her to see. Trying to see the whole collection would be exhausting and nigh on impossible. This way she could get a general feel for the place and hopefully see some examples of the giants of art history she might have read about in Gombrich. Maggie nods excitedly, oh yes, she had already read it cover to cover. *Really?* Peter is impressed. Well, he hopes she approves of his choices then, for she may already be more of an expert than him.

Maggie walks next to Peter, her eyes wide, neck craning to the left and right, savouring the muted light and downy hush of whispered comments and exchanges. One moment she is transfixed by the marble lines of the sculptures that dominate the space of the main hallway, the next her eyes drink in the loftiness and grandeur of the building itself and she stands stock-still, gaze turned upwards to take in the play of light on the stucco work of the ceiling and arches. From time to time, Peter finds he must take her by the arm to gently guide her out of the path of an oncoming gaggle of gallery visitors. He cannot help but smile at the refreshing naivete of an awe unpolluted by the need to appear culturally *au fait* or sophisticated.

He wonders what it must be like to see the greatest achievements of Western Art through fresh and untired eyes, and for a moment is forced to acknowledge that he is actually feeling a little envious. He had been trailed around galleries on Sunday afternoons since he could remember, and for the longest time, the marvels of Reynolds and Ingres had become like so much background wallpaper. He had, thank the Lord, eventually learned to rediscover the genius in the oh-so-familiar, through his own relationship with paint and charcoal, and of course, once the shine had rubbed off the beguiling distractions of Pollack and De Kooning. Not that he admired them less, it was more than he had come to admire their forebears more.

Peter is about to signal to Maggie that they have arrived at the first exhibit, he wants to show her, when he realises that she has disappeared from his side. He experiences a momentary sense of panic. The gallery has been steadily filling up and it is almost impossible to pick an individual out amid the sea of heads clustered around the paintings and statues, or filing in and out of adjacent rooms. He tries to recall what she is wearing, but he has never been one to notice such things; just ask Wendy. His capacity to fail to notice a new dress or hairstyle would drive her to despair. He knows that Maggie looked nice, pretty even, if he is honest. He seems to recall she was wearing her hair long and free. Indeed, now he comes to think of it, he had noticed it was a rather beautiful shade of auburn, tinged with silver threads of grey. He is surprised at this uncustomary attention to detail but brushes this thought aside and scans around him. Look. Over there. Isn't that she? He sees the back of a woman's head, thick copper-toned tresses of hair tumbling down her back, gazing at a picture some yards away. He approaches. It is Maggie. She is standing, as though in a trance, eyes fixed upon Fra Filippo Lippi's jewel-like depiction of The Annunciation. She seems to sense that he is close as he approaches her, though she does not move.

"Oh, Peter, look, it is Gabriel. Isn't he just beautiful?"

"Maggie, I thought I had lost you," says Peter, a tremble in his voice betraying his relief. He quickly continues:

"And if it is angels you want, I promise you I have the most beautiful angel of all on my list for you today. You wait and see".

Maggie turns away from the painting and looks at Peter with shining eyes.

"Not the most beautiful, Peter," she says quietly, and Peter thinks he sees the glisten of a solitary teardrop on her cheek, "for I'll not see him again, not in this life anyway."

Peter looks at her quizzically, but she just smiles a small sad smile and takes his arm.

"Now, what are we looking at first?"

The afternoon passes in a blur of joyful discovery for Maggie. Peter leads her from the arresting chiaroscuro of Caravaggio's Supper at Emmaus to the mesmerising tenderness of Raphael's Madonna with Pinks. They both smile as they remember Roger's drawing of her and how they had all first met. Maggie drinks in the images as one who has been near dying with thirst. She listens with unfeigned fascination as Peter expounds the formal qualities of each painting, and giggles when they notice that he has attracted a growing audience of attentive listeners from amongst the gallery-goers. Peter bows his head in embarrassment and taking Maggie by the elbow, mutters something entirely inaudible and ushers them both away, as quickly as politeness will permit.

Next, they pay a visit to Rembrandt Van Rijn, and it is all Peter can do to restrain Maggie from touching the luscious textures of the brushwork with her fingers.

Peter throws in Turner's Fighting Temeraire for good measure and delights in Maggie's pure delight at the audacity of the wild man's vision. He realises that he has not enjoyed a Sunday afternoon so much for many years, perhaps not since Annie was a little girl. But he can see that Maggie, for all her enthusiasm, is approaching exhaustion. He leads her at last to the angel he had promised. Da Vinci's Virgin of The Rocks.

The crowd is thinning out now and the galleries are becoming increasingly gloomy as the afternoon wears on, but Maggie can scarcely take her eyes off the sublime face of Leonardo's celestial messenger. There is a seat free in front of the painting, so the two of them sit in silent contemplation. Peter is half wishing that they could stay there like this forever.

He takes a sideways glance at Maggie. The copper tint of her hair seems almost to gleam in the muted light and all but creates an aura around her head and shoulders. Meanwhile, the softness of the shadows has dissolved the furrows of worry, (or could it be sorrow?) that line her face and suddenly she appears as one untouched by the passing of the years. Peter feels his skin all at once a-prickle with the proximity between their two bodies. He wonders if she feels it too, but if she does, she does not betray it in her looks. *Time to go home* he thinks and making a small cough, signals that the lesson for today is over. However:

"There is one final painting I wanted to show you, if you are not too tired and since it is on the way out," says Peter. He has paused before a canvas mounted in a heavy golden frame.

"Ha! Now, you didn't think I would know this one, did you?" Maggie beams with glee. "It is one of Van Gogh's sunflower series. Sure, but didn't I have it on a calendar in me old kitchen. I'm thinking he had a way with paint, even if the man did slice off his poor wee ear!"

Peter smiles. That childlike candour again.

"But Peter," continues Maggie, "that makes me think, I can't tell you how much I love the paintings here, but they are all very, well - old. Do they not have anything - you know, done this century? I would love to see some, you know, *modern art.*" She drops her voice and mouths the last two words as though the very notion might be forbidden in such a place.

"Well," replies Peter sternly "that makes it necessary for us to visit the Tate next weekend".

"Oh, Peter, you really mean it?"

"Well, we can't be leaving your art education half-finished, that would be sadly remiss, don't you think?" Maggie grins. Peter shakes his head. He wonders if he knows what he is doing. He searches his heart for caution but finds only a giddy recklessness he thought he had left behind with his youth.

Islington

Wendy shoos Ollie off her favourite spot on the sofa and sinks into the familiar softness of its old and battered cushions. She had thought about getting it reupholstered this year. She had seen exactly the right fabric in John Lewis, last time she had been in Oxford Street, but it hardly seems worth it now. She sighs and balances the old photo album on her knees. Perhaps she is being a little sentimental, maudlin even, but you don't just walk away from almost twenty-five years of marriage without a backwards glance. She purses her lips and opens the cover. There it is. That old black and white portrait, the one she had always loved so much. It had been the first photograph she had ever taken of Peter, not long after they had met. She had had her own darkroom back then, although she had considered her dabbling with developing and printing a relaxing hobby, rather than any serious attempt to become a photographer. Still, it was not a bad photograph, if she said so herself. It had captured something about Peter, something that even now she finds difficult to articulate.

She turns the pages of the old album, whilst Ollie rubs against her shins, purring. She leans down to tickle his ear, without shifting her attention. So many memories. The next photograph depicts a young woman with long blonde hair, in a black polo neck sweater, matching close-fitting slacks and bare feet. The signature beatnik style. She smiles at the irony. How quickly the kick against conformity, becomes the uniform of every fresh generation. Look how serious she is trying to appear, an undergraduate with all her life before her. How she had adored Kerouac and Ginsberg; until she met Peter, and then there was only room for him. Eight years her senior, he seems so worldly and sophisticated. She never stood a chance.

There is a solitary snap of the two of them at a "happening" that she cannot even remember now, but nothing else to document their courtship. Her graduation photograph with mortarboard and gown. She had been the first woman in her family to gain a degree. Something we take so much for granted now, she reflects, but it still *meant* something back in the fifties. The next page reveals a shot of Peter and herself outside the little Registry Office in Islington. Mr and Mrs Carmichael. How long ago it all seems now. She had been insistent on rejecting the bourgeois notion of the white wedding, something for which her parents had never quite forgiven her. Besides she was already pregnant with Annie. Now she is organising the wedding of her own, only daughter, she wonders whether, after all, they had merely felt cheated out of the wedding day they had dreamed off since she had been a babe in her cot. Strange how our perspectives shift with the passing of time.

The following pages provide a peek into the comfortable domesticity of the newly-weds. Peter at his easel; digging the garden; playing with Seamus the enormous and lovable Red Setter they had bought back from Battersea Dog's home. How they had grieved when he had been knocked over and killed on the road outside their first flat. Then she comes across the shot of herself holding Annie in the hospital. She looks so drained. So vacant. The image still chills her heart and it is a time she does not like to remember. Yet Peter had been so full of joy, with an energy she had not known he possessed, until then. And just as well. Again, there are woefully few photographs, though perhaps this is not so surprising. But those there are, tell the story. Peter holding Annie; Peter changing her nappy; feeding her, bathing her. She wonders who took them. There is not a single photograph of her herself with Annie as a baby. Wendy experiences a moment of painful guilt. She knows she was not to blame, yet she feels it none-the-less.

She turns the page hurriedly, glad to move on from that dark time. The three of them outside the little caravan they had rented in St Ives, that year Peter had been Artist-in-Residence for the summer. Annie can only have been three. How small she seems. Why didn't they look happier? Surely, they had been by then? She turns the pages, memories coming back to her thick and fast. Peter digging the garden, again; in shorts on a beach paddling; in the rock pools with Annie; Peter riding a bike, Annie balanced on the handlebars. Herself and Annie having a teddy bears' picnic on the back lawn. Annie the solemn hostess; her favourite bears, impeccable in their manners, with plates of cake untouched, until Annie had poured the tea. Wendy smiles. This had always been Pete's favourite picture. Ollie jumps up beside her and snuggles against her hip. Stan, not wishing to miss out on his share of the attention, leaps up and onto the arm of the sofa and mews cheerfully. Wendy leaves through the remaining pages, family holidays, Christmases and birthdays. These were the very happy times, the glue of their marriage and family life. There are more albums, testaments to Annie's blossoming through the years of teenage rebellion into the beautiful young woman she is today, their mutual and finest creation. But these can wait for another day.

She rubs her forehead against Stan's and he trills happily. She closes the album and re-opens it at the first page. That portrait of Peter. So youthful for his age, her Peter Pan, yet so earnest. All at once, an insight occurs to her as to why he might choose to hang out with students less than half his age. How could she not have seen it before? He had never really spoken about it, at least not in any detail, but in those days people seldom did. He had been robbed of the normal exuberance and carefree optimism that you are supposed to enjoy in your early twenties. Instead of hanging around cafes and listening to Jazz in smoky dives, Peter had been subjected to sights and experiences for which no young mind can be fully prepared. Plucked out of art school and posted off to Italy to capture the suffering of the wounded and dying in pencil and paint, he had had to grow up very fast and had missed the heady comradery of student life. And then, once he was home, just as he was starting to recover, hadn't he been doubly robbed?

She had to admit it to herself. Pete had been prone to bouts of melancholia when she had first met him, it was probably part of the attraction, if she is honest. She raises her eyebrows at Stan, who takes this as an opportunity to remind her it is getting close to tea time, with a dab of is paw on her upper arm. So, wasn't she supposed to be his Wendy, the girl who comes to his rescue, with her youthfulness and optimism about the world? But it had not worked out that way. Wendy gathers Stan up in her arms and cuddles him. If only she had been able to do such a thing with her own child. Yet she had been crushed beneath the deadening weight of post-natal depression and that one simple act, which is so natural and instinctive for most new mothers, had seemed completely beyond her. God knows what would have become of them, had Peter not taken over the parenting role in those early months. He had even given up the teaching post he had taken by then, so that he could be at home fulltime and care for both of them.

Wendy nuzzles Stan, who is starting to wriggle hungrily. He had had little chance to savour that joy that he had felt on that first day, though Peter would never have it said. Little chance to be a carefree Dad in a happy family. Not in those early days at least. And then, once Annie had started school, he had given his young wife so much encouragement to forge a career for herself, to rebuild her shattered self-confidence. Yet what of his own ambition? She had been serious the other day at breakfast. Peter had shown great promise amongst his peers. There had been great hopes for his future as a painter, yet he never seemed able to translate it into success. Even as a teacher, and he is a very talented teacher, Wendy is in no doubt of that, he had seemed to lack the drive to apply for more senior positions and almost to shy away from professional advancement. Wendy, who had seized the bit between her teeth and fought her way into the still patriarchal world of academia, had felt nothing but frustration with the man she had once revered.

She cringes when she recalls how often she had taken to belittling him for seeming to prefer the company of his students to achievement and status. And sadly, although once they had enjoyed the same interest in theatre and the arts, their preferences had become more diverse over the years, their lives more separate. Wendy had no time for Peter's love of Opera or even jazz, for all her beatnik pretensions, and preferred the Beatles and the Rolling Stones. She suddenly wishes she had made a little more effort. She looks at the face of the man she used to know. Why had she not understood that he had been trying to recapture a youth he had never really had? How could she have failed him so badly? But it is all too late now, and she knows it. She hopes he finds the happiness he deserves, she truly does.

"Now what are we going to get you for your supper?" she coos to Stan and Ollie, as her eyes threaten to moisten. The two cats scatter to the floor in unison, tails high in the air, arching their backs and stretching, ready to tuck in their napkins. Animals can be such a wonderful distraction at times.

A lot can happen in six weeks. The weekend after they had visited The National, Peter escorts Maggie to the Tate Gallery, where he shows her the marvels of twentieth-century painting. Maggie drinks in the masterpieces by Cezanne, Matisse and Picasso and their contemporaries. She thrills at the audacious canvases of Franz Klein and Barnett Newman, and approaches a state of near bliss in the room dedicated to Mark Rothko. Yet, and rather to Peter's surprise, nothing could compare with her reaction when they happen upon Waterhouse's Lady of Shalott. For on seeing her, Maggie whispers,

> *And as the boat-head wound along*
> *The willowy hills and fields among*
> *They heard her singing her last song,*
> *The Lady of Shalott.*

Then, inexplicably, she bursts into tears. Feeling very uncool, she brushes it off as maudlin sentimentality, yet Peter can see there is more to it than that. He is deeply intrigued. Indeed, it would be no exaggeration to say that he is beginning to find himself ensnared within a web of beguilement, every bit as enchanted as the one of Shalott's weaving.

Over the next three consecutive Sunday afternoons, Maggie and Peter visit The Courtauld Institute, The Institute of Contemporary Art and an oblique an excruciatingly dull touring exhibit at The Serpentine Gallery in Kensington Gardens, which proves a test even for Maggie's ebullience.

Rounding off the whistle-stop tour with the latest offerings at the Whitechapel Gallery, Peter has now pretty much run out of galleries and therefore excuses to spend time with his protege. Thus, for the first time since he and Wendy had begun to disentangle the long threads of their lives, Peter finds himself obliged to spend an entire miserable weekend in his own company, with only the condescending attentions of Stan and Ollie for companionship. Even Wendy seems moved to pity when she returns from a weekend walking with friends and, finding him in unusually low spirits, invites him to share her evening meal. Peter reflects on what a good woman she is. Perhaps he was crazy to let the marriage go without more of a fight, but he is dreaming of shining auburn hair, even as he thinks it.

Maggie meanwhile had been offered an interview for the foundation course at the art college and is fast becoming one of the most popular regular life models, whilst continuing to attend the Tuesday evening class as a student herself. She works all the shifts she can at the Russell, to have some money to put away, but no longer begrudges the work, as the role of chambermaid no longer defines her being. It is just something she does.

"And wouldn't that old fellow Jean-Paul Sartre have been proud of me," she thinks to herself; for in addition to expanding her knowledge of the Fine Arts, and guided by Peter's direction, she has begun to read avidly. She needs to, for hasn't she a lifetime of learning to catch up with? And sure now, doesn't every book she reads, take her a step further away from her old life, her old self, the old Margaret Doyle? *The further the better,* thinks Maggie. *The further the better.*

The first Thursday evening in June, after she had been modelling all day for the first and second years, Maggie has gathered together Peter and the gang in the Princess Louise and after insisting on buying the first round, stands up, clears her throat and makes an announcement.

"I thought I would let you all know, I have been offered a place on the foundation course, so I have. I am going to be an art student. Can you imagine it?" Her grin threatens to stretch from ear to ear.

Peter offers a warm handshake of congratulations, whilst the lads whoop and whistle and clap, and the girls get up and take turns to embrace her warmly. Then, all raising their glasses, they cry "Whiskey and Butter" in unison and laugh with delight.

"One thing though," cautions Summer wagging a finger at Maggie,

"Now you are one of us - we have just got to get you some cooler clothing. You and me girl, we are heading to Camden Market this weekend and no arguments!"

Maggie opens her mouth, then closes it. She looks down at her floral print blouse, Marks and Spencer's 'A' line skirt and low-heeled court shoes and bursts out laughing.

"I wouldn't want to change a thing" offers Roger gallantly, "you are, and always will be the Madonna of Southampton Row - whatever you are wearing."

Tony cuffs him playfully, "And he has only had one pint!"

Sarah, meanwhile, is studying Peter. She has long since suspected that he is carrying a smouldering torch for their new friend, and although she is as fond of Maggie as any of the others, her pleasure in learning that she will be staying around is somewhat tainted by the ugly green stain of jealousy. It is bad enough that Roger is fawning over her as usual, and alright, she knows that Peter is old enough to be her father, perhaps, if she is being honest, even her grandfather, but there is something so attractive about the silver hairs around his temples, the ruggedness of his face and the mellow timbre of his voice that makes her want to melt like butter in the sun. But whilst it is clear he enjoys the youthful company and adulation of his younger students, there is something quite different in his interaction with Maggie. She is, Sarah supposes, closer to his age, although of course at the tender age of twenty, anyone over thirty is lumped in the category of middle age. Maggie may not quite be old enough to be Sarah's mother, but she is not far off it. *She has it!* Whilst Peter benevolently indulges the attempts of Roger, Tony, Summer's and her own attempts to impress him, it is *he* who is trying to impress Maggie. He is watching her now, an unmistakable glow of admiration in his eyes, for all her plainness of dress and lack of make-up. Sarah thinks about going home for an early night, but she knows how transparent this would be. She wants to be happy for Maggie, she does, but couldn't she have found somewhere else to do her foundation year?

"You'll come won't you, Sarah?" Summer is back on the make-over campaign. "Sarah has such style," she chatters on, "she just knows how to put things together and make a look work."

Now they are all looking at her, even Peter. She smiles cheerfully into her rival's face, but the smile does little to mask the barb in her tone.

"Sure, I'd love to help remodel our Maggie. You know me, always up for a challenge. Where shall we meet?"

On the Thursday of the following week, Peter sticks his head around the door of the life drawing studio. He is hoping to catch Maggie before she starts her modelling stint. She customarily arrives well before time, and the students do not usually breeze in until five minutes before the model takes up her first pose. This morning there is no sign of Maggie, however, though he spots a slim young woman, whom he fails to recognise, standing with her back towards the door, sorting through a voluminous bag she has perched on one of the high stools. She is dressed in a striped men's shirt and denim dungarees, gathered tightly around her waist in a wide leather belt. On her feet, she wears green Doc Martens, and around a head is coiled a brightly coloured scarf, over and through which curls of copper hair trail, as though she were a shepherdess from some ancient Greek pastoral scene. Peter finds himself quite charmed for a moment, then coughs and asks if she has seen Maggie, the life model, yet?

Maggie turns with a dramatic flourish and enjoys Peter's temporary loss of composure. Bejeebers, but she is not sure whether to be pleased or insulted by the look of surprise on his face. He stands unmoving and speechless for so long that Maggie starts to feel more self-conscious than in all the times she has stood before the room full of students without a stitch of clothing to hide her modesty. *Does he think she is too old for all this?* She asks in a faltering voice, touching her scarf and hair with her long fingers. *Only Summer and Sarah had been so persuasive…*

"I think you look beautiful, Maggie" Peter replies in a moment of unguarded candour. Now neither of them knows what to say or do and the moment hangs between them in awkward silence until the tension is broken by the noisy entrance of a handful of students. Maggie turns away and lights a cigarette. She takes a couple of draws from it then heads for the sanctuary of the changing screen. Peter busies himself with arranging the dais for a pose and soon the room is full and the class begins. He has quite forgotten what it was he wanted to talk to her about.

Maggie finds it hard to focus this morning, and never have the minutes seemed so long. At break time, she avoids Peter and enters into a lively discussion with Tony and Roger, who are effusive in their compliments about her new hairstyle. They half-jokingly declare her as their official muse and Maggie's blushes add an even deeper prettiness to her face.

At lunch-hour, Maggie hurriedly pulls on new clothes and rushes out on the pretext of an urgent errand. Peter is left to upbraid himself for having put his foot in it. Why did he have to go and behave like a complete idiot? And how had this little Irish woman been able to get under his skin so? He and Wendy were only just in the process of ending their relationship, why would he even be thinking about trying to start a new one? Because he did not want to be alone? That would be pathetic. But no, it isn't that. It is Maggie. Goodness knows he has had plenty of young women flirting with him over his years as a lecturer, and he has just come to accept it as an occupational hazard. And yes, he had sometimes enjoyed the spark of a mutual flirtation, even if perhaps he should not have done. But he had never let it go too far.

But this is different. Maggie! There is something about her, something that stirs his blood and makes him think back to his days as a younger man. Perhaps that is it. He does not feel old when he is around Maggie, although the reflection in the shaving mirror assures him that he is. He feels a vividness of life he had thought lost to him. Maybe he is just getting to be a sentimental old fool. Wendy would certainly say as much. Wendy who knows him inside and out, even when he wants to believe she does not. And suddenly he wishes he could talk to her about it, although that is obviously out of the question. People always talk about second childhood, maybe this is the start of second adolescence. He sighs and decides that maybe he should go out and get himself a sandwich for lunch after all. Anything to distract him from this ridiculous moping.

The remainder of the day passes with similar discomfort for Peter and Maggie. Maggie finds herself unable to avoid him at the finish of the class, as she must get him to sign off her hours. She is hoping to approach him whilst there are still plenty of students loitering about, but this afternoon, as fate would have it, the studio has all but emptied by the time she has finished dressing. Peter, meanwhile, has resolved to take the bull by the horns.

"Maggie," he says, "about earlier, I am so sorry, it was the aesthetic observation of an artist, nothing more. I do hope you can forgive any embarrassment, or awkwardness it may have caused. But your new look does really bring out your best features".

He hopes it sounds as matter-of-fact and disinterested as he would like it to be.

"Sure, it would be a sad world if we fell out over a compliment," smiles Maggie, but she cannot tell whether she is relieved or disappointed. "You have been a real friend to me Peter, so you have, and it'll take a bit more than a silly misunderstanding to change that, to be sure." And with that, she squeezes his hand, as though to demonstrate the platonic in the relationship. But they both feel a tingle of static and they both wonder who they are fooling.

Early that evening, when Maggie gets home to an empty flat, she goes to her room and lies down on the bed. She stares at the walls, willing herself to rid her mind of the image of Peter's eyes fixed upon her, tongue-tied and awkward as a teenage boy. Then, almost as though a veil has been drawn aside, and she is seeing them for the first time, her gaze is arrested by the roses on the wallpaper. The faded paper blooms stir the reminiscence of other roses on other walls. A visceral memory of her lovemaking with Father John in that other rosy bedroom overtakes her. The feel of his thigh against hers, the scent of his flesh, the warm moistness of his mouth, the yearning in her groin. Maggie sits up with a start and shakes her head as if to empty it of such dangerous recollections, though in truth it is her body that remembers, and all the shaking of her brains will do no good at all. She paces around the room, chewing her lip. She knew there was something about this bedroom that made her uncomfortable. *This will not do, t'will not do at all.*

As soon as Kathleen arrives home from her shift, Maggie asks if it would be alright if she re-painted the bedroom, perhaps make it a bit brighter and modern. Kathleen smiles;

"First you make-over yourself and now you want to make my flat over, it's me you'll be making over next. Though the Lord knows, it would do me no harm! Go on! This is your home, now, you make it how you want it."

Maggie hugs her. She would have her coat on already to get to John Lewis to choose some paint if the hour were not so late, and you can be sure she will be up first thing tomorrow.

The painting of the bedroom is of course an utter failure. It certainly looks bright and cheery, as Maggie has picked out a sunshine yellow and treated herself to some inexpensive prints by Matisse and Chagall, her favourite painters, as well as a brightly coloured duvet cover. And when it was finished and the rollers and brushes washed and put away, Maggie had stood in her room and beamed with pleasure. But in the early morning half-light, the obvious absence of the damned roses only serves to remind her of them all the more. She tosses and turns and feels the unwelcome ache of desire, made more acute by a vague impression of having dreamed of some lover during the night, a lover who was not wholly Father John nor yet wholly Peter. She is used to the other dreams, the ones that haunt her in the small hours, and cause her to wake up sobbing, but this is different. Surely a woman of her age should be beyond such things? But then, of course, she is still having her monthly bleed, so she supposes she is not. How strange to wish yourself older than you are, when most folk long to be younger again. Maggie shrugs. It seems that Life had not done with her yet. How sad to think of the wasted years she had spent believing it had.

For the first time in many long months, she thinks of her husband. Till death us do part, the priest had pronounced, and in her faith that meant what it said. No divorce for a Catholic, no second bites of the apple. (That bloody apple!) What God has joined together let no man put asunder. Yet they are asunder and she does not even know where her spouse might be. For a moment she feels a deep throb of pity for him. But it does not last long. The memory of a life of emotional drudgery and cold embraces is too strong. She is sorry that she caused him pain, but the marriage had sucked the life out of her without replacing it with the new life she so craved. She shudders. Well, she had experienced God's unbridled retribution and she was done with it now. Maggie is shocked by her own defiance. Is that what this new life of hers is all about, after all? Is it just a two-fingers up to God? Doubtless, her husband, wherever he was, would think so in his stultifying piety. Yet she knows it is not. There is something in this new Maggie that rings pure and true within her soul, and how could something so pristine offend a loving God?

But what of her feelings for Peter? He is a married man, and she, in the eyes of the church, a married woman. *Lead us not into temptation!* Can it be the devil himself tempting her again? No, she will not delude herself on that point. It never was the Devil that led her astray, and neither had it been God putting her to the test. Maggie is not the one to avoid shouldering the responsibility for her actions. She makes a private vow to keep this man at arms' length. *Sure, doesn't she have enough complications in her life, without creating more?*

She takes out her notebook and pencil from the bedside drawer and inserts Peter's name into the list of compulsions she has vowed to overcome; right beneath handwashing, then smoking and just above chocolate digestives.

By the time Maggie has done wrestling with such thoughts, it is daylight. The yellow sunshine of the newly painted walls, blazes with the borrowed brightness of the summer sun. Maggie rises bleary-eyed and pulls back the curtains. And in the light of the new day, things don't seem so bad, or so complicated, after all.

Verse 2

Autumn 1980

Sarah sits at the table in the Pizza House in Sicilian Avenue, lost in a little world of her own. She is scrutinizing Maggie's "new look", though in truth, the term "new" is hardly accurate now. Maggie seems unconscious of her attention and is laughing and smiling over her profiteroles, trying to tempt Tony to try some. Tony is pulling a face. He has a lifelong distaste for fresh cream and despite the lure of the rich chocolate sauce, he feels a little nauseated at the idea. Summer and Roger are arguing about painting as usual, but the banter is good-natured and their mutual enjoyment in all seeing each other again lends a summer warmth to the coolness of the fading September evening.

It is the first time all five of them have met up since the end of last term and there is much excitement about the year that lies ahead. Maggie has completed her introductory week on the foundation course, whilst the others have graduated to the second year and the status of "old hands." There is much talk of how "the real work is just beginning," in tones that betray a mixture of relish and anxiety, as each must meet the challenge of establishing a unique artistic voice. Meanwhile, there are the more mundane details of life to catch up on. Tony and Sarah had gone home to spend time with their respective families and do not have much of interest to relate. Summer, on the other hand, had spent the summer backpacking around India. Summer's mother had had a somewhat bohemian youth and had followed the hippy trail along the silk route. She had, therefore, actively encouraged Summer to go, regarding it an essential part of her daughter's education. It has bought about quite a transformation. Summer's face, though thinner thanks to an inevitable episode of gastroenteritis, glows with health and she is inflamed with enthusiasm for all the rich and exotic colours that had assailed her eyes during her travels.

Only Roger had stayed in London for the entire summer and, lacking the necessary funds, could not boast of much in the way of a holiday at all. Maggie had managed to wangle him a couple of weekly shifts as a porter at the Russell, where she herself had continued to work throughout the summer months. Of course, he had had to remove the rings in his ears and leave off the eye-liner, such things were hardly in line with the Russell's rather grand image, and when Maggie had seen him in his white shirt and plain black trousers, she had felt touched by how like a little boy he suddenly appeared. The times they had subsequently spent together had cemented a friendship that had become equally precious to both, despite the difference in their ages.

Maggie meanwhile, had initially done her best to avoid Peter when she was not at work, spending her free days up at St Albans with Kath and Vonnie. After a difficult couple of months during the Spring, Vonnie had finally reached the point where the burden of caring for her mother, on her own, had become too much for her and had been obliged to place the increasingly frail old lady in a nursing home, close by. It was everything that Vonnie had tried so desperately to avoid so had been a painful time for her. Still, nothing cheered up her depressed spirits like time in her mother's allotment, and Maggie would join her for company, spending long days in happily silent toil, until she had come to love digging and planting out almost as much as Vonnie herself.

Rather to Maggie's relief, Peter had taken off to France in the third week of the summer break. Eager to escape the loneliness of his empty days, he had volunteered to stay with old friends and help them restore an old farmhouse they had bought in Provence. Thankfully, there was little risk of seeing much of him in the department where she was doing her foundation year, as he had no teaching input on the course. She had fretted over whether she should even sign up to model for the evening life class this term, but discovering it had been taken over by Mark Aldiss, a colleague of Peter's, had decided that she could not afford to forego the extra income. After all, there was no reason to avoid him altogether, now was there?

Sarah twists her mouth critically. She has to admit she did a good job. It is over three months since she and Summer had hauled the dowdy Maggie off to the Camden markets and helped her pick out a whole new wardrobe, with Summer always deferring to Sarah's superior judgement as to what would work and what would not. It had certainly bought about a transformation, the words ugly duckling and swan spring to mind. But Maggie had been no personality-less clothes horse; on the contrary, she had taken Sarah's ideas and made the clothes work for her with a flair that was all her own. And she looks great; she really does, Sarah cannot begrudge her that. But really, she could not have shot herself in the foot more effectively with a twelve-bore shotgun at point-blank range. It had been clear to anyone with eyes that Maggie's transmogrification had cast a spell over Peter.

Sarah sighs. She might as well be invisible and has no chance at all, (as if she ever had one in the first place), and okay she probably did not, but at least she could foster the fantasy of a chance. Now even that has been crushed underfoot like one of Maggie's roll-ups. And that is another thing, Maggie the chain smoker with her ashtray breath and nicotine-stained fingers seems to have morphed into Maggie the social smoker, who holds her roll-up with such effortless coolness, that she is in danger of making smoking fashionable all over again. Life just seems so unfair sometimes.

Peter is not with them this evening, so that is something to feel grateful for, she supposes. It had been clear from the way his eyes had lit up when he had glimpsed Maggie, across the canteen on the first day of the new term, that his feelings had not been changed by a vacation in the French countryside. If there is anything more painful than unrequited love, it is having your nose rubbed in it by having to witness the object of your affections moon over somebody else.

"Sarah, hullo! Anyone home?" Tony is snapping his fingers in front of Sarah's face and chuckling.

"She lives in a dream, this one," he says to the rest of the little party.

"Sorry? What?" Sarah replies. "I was miles away."

Tony ignores the icy snap in her tone and ploughs on.

"We were just saying, apparently there are student discount tickets available for the Dario Fo production, *The Accidental Death of An Anarchist.* Maggie has never been to a West End theatre. It should be a bloody great play. Are you up for it?"

"Golly, yeah," Sarah smiles at Maggie, the frost all melted by pure delight at the plan. "It would be great." And then she wishes she could kick herself because the words - "Do you think Peter would like to tag along?"- are out of her mouth before she can help herself. *Why on Earth did she have to say it?*

"Well, maybe, although he would not have a student card, so not sure about the discount. But he is probably glad for any distraction now he is all by himself."

Maggie and Sarah both look at Tony together, the question clear on their faces. But it is Summer who breaks the news:

"Oh, yeah, didn't you guys know?" she drawls, twisting her mouth meaningfully, "Peter and his wife have separated. By all accounts, she has gone off to Suffolk to write a book, and she is not planning to come back."

"And how in Heaven's name would you know that?" demands Maggie. The note of outrage in her voice makes them suddenly feel like children being scolded by an adult.

"Well, you know, Central gossip," replies Summer uncomfortably, "I don't think it is any big secret…"

"Well, I am sorry," continues Maggie, trying to sound a bit more conciliatory, "I just think that a lot of harm is done by idle gossip, so it is, and I should hope we have a bit more respect for a friend than to be spreading it."

The little group falls silent for a moment, suitably chastised.

"All the same, Maggie," adds Sarah, with perhaps just a hint of jealous spite in her voice, "You have to admit it *is* an interesting bit of news."

Her arrow hits the mark. Maggie turns red and dare not say any more. Tony and Summer exchange a glance with raised eyebrows and everyone tacitly agrees to change the subject.

Bethnal Green 1980

A cold, damp and dreary November morning. The day is taking its time to break and the weak rays of the winter sun struggle to pierce the East London gloom of shadow and diesel fumes. A few heroic birds, or perhaps those lacking the wit to flee to warmer climes, are twittering in the now bare trees, but any bird song is lost amid the din of thundering buses and lorries and goes unheard by the crowds of commuters emerging from the Bethnal Green tube station.

The large clock in the deserted entrance foyer reads 8.30 am. Jack O'Donnell paces the empty corridors of St James of the Marches school. Through mesh enforced glass fire doors and past well-worn iron bannisters and pitted cement staircases he makes his way; details so sharp in their novelty not three months ago, blending now into overlooked familiarity. The soles of his shoes squeak unforgivingly on the scuffed linoleum. Would that his mortal soul could find such unapologetic a voice. But the sorrows of his heart have congealed into dumbness like dried blood.

Rounding the corner towards the glazed lobby and student entrance which leads into the fading grandeur of the assembly hall, his footsteps echo in the now silent, but soon to be thronging cloakrooms. Lined up in orderly file along the length of their racks, the coat hooks bow their coloured billiard ball heads as if in silent Matins. He savours this quiet time of day, before the morning bell, yet cannot ignore a lurching discomfort in his stomach. *Dread*. There, he has owned it. As he has owned it every weekday for the past eleven weeks. A feeling that neither diminishes with habituation nor escalates so far that it is wholly incapacitating, yet permeates through into his evenings and weekends, polluting any leisure time with uninvited preoccupation and foreboding. Jack tries to recall the last time he truly enjoyed his free-time, but it is like peering through a fog. He lets out a deep sigh then gazes round.

Through the picture windows, he spies the first arrivals in the schoolyard, a gaggle of swaggering toilet-mouthed youths who shove one another with whoops of exaggerated coarseness. Jack shudders and touches the cold glass that separates their worlds. One of the youths look his way, his animal instincts alert to the fact he is observed, and holds his gaze in a glare of defiance but, shrugging contemptuously, cannot even be bothered to make a rude gesture. Jack knows the boy but cannot recall his name. An Unteachable. Jack looks away. He knows that any other schoolmaster would summon the boy in and chastise him. Reinforce the order of things. But he is intimidated to his core by these strange beings, whose very speech renders them at times almost unintelligible to him. He is reminded, as if he needs any reminder, that he is in an alien land. A land far from home and everything he understands; a land where respect for adults, authority and even the Holy Church itself appear to be phenomena assigned to the distant past.

The dull ache of homesickness throbs through the flatness of his mood; a longing for green fields, soft rain and wind-blown skies. The smell of peat and the sea breezes, the burn of a fine Irish malt on the back of the throat or the creamy bitterness of a Murphys stout. He longs for the vividness of experience that reminds him he is alive and wonders some days if, indeed, he still is. For in this Limbo of his own creating, it has become difficult to tell. Two very long years since he stepped off the boat in Liverpool, with only a hold-all and a wish to be away, to be somebody else, anybody else. But even as he had left the cassock and collar behind, who is Jack O'Donnell without them? The Holy Roman church was all he knew. The Word of God all he had to offer.

The yard is filling up now and soon the morning bell will sound. He turns his back to the entrance and heads for the staff room to look for any chits in his pigeon hole. He nods to Phil 'Chemistry' Jones on his way in and almost collides with Jill Tuffin, who has spilt a pile of exercise books in the doorway. He stoops to assist her in gathering them up and is struck by the warm spicy notes of a not inexpensive perfume. He notices a deep flush around her neck and throat. She thanks him, averting her eyes with a coyness that he half suspects is flirtation, then hurries off. She is not unattractive, thinks Jack, watching her go, but it seems more a registering of a fact than an emotional response and he is taken aback by his own detachment.

He checks his pigeon hole and finds it mercifully empty, save for the form register: No chit requesting him to cover classes for absent masters today. Did he sigh with relief? Every teacher knows the Hell of covering for an absent staff member. It is a Hell that most would seek to avoid, and none more so than Jack O'Donnell.

He feels a clap on his back, then shame at his exaggerated startle reflex. He spins around to find Jim Morris, in tracksuit as always, laughing at him. But it is a warm good-natured laugh and Jack finds he can join in. Jim seizes Jack's hand and tries to execute a bewildering dap handshake, and as usual, Jack messes it up. "One day…" grins Jim, wagging a finger at him. To be sure. *One day; but will that day ever come?*

The staff room is emptying and the raucous racket of the bell ringing soon drives out any stragglers, who like Jack, find their feet a-dragging.

Jack tucks an attendance register under his arm and head for his form room. He finds himself swept along with the stream of students heading down the main corridors towards the staircases. He experiences a fleeting sense of watching himself in the opening credits of a film in a long tracking-in shot, and his head swims momentarily. Reaching the safe moorings of his form room on the second floor, he takes the register - all the boys are present. One less headache for the day.

During school assembly, Jack stands at the back, scanning the sea of tousled schoolboy locks; looking for a landmark he recognises. But even the length of hair, curling around sweat-stained collars and grubby half-washed necks is all wrong to him. Jack is dubious that they can truly be catholic at all. They speak the words Amen but mean Fuck You. Perhaps he envies them. They play the game without it cowing their spirit and twisting their souls with guilt and shame. He has overheard them talk about confession as though it were an opportunity to boast - a competition as to who wins the most Hail Marys. His hero is John Lennon with his message of love and peace. Their allegiances seem to lie more with Sid Vicious and an altogether more aggressive spirit of teenage rebelliousness. Perhaps he even likes them. He has to admit that part of him harbours an admiration of such open rebelliousness and wonders if it is an English thing, the corruption of the prevailing protestant capitalism; a corruption that has turned football stadiums and department stores into the true Cathedrals of contemporary British life. Still, one man's corruption is another's liberation. He is hardly in a position to cast the first stone.

Jack tries to hang onto the familiar murmurs of the Lord's Prayer to pull himself back to a shore of here and now, but the meaningless drone washes over him and he is flotsam on an ocean of dislocation. Mouthing the all too well-known words of the hymns, but making no sound, Jack feels an almost overwhelming impulse to run out of the hall, to run as fast as he can, but there is nowhere to run so he fidgets instead. Mrs Jenkins turns her head, a signal of disapproval. There is an odd comfort in it. It is something familiar, something he can understand.

Somehow the morning passes soon enough. First period is general R.E with the third years. Jack tries his best with a class of boisterous lads who neither know nor care about the catechism, the history of the Saints or the difference between venial or mortal sin, though their ears prick up well enough whenever sins of the flesh or carnal knowledge are mentioned. Even the words Holy Virgin can be enough to provoke a fit of sniggering, and it is at times all Jack can do to keep his patience, reminding himself that he was once an adolescent too.

It is not as though they are altogether bad kids. They like Jack well enough and regard him as a sort of curiosity with his exotically Irish lilt, soft manners and handsome regular features. They find particular enjoyment in his large, dark-framed spectacles and call him Clark Kent behind his back, but not out of earshot. Not exactly original, he thinks, but he has heard worse. He has heard a lot worse.

After break, it is double GCE Latin with the fifth years who are preparing for mock exams after the Christmas break. He tries to warm them up with noun declensions - bellus, bellum, belli, belah, blah, blah, then proceeds onto reading. He selects a section of the Aneaid and singles out an unwilling volunteer. Giles, a lad whose voice is croaking under the assault of an adolescence testosterone surge, stutters through the passage at a painfully slow rate. Jack, for whom Latin is like a second tongue, winces at the clumsy handling of words which for most of his life have conveyed all the majesty and mystery of the Divine. By the time Giles is through, the mercifully already dead language has been more mangled than poor Hector's dragged and broken body. After that, even the painful struggle of translation comes as a sweet relief.

At lunchtime, his head thumping, Jack heads back to the staff room and his newspaper and Tupperware box of tasteless sandwiches. He takes a seat in the far corner, there is an empty armchair next to him, but failing as he does to raise his eyes from his paper, he is startled by a soft voice addressing him. Jack looks up. Janet Hazelwood is standing with her hand on the back of the vacant chair, asking if it is free. He notices a sing-song turn in her speech and staring up at her tries to place the accent. She flushes and asks again. Janet teaches English and has been at St James for several years. He has seen her in staff meetings, yet they have barely had a conversation in all the weeks he has been here. She waits patiently for his response.

"By all means," he replies softly. Janet smiles, almost laughing. Jack is unsure how to react. Is she laughing at him? Janet is perceptive; she picks up on his thoughts, his dismay.

"I am so sorry - I just love to hear you speak. I adore the Irish accent".

This time it is Jack whose cheeks redden and Janet finds herself apologising again.

"Oh gosh. Sorry, I did not mean to embarrass you. I just meant, well, be a dear and help me out of this hole I am digging for myself."

Jack knows how to be gallant. He nods and smiles

"I do seem to be a stranger in a strange land."

"That is remarkable - I am reading that very book at the moment." And as though he might doubt her, she dives into her roomy bag and hauls out a well-thumbed paperback, bearing the title A Stranger in a Strange Land by an author, whose name he does not recognise.

"And did you know that David Bowie wanted to make the film before doing The Man Who fell to Earth?"

"The man who - sorry?"

"My, you really are a stranger," murmurs Janet, crossing her long legs and resting her chin on her hand. She seems to be observing him. She could hardly fail to miss his eyes as they flick to her ankles, though he is scarcely aware of it himself. But she does not recoil and settles herself into the chair.

Jack catches his lip in his teeth, glances over his spectacles, as though at something across the room, then returns to the sanctuary of his newspaper. Janet wrinkles her nose, opens her book and begins to read.

Engrossed, however, as he might seem, Jack's thoughts are not on the words of the narrow columns of yesterday's Evening Standard. He is pondering instead upon the theme of alienation. He half misses the long lain aside vestments of his clerical garb, instant indicators of his identity and social standing. On formal occasions, the entire teaching staff still don the traditional gowns and mortarboards, yet these days only one or two of the die-hards insist on wearing them for teaching. In any case, it is a uniform that has lost the respect it used to demand. So, here he sits in his slacks, V-neck pullover and clip-on knitted tie; a turtle stripped of its shell. A mere man. The trouble is, as a mere man, he simply has no idea what to say, or how to be. And thus, they remain, until the afternoon bell bursts the fragile bubble of their companionship. Janet catches his eye.

"We must do this again sometime…" And pulling together her things, is gone.

Was she teasing him? Jack folds his paper, collects his textbooks and steels himself for the afternoon. He has little time to give it any further thought for the present. There are more challenging waters to negotiate.

Though Jack had naturally gravitated to teaching the subjects most familiar to him, Religious Education and Latin, he had soon discovered that the former, at least, incurred some major drawbacks. Latin apart, most of the lessons he takes are weekly general Religious Instruction, which along with Physical Education, form part of the basic curriculum for every boy at St James regardless of their chosen exam subjects and, all too frequently, their lack of interest in it. On the upside, there were no examination results to worry about and a good deal less homework. Yet even this had its drawbacks. It was all very well for the other teachers to tease and congratulate him on being able to coast and put his feet up but, in reality, cover for absent teachers would inevitably fall to those members of staff who did not have to prioritise free periods for marking. What is more, although the banter was friendly enough, he found it difficult to dismiss the impression that both he and Jim Morris were regarded as didactic also-rans. But then, perhaps it was this shared lot in life that had drawn the two men together.

This afternoon, however, being a Monday, he can look forward to a bit of "real teaching," as his colleagues would put it. As is usually the case in a Catholic school, a small number amongst the fifth form students have elected to study religious studies at examination level. It is true that he has yet to get any "A" level students, but he is only in his probation year. Besides, he is beginning to foster hopes for one or two of his "acolytes", a soubriquet he uses for the small group of lads in the class. Not that he is under any allusions. It is highly likely that many of the boys are only in the class because they regard R.E as a cushy option. Still, as is the case for Latin, the handful of boys in these classes come mainly from higher economic status families. On the whole, therefore, though mischievous and cheeky, his "acolytes" are not given to outright aggression or insubordination. Hence double R.E on a Mondays afternoon has become the one time in the week when he feels more at ease. Indeed, at times, he even catches himself feeling *almost* like a teacher.

Jack has been pleasantly surprised by the sophistication of the syllabus, which picks out key theological themes in both the Old and New Testament. In the right mood, the lads are apt to demonstrate genuine curiosity, asking questions and quizzing him in-depth about doctrinal complexities.

This afternoon they demonstrate especial zeal around the subject of original sin and the story of Eden and the Tree of The Knowledge of Good and Evil. Collins asserts that surely it was unfair of God to condemn mankind for all eternity, for acting on a curiosity and thirst for knowledge which God must have created in them. *Surely Mr O'Donnell must agree?* Jack replies that neither of them is there to sit in judgement upon God, rather it is a matter of becoming familiar with the biblical account and how it had played out through key doctrinal edicts.

But today the Devil is in Collins and he presses the point. *Can he, Mr O'Donnell, really sustain the assertion that these are the actions of a loving father? To punish His children eternally for something He created in them?*

Jack finds himself lacking the confidence to close down this line of enquiry with an authoritative refusal or silence, and all too quickly finds himself obfuscating the point, in an attempt to change the focus. But the boys are on the scent now. They would have God Himself in the dock, were it left to them, with Mr O'Donnell himself on the stand as the witness for the prosecution. For them, it is a bit of harmless fun. They do not see the pain in his eyes or the conflict in his heart. They cannot read his thoughts or guess that, behind his mild words, he is silently resolving that he will have to leave teaching.

And then, as though in some act of unconscious empathy they sense that they had gone too far and drop it. Collins himself changes tack, steers the discussion to a safer course. Thankfully the other students are content to follow his lead. But Jack is left with a deep sense of shame. They have seen him drowning. They have put him to the test and he has failed.

The lesson continues, though the whole class seems in depressed spirits, and when the bell rings out the signal for his release, Jack does not meet their eyes or make his usual farewell. They shuffle out without their customary animation. Jack sits crushed, his brow in his hand, forcing back the darkness that threatens his thoughts. And then he notices that not all the boys had left the room. Collins, halting and fiddling self-consciously with his satchel, approaches, his head bowed slightly.

"I am sorry, Sir," he says and smiles weakly. "I overstepped the mark. It was disrespectful and unfair." His voice is all earnestness and for a moment, Jack marvels at this unexpected maturity. It is all he can do to acknowledge the apology with a tacit nod without surrendering to choking emotion. Collins senses that his words have been sufficient, purses his lips ruefully and leaves, head still hung in penitence.

Jack sits for a moment and contemplates the turnaround in his heart. *Are a man's life and soul so easily saved after all? Can it really be that all we need is love? Forgiveness? Compassion? And how can we forgive when God does not? How is it that the compassion of a fifteen-year-old schoolboy has stirred a hope and sense of faith in humanity within him which has seemed so long dead?* Jack collects his books, thankful that the day is almost over.

The next morning, and somewhat to his surprise, Jack finds himself looking out for his lunchtime companion, though she seems nowhere to be seen.

Later in the afternoon, during lesson change over, he thinks he catches a glimpse of her and is fleetingly aware of some heat in his face. But, if it is she, then she is quickly lost in the crowd of students and teachers that streams through the corridors and up the stairways.

The week passes, and there is still no sign of her in either the staff room or in assembly. Jack is almost beginning to wonder if he had imagined her. By Thursday he had spent two long lunch hours staring out of the windows as Geography Jones had extolled the virtues of The Gunners in the upcoming weekend third round play-off with Crystal Palace, to anyone who might be listening. Jack had wondered who cared, but this was England and unaccountably most of the other male staff members evidently did, so would throw fuel upon the unquenchable fire of match statistics, goal averages and transfer speculations that spewed from the otherwise tepid Geography teacher's mouth.

At least he has passion, thinks Jack, looking up at the staff room clock for the fifth time, but he is aware that this concession is tainted with a kind of sullen resentment, which he fears must show on his face. It is only when Jim tumbles in and pulls up a chair next to him, and he messes up yet another convoluted handshake, that he finds his smile again.

"We still on for tomorrow, me Old China?" asks Jim with a wink.

Jack nods cheerfully. "That's what it says on the roster, mate."

"Cool, man." grins Jim, "catch you then." And as quickly as he had arrived, he is gone.

Sure enough, the next day finds Jack and Jim on lunchtime school yard supervision duty together, though it would be fair to say that the burden of the duty is undertaken by the prefects. Protected only by the status signalled by their enamel badges of office, they patrol the cloakrooms and corridor in pairs and take turns to brave the elements around the yard and popular smoking hideaways. The prefects know they can call upon the teaching staff when *absolutely* necessary. But *only* when *absolutely* necessary. For Jack and Jim therefore, it provides a regular opportunity to spend time in each other's company, and over time it has become a highlight in each man's week.

"I'll tell you what, you should have seen me finish in last weekend's half marathon, mate. Put on a regular sprint at the end. My best time yet. I beat dozens of lads nearly half my age." Jim puffs out his chest like a prizewinning racing-pigeon.

"Aye, so I heard," responds Jack with a knowing eye and gentle nod.

"No kidding, I reckon I am at my physical peak, mate. And I'll tell you what, the birds love it!"

"Aye, is that a fact now?"

"Too bloody right. I was in the bar after and this bird came up to me, Sharon or Sandra, I can't bloody remember now, but she was making it pretty clear what she was after, and it wasn't my brain."

Jacks smiles. It is such a little smile, but the animation of it transforms the dullness of his features.

"To be sure, I'd have thought you'd not have much energy left, after a run like that".

"You bloody joking, my son? This is Jim lad you are talking to. I'll tell you what, we had another little marathon of our own that night, if you take my meaning."

"Well, now I would call that impressive, so I would. And will you be seeing this young lady - Sharon? Sandra? again, I wonder?"

"Not me mate. I like to spread myself around, only fair to the other birds, in'it? They'd have to be bleedin' sprinters themselves to catch old Jim," and he laughs at his own joke.

Jack laughs with him. Jim watches him out of the corner of his eye and feels a little victory inside. He likes Jack, but he sees in him a deep sadness, so he tries to make him laugh. It is perhaps a role for which he has been rehearsing his whole life.

Jack, in his turn, likes Jim and sees through the defence of class clown. He had met so many of them before; lads so crippled by a sense of their intrinsic inadequacy, that they hide behind perpetual high jinks and constant tomfoolery. In an unguarded moment, Jim had confided to Jack that he had been hindered by undiagnosed dyslexia throughout his own schooling. Indeed, it had been his athletic prowess and determination to excel on the sports fields, no matter what the game, that had saved him from being consigned to factory work or labouring, and with a couple of retakes he had scraped good enough grades to win a place in teacher training. So, Jack's respect for Jim is real and deep. But there is something else about Jim. Something that truly endears him to Jack. Jim does not think that Jack knows what he is up to with his outrageous accounts of his physical and sexual prowess, but Jack is fully sensible as to how pleased Jim is to have made him smile. And he is deeply touched.

"So, what about you?" Jim has changed the focus. "What did you get up to at the weekend?" He tries hard not to sound as though he is prying. He rarely asks Jack about himself or expects a mutual exchange of confidences. Or at least, not since the first time he had tried when he sensed that his curiosity had been unwelcome.

"Sure, nothing special. Did some reading, watched the football on the T.V."

"You should come out with me one Saturday, my friend…" He notices the poorly disguised look of alarm on his friend's face. "I don't mean a pick-up bar or anything like that. Just a pint, a game of darts, something to get you out of that flat of yours. A proper mates' night out. What d'ye say?"

Jack shrugs.

"Well, it if was just a pint, now. Sure, that would be great."

"Such a waste though," sighs Jim, thoroughly satisfied, "what with your good looks and my dynamite personality, we would have the birds eating out of our hands!"

"Sure, perhaps we could stop and feed the ducks on the way home, then," jokes Jack.

Jim rolls his eyes.

"Hey, I'm the joker here, son. You're the one with the looks. You gotta leave me something!"

And they both laugh.

The remainder of the dinner hour flies by, with Jack envying Jim his self-assurance, even as Jim envies Jack his quiet reserve and self-containment. In a way, they make the perfect team. One who loves to talk and the other who prefers to listen. Even if Jack is secretly disappointed at not seeing Janet again, at least the week is going to end on a good note.

Camden Town. Monday 8.30 am

"So, you are saying that I am making the same mistake all over again, is that it?"

Bernard breathes out a little louder than he had intended but remains silent. He notices that his patient's breasts are rising and falling and feels an unwelcome stirring in his groin. He reminds himself of the perils of the erotic countertransference. He needs to focus, not allow himself to be distracted from the therapeutic task.

Janet becomes fidgety. She is exasperated. As she often is. It had become a defining feature of the therapeutic relationship. He had become the eternally frustrating and disappointing father. It is a classic case of Transference in one of its many glorious vicissitudes.

"No, but really - I can feel your disapproval..." Janet continues.

"Janet -" Bernard begins choosing his words carefully. "I think you are projecting that disapproval. You tell me about a man who is unresponsive and you expect disapprobation because, once again, you know that you are walking into a situation..."

"I knew it. You disapprove..."

"I am simply noticing a repetition of...."

"Oh, I know, I know". She is virtually wailing now. "Along comes this man. Nice enough looking, charming in his way, but nothing special. But he's got this whole disengagement from the rest of the world thing going on, so I want him to notice me and it is like a challenge."

"Perhaps this is what you want of me?" Bernard cautiously suggests.

"What?"

"To notice you - I mean have you figure in my world. I mean, *really* figure in it."

"Oh please, not this again..."

Bernard shrugs despite himself. Impasse. But Janet knows he is right and that is exactly why she is so pissed off.

"Well, we seem to be out of time."

Janet rises from the couch, brushes off her slacks and turning, shoots an impish glance at Bernard. Full of mischief. He cannot help but smile. He does not want to. But he cannot help himself. He makes a mental note to discuss it when he next meets with his supervisor. He is feeding the transference. He frowns and wonders briefly just what could have happened to Janet's father, that had left him so unable to respond emotionally to such a bright and intelligent being as his daughter.

"See you next week."

Janet makes her way to the school. She knows Bernard has a point. She had made the link herself, almost as soon as

Jack and she had exchanged their first words. What a cliché she must seem. She wants to kick herself. Jack O'Donnell was her father right enough. Good looking, charming when he needed to be, but cut off by God knows what kind of trauma and begging to be rescued. She feels like crying. Two years of lying on that couch and how many thousands of pounds and here she is again. Surely you must be able to demand your money back, she thinks bitterly as she boards the eastbound central line tube to Bethnal Green, but at least she is not walking into it blindly this time. Who is she kidding? She opens her bag and takes out a pen and the paperback crossword book she reserves for the tube journey back from her therapy session. She opens a page and slips into the familiar decompression routine. She would need to have all her equilibrium restored for 4J and Macbeth first period.

By morning break, Shakespeare and the three witches and 4J not-with-standing, she has resolved not to purposely seek Jack out at lunchtime. But isn't this just playing games? Surely it is. Perhaps instead she should change the rules, take control. It is something to think about.

She thinks back to what she had told Bernard.

"And then he said *I feel like a stranger in a strange land*, and there it was, a plea for help - that had been the hook."

She wonders why she had not told him the other part, the part about how strongly Jack had reminded her of her father. But she knows why. Because he would have been so bloody smug, that was why. But what is she doing? She sounds like a teenager. She rebukes herself for such childishness and resolves not to do anything rash until she can discuss it further with Bernard. She will be open with him this time. She will.

Nevertheless, when she enters the staff room at lunchtime, she cannot help scanning the sea of heads until her eyes settle upon that gentle and grave face. He looks up and smiles. Her resolve, however well-intentioned, is useless. She knows it.

She looks over and catches Jack's eye, grins and makes her way to the vacant chair next to him. She extends her right hand and formally presents herself:

"I am sorry I don't think we were properly introduced last week, I'm Janet - Janet Hazelwood. Pleased to meet you."

Jack plays his part in return and invites her to sit. He comments that he had not seen her around for the rest of the previous week, then wishes he had not, but Janet, if she is aware that he has a betrayed an interest keener than he might wish to reveal, does not show it. She explains that she has been on study leave, as she is doing a diploma in counselling; *she is studying at The Westminster Pastoral Foundation in Kensington. Does he know it?* Jack thinks he has heard the name but is unfamiliar with the Institution himself. Janet continues, *anyway she is often not in for assembly as she has her own therapy two mornings a week. One of the perks of having been there for so long is that the school is supporting her in this and allow her a late start, she supposes.*

Jack is a little taken aback by her frankness. He would have thought that being in therapy would be a matter of some privacy, yet Janet refers to it as though she was talking of an appointment with her hairdresser. It is clear he still has much to learn about life on the mainland.

Janet chats on, she tells him about her morning with the ferocious fourth form, enacting the witches' scene from The Bard's Macbeth. She has a real way with words and paints a picture so delightfully absurd that Jack cannot help but smile. Jack is suddenly reminded of Jim. He begins to realise that, far from self-centred, her garrulousness is a genuinely altruistic attempt to entertain him and put him at his ease. He wonders what it can be about him that invites such generosity of spirit. Janet continues on in the same vein. She demands nothing from him, until:

"Do you get a little homesick Jack? You seem a little - I don't know, sad somehow," she asks gently, but it is an invitation, not an interrogation.

"I like it just fine where I am, just now," he replies to his own surprise and without the merest hint of flirtation.

But it is enough for Janet, and after this, they find that they can sit in comfortable silence. It is such a small step. Nonetheless, it is the tentative template for what will become a daily routine.

9th December 1980

"Why Jack, whatever is the matter?" Janet is peering into her companion's face. It is not yet nine o'clock and the staff room is filling up. She is taken aback by the look of shock that seems to have paralysed his features. The radio is on in the background. Janet is not paying attention but is all at once aware that a stunned silence has replaced the usual racket of pre-school-day coffee and chatter. The newsreader is announcing that John Lennon has been shot and killed outside his New York home. You can hear the distress in his voice.

Jack stands up, looks wildly around and then sits down again. He appears insensible of Janet or any other soul. The world seems to be slipping away. Suddenly everyone is talking at once. Janet places her hand on Jack's arm. The notion that he has had a stroke flashes through her mind, but she knows this is nonsense. The nine o'clock bell rings, drowning out the sound of the radio. Jack startles into automatic motion and heads wordlessly towards the door. He is deaf to Janet's entreaties and blind to the look of gentle concern that clouds her anxious face.

"Come on mate, it's not the end of the world!" chirps chemistry Jones, who catches Janet's look of anxiety as Jack passes.

Jack stares at him in incomprehension. *What part of John Lennon is slain do they not understand? And how can Hope remain in such a world? The world may not have ended, but it can never be the same again.*

It is lunchtime, with only a week and a half to endure before the Christmas break. The world had kept on turning, though it is a colder place and not only because of the winter chill. Mark Chapman had earned his dubious place in history, though it is a fame pitifully eclipsed by the meteoric brilliance of Lennon's own. Jack had drowned his sorrow, binging on Irish malt and the repeated playing of *Imagine*. He had woken the next morning with a headache and broken cassette player, which had somehow seemed entirely fitting.

Just now, Jack and Jim are standing arms crossed in the corridor before the great extension of plate glass that separates them from the chill December air. Outside, in the schoolyard, small groups of boys huddle in sunlit corners of the recreational quadrangle below or chase one another around in an attempt to shrug off the shiver of winter. Jim is expounding his account of last year's London Marathon, in which he had competed for the third time, but Jack's attention is drawn to the world on the other side of the glass.

On the far side of the yard, where the tarmac still lies in shadow, some of the boys are making use of an unthawed frosted path as a slide. One by one they hurtle towards the top of the glistening track then skid along with yelps of delight, occasionally losing their balance and crashing to the ground to painfully skinned knees. The vapour of their panted breath hangs on the air making Jack glad of the ancient radiator that pumps out heat into the cloakroom and vestibule. Jack rubs his upper arms involuntarily as he regards the boys who have not the sense to keep active. He has often reflected on the dubious rationale for enforced outdoor playtime, even in the coldest weather, especially for those younger lads who continue to sport short trousers, even in the winter months. He suspects that there may be more than a hint of sadism in the tradition, for thus it had been since before he had himself been a school lad. He can still recall the misery of freezing hands and stinging ears, the agony of blood returning into blue-hued fingers when, back indoors, they began at last to thaw.

Jack turns his attention back to Jim, who is nearing the climax of his narrative, when he is interrupted by a loud yelling from outside. At the far end of the lower playground, a fight has broken out between two lads in the fourth form. It is not a bully picking on a weaker victim, but two equally matched peers, who might on any other day be the best of mates. A large crowd of eager boys gather around, shouldering the prefects, who are trying to intervene, out of the circle. From their position of elevation, Jim and Jack have a reasonably clear view of the protagonists, despite the wall of uniformed spectators, and find themselves pressing their noses up against the coldness of the large window to follow the action.

The one lad, who is slightly taller than the other, flails at his opponent, landing closed fists on his head, but his smaller opponent grips him around the waist and drags him to the frozen ground. There ensues some wrestling and untidy scrabbling, and the lads in the circle have all begun yelling and chanting a chorus of "Fight! Fight! Fight!" The war cry is attracting the remaining boys in the yard and it soon becomes clear that the prefects are failing in their struggle to take control of the situation.

The boy who had hit the floor first has struggled back to his feet with a bloodied nose. Now, he jumps on to the back of his nemesis, who bucks and twists, trying to catch his tormentor with a backwards head butt.

Jim and Jack stand coolly behind the glass, judging the moment to take charge.

"You know what these lads need?" remarks Jim casually.

"And what would that be, now?"

"They need to learn to box."

"I couldn't agree more." Jack nods, flexing his hands automatically and tugging up his jacket sleeves. Jim grins at him, gestures with a flick of his eyes to the scene outside and they head out to break up the circle. There will be detention for at least two lads this afternoon.

Just two days later, Jim and Jack present themselves to Father O'Leary, in his private office. Jack has only been in the Head's office once before, when interviewed for his post, and was happy to avoid the Head Master as far as possible, even though he seems to be the most affable of gentlemen. For affable as he may be, Father O'Leary is the only person currently aware of Jack's earlier incarnation as a member of the cloth. It had after all been out of the question to omit such a large portion of his life from his curriculum vitae. Father O'Leary has never made the slightest reference to it, yet Jack never-the-less finds himself ill at ease in the old priest's presence, lest it somehow becomes a topic for discussion. He leaves the talking to Jim and in a bid to avoid the ageing Father's scrutiny, gazes around the office at the assortment of framed and mounted certificates and numerous elongated wide-angle school year photographs which adorn the walls.

Jim lays out his proposal to run a boxing club for the boys. In the school gym to begin with, but eventually linking up with the local boxing club. Jack, who had been an experienced pugilist in his youth had offered to help out and the school already boasted some antiquated basic equipment, though it rarely saw the much use these days. It was simply just a matter of organisation and commitment. And a little goodwill.

There is no need to labour the rationale for the project. Like Jack, Father O'Leary had grown up with boxing, sometimes bare-knuckle mind you, and sparring had been a part of seminary life; the perfect remedy for celibate young men awash with testosterone. Father O'Leary embarks on a reminiscence about his own days as a young neophyte back in County Down and is just about to share this remembrance with Jack, when he notices that the one-time priest is looking a little uneasy. Well now, perhaps Jack's former calling is not common knowledge? The older man, therefore, checks himself, clasps his hands together and comments that *the three of them clearly share a belief in the value of discipline and of the healthy channelling of aggression. Besides, it is nearly Christmas, the season of Good Will. He is more than happy to endorse the project. Furthermore, he is sure that the school budget could be stretched to cover the purchase of additional safety helmets and mouth guards, to allay any concerns expressed by overprotective parents. Why, to be sure, he might even be tempted to don his vest and shorts and join in, as there might be life in the old dog yet.* With this remark, he winks at Jack, but Jack's attention has been arrested by a large framed photograph above the Headmaster's desk; a photograph he had missed during his first visit to this room, when he had been a good deal too anxious to take much notice of his surroundings. Its impact today is, however, unmistakable. Father O'Leary follows Jack's gaze, then smiles.

"Oh well now, yes, of course, our namesake - St James of the Marches. He was an incorruptible, as you see. His body lies in a crystal casket in a Franciscan chapel in Naples, I took the photograph, meself, so I did, when I visited many years ago. Do you know, he is said to have a sweet fragrance about him even after all these centuries? Remarkable, isn't it now? The mysteries of God's works. But sure, I don't need to be telling you lads that, now do I?"

Then looking at his watch, he rises from behind the desk, as though recollecting he has another appointment, wishes them luck and warmly shakes hands with Jim and Jack in turn. They can still hear him chuckling to himself as they leave the office.

"What was all that about?" Jim asks when they are back in the corridor. He had seen the photograph enough times, but it had never really registered with him that it had any particular relationship to the school itself.

"His body does not decay - you know. Incorruptible. As in, corruption of the flesh."

Jim pulls a face.

"Blimey, really? I thought it meant he, you know, declined the odd backhander or something. And he is just lying there in that glass coffin thing like Snow White? That is pretty bloody creepy if you ask me!"

Jack cannot help but smile.

"Well, they say that he converted thirty-six fallen women in one sermon on Mary Magdalene, so they do. So, I'm after thinking he must have had quite the way with him."

"Shit. I knew there was something I did not like about the look of him. The guy sounds like a regular party-pooper to me." Jim grimaces as though he has a bad taste in his mouth.

"Jim, don't take this the wrong way, but you are a Catholic, are you not?" Jack had never asked and had just presumed that Jim must be, to be teaching in a catholic school.

"Well technically..." replies Jim, "I mean I am, but let's just say I wasn't exactly an altar boy and the truth is I spent most of my Sunday mornings on the football pitch, rather than at mass."

Jack's mind flashes back to his childhood in Ireland and smiles again.

"O, you happy breed of men..."

"And, what does the Bleedin' Hell does that mean?" Jack grins with closed lips and widens his eyes.

"It means you are English while I am Irish and there is a gulf wider than just the Irish sea between us, so there is."
"Yeah, well stuff that. You can't help it, can you? We've got our boxing club. You and me against the world, mate!" With this, he gives Jack a friendly punch to the upper arm. Jack winces and rubs his bicep with a look of mock injury.
"We are going to have to toughen you up, I can see." laughs Jim.
Jack nods. There is probably some truth in that.

Camden Town.

"What if I take charge, set the rules as it were, and then - and then at least I will know. I will not be waiting around for crumbs. That would be different, wouldn't it? Not just being passive, I mean..."
"Well," muses Bernard, "I suppose there is something in that..." He is feeling bamboozled, as he often does. "But here, it is not so much a case of what you do or do not do, but being aware of how those actions are being driven by unconscious...."
"Oh, so I can walk into a burning building, so long as I know I am going to burn, is that it?"
"Hmmm..." Bernard rubs the top of his skull cap, finding little comfort there.
"Well, I already did."
"Did what?" Bernard is feeling confused now.
"Walked into the burning building, took control. I introduced myself and - and well, chatted him up, I suppose." Janet is not sure she likes the way this sounds. She qualifies it. "Not in a predatory way. Just friendly - but I definitely took control. In fact, that is what we are now, friends, I mean."
"Uh-huh? And how did that feel?"

"Well actually, it felt good. Not hanging around hoping to be noticed. I made him notice me. And I think he likes me…"

Janet falls silent feeling a little guilty that she had not mentioned it before. Bernard studies the veins on the back of his hands. The skin looks thinner somehow and oddly translucent. *When did he become an old man?*

"What? You don't think it is possible for him to like me?" Janet is responding to the lack of response with distress, this is familiar ground. Bernard pauses a little longer.

"As it happens, I was thinking what a step forward it might be, that you can perceive that this man likes you and tell me about it with such certainty."

"It is. It is, isn't it? And I am going to act on that when it feels right. I am going to take a risk. And if he knocks me back, then that is okay. At least I will know where I am with him and if he does not want to take things further, I will not be hanging around just hoping."

Bernard cannot hold back the gentlest of sighs.

"Oh, come on Bernard, what do you think?

"I think our time is up."

And it is all Janet can do, not to lob a cushion at him on her way out. She must, instead, content herself with picturing it in her mind during the journey back to Bethnal Green.

The term is drawing to its hectic end. Janet has not been a party to Jack and Jim's fledgeling boxing club schemes, as it has simply not occurred to Jack that she would have any interest in it. Still, she detects a buoyancy in his mood and is herself aglow with the festive spirit. She decides to take her chances.

"Don't you think it is time you asked me out?" she chirps one afternoon in the break between rehearsals for the school nativity play. She is fiddling with the tinsel and wire for the little Baby Jesus' halo and prising open a paper clip with her teeth. The cramped staff room is festooned with paper chains and Chinese lanterns, and someone, either in humour or optimism, or perhaps both, has hung a small bunch of mistletoe from the pendant light shade in the centre of the room. Jack and Janet's usual corner has been overtaken by an artificial Christmas tree, with cheerfully winking lights, brightly coloured glass baubles and garlands of glittering tinsel.

Jack stares at her blankly. Janet swallows uncomfortably. This is not going well.

"You know - on a date, walking out together - I am sure they do it in Ireland." Janet tries to disguise her anxiety with levity. Her stomach turns suddenly cold.

"I um, I - I". Jack is hardly erudite in his reply.

For a moment Janet looks floored. Jack can see that her customary self-composure is slipping but is unable to come to her rescue. He puts his hands over his eyes, then pinches the bridge of his nose. What was he thinking? Surely, he did not think things would just carry on in the cosy companionship they had established? Jack feels suddenly angry with himself, and, still, he cannot think of anything to say.

"I am sorry - have I got it so wrong? You aren't married, are you? You don't wear a ring and you've never mentioned…" Janet's carefully plucked brows knit in puzzlement. She lets drop the tinsel and paper clips.

"No, to be sure…" he manages at last but finds he does not know how to elaborate. Memories of back home and the stolen hours spent in Margaret Doyle's bedroom crowd his thoughts. The roses on the wallpaper, the smell of freshly laundered sheets, and the soft corners of her hips and the feel of her skin. He has not so much as touched a woman since. He certainly has not felt that ecstasy made more intoxicating still by its sinfulness. But he remembers also the betrayal and the terrible cost.

"I am sorry, Janet, it's not what you think," but he is still unable to find words.

Janet sees the pain in his eyes. The counsellor in her takes charge.

"Jack, I don't think I can be reading the signals that poorly, but if I have got the wrong end of the stick, then please accept my apology. I guess it is just the Christmas spirit - all this ridiculous mistletoe..." she is trying to be a comic now, but she is gathering her bits and pieces and rising to leave.

"I'll see you around."

She is gone. Jack remains sitting next to the Christmas tree, his face dappled by the twinkling of the fairy lights. He looks around the room hoping to spot Jim, but Jim is nowhere to be seen and what use would he be? Besides, Jack already knows what he would say, for hasn't he already tried to egg him on to get a move on with Janet a dozen times and in a dozen different ways. But how could Jim or anyone else understand? Jack envies Janet her Bernard, though she talks about him with such mixed feelings.

And then he remembers Father Frank. "I'm always here for you," he had told Jack, shaking his hand warmly as they had parted, and Jack had felt the full force of his sincerity. Frank had been above all, the one person in the world he had trusted enough to contact on his exodus from Ireland. He had put him up when he had first arrived in Liverpool and encouraged him in his plans to train as a teacher and build a new life, without questions or attempts to dissuade. He recalls the gentleness with which Frank commiserated over the death of Jack's infant son and the terrible circumstances around it; never once a judgement, never once a reproach. So, although they had only exchanged infrequent letters since Jack had moved down to London, Jack knows that he could phone him. And perhaps, that is exactly what he should do.

"Damnation," breathes Janet through gritted teeth as she makes her way back to where the third years are holding rehearsals. "Damn you, Jack O'Donnell," but the tears are stinging her eyes. And what in Hell is Bernard going to say? Who is she kidding? She knows exactly what he will say and that is the worst part. Perhaps she will not tell him. But what is the point of paying a fucking therapist if you cannot confide this pain, this rejection? Janet takes a long sigh. A group of kids rush past on the stairs singing a corrupted version of jingle bells. She hates Christmas and fucking Bernard will be on a break after the next session. Could she have made it any worse for herself? Christ, perhaps she has done so deliberately, unconsciously that is. If Bernard even hints at this she will scream, truly. She will. She is such an unholy mess. How can she hope to be a counsellor when her own life is so royally screwed up. But at this moment, a more benevolent aspect of Bernard comes to the rescue.

"You are too hard on yourself," she hears him say. "Sometimes we are all just human beings – frail but doing our best."

Janet feels the tears prick her eyes and the muscles in her neck and shoulders soften. She pulls out a handkerchief from her sleeve, blows her nose and exhaling sharply pushes open the hall doors. Thank God the day is almost over. And if she is a little over sharp with a tea towel-hooded Joseph, when he drops his crook and nearly brains the hapless donkey slumbering beside the cardboard crib, then who can blame her?

The following day Jack looks out for Janet, but she is nowhere to be seen. He wonders if she is deliberately avoiding him. He would not blame her. Perhaps she is not as emotionally robust as her outward confidence would have him believe. Whatever the case, it is clear that he has hurt her pride or her feeling, and most likely both. He wonders if he just has some innate talent for it, despite his best intentions. He had been trying to protect Janet, by not rushing into something before he is genuinely ready, but now he has hurt her anyway. Yet, if he is truly honest, is it only really himself he is trying to protect again? Either way, he does not seem to be able to get a handle on this relationship business. Jack can feel his head spinning.

He recalls his phone call with Frank last night. Frank who had been so pleased to hear from him, so ready to listen and offer wise counsel. And for someone who usually avoided giving outright advice, Frank had been pretty direct; *Jack was no longer a priest so he needed to stop acting like one.* He had not meant to be unkind but, as usual, he had hit the nail on the head. The irony in his self-imposed celibacy since quitting the priesthood had hardly escaped Jack's attention. How much easier it seemed now, and how contrary. Jack had sighed and professed himself a sad case. But Frank would have no truck with self-pity. *The risk of getting hurt and hurting others was grist for the mill, a normal part of normal life. If Jack wanted to enter back into life, he had better start to live it, instead of hanging around on the periphery, a detached observer. He could not remain in no man's land for the rest of his days.* If Frank had been there in person instead of on the end of the telephone receiver, he might have taken Jack by the shoulders and shaken him, but a metaphorical shaking had had to suffice.

Yet, if Janet is steering clear of him then he may already have blown his chances.

The last day of term arrives and at the Christmas get-together in the staff room, and much as she would like to, Janet finds she can no longer hide from Jack. She tries not to catch his eye, turning her back to him in conversation with Jill Tuffin, but he sees the flush on her cheeks as he approaches. Jill sees it too and tactfully moves off to claim another of the mince pies, which are after all, exceedingly good.

Janet wishes Jack an over-cheerful Merry Christmas then stares down into her sherry glass. Jack clears his throat.

"Janet, would you do me the honour of allowing me to take you out for dinner?" His tone is formal yet warm. Janet screws up her eyes then looks up with a lopsided smile.

"As long as we go Dutch," she says firmly.

"Sure. Why not? I dare say I would like Dutch food, although I have never tried it..."

"Oh, Jack. You are such a treasure," she squeezes his arm. "It means splitting the bill."

Jack shakes his head. There does indeed seem to be rather a lot he is going to have to learn.

Spring 1981

"Give it a bit of welly, lad! It's not a rice pudding." Jim is holding the battered leathered punch bag in place whilst a pasty fourth-year jabs at it with his right fist. The boy's small freckled face is turning puce and he is panting heavily, but Jim will not allow him to let up.

"You gotta punch from the shoulder and follow-through, you see." The boy stands back, shrugs his shoulders to loosen the tightness in his deltoids, then taking an almighty swing lands a heavy punch right in the centre of the bag, almost sending Jim, who is taken off his guard, sprawling.

"Now you got it!" whoops Jim in delight. He ruffles the lad's hair. "We'll make a Henry Cooper of you yet, Jenkins."

The boy beams with delight and continues pummelling the bag with renewed enthusiasm, as Jim leaves him behind to make a tour of the gym.

"Put some speed into it, this isn't the girl's playground," he hollers at a couple of well-muscled older lads with whirring skipping ropes, and "Don't be afraid to hit him, he won't break." This last remark is made to a lad who is directing puny punches at Jack's upheld glove, as though in terror that he might knock his teacher out. The danger seems small since he is hardly less skinny than a strand of spaghetti. "Fat chance!" thinks Jim to himself, whilst Jack tries hard to keep a serious expression on his face.

Jim finishes the tour of his domain, with a word of encouragement or piece of advice for every one of the fifteen lads who are hard at work at their respective training activity. He stands in the corner and folds his arms then looks around with a sigh of satisfaction. He strokes his chin in thought. Then signalling to the two lads who have now completed their skipping quotient, he enlists their help in laying down some gym mats in the centre of the room. Next, he places some protective belts and headgear in a pile to one side, puts his two fingers between his lips and whistles loudly.

"Right now, time for today's bit of sparring practice, I think. Can we have two volunteers, please!" and without waiting for any hands to go up - "Griggs, Petersen you first."

The lads descend on the protective gear with glee, and Jim, who is the only member of the group whose hands are not hampered by padded boxing gloves, assists them in fastening the helmets and belts in place.

"Oh, and better not forget your gumshields, lads, we don't want any stitches in lips today!"

A titter of laughter runs through the circle of lads that has formed around the makeshift sparring ring. Jenkins turns pink and rubs his mouth where his tooth had lacerated the skin a few weeks ago, after he had overlooked inserting his mouthguard. The lad who had been sparring with Jenkins was the spaghetti-thin lad who could boast about as much force behind his right hook as a spicy meatball, and the blow that had done the damage was almost certainly a mis-hit, in what had become an ungainly tussle. Never-the-less the wound inflicted had bled for England, and Jenkins was not the only lad amongst them to turn a little faint. Once they had got the wounded soul to Casualty at Mile End hospital, it turned out that the damage was, in fact, pretty superficial after all. All the same, Jenkin's lower lip had swollen to the size of a sparrow's egg.

Superficial or not, the unfortunate debacle had nearly bought about a premature termination of the fledgeling little boxing club and had certainly caused outrage amongst some of the staff at St James who questioned the fostering of gratuitous violence and muttered about "retrogressive values" and "the brutalisation of minors". But Jim was unapologetic.

"Jeez, this is boxing, not making fairy cakes, and besides we have had much worse injuries on the football pitch and no one bleats on about the fostering of aggression, or health and safety then. We are teaching these lads self-discipline and resilience for Christ's sake. How is that retrogressive?"

Fortunately, Jenkin's father, if not his mother, had shared this point of view, and Jenkins himself, keen not to become an easy target for any bully who was on the lookout for a bit of fun, insisted that he wished to continue. Given Father O'Leary's continuingly cheery endorsement, the club was saved. Indeed, it had begun to attract even more new members, as it had now assumed a reputation for meaning business. As for Jenkins, his bulging mouth and stitches, though painful, had purchased him a week or so of heroic notoriety and the kind of kudos that pocket-money cannot buy.

Griggs and Petersen, gumshields, body belts and helmets in place, square up to each other in the centre of the mats and start to jig around each other, making quick little movements with their fists, but landing no blows. Jim stands with his hands on his hips then claps his hands loudly.

"This is sparring lads, not a bloody tea dance. Get on with it, there are other people waiting to have a go."

Petersen, taking the cue, shoots out a right hook and connects with Grigg's waiting left guard.

"Well done. That is more like it," roars Jim.

Griggs keeping his defence up with his left, strikes out with his right fist. The jab pushes through the other boy's guard, which is low and weak. His glove glances off Petersen's left cheek. Petersen is galvanised by the shock of the blow, however minor. He responds with an impressively fast repost which finds its mark and knocks Griggs off balance and tottering across the mat. Jim calls time and checking that Petersen is okay, pats them both warmly on the back.

Jenkins and the spaghetti boy are up next, in what is less than a historic rematch. They make a comic sight, as they touch gloves then flail around, weaving and ducking imaginary blows, gloves held up to their faces, as though they are trying to hide from one another. Jim tries hard to resist laughing but congratulates them for their efforts all the same. The remainder of the boys pair off until there is one left standing alone. The last of the fifteen. The last, who just happens to be the largest and most well-developed lad, despite being junior to several of the others. This boy is naturally endowed with spectacular musculature or he works out regularly at a gym. Either way, his physique is impressive in one so tender in years. Jim grins and drawls out his name.

"Ah, Lanigan! No one in the mood to take you on this morning, I see. What are we going to do about that then? Any volunteers amongst our brave little band?"

The circle of lads, some of them seated cross-legged by this time, fiddle with their glove laces, or stare at the gym mats, as though cogitating on one of life's really big questions. Lanigan takes the silence as a compliment and smirks. This is not rejection. This is not being left last to be picked for a team. This is duty due to the alpha male and he knows it. Jim knows it too and is in the mood to bring him down a peg or two. He clears his throat.

"Er, Mr O'Donnell, I see you still have your pugilist's mittens on, would you do us the honour?"

Jack stares at Jim in a kind of stunned silence then scratches his head. He is trying to weigh up the potential effectiveness of any number of possible responses when he is temporarily saved by Jenkins' hand shooting up into the air.

"Yes, Jenkins? Are you volunteering?" asks Jim in a deadpan tone.

"No - no Sir. But Sir, I was just wondering. What is a pugilist, sir?"

The question breaks the tension. Jim and Jack both have to chuckle.

"Well, I suppose I am, or was - in my day, that is," admits Jack sheepishly. "A bit of a boxer, that is. But it has been a while," he adds glaring pointedly at Jim.

"Perfect then," says Jim. "We wouldn't want it to be an unfair contest, now would we?"

Jack shakes his head, peels off his tracksuit bottoms and heads over to where he had left his hold-all to find his gum guard. Meanwhile, Jim holds forth on the majesty and history of the noble art of pugilism and the Queensbury Rules, whilst Lanigan shifts uneasily from foot to foot. He sizes up his opponent from across the room as he leans over his bag.

Jack meanwhile is contending with his racing thoughts. He is by no means in poor shape for his thirty-odd years but has become skinny of limb and slack around the abdomen since he left Ireland. He wonders if Lanigan is as powerful as he looks and wishes he had paid him more attention during training exercises. He becomes suddenly aware of the blood beginning to throb in his veins and, at that moment, realises how much he has come to relish the re-quickening that the regular increase in physical exertion brings. That and the intense sense of camaraderie with Jim that their joint investment in the project has fostered. Small wonder then that the boxing club has become an oasis of vitality in the deadening desert of his week. Jack shakes his head. Yet it only feels like only yesterday, that he could never have thought such a thing possible. Right now, however, he has other things to think about and something tells him, he is going to need one hundred per cent of his focus.

He moistens his lips, slips in the gum shield, pushing it into place with his tongue. He straightens up and strides back to Jim, the waiting circle and Lanigan.

The two combatants touch gloves. Lanigan directs a look of sly meanness at Jack, hoping to intimidate him, and they both take a step back. Jack raises his gloves, but Lanigan, hoping to use the alacrity of youth to his advantage, is already at him with relentless jabs. Jack parries the blows but is already puffing. He feels the instinct to lash out with all his adult power against such ferocity but forces himself to hold back, aware of the inequity of the match, in maturity and experience, if not weight. Lanigan is operating under no such inhibitions. Perhaps more threatened than he cares to admit, he might be fighting for his life. Still, Jack's strong point was always his guard and it serves him well. Suddenly his concentration is broken as he spies Jim from the corner of his eye. Jim is mouthing something, but he cannot catch it and then WHAM! A wrecking ball of pain crashes through his cheek and skull as Lanigan's fist makes contact with the bone of his left eye socket. Jack reels for a moment, his head swimming. Then, as quick as you like, Jim is there, arms around his shoulders, looking intently into his face. Jack shakes his head briskly and returns his gaze with a steadiness less equal, then sinks to sit, legs splayed out before him on the green mat. He can see two Lanigan's standing to one side; both have a look of anxious horror on their faces.

Jacks ears are ringing and the sting of the blow continues to reverberate around the inside of his head like an echo. Searing pain continues to jar his senses and he struggles to catch his breath. Jim squats down beside him now with a;

"Steady there, mate. Are you okay?"

If Jack was more with it, he might notice a tone of genuine concern has replaced his friend's usual cockiness. As it is, it is all he can do to grunt and nod. Jim remains squatting next to him. He beckons to one of the other boys to fetch a cold sponge and mops his mate's brow with all the assiduousness of a regular Florence Nightingale. Jack rubs the side of his face and moves his jaws from side to side with his gloved hand. Then, looking from Lanigan to Jim and back, he bursts into laughter.

"Bejeebers, it hurts..." he says "but, sure I never felt better or more alive in me whole life!"

Jim laughs back, clasping his hand to raise him from the mat, and Lanigan's expression of anxiety softens into a curious blend of cautious smugness and relief.

"But I tell you no lie, now," he says to Jim later in the changing room "it's the first time I've *truly felt anything* since I stepped off that bloody boat, so it is."

Jim smiles. "Put it there, mate," and they bump fists, "and no worries," adds Jim. "Thompson of the sixth form said he would come next week, and *he* has been in training at the local amateur club since he was in junior school. He'll sort the little shit out, you see if he doesn't!"

"Jim. You are incorrigible," grins Jack.

"That I am," nods Jim. "But I tell you what, today the drinks are on me."

Janet awakens into an awareness of the unfamiliar warmth of another human body next to hers. It is a warmth that has pervaded her dreams, lending a deepness to her slumbers that she has not experienced in many years. For a moment she wonders if she is still dreaming, but the memories are returning, even as she struggles to open her eyes.

Janet had been horrified when Jack turned up yesterday evening to take her out to their favourite Indian restaurant for dinner. His eye socket and cheek had become shiny and black by late in the afternoon, despite the packet of frozen peas he had held to it for over an hour after he got home from the pub. *It was monstrous* she said, *children, being encouraged to wallop one another and their teachers*. Though she supposed there might be a case for sublimation and the diversion of inherent aggressive drives that might otherwise manifest in more antisocial behaviour. *But it was all the fault of that Neanderthal Jim Morris. He was exactly the macho type that gave men a bad name. Really, she was surprised Jack went along with it.* But at that point, Janet had caught the sound of the scolding harpy in her own voice and fallen silent. Good grief, was she turning in her mother so soon? So critical, so judgemental, so old!

She had not felt half so outraged, however, when after seeing her home, Jack had kissed her with a new and very welcome urgency, and had asked if he might stay the night. Janet had agreed without demur. This was not a moment for maidenly coyness. Yet things are rarely that simple, even when they seem it. Even as she and Jack were sinking onto her bed, fumbling with each other's clothes, Jack had suddenly frozen. A look of panic crossed his face. He pulled away.

"Janet, darling, I am so sorry," he whispered, "we have to stop. Sure, what was I thinking? I can't take the risk of making you pregnant."

Janet was impressed. Here was a man who was ready to take responsibility, even in the heat of passion. Rare indeed. Yet at the same time, she had been puzzled by the intensity of his reaction. Still, that could wait.

"Goodness, is that all?" she smiled drawing him close again. "Well, you don't have to worry about that. I am on the pill."

"I thought you were a Catholic…"

Janet could almost have laughed at the look of perplexity that knitted his brows.

"Well, so I am, I guess, but that does not mean I buy every word that issues from the Pope's mouth wholesale. And as far as I know, sex outside marriage is considered a sin, so I might as well be hung for a sheep. Besides don't you think being a little sinful makes it even more fun?"

Jack, relieved beyond words, had simply nodded and kissed her again.

"There is certainly still a lot more I have to learn about English Catholicism," he breathed nuzzling her neck.

"Well, believe me, you have come to the right place. Now call me a heretic and get that shirt off!"

Janet raises herself on one elbow and gazes into Jack's still sleeping face. She feels her body almost physically lurch in the wake of the wave of intense love that sweeps over her, taking her by complete surprise. It had not been the most spectacular lovemaking she had ever enjoyed, indeed there was something a little inexperienced in Jack's tentative embraces that made her silently wonder just how few sexual partners he may have had. She grimaces. She would hardly have described herself as a loose woman, but last night she had felt like a Mrs Robinson to his Benjamin Braddock, without the age difference of course. It would certainly go some way to explaining his reticence. But what Jack had lacked in finesse he had certainly made up for with gentleness and a touch so tender it makes her thrill just to recall it. She watches him sleep for a while, still flinching at the blackness around his eye, then wakes him with a deep kiss. It is Sunday morning. Catholic or not, Janet will be worshipping in her own fashion.

Her Monday morning appointment with Bernard might be the opportunity for coyness, but Bernard cannot help but see the glow about her, and Janet is almost bursting to tell him, despite her promise to herself to play it cool.

"I am a fallen woman," she admits. "I have fallen in deep, and I can't see myself getting out."

"Would you wish to get out of it?"

"Oh, Bernard, of course not."

Bernard sighs. In his experience, once people fall in love, psychotherapy is more or less a waste of time. It is a kind of untreatable madness, *a folie a deux*. He feels himself preparing to make some scathing observation, but catches himself just in time. Could it be that what he feels is, in fact, a hint of jealousy? He holds his tongue and half listens whilst Janet rattles on in a kind of ecstatic delirium. He ponders silently. She has found what she was looking for. Surely that is something. Couldn't he just let her have that for a change?

"But you don't think it will last? Do you?" Janet's tone has shifted from major to minor, and the change in key jolts Bernard out of his reverie.

"You say *I* don't believe it will last? I wonder what *you* think?"

"He has opened up to me, I really felt connected to him this weekend, but there is still so much about him that, you know, is closed off somehow."

"Would he be quite so attractive if he was less mysterious?" *Why had he said that?* Bernard castigates himself internally. *There may have been some truth in it, but it was cruel and unnecessary. Janet was smart and perfectly able to ask these questions herself.* Yet Janet seems strangely immune to the edge of sarcasm for once.

"It is true, I know," she admits miserably. "I guess I am still stuck on the challenge thing, or the rescue, or both probably. And it is the precious moment of connection that is the hook, isn't it? And once you have had it, you want it again. Like a damn junkie!"

Bernard is shocked by her sudden anger at herself. His compassion permits him a little largess:

"I think you are being a little hard on yourself again there, but perhaps there is some insight in there too".

"Bernard, can I ask you a question?"

"You can ask…"

"Do you honestly think there are any normal men out there? I mean ones without issues who can just love and be loved in return?" Bernard pauses. He tries to respond with all the neutrality he can muster.

"The real question is, I think, if you met one would you recognise it, and would you want it?"

Janet falls silent. She is thinking of some of the perfectly lovely and happily married men she had known. There had not been one of them that she found the least little bit attractive.

"I hate this unconscious shit, I hate to feel at the mercy of it," she protests at last, "it is so unfair." She could be a little girl stamping her foot in frustration.

"Well, I guess that is what we are trying to do here," muses Bernard with uncustomary sympathy, "bring it into consciousness, so you can be less at its mercy."

"Do you know what it is like?"

"Hmmm?"

"It is like when you are very little, the grain in the wood of the wardrobe door, or the patterns in the wallpaper and curtains all look like scary monsters in the dark. You feel alone and frightened but when someone switches the lights on, you can see them for what they truly are, just patterns. That is all!"

"Do you know, I like that," says Bernard with a smile.

"And you see, there I go again. Saying something clever to please Daddy." But, this time, Janet is laughing.

Then Bernard says something, he never thought he would hear himself say.

"Perhaps you could just enjoy the feeling of being in love for what it is and not look for the patterns, just for now. Giving one's heart is always a risk, at least you are taking that risk. Perhaps that in itself is a step forward."

"And you will always be here to pick up the pieces, right?"

"As long as you need me to be, Janet, as long as you need me to be."

Easter 1981

Janet puts aside her pen. She has spent the best part of the Easter break writing up her case study for the final submission for her counselling diploma. She had been lucky enough to have a number of clients from whom to pick, as all but one of the training cases, she had taken on at the low-cost clinic of the Westminster Pastoral Foundation, had stayed the distance.

She wonders about Jaime, the lad who had dropped out after only five sessions. Perhaps he had got a raw deal having such a novice as herself, and perhaps now, with some more experience behind her, she would not have felt so easily thrown by his wilful attempts to misunderstand her responses and feel judged. Still, that was the way it worked, people could access low-cost counselling because they were willing to see a trainee, it was all quite transparent. Yet he had used her inexperience against her like a weapon, pushing every single one of the buttons guaranteed to trigger her deepest insecurities, until she could hardly think straight. She shakes her head. Thank goodness for her training supervisor and Bernard. She had been almost at the point of throwing in the towel, and might have done, had they not helped her see that it had been the perfect set up. Jaime had needed the therapist to feel like a failure. If anyone had made an error, it was the senior therapist who had assessed the young man as suitable for a trainee.

"Even therapists with years of expertise can make a wrong call," Bernard had said. "Your client was, perhaps despite initial appearances, unable to articulate the deepest level of his distress and therefore needed to convey to his therapist exactly what it is like to feel like a total waste of space, through projective identification. He got you to feel exactly as he does. It can be very effective, but very difficult to endure. It can take years of skill and experience to withstand such a powerful onslaught, then understand and respond to it as a communication rather than an assault; and even then, we all have weak spots. We are still human beings at the end of the day - even me."

Privately, Janet doubts that Bernard could actually believe this to be true of himself. At the same time, even she can see this is unfair and is ashamed of her ingratitude. Such conflicting ideas seem to encapsulate the contrary twinning of idealisation and frustration that characterises her relationship with him.

In any case, the clients that she had continued to work with had provided her with a rewarding, though by no mean always easy, training experience, and she could honestly say that at least one or two seemed to have made significant improvement. *But was that because she needed them to?* Janet knows she is prone to torture herself with this old chestnut. In therapy, who exactly needs who? And isn't that why therapists have therapy themselves, to at least try and unknot the whole unholy tangle. After all, there would be no therapists to go to, if you weeded out any of the trainees with some kind of pathology; some kind of unresolved neurotic compulsion to feel needed or helpful.

Bernard would joke that you knew you were truly cured when you realised that you no longer wanted to be a counsellor or therapist. Janet cannot begin to imagine that. She finds sitting in a room with someone talking about the things that deeply matter to them, the most fascinating and engaging moments in her life. It is true, that perhaps, after that, social interactions seem superficial and bland, and she knows all too well that the intimacy of the counselling room should never be a substitute for the intimacy of a real relationship. Goodness knows she had beaten herself up about that often enough. Well, at least she is in a relationship now, although if she is honest, she knows there is a lack of true intimacy despite the tender albeit increasingly adventurous sex. Or perhaps, if she is being fair to herself, it is more that there seems to be such a gulf between sexual and emotional intimacy; for no matter how strong a connection she feels when she is alone with Jack in bed at night, and for her it is very strong, it seems inevitably to evaporate with the light of day. Perhaps that is being in love for you; the toxic blend of self-deception and idealisation. Nevertheless, she *is* in love with him. She cannot deny it. *What is a girl going to do?*

She pushes the pad and paper away. She will be no good for anything until she has had a coffee and cleared her mind. She puts the kettle on, then settles back at her desk, waiting for it to boil. She reaches for the Evening Standard that lies on the shelf next to her and turns absent-mindedly to the classified and jobs vacancy section. A small block advertisement at the bottom of the page catches her eye. *The Central School of Art and Design seeks a student counsellor.* Janet peers more closely at the small writing. The position will become available at the start of the new academic year. The post is full time and includes the provision of counselling and support across a range of student needs. The ad suggests that the post would suit someone with a qualification in student or general counselling and experience within teaching or an educational setting would be an advantage. There is a telephone number and a name to contact for further information. The closing date is the end of May.

Janet sits back and thinks. The kettle is whistling its readiness. She stalks over to the kitchen area and takes it off the hob. *Isn't this everything she had dreamed of? Getting out of teaching, doing what she loves best? She will have her diploma by July. In teaching, it is par for the course to start applying for posts before completion of training due to the practicalities of term planning. She has heard other students on her training- course talking about applying for posts already. Why shouldn't she?* Janet places a teaspoon of instant coffee in a mug, adds the steaming water and shakes her head. *No, no chance. And yet -* and surely this is Bernard's voice and not her own - *If you don't try, you will never know?*

The Greenwich Tunnel.

The tea roses in Victoria Park are beginning to blossom. The unmistakable sweetness of freshly mown grass and the promise of the first rain of summer linger intoxicatingly in the air, beckoning all outdoors. Janet and Jack, for two, are in no mood to be cooped up all afternoon and have been enjoying the kind of heady late Sunday morning stroll that lovers often take. Inspired by a sudden happy idea, Janet squeezes Jack's arm and suggests that it is the perfect day to catch a bus down to The Island Gardens on the Isle of Dogs and take the foot tunnel under the Thames across to Greenwich; *Jack has never been, and really it is an experience not to be missed. They can grab a bite to eat at the pie and mash shop, another first for Jack, and although it might be a bit late to catch the best of the markets, Greenwich Park will be a lovely place to hang out for a few hours. And they could even have a look around the Cutty Sark if it is not too overrun with tourists.* Jack nods happily. *That sounds grand to him.* He is still so much a tourist himself and is happy to be guided around.

Twenty minutes later, they are sitting on the top deck of the number 277 heading down to Lime House and beyond there, the Isle of Dogs. Janet chatters on about the history of the areas they pass through, pointing out the canal and old seaman's rest home whilst Jack gazes through the windows at the unfamiliar streets and buildings.

As the bus trundles deeper into the Docklands, boarded-up bomb sites and tumble-down houses, give way to empty warehouses, long-abandoned pubs and the blank face of the long Dock wall, beyond which hunker grim housing estates and sordid tower blocks. Everything about the area speaks of poverty and despair and the people on the streets shuffle past as though anxious to be back indoors, despite the bright early summer sunshine. Jack wonders momentarily if Janet has taken them the wrong way but they alight, at last, at the so-called Island Gardens, along with a couple of other somewhat shell-shocked looking tourists. Jack wonders how ever a location could have been so misleadingly named, yet taking Jack's hand in hers, Janet skips happily in the direction of the river.

"You see," points Janet, indicating a squat little brick edifice with a domed glass roof on the far shore of the river, "we go down in the lift here and walk right underneath The Thames and come out over there. Isn't it wild?"

Jack is not so sure. He has never thought of himself as claustrophobic, but the thought of all that water bearing down above his head is making him feel a little uneasy.

"It is perfectly safe, Silly. It was constructed by Brunel in Victorian times and opened the year after she died. Queen Victoria I mean. There were no bulldozers or earthmovers back then of course. Can you imagine how on Earth they ever built it?"

Jack fails to see how this is supposed to be reassuring but trudges dutifully behind her along a little tree-lined path to where another building, a mirror image of the edifice on the opposite bank, forms the entrance to the tunnel. Inside, he sees a staircase spiralling downwards away to the left and around a lift shaft that forms its core which, in turn, plunges to the level of the tunnel below. Jack has to admit it is impressive. Janet leads Jack around to the far side of the caged lift shaft, where they are just in time to hop into the great wood-panelled lift. She pulls Jack towards one of the vacant padded seats along the wall. Her face shines with excitement as, with a smile, the attendant draws closed the great concertina steel doors and sets the lift in descent.

The lift takes only a minute, but to Jack, the descent seems to take an eternity. The air feels chill and damp and he can hear echoing voices through the grated walls of the lift shaft. He is aware that his face is beginning to perspire, but Janet is looking around her, beaming at their fellow travellers, blithely unaware of his uneasiness.

When they reach the bottom, the attendant pulls open the doors once more and out they file. The flag-stoned tunnel path leads gently downwards and away to one side. Jack realises that he cannot see the other end. He swallows hard. This is not quite what he had expected. The tunnel is lined by the kind of white ceramic tiles he associates with public lavatories and lit with flickering fluorescent strips, which cast tremulous and ghastly shadows along the walls.

He shivers in the cold dank air, taken by surprise by the subterranean drop in temperature. He can hear the echoing drip of water. The voices that he had heard in the lift sound louder now and barely human somehow, as they resonate around the arching passageway. Janet grasps his hand and, seemingly oblivious to the clamminess of his palm, marches blithely onwards towards their unseen destination. The echo of the slap of their footfall clangs uncomfortably in his ears and merges with the general cacophony, which by and by seems to engulf them from all sides.

Jack proceeds onwards, a grim expression on his face, scarcely able to return Janet's smiling glances. They step across shallow puddles which gather in the pitted flagstone paving and the air grows damper. Jack notes, with some discomfiture, the trails of limestone that stain the ceramic tiles above their heads and the odd unnerving trickle of water.

They are heading gently downhill now, towards what Jack hopes is the middle of the path. By and by, they pass a gaggle of Japanese sight-seers, who whisper in hushed tones. They seem to clasp their cameras to their breasts, as though for safety. Jack tries to envisage the massive body of water of Old Father Thames above their heads, but the thought is hardly comforting. He tugs at his collar. Can the air really be so thin, down here?

At last, Janet stops and declares that they have reached the half-way point. Her words brim with such pride that one might be forgiven for thinking that she herself had some part in the construction of this netherworld way-fare. She starts to say more but, before she has a chance to extol the further marvels of Victorian engineering, she notices the pallor of her lover's face and exclaims,

"Jack, why whatever is the matter, are you okay?"

"Can you hear flapping - wings flapping?" Jack's voice is hoarse and shrill. He is staring into Janet's eyes, his face rigid with fright, his skin almost green in the artificial light.

"Well, no, I can't, but maybe there is a pigeon down here, I know they get down here sometimes. The sounds do carry in a strange…"

But her words are lost in the roaring echo that is now in his head, and at that moment a shrieking from one end of the tunnel, or is it from all around, commences. Jack claps his hands to his ears, screws up his eyes and cowers as though to evade the beating wings that seem to be descending upon him. Surely these are the cries of demons, or souls in torment and he and Janet are treading the path to Gehenna, or Purgatory. He starts to weep. He cannot help himself. He slumps against the cold tiles of the tunnel wall. He is lost. There can be no redemption for him. Janet, her own heart in her mouth, is shaking him with urgent gentleness, pressing her fingers against his neck to find his pulse.

"Jack! Jack, talk to me. Are you having chest pains? Shall I run for help? Should I call an ambulance?"

She looks around in desperation, but the tunnel seems suddenly empty. She places a hand on his cheek.

"Please Jack, please talk to me."

Her pleas seem to throb in his skull. He forces open his eyes, his vision is blurred, but all is silent around and the terror has passed.

"No - I'm fine. Just need a minute. Help me to the end, can you?" he pants, and placing his arm around her shoulders, they stumble onwards until the far lift comes into view. The great metal-latticed doors stand open and the interior is empty save for the attendant, a middle-aged peroxide blonde, with bright red lipstick. She awaits their arrival with patient friendliness. Jack and Janet tumble into the lift and onto the bench. Jack has his eyes closed and is breathing heavily.

"Get a lot of them like that, Luv. I've seen it many-a-time," remarks the attendant in a kindly voice, as she pulls the doors too. "You'll be right as rain as soon as you get back up into the fresh air, Ducky, you wait and see."

And she is right. Once she has let them out with a sympathetic farewell and Jack feels the fresh air and sunshine on his face, it is as though he has awoken from a nightmarish slumber.

"Oh, Jack! I am so sorry. I had no idea you were claustrophobic." Janet's voice is all concerned contrition.

"Phew! To tell the truth, neither did I." Jack tries to joke, but his eyes do not smile, and he quickly tries to change the subject. He sets off at a stride, hoping to put as much distance as he can between himself and the tunnel entrance, and Janet must trot along to keep up. And if there is one thing she understands by now, it is when to let things go.

Jack and Janet wander around the pretty little village of Greenwich for an hour or so, gazing up amongst the masts of the Cutty Sark and stopping for a bite to eat at the popular and crowded pie and mash shop, just managing to grab a corner table, as another couple rise to leave. Jack is unimpressed by the mash and liquor. He feels a sudden longing for his homeland and a good Irish stew with potatoes and their skins. Still, he smiles and fakes enthusiasm for Janet's benefit, even though she knows him well enough by now to see through it.

The shadows lengthen in the fading evening sunshine and it is time to make tracks homewards. Janet catches the look of anxiety on Jack's face. *It is okay, they can catch the river bus, then take the tube; that is unless Jack has not told her about any fear of water, he might hav.!* Janet jokes then realises the insensitivity of her flippancy. But Jack is all smiles.

"Sure, that would be grand now, so it would. I would rather be *on* the water than *under* it, even it if means swimming for it, believe you me."

And with that, he finally makes Janet's afternoon. There is nothing like the romance of a trip along the Thames in the dusk, and she wonders why she had not thought of it before. Jack makes an effort to be especially attentive as they sit with arms entwined and watch the passing riverside lights begin to twinkle.

The tunnel and its drama seem quite forgotten, but when he is not looking, Janet's eyes rest on his face with sad puzzlement. That night, after he has escorted home, Jack recalls he has some marking that he must complete before the morning and declines to stay over. Janet nods understandingly, though her words conceal an unspoken hurt. *She will see him at school tomorrow then.*

Camden Town. Monday 8.30 am

"I just know there is something, something he is keeping to himself. And yes, I know I have to wait until he is ready to share it with me, but what do I have to do for him to trust me?"

Janet's words meet a wearied silence.

"Well?" she asks a little petulantly. "You are listening, I suppose? You do usually at least make the effort to grunt, or something…." Her words sting. Bernard tries his best not to retaliate. To stay off this particular round-a-bout.

"You sound angry with me when in reality I think you are angry with this man who will not let you in." He tries to make it neutral, keep the judgement, criticism, whatever it will be heard as, out of his tone.

"What is your point?" demands Janet. She knows she is being unreasonably hostile, but cannot help herself. She hates herself when she is like this. Such a child.

Bernard sighs. He decides to take a risk.

"Well, it seems to me, time was we used to talk about you. About Janet, *her* fears, *her* desires…"

"And, now..?"

"Now we only seem to talk about Jack. His problems, his feelings."

"Okay, Bernard. I get the picture…" The child is being ticked off.

"The point is," continues Bernard determined to make it, "I want to know about Janet, I want to know about her feelings, her fears and desires - it is *you* I am concerned with, and I think you are hiding behind this man's difficulties…"

The tears spring into Janet's eyes.

"You know what, Bernard?" she snivels.

"Uh-hum?"

"Sometimes, I just really hate you!"

"Uh-huh." replies Bernard.

Central London. May.

The afternoon tea break is almost finished in the popular little student refectory which nestles in a corner of the ground floor overlooking Southampton Row. Most of the punters have drifted out, and Ada, the cheery cockney proprietor, has already started wiping down tables and stacking chairs, in preparation for closing up. She whistles a little tune as she works, now and then breaking into song as she recalls the words. For anyone interested, the tune and lyrics might be recognisable as Noel Coward's *London Pride*. But doubtless, there is nobody old enough there to identify them as such, let alone care. If anyone were to be paying attention, however, they would notice that she adopts a different Coward classic every day. Yesterday it had been *Don't Put Your Daughter on The Stage Mrs Worthington*, Tomorrow, it is looking as though it will be *Mad Dogs and Englishmen,* but she will see how she feels in the morning.

Maggie and the Gang remain sitting at one of the long tables in the centre of the cafeteria. For the last ten minutes, Maggie has been absent-mindedly tearing bits of polystyrene off her empty disposable coffee cup, and now little of it remains. The others can see that she is anxious and are doing their best to bolster her confidence.

"Oh, come on, Maggie. You'll breeze through it, you know you will. You've seen the kind of work everyone in our year does. It is not that special. Honest, you have nothing to worry about." Summer nudges Roger to lend support to her argument. He obliges.

"Fuck it, Maggs. You know Summer is right. You have more talent in your little finger than most of our lot do. Look at Chisholm, he is a proper wanker. He couldn't paint anything original or interesting to save his life and they accepted him. I reckon he took someone else's portfolio to the interview. Beats me how he even made it onto a foundation course, let alone a degree."

"Hey, now!" Summer interjects. "Just because you don't like his stuff, Roger, doesn't mean you should be disrespectful. I think he has a kind of brute powerfulness going on. It does not always have to be about the aesthetic you know."

"Oh, come off it, Summer. You loathe his stuff, you know you do. It is so goddamn ugly and contrived. I just don't get why you always have to stick up for other people."

"Whoa, you two. This is not helping Maggie, is it?" Sarah steps in to separate her friends. This argument could go on for hours. And often does.

"I think what Roger is trying to do, is point out that you make the rest of us look like amateurs already, Roger excluded, of course."

"Oh, right thanks, Sarah. Yeah, I know you think I am full of myself. But you gotta believe in your talent, or why bother? I can't stand fucking false modesty, really I can't."

"Well, I think we all know that," replies Sarah acidly.

The others snort. Maggie laughs, she cannot help herself. Roger sees the look on her face and laughs as well.

"Seriously though, Maggs, you gotta believe in yourself when you go in there. You gotta convince them of your passion. Don't assume they know how much this means to you."

"Sure, and what if I can't? What if I can't put it into words?"

"Then just talk about the paintings. That way, your passion will speak for itself. Just talk about what you know, what you feel."

Maggie almost jumps. The words had come from behind her. Peter has slipped into the café unseen, and approaching the little group, had caught the tail end of the conversation. Tony shifts over on the bench to make room for him, and he seats himself next to Maggie. He smiles at her with an earnest expression. Maggie flushes, inordinately perturbed by this unexpected proximity. Sarah throws him a shy grin, but she might as well be invisible. She should know, by now, he only has eyes for Maggie.

"When is your interview slot?" he asks gently.

"Tomorrow at eleven. Sure, I never felt so nervous in me whole life."

"That's okay, Maggie. Everyone else will be just as nervous as you, don't forget. But Roger is right, lots of kids will bring along some great stuff but it is the passion and commitment they are looking for."

Roger smirks and nods. Summer pokes her tongue out at him, but Peter ignores them and continues.

"Have you sorted out what you are going to take to show them?"

"Well, yes - no. That is, I keep changing my mind, so I do."

"Well, if you want some advice. Don't take too much. You don't want to overwhelm the interview panel. Take the things that you really feel say something about how you see the creative process, and take a good few life-drawings, as technically they are very strong. And something else. Take something that you feel was a disaster, and talk about why. Everyone takes their 'best' work, as they want to make a good impression. Being able to think about what did not work, and why, will impress them more. Take it from me."

"Sure, I'd have no trouble with that," jokes Maggie, but she is profoundly grateful for the tip. It is not something she would have thought of herself.

"Most importantly," adds Peter. "Just be yourself, Maggie. Trust me, that will be enough."

Peter, gets up to leave. He goes to place his hand on Maggie's shoulder, then thinks again.

"Let me know how it goes," he concludes with a wink and is gone.

The little Gang sits in silence. Sarah feels faintly sick. Roger is recalling his own interview, his lips curled in a little smile of self-satisfaction. Tony is gazing out of one of the windows. Maggie stares down at her demolished coffee cup and crumples it into a ball. Summer reaches across to put her hand on Maggie's and mouths. "It's going to be alright, Maggie. They will just love you. I know they will."

All evening long, Peter finds himself thinking of Maggie and humming the tune to *London Pride*. He wonders about the connection but cannot for the life of him find one. In the end, he selects *A Kind of Blue* from his LP collection, places it on the stereo turntable, drops the needle into the groove and pours himself a scotch. If anyone can drive out an earworm it is Miles Davis. He is not so sure that anything can drive out the thoughts of Maggie, however, so sighs in resignation. "Butter and Whiskey. What cannot be cured, eh?"

Bethnal Green. June.

The Saturday morning session is almost over. The windows of the old gym are clouded by the steam of testosterone-infused perspiration. The little band of boys lining up for their first boxing gloves has swelled to twenty, and there is barely enough gear to go around. The older and more experienced lads have begun to take on a mentoring role with the younger, and lads who had been regularly in trouble with their insubordinate behaviour were now showing signs of self-discipline and motivation. Even those among the staff, who had initially voiced the staunchest opposition to the project, had found themselves conceding that the boxing club was having a measurable and positive impact on the school as a whole. Lately, for those members who had transgressed, it had become common practice to substitute traditional detention with a week's suspension from Boxing Club, and this was already proving a far more effective deterrent.

Jim looks around the gym and surveys his creation and sees that it is good. Yet he does not feel happy; well not as happy as he should be. His eyes swivel to the far side of the gymnasium where Jack is holding up a focus mitt, encouraging a sandy headed fourth-year, with nods and praise. *What is it with Jack?* To anyone else, he might appear fine. Indeed, Jim had been genuinely chuffed when Jack had seemed to come out of his shell during the first few meetings of the club, and it is true that this change has lasted. But Jim *knows* Jack and more importantly has come to care deeply about him, and 'fine' is simply not enough. He knows that Jack has finally settled into teaching, rocky though that had been for a while, and what's more he now has a steady thing with Janet, who let's face it, is drop-dead gorgeous, and if Jim could find a woman like that, well, he might be a very different man himself. But that is not the case in point.

Jim knows, can feel it in his water, that despite all this, there is something still lacking, something shut off maybe, in his friend. As though he is going through the motions, contented enough perhaps, *but for Christ's sake where is the oomph, the vitality, the fight? Life is not a warm-up, it is the one shot. You have to be a contender, not a journeyman.* Sometimes Jim wants to just shake him into animation; shake him, or hit him. Anything. *Hold on! Perhaps that is not such a bad idea.* Jim strolls over to the equipment box, places a protective helmet on his head and takes out a pair of sparring gloves, his eyes still fixed on Jack.

"You there," he calls to Jenkins, who is sitting panting, a skipping rope wrapped around one ankle, "come and lace me up". Then, while Jenkins fumbles with the first lace, he takes a second pair of gloves with his free hand and lobs them at Jack.

"Jack! You're on. You and me, mate. A quick demonstration to round things off!"

Jack drops his hands, stands up straight and gapes. He pulls a face and shakes his head.

"This isn't an invitation to dance. This ain't no disco. Get yourself over here!" There is an edge in his voice that silences the boys who, ceasing their exercises and looking towards the two teachers, have started to giggle nervously. Jack makes towards him and signals he wants to discuss the idea. But Jim beats him to it:

"This is a boxing club, not a god damn debating society. How are the lads ever going to learn if they never see the real thing?"

Jack finds this reasoning a little difficult to counter, he steps back and snatches up the gloves, but Jim can see he is not happy. *So much the better.* The sandy headed lad moves to his side to help with the bindings. Jim gathers the boys around the gym mats that are laid out in the centre of the room, whilst Jenkins helps with Jack's headgear.

"I'd better warn you, I am a southpaw," grins Jim shrugging off his tracksuit jacket, and swiping at the empty air with his left fist.

Jack raises an eyebrow with pursed lips. This he knows already; he also knows that despite his shortness in stature Jim has a surprisingly long reach. He gets the sense that Jim is deliberately trying to needle him. He tries to look into Jim's face, to work out what is going on behind those quick eyes, but Jim evades him, jumping around like Mohammed Ali performing for the crowds. Jack hands Jenkins his watch and the bell. *Three minutes. This is an important job.*

The two men slip in their gum guards then face each other and touch gloves. Jim winks infuriatingly. Jack sets his jaw and wishes he were elsewhere.

Jenkins strikes the bell. Jack puts up his guard and skips from foot to foot. Jim takes a jab, but it fails to find its mark and glances off Jack's left fist. Jim bobs and weaves and tries a one-two combo, but once again Jack blocks him nimbly.

"You are supposed to try and hit me back," hisses Jim through his gumshield, then sends a cross punch that glances off Jack's helmet, and sends him staggering sideways for a moment.

"I said, hit me!" Jim's frustration is evident.

Jack shrugs his shoulders and takes a jab, connecting with Jim's gloves, but Jim makes a counter punch and then in immediate succession a mighty uppercut which catches Jack unprepared, right in the solar plexus, winding him painfully. A hush of shock falls on the ring of boys who have been cheering them on up until now. Jack finds his breath and glares at Jim, who is laughing, taunting him. Jack pulls himself up to his full height and renews his guard. The blood is pulsating through the veins in his neck and head and he suddenly experiences a flash of white-hot rage. Jim skips forward and tries another cross but Jack, anticipating the move and the gap in Jim's guard, takes an almighty swing and makes full contact with Jim's chin. Jim staggers back, his glove over his face, and drops to the gym mats on his backside with a heavy thud. Jenkins hits the bell. The trickle of blood oozing from Jim's lip is already making crimson stains on the whiteness of his vest.

Jack spits out his gum shield and squats next to his fallen opponent to ascertain the damage, and help him to his feet.

"Oh Christ, Jim. I am so sorry!" But the words are hardly sincere. Jack should be beside himself with chagrin, he knows he should, but the truth is, it felt good; it felt bloody good.

"*I'm* not," laughs Jim heartily, dabbing his lip, "I knew you had it in you, mate, you just needed someone to press the right buttons."

Jack looks at his friend shaking his head, then wraps his great arms around him, patting the back of his head with his glove.

"Hey, steady now," grins Jim, breaking free with a slight squirm, "I told you this ain't no discotheque!" But his eyes twinkle with happiness.

"I think that will do for today, lads. Get the equipment and mats put away, then off to the showers. And see you all next time."

Jim begins pulling off his gloves chuckling to himself. Jenkins helps Jack untie his laces with a stolen glance of admiration. Jack looks at his sweat covered arms and stretches wide his fingers which are still tingling. He shakes his head, then looks over and catches Jim's eye.

"I owe you one," he nods.

"You can make that with a whisky chaser, then."

"What on earth happened to Jim?" Janet corners Jack in the staff room, on the following Monday afternoon. She has not seen Jack since Friday, as she had been up to Sheffield to visit her mother and father. She had invited Jack along, but he was not about to be prised away from his beloved Saturday Boxing Club. And besides, he is not entirely sure he is ready to 'meet the family.' Janet had had more sense than to try to pressure him. It is early days and they are doing okay as they are. They had spoken on the phone late the previous night, but Jack had mentioned nothing about the fight.

Meanwhile, Jim's lip has swollen to the size of a misshapen mushroom and is an ugly shade of purple, though he assures one and all that it looks much worse than it is. Janet is doing all she can to keep her cool.

"We had a bit of a sparring match…"

"What you mean "we"- as in you and Jim, or you and one of the boys?"

She is not at all sure which would be the worse answer.

"I mean I - I caught him on the lip, so I did."

"Caught him?"

"Punched him, then…"

Janet is reeling. "And you just, what, forgot to tell me? You maim your mate and you just don't think to mention it?"

"Well, I would hardly say maim..."

"Really? Have you seen Jim today?"

"You see, this is why I didn't mention it."

"Sorry?"

"Because I knew you would be – upset."

"Upset? You think I am upset?"

"Well, you certainly sound it, so you do..."

"I - I just don't get it. You must have hit him pretty hard..."

"Aye, that I did, there's no denying. I could have hit him harder, sure that is the truth of it. My blood was up, and no mistaking."

"You were angry?" This is worse than Janet could have imagined. "Let me get this straight, you hit him in anger?"

"Aye. I did indeed. He made me angry, so that I would hit him. He wanted me to. You can ask him if you like".

But it is Janet who is angry now.

"I am sorry Jack. But I just don't get it. Is this some macho shit?"

"Janet..." He takes her hand, but she tries to pull away. Perhaps she has been all wrong about him after all.

"Janet, listen. I've got things I need to talk to you about. Things about my past, about, well about why I am - well the way I am. I thought I could keep it all shut away. But I can't, not at such a cost. Jim showed me that."

"Jim?" Janet is having difficulty making sense of all this "Jim? What does Jim know about such things?"

"Ah, now there you might be surprised. Can we talk about it later, tonight? Please. I'll make it up to you, so I will."

Janet is left scratching her head. She needs to talk to Jack in any case and the notion that he is ready to share is bait she cannot resist. Whatever her misgivings about Jim's methods, she cannot doubt that something is different. She gathers her books and heads for the last period of the day, though the lesson seems interminable and the hands of the clock seem glued in place.

It is evening. The world seems unusually at ease with itself. Maybe it is the warmness of the breeze that gently rustles through the plane trees or the merest hint of Jasmin that wafts across from the park. Or perhaps it is just Jack. He feels a lightness in his step that is both welcome and curious to him, like a long-forgotten favourite song. He even finds himself whistling as he makes his way to Mile End Tube station, where he is meeting Janet. He smiles when he sees her and they greet each other with a warm embrace. *Does she know a nice quiet pub?* Tonight, he would prefer to go somewhere where they can talk, he has somethings he needs, no that is not right, *wants* to tell her. Janet is all compliance, the anger about Jim's lip a thing of the past, the idea of Jack wanting to talk is incentive enough. And besides, she has something to tell him too. The couple walks arm in arm to the nearest pub, exchanging light-hearted banter, yet the banter conceals a mutual nervousness, a mutually unspoken recognition that something is changing.

When the drinks are on the table, a gin and tonic for Janet and a pint of Guinness for her Irish lover, Jack begins by telling her what had passed between himself and Jim that Saturday morning. He hushes her protests with a finger to his lips and goes on to describes what he likens to the unblocking of an artery to his heart. He knows he has been holding back, has been emotionally shut down, but at the weekend Jim had kicked open the sluice gates, and he does not want them to close up again.

Janet sits and listens and wrestles with her thoughts, then wrestles with her feelings about her thoughts. She is pleased, of course she is, that Jack has made a kind of breakthrough. She can see the difference already. But did it have to be Jim? Why couldn't she have been the one who was able to help Jack? She is the one who has trained as a counsellor, for Christ's sake. And here is Jim, kissing cousin to a caveman, (so okay, maybe she is being a little unfair there), but here is Jim managing to achieve with a single punch to the stomach, what the offer of all the love in her heart for this man could not. At the same time, she is ashamed, ashamed of this need to be everything to this man. Why can't it be enough for her? Of course, she understands why. Haven't she and Bernard discussed it often enough? Still understanding alone is not yet sufficient to remove the sting, and she feels the tears well into her eyes, then realizes that she is no longer hearing Jack's words.

She apologises. *It is such a lot to take in, make sense of.* Jack is all patience, all understanding, *but he needs her to listen to what else he has to say now because this will not be easy for him.* Janet is all attention once more. She has waited so long for this confidence, this moment of real intimacy. Jack takes a deep breath. *He knows he should have told her about his past before this, but it has just been so difficult for him. The truth is he used to be a priest. As a novice he had felt sure he had heard the call, sure he had heard God's voice, right enough, but the life was hard, harder than he had imagined. He had hoped that the love of Christ would be enough for him, but he found he could not keep his vows of celibacy. He cannot tell her how deeply he feels the shame of this, but that was not all. There was a child...*

But now Jack's story tails off. He is distracted by Janet's reaction. Has she even heard what he is saying? She seems so obviously preoccupied with something else, again. He can see that she is trying to strangle some response, the struggle is written all over her face. *What is it? What has upset her so?* Janet tries to dismiss it. *It is nothing*, but she finally blurts it out:

"And does Jim know about this?"

"About what?"

"About the little detail of your having been a priest?"

"Well, aye. As a matter of fact, I told him a while back, so I did..."

"Oh, I see." Janet is numb with hurt. The green-eyed monster has her clamped firmly in its jaws.

"And this is all you care about? The fact that I told Jim before I told you." Jack recoils, dazed by this unlooked-for response. He falls silent.

Janet is distraught. *He knows how insecure she is. He has to forgive her.* But there is only puzzlement and disappointment in his eyes. He had meant to offer her a gift, a gift of his trust, a window into his vulnerability, but now that offering lies shattered and in ruins. They sit in silence for some time, until Jack's anger begins to melt, softened by seeing the dullness of genuine remorse in Janet's usually vibrant eyes. They exchange a sad smile and he reaches for her hand. The tears run down her cheeks, smearing her oh-so-carefully applied eyeliner and mascara. Now it is down to Jack to comfort her. He takes out a handkerchief and dabs at her face with undeserved tenderness. *It is not so bad, really, it is not for nothing that envy is one of the seven deadly sins. But look at him, he could hardly be the one to cast stones when it came to sin!* Janet sniffs and smiles. He hands her the hanky and she blows her nose.

"To tell you the truth, Jim had guessed, so he had, and asked me right out?"

"Truthfully?"

"You may not believe it, but the man has hidden depths, so he does,"

"Very well hidden!" laughs Janet, but this time with a twinkle of kindness for her rival in her eye.

"The thing about Jim is, he - well, I think you would actually like him if you gave him a chance. And I would like you to. He has been a very good friend to me."

"Really, Jack?" Janet's voice is all relief. "I would truly like to do that for you, Jack, if you will give me the chance. I mean it. If he is important to you, then he is important to me."

And the rift seems healed. But, like that one precious fleeting glimpse of a timid wild animal, the moment for Jack to share his past has come and gone and Jack simply cannot find the courage or will to summon it back. He wonders if it will ever come around again.

"Well now, I've told you my secret. Now what was yours?" he asks by way of deflection.

"Oh, Jack! You know I am completing my counselling qualification at the end of the month. Well, I have been offered the job I went for as student counsellor at the Central School of Art and Design, conditional on my getting my qualification, of course. I didn't think I stood a chance, but they called me first thing this morning. And they want me! The post starts in September."

Jack pauses:

"And have you accepted the job?"

Janet nods.

"Oh, Jack I shall miss seeing you every day at school, but this all that I have been working for...."

"Well, Of course, it is, me darling girl. I could not be more pleased for you. I know how hard you have studied for this. And you know if we moved in together, well we could still see each other every day, now couldn't we?"

Janet stares at Jack in disbelief.

"You mean it? Seriously? You feel ready to take that step - make that commitment?"

Jack shrugs his shoulders with a sheepish grin:

"Well, you didn't run a mile when I said I used to be a priest..."

And there *is* real truth in this. For on reflection, whilst Jack had felt dismayed at Janet's reaction to his revelation, it was clear that the issue of his having been a priest had not fazed her. That in itself had been a huge relief. As for the rest, well, he struggles sometimes himself to believe it ever really happened, and the more time passes, the more it impossible it seems, though the guilt he continues to feel, is real enough. Perhaps asking someone else to believe it, would ultimately be asking too much.

Yet Janet is looking shamefaced. In the upset of the conversation and her eagerness to tell Jack about her own news, the fact that he had confided in her about his past had been lost. His reminder causes her no little grief. She apologises with a sincerity that cannot but touch his heart. *Of course, she wants to know more, though who or whatever Jack was in the past could not diminish or alter her feelings about him. He is the best man she has ever known, and more to the point, she loves him.* She places her arm through his, *what matters now is the future, and they have a wonderful future to look forward to together.* Jack plants a kiss on her nose. Is the past really behind him? Can life truly be that straightforward? Jack wants to believe it can, and for the rest of the evening as they excitedly discuss flat hunting together, maybe he does.

The following lunchtime Janet spots Jim collecting messages from his pigeon hole in the staff room, and sidles over. Jim's face betrays a momentary expression of anxiety, but Janet leans over, and whispering - "Thank you," kisses him softly on the cheek. Jim blushes and is suddenly bashful. He mutters something about her "being welcome", and then she is gone. Jim strokes his face, where her lips have left the merest trace of pale pink lipstick, and smiles a rather sad little smile. He chews his thumbnail for a moment, then gathers his papers and hurries off, checking all around him to make sure no one has witnessed him drop his guard.

Covent Garden. 29th July 1981.

"Maggie!" Kathleen calls as she enters the little hall in the flat, taking off her summer cardigan and folding it over a kitchen chair. It is a beautiful summer's day and her nylon uniform feels sticky and uncomfortable after the journey home from her morning shift.

"Maggie May!"

"Yes Kath, sorry, I was just working on a little project." Maggie appears from within her bedroom. She has ink smudges on her face and hands and it is all Kathleen can do not to laugh. Suddenly, however, she experiences a nagging worry about Maggie's inky hands on her sofa. She bites her lip, loath to suggest that her sister wash her hands. Sure, with her doing so well just now with the compulsive handwashing that had made her poor hands so sore, wouldn't it be better just to let it go? She eyes the sofa and smiles brightly.

"Why Maggie, whatever are you doing in on a fine day like this when half the world is out enjoying the celebrations? There is bunting and balloons everywhere and half of Long Acre is closed off for a street party. People are saying there has not been anything like it since V.E day, not that we had any such thing back home, of course."

Maggie lifts the blind and peers into the side street. Sure enough, she spies revellers trotting up and down in their party finery, Union Jacks in hands, and she can hear the strains of live music, drifting across from a temporary stage.

"Did you not even watch it on the T.V, Maggie May?" asks Kathleen, without waiting for the reply. "Sure, we had the television on all morning on the ward, it gave the patients a real lift, so it did, and we tried to make a bit of a party of it over lunch."

"Why Kathleen O'Reagon, I never took you for a loyalist," sings Maggie tauntingly. "And yes, I did have the T.V on for a while there, but I thought she looked like an overblown meringue in that dress, and all that pomp and ceremony. Sure, tis all just a front anyhow."

"Oh, Maggie Love, do you not have a romantic bone in your body? The Princess is marrying her Prince. Now, doesn't everyone love a happy ending?"

Maggie rolls her eyes.

"Ever-after is a long time," she drawls, "I'd be hedging my bets if I were you, so I would." She winks.

Kathleen cannot help but laugh. But now she becomes serious and seating herself at the table, pats the seat next to her.

"Now Maggie, since you are here, come sit down with me, I have something I need to talk to you about".

A look of concern crosses Maggie's face.

"Do I need to put the kettle on?" she asks earnestly.

"Well, that would be grand," replies Kathleen, "though not absolutely essential. I don't think it is bad news, well not wholly. Leastways I *hope* it will not be."

Maggie sits down next to Kathleen, taking care to wipe her hands first on a kitchen towel. They exchange a knowing smile. Maggie has come such a long way since Kathleen first bought her home from that terrible place. Sure, Kathleen would hardly recognise her. She feels her eyes beginning to well up, so starts to talk. *The situation has changed with Yvonne; yesterday, and hardly unexpectedly, her mother finally passed away.* (Maggie makes a noise of condolence). *Well, Yvonne's mother has left the house and everything to Yvonne, so,* and here Kathleen takes a breath, *so Vonnie wants the two of them to live there, together. It is such a lovely house, so it is, and St Albans such a nice little town and Maggie knows how lovely the garden is. They can keep chickens if they want, and she and Vonnie could have the life they always dreamed of…*

"But you are worried about what will happen to me," interrupts Maggie taking her sister's hand.

"Sure, in a way Maggie, and is that so surprising? But hear me out. You see, now you have been offered a place on the degree course," (she raises Maggie's hand to her lips and kisses it with pride,) "well, of course, you'll be needing to stay near the art school. So, I want you to stay on in the flat, but it will still be in my name and I can continue paying the rent - No, Maggie, let me finish. The truth is, I know I am not getting any younger but I am not quite eligible for me pension just yet, for all that I might feel as though I am, some days. So, you see, if I take the Friday, Saturday and Sunday night shifts every fortnight, I can get by on that right enough and I can come up and stay those weekends, tis only half an hour on the train, after all. And don't be thinking I'll be getting in your way, as I'll be spark-out all day and working all night. And…"

"And you'll be able to keep an eye on me…"

"Well, that too," laughs Kathleen. "But now tell me truly, Maggie May, do you feel ready to go it alone, because if you are not, you know that Vonnie and I can wait…

Maggie looks into Kathleen's eyes. They are steady and bright with earnest concern.

"Kathleen Mary O'Reagon, if you don't get a move on up to St Pancras station right this minute and catch the next train for St Albans, I'll take you on my back, so I will. There will be some trains running, even if it is a public holiday, and Vonnie will be needing you more than I do, right now. And don't you even be dreaming of paying the rent for me. I'll have my grant and the life modelling and still intend to do some occasional shifts at the Hotel. I'm as ready to stand on me own two feet as I will ever be."

Maggie pauses here because she wants to say so much of her gratefulness to Kathleen but hardly knows where to start. Kathleen senses a speech is imminent so bustles off to begin packing before Maggie can open her mouth. She never was one for sentiment and fuss. Maggie shakes her head with a fond smile. Her sister may have been a stranger to her for all those years, but she is beginning to be able to read her like a book. So, if Kathleen thinks that Maggie is going to let her escape that easily, she is mistaken. On her return from St

Albans the following weekend, Kathleen finds a card and enormous bouquet of roses waiting for her. The card reads: *To my dearest sister Kathleen with eternal Thanks and Love. You have saved my life, so you have! And if you'll not let express all that is in my heart in words, then I'll just have to say it with flowers.*

Verse 3

Autumn 1981

It is the end of a long Friday afternoon in mid-September, that tender time of year when the evenings mellow and after-work-drinkers sit outside public houses and tarry until dark, savouring the last dregs of summer. The teaching day has ended and most of Maggie's peers have left, making weary tracks for home or the student bar. In the open space of the deserted first-year studio, groups of lanky wooden easels cluster together in subtle formations, tentative attempts at preliminary territorial marking. Uncleaned palettes rest discarded on every chair and stool, while brushes soak uncared-for in the jam jars of turpentine that crowd the draining board of the old and much-stained butler's sink. Only Maggie and a couple of other first years, Leslie and Tom, whom she knows from the foundation course, remain.

Maggie has struck it off well enough with the other students in her year, though it is, of course, only the end of the first week of term. Her loyalty, however, remains firmly with The Gang. Seniors now, each occupies their own sectioned-off studio-spaces in the ateliers further along the corridor. She wonders how they are getting on and smiles as she works. Just then, her thoughts are interrupted by Leslie and Tom, who call out from the other end of the room. Maggie looks up from the business of carefully wiping the paint from her brushes with a soft rag. Tom signals that they are leaving now, Maggie nods her farewell and they head out through the door.

For a few moments, Maggie sits all alone, drinking in the reality. This is it. She is really here. Margaret Doyle, an art student, of all things, on an actual degree course. Margaret Doyle BA(Hons). Okay, she might be getting ahead of herself, but she likes the sound of it. She sits enjoying the novelty of her situation then looks at her canvas and scowls. She is not at all sure that still-life is her forté. But term one is structured around set projects and formal teaching, so still life it is. *Start with the basics*, Matt, their year tutor had said, and who was she to argue with so many years of experience? And Maggie had found herself marvelling at just how varied the paintings of fifteen people all painting the same subject could be. And sure, that alone is food for thought.

Maggie finishes cleaning her brushes, carefully softening the bristles with washing up liquid then drying them off with a soft cloth. She glances up at the clock and thinks about going to find her little gang of friends. Driven by the looming prospect of the final show, Sarah, Summer, Roger and Tony and the rest of the third years have taken to hanging out in their studios until well into the evening. Leaving in daylight is for first years.

Maggie collects her belongings and heads around the corner and up the steps to the main corridor. She pauses and looks out across the dome of the exhibition hall and remembers the first time she set foot in this building. Even now, its hidden playfulness still makes her smile. Across the quadrangle she recognises the silhouette of Summer, heading for the main stairway; heading out to find supper she supposes. She waves, but Summer does not see.

The first studio she comes to seems unusually quiet as she enters and, for a moment, Maggie feels unsure of herself. Peering around one of the alcove screens however, she spies Roger, coat on and rummaging through his canvas satchel. Hearing her footsteps, he looks up and smiles that impish grin of his. *The others have gone to the student bar, it is cocktail night. All cocktails half price before six o'clock. They left him behind to tell Maggie to follow them on over, they wanted to make sure they got a table. Roger cannot face it, still hungover from the night before, he fears, and to be frank a cocktail would be enough to make him puke right now.*

Maggie raises a sympathetic eyebrow. Roger cannot hold his drink as well as the others and should know better than to try by now. But excess goes with the territory at his age. She feels a pang of maternal protectiveness. Well, she may not quite be old enough to have been his mother, but were he just a couple of years younger. And suddenly she wonders what his mother is like. Sure, she must dote on him so. So talented, so sensitive, Maggie wonders how she can ever bear to let him out of her sight.

Maggie wrinkles her nose and decides that she is not up for cocktails either. *If it is okay with him, she would like to just hang out in his space for a while. She has some reading to do.* Roger is delighted. Only if she does not mind, he is just going to nip out and grab a bag of chips. *He has not eaten all day, and it will probably help. Does she want to come along?* Maggie shakes her head; she is happy to wait here. Roger stuffs his wallet into his duffle coat pocket and hurries out. Maggie smiles to herself, a duffle coat seems hardly necessary, yet Roger insists on wearing it on all but the hottest of days.

She throws her bag down beside the radiator beneath the window and places herself next to it on the scuffed and paint-splattered parquet floor. She has a sudden thought that the floor must once have been quite beautiful. All those wooden blocks so skilfully laid and polished. The thought of so much carelessness makes her a little sad. *What a lot of vandals, we painters are.*

She leans back against the wall, fishes a paperback out of her bag and opens the pages at a place marked by a scrap of coloured fabric. It strikes her as very peaceful in the stillness of the empty studio, though all is not entirely quiet. In the background, Maggie hears the sound of laughter and the thump of the bass from a radio in the room next door. The idea of smoking a roll-up pricks at the edge of her thoughts, but fades just as quickly. She looks up momentarily then sighs with contentment and re-reads the passage she had just completed.

"All alone?" A familiar voice breaks her concentration. Peter has stuck his head around the door and has spotted Maggie in the corner of Roger's alcove.

"For the moment, to be sure. Roger has just popped over to the chippy." Maggie looks at her watch, wishing him back soon. Why must she feel so uncomfortable around Peter? Sure, anyone would think she was a teenage girl.

"What are you reading, Maggie?" Peter asks.

"Stoppard. Rosencrantz and Guildenstern are Dead. For English Literature homework," she adds by way of an explanation.

"Hmm, I see," grins Peter. "I know it well. Mind if I join you for a moment, Maggie. There was something I wanted to talk to you about."

"To be sure," replies Maggie with a nervous smile. *Where on earth is Roger? The queue in the fish and chip shop must be particularly long this evening.*

Peter seats himself beside her, stretching out his long legs. He wonders how much difficulty he will have getting up again. He is feeling his age.

"Well?" enquires Maggie, a flush spreading around her neck, and very becoming it is too. Peter clears his throat. His body seems almost to fizz in proximity to this woman. He wonders if she feels it as well. Or is he going to make a massive fool of himself? It is surely not just his imagination that she has spent the last twelve months trying to avoid being alone with him, any more that it can be his imagination that the dark centres of her lovely green eyes widen whenever she sees him.

He reaches inside his jacket pocket for a slim embossed silver case and takes out a cigarette. He offers one to Maggie. She wrinkles her nose, unable to decide, then declines. Peter lights up, then looking at Maggie mischievously, offers her a drag. Maggie sighs and relents. Peter passes the cigarette to

Maggie, who takes a draw and sends a ring of smoke undulating into the still air. She hands it back with a shy glance. Peter cannot help but notice the stain left by her lipstick. He takes a drag, his own lips tingling as they touch the paper where hers have been. They exchange a smile. Peter has not shared a moment of such intimacy, such genuine intimacy with a woman, any woman, since he can remember, and for a moment words seem unnecessary. He gazes at Maggie's soft mouth. The moment, at last, seems right. He is just leaning towards her when there is the sound of a sharp intake of breath. Peter and Maggie jerk apart, as though caught in some illicit act. Sarah is standing in the doorway, flanked by Roger, who is absorbed in tearing the wrapping from his supper. Sarah had returned to the studio to look for Maggie and had bumped into Roger on his way back up the stairs. The gasp had been quite involuntarily, and feeling mortified, she turns on her heel and flees the studio, forcing back the tears. Roger calls after her, but she pays no heed and is gone. Roger shrugs his shoulders and looks quizzically at Maggie and Peter, holding out his bundle of papers.

"Anyone fancy a chip?"

Peter scrambles stiffly to his feet. He signals to Maggie to stay where she is but whispers - "I really do need to talk to you Maggie, I'll be in the life-studio." With that, he brushes himself down, nods to Roger and also takes his leave.

"What's eating Sarah?" Roger asks, stuffing a handful of fries into his mouth, his fingers and chin already shiny with grease. The pungent reek of vinegar and deep-fried fat reminds Maggie that she has not eaten, though she had not thought she had much appetite. She shrugs her shoulders and stares back into her book. But she does not see the words and all she can hear is the beating of her own heart. *As if we need to study the absurd*, she thinks, when *there is such absurdity in our lives* already.

Sarah retreats to the safety of the student bar and squeezes through the crowded room to the little table where she had left Tony and Summer sitting. They shout their greeting over the thumping bass of UB40's *One in Ten* and gesture to her to help herself to one of the brightly coloured drinks, which sit on the table in front of them. Sarah stares at the little paper parasols and pieces of fruit and cucumber that decorate the cocktails and scowls. Summer attempts to enquire about Maggie, but her voice is already hoarse from the effort of trying to make herself heard over the music, so she just waves her hand in defeat. Sarah, realising what her friend is trying to ask, makes an exaggerated shrug of her shoulders. She selects a sugar-rimmed glass full of bright blue liquid and shuffles along the bench to sit herself next to Tony. Giving a forced laugh, she twirls the tiny parasol in front of his face then drains the cocktail in one swallow. She wipes her mouth with the back of her hand, glances at Tony and helps herself to a second drink, this time of some coconut confection. Summer rolls her eyes and frowns at Tony, who shakes his head. *What is he supposed to do about it?*

Sarah takes a little longer over the second cocktail, it is sickly sweet and she is not all that sure she likes it. Then when the glass is empty, she holds it up and pulls on Tony's sleeve like a demanding child. Tony knits his brows; he can feel Summer glowering across at him. *Why does she always have to play the grown-up?* His head feels pleasantly light and the music is throbbing in time with his heart and Sarah is pleading with him with those big brown eyes. He stands up, retrieves his wallet from his jeans pocket and elbows his way to the bar. Summer reaches across to touch Sarah's wrist, but Sarah will not meet her gaze and sits eyes closed, mouthing along with the lyrics of her favourite Pretender's track, which plays over the P.A.

The bar is busy and Chrissie Hynde has made way for Tears For Fears and Simple Minds by the time Tony returns with the drinks. By the end of the next few songs, Sarah is leaning against him, giggling in a way, that signifies she has almost certainly had enough now. Tony puts his arm around her, to steady her. How is it that she has never been able to see how crazy he is about her? But she only ever has eyes for Peter. A man, mature - no, old enough to be her father. Goddammit, possibly even her grandfather. Tony curses his inexperience and lack of worldly sophistication. Still, he has to admit that he does idolise Peter a little also, and if it were not for him, he would probably never had got to spend so much time with Sarah in any case. Still, life can be a real bastard sometimes.

She is so close to him now, that despite the heavy tobacco smoke in the crowded bar, he can smell the fragrance of her shampoo. Apples - her hair always smells of fresh green apples. He closes his eyes, breathes her in. Suddenly, he feels the touch of her hands and fingers on his neck and face as she pulls him towards her for a deep kiss. Tony knows she is a little the worse for alcohol and knows, all too well, that this is some game she is playing, but he cannot find it in himself to care. He has wanted it for too long. So even if it is not real, he cannot resist. He returns the kiss then feels himself reeling. He looks up. Summer is sitting with her arms crossed in silent reproach on the other side of the table. *What does she know? And why does he feel like weeping?*

Back in Roger's studio space, Maggie sits deep in thought, making a show of reading her play, whilst Roger finishes off his supper, then wipes his fingers and picks up his palette and brushes. The two of them are used to comfortable silences, but this evening Roger senses a tension in the air and seeks to break it. He reminds his muse that he is still hoping she will model for his Madonna painting. He is planning for it to be the central piece in his show. Maggie smiles, of course, she would be delighted. *But not just yet*, adds Roger, *the light must be just right, the afternoon light of Spring. There is softness in that light like no other, and only that will do.*

Maggie smiles at his earnestness. *Of course, any time that he wishes.* Roger nods contentedly. Poor Roger, born in the wrong time. She imagines him as an apprentice in the studios of Raphael or Da Vinci, how at home he would have been. She tries to picture him grinding raw minerals for pigments; lapis lazuli for blue, crushed madder root for red. How close to alchemy a painter's lot must have been in such times. And, sure, wasn't it magic they wrought in their own way? The picture enchants her briefly, but it is not long before Maggie finds her thoughts wrenched back to more present matters. She thinks about Peter in the Life studio. He is waiting for her. She knows he is. They have both waited so long. Peter is free now, and so is she, at least as free as she will ever be; for even if she were free in the eyes of the law, she can never be in the eyes of the Church. Can that freedom be enough for him though? Maggie shakes her head. It would not be enough for most men; but then Peter is not most men.

And if it is not? Well, she has her own life now and that is more than ever she could have hoped; and surely more than she deserves. Even so, she wants more. She feels it as surely as she feels hunger. Sure, are not human beings made for love and companionship? She has been too long alone. Besides, there are different kinds of freedom.

She rises from her spot in the corner and nods a goodnight to Roger. He returns her farewell with a distracted wave, then resumes his painting. She makes her way to the life studio and steps in, quietly closing the door behind her and flipping the latch on the antiquated snib lock.

Peter is sitting on a donkey near the dais with his back to the door and turns at the sound. Maggie presses a finger to her lips and moves across to stand in front of him. Without a word, she kicks off her shoes, unfastens the clips of her dungarees and steps out of them. Now, she unbuttons her shirt, her eyes all the while fixed on Peter's face. She wears no bra and is standing before Peter in only her briefs. Peter has seen many women, and indeed Maggie herself in this room, wearing less, but never has he felt so aroused. He feels breathless at her sensuality and for a moment wonders whether his heart will hold out.

Maggie draws closer to him, then takes his hand and kisses the palm. Peter feels his body tremble as he embraces her, then leads her up to the mattress on the modelling dais and the two of them sink into its softness as one. There are no roses on the walls, no guilt, no worry - only Maggie and Peter. But even so, Maggie tenses with anxiety at a sudden thought and almost pulls away.

"Peter - I can't be getting pregnant, have you got any…well, you know?"

"Shhhh," whispers Peter with a wink. "I had a vasectomy over twenty years ago. We don't need to worry about all that…"

"Tony, take me home with you," slurs Sarah at the end of the evening when the bar is closing and more than one tipsy student is tottering unsteadily towards the exit.

"She's had far too much to drink, you know that." Summer says accusingly to Tony, as though the gentle Jeckle she has known for the last two years has suddenly transformed into a profligate and predatory Hyde.

"It's okay, Summer. I will look after her," he says earnestly.

"Yeah, mind your own business, Summer," adds Sarah with uncensored spitefulness. Tony sees the hurt in Summer's eyes.

"She's completely pissed," he says, as though this is not obvious. "She doesn't mean it - you know she doesn't. She won't even remember tomorrow."

"No," thinks Summer to herself, "But *I* shall." *Why does she always have to be the sensible one, the one who tiptoes around other people's feelings? Fat good it does her.*

"It's the Peter thing," adds Tony, feeling a need to explain away Sarah's unkindness. "You know how bad she has it for him."

Summer softens.

"Well, none of us are strangers to a broken heart," she smiles.

Tell me about it, thinks Tony, waving farewell.

"Come on, Princess, let's see if we can hail a cab, I don't fancy our chances on the night bus."

The next morning Maggie wakens early in her flat, to find Peter snoring softly beside her. The morning sunshine highlights the wires of silver in his hair and deep furrows around his eyes, and Maggie realises he may be almost old enough to be *her* father, let alone Sarah's. But she does not care. Last night he demonstrated a sexual prowess worthy of a man half his age. Maggie strokes his greying locks with the back of her fingers, then pulling on her dressing gown, pads to the kitchen to make some coffee, grateful that Kathleen is not on duty this weekend. When she returns, two steaming mugs in hands, Peter is awake, his hands clasped behind his head. He smiles and gestures with a nod of his head to the space next to him in the bed.

"Have I told you, Maggie, just what a spectacular woman you are?"

"Maybe just the once or twice, or fifty times," laughs Maggie sitting next to him and kissing his lips, trying valiantly to keep the mugs upright, what with Peter all the time trying to pull her back into bed. Finally, she sets both the mugs down on the cabinet next to her and falls into Peter's arms. She kisses him again then gazes up into his eyes.

"Do you know, I feel like that woman in the song?"

"What song would that be my Maggie," asks Peter nuzzling her neck.

"You know, that one by Aretha Franklin, is it? *You Make Me Feel Like a Natural Woman!* Sure, tis exactly how you make me feel, it is."

"Maggie," says Peter shaking his head "You truly are the most remarkable woman I ever met. Now take off that robe and get back in this bed."

But Maggie resists, wagging an admonishing finger.

"We'll be having none of that this morning, so we won't. Now, drink your coffee and be off home with you." Peter opens his mouth in dismay.

"It may be Saturday, your Lordship, but some of us peasants have jobs to go to. I've a nine o'clock shift at the hotel and I can't be late."

"Oh, Christ! Stan and Ollie!" exclaims Peter.

"I beg your pardon?" Maggie is mystified.

"Stan Laurel and Oliver Hardy, our - my two cats. They will be starving. They did not get their dinner last night. Christ, I really do have to get home before they demolish the place looking for breakfast."

"And where is home now, Peter? I don't think I ever heard you say."

"Why I live at the Angel. The Angel, Islington."

Maggie collapses in laughter next to a bemused Peter, sure wouldn't Tom Stoppard just love this? And when she has stopped shaking with mirth, they agree to meet tomorrow morning to spend the day together

"On the steps of the National Gallery," pleads Maggie, "where we had our first date."

In a different part of town, Sarah awakes and cringes at the light streaming through the unclosed curtains. Her mouth feels dry and somewhat gritty, but apart from that she is feeling surprisingly good; probably better than she has a right to. There is a glass of water on the nightstand next to the bed, where somebody has thoughtfully left it. She reaches out for it and takes a long gulp. That feels so much better.

She squints around her. She is not in her own bed, or even her own room. She feels a moment of alarm and explores her chest and shoulders with anxious fingers. She is still wearing her T-shirt and bra. Thank God for that, at least. She stretches out her arm behind her and feels the warm body of Tony next to her. A hazy memory comes floating back. She turns onto her other side and looks at Tony's sleeping face. She never really gave much thought to how sweet-looking he was, but right now she is moved by a desire to kiss him, which is fuelled neither by alcohol nor self-pity But, first she is dying to pee.

Sarah sidles out of the bed and tiptoes to the bedroom door. Holding it open a fraction, she peers out and strains her ears for any sound of activity. There is no one stirring. Across the hallway, she spots the bathroom door ajar. She makes her way over as noiselessly as she can, shivering with the early morning chill. The hallway is full of clutter. It must be a student flat. She reaches the bathroom. She grimaces. It must be a *male* student flat. She wonders what it is with young men. Don't their mothers teach them how to clean a sink or bath, or wash a towel for that matter? But the urgency to pass water overrides her scruples. At least there is a roll of toilet paper. She supposes she should consider herself lucky. She pulls the toilet chain, cringing at the ancient cistern's tell-tale gurgle, then creeps back to Tony's room.

Tony is still sprawled out in oblivious slumber. He looks even cuter, without the pressure on her bladder. She lies down on the bed next to him.

"Tony," she nudges him gently.

"Waaa..?" Tony yawns his way into consciousness and rubs his eyes.

"Oh hey, morning Sarah. You okay? What the Hell time is it? Can I get you a coffee or anything?"

"Um, that would be nice, in a minute maybe. Tony, last night did we - you know?"

"Oh, no. No, no. You wanted to…"(remembering how he had almost had to fight her off), "but you were, well, way too drunk, and well, you know…"

"You mean you didn't want to…"

"Hell no, I mean yes, of course, I did. You *know* I did not mean that. I've dreamed of nothing else. But not like that…" Tony colours. Now he has completely given himself away.

"Well, what about now?"

"What about it?" Tony is confused.

"I am not drunk now, am I?"

"No…?"

"Oh, Shit Tony! Do I have to spell it out for you…" and pulling him across to her, they share a long, sensuous and unmistakably sober morning kiss.

"I guess the coffee can wait, then?" smiles Tony.

"I reckon it can. I don't know about you, but it's the weekend and I've got all day. And we've got a lot of catching up to do."

Maggie saunters through Long Acre and down to St Martins Lane. She is in no hurry, for there is plenty of time before she is due to meet Peter at the National Gallery. She wears a close-fitting fifties' sweater and pedal pushers, a delightful find in a local vintage shop. She has pinned her hair up into a French pleat and applied eyeliner and a flatteringly pale lipstick with the utmost of precision. Maggie is not normally given to vanity, but this afternoon she knows that she looks a knock-out. Love can do that for you.

The sun is still bright for the time of year and there are still plenty of tourists and Sunday day-trippers around, drawn to the delights of the famous market. Maggie would have preferred it when they still sold flowers there, but like the man said, *the times they are a-changing*. She looks about her, smiling to herself and humming *Drowsy Maggie* - an old Irish ditty, she remembers from childhood.

All at once, something in the periphery of her visual field catches her attention. The blood in her veins turns to ice water. Her happy insouciance evaporates in an instant. She turns her head, trying to act as casually as she is able, gripped as she is by a dread that crushes the very air out of her lungs. She sees him. A tall, dark man, of Mediterranean appearance, in sporting jacket and slacks. The kind of man you see on every corner of London during the season. He stands, camera around his neck, gazing up and down the street, playing the hapless sightseer but she has seen him before and not just once or twice, either. At first, she had told herself that he might just be a guest at The Russell, hence the familiarity. The first couple of times, she had even managed to talk herself into believing it. Yet, here he is again, and somewhere deep within warning bells are ringing. This is no coincidence. He is following her. She is sure of it. Her heart racing, Maggie ducks into a newsagent's. She creeps up to the window behind the shopfront display and peers out into the street. The man has turned and is heading the other way up Long Acre towards the tube station. He gives no hint that he is aware of Maggie's movements and is soon out of sight.

Maggie heaves a sigh of relief. Perhaps she is letting her imagination run away with her, after all. She covers her face with her hands and groans, then conscious suddenly of her odd behaviour Maggie turns towards the bemused shopkeeper, flashes him her widest smile and asks for an ounce of Old Holborn. She is doubtless not the first pretty woman to take refuge from some unwanted male admirer who is making a pest of himself, nor will she be the last. The streets are full of Italian men at this time of year, and their reputation does, after all, run before them. And there would be plenty of pinched backsides to prove it.

Back on the pavement, Maggie hastens her steps and gives herself a stern talking to. She had rather hoped that she had left all that behind her. She really must get a grip. This is such a wonderful day, why ruin it with her ridiculous suspicions? Perhaps it all just seems too good to be true, so she is trying to find a way to spoil it. *Well, we'll be having none of that nonsense now, Maggie Doyle.*

By the time she spots Peter waiting for her on the broad stones steps that rise up from Trafalgar Square, she has almost convinced herself. And Bless him, he would be early, so soon her head is full of other, much more pleasant things.

"What would you like to do now, My Maggie?"

Peter sits next to Maggie on the steps. They have spent a happy hour giggling over the voluptuous proportions of Reuben's women and marvelling at the luminosity of Vermeer's brushwork. Maggie is fairly brimming over with the excitement of it all. She closes her eyes and leans back to feel the sun on her face. She wants to sit awhile if that is okay. Peter nods and gazes at her. It certainly is. A lock of her hair has escaped its pins, and he twists it playfully around his finger. Roger had got it wrong - she is not one of Raphael's Madonnas, no submissive vessel. She is more like Rossetti's muse. Beautiful, yet fearless and independent. A woman to hold in awe. And yet, at the same time, it is her childlike freshness and enthusiasm, he finds so completely charming. He makes a silent prayer that she never assumes the kind of cool ennui he has met with, in so many of his younger students. That brand of seen it, done it, threw away the T-shirt, that haunts the world of contemporary art, replacing the joy of creativity with the cynicism of the world-weary.

"Can you imagine," she is asking, as if in answer to his prayer, "really imagine what it must have been like to be an artist when people saw these paintings for the first time? The sheer impact that these images must have made when first revealed. I mean, today, we are surrounded by pictures, and photographs on billboards, magazines, film, T.V. It is almost as if we cannot escape them. Graphic representation has become background noise, visual pollution. The same with music. But imagine, back in those days, what it was *really* like to see one of these great paintings, or hear music by Vivaldi or Bach for the first time! Sure, it must have felt, I don't know - miraculous, truly. Miraculous. Don't you think?"

Peter nods, but in truth, next to her, he feels like a jaded old man. Maggie opens her eyes and sits up, *her* passion in no way blunted by his lack-lustre response.

"But Peter, I have never seen *your* work. Your paintings I mean. Of course, I've seen some of your life drawings, but nothing else. Sure, how can that be? Do you have a studio of your own? What is it like? Can I see it? Oh *please*, Peter, I would love to see it. Couldn't we go and visit this afternoon?" Maggie's questions tumble out and Peter puts up his hands to stay the avalanche.

"Well, for a start. I used to have a studio on the Hackney side of Islington but, what with teaching becoming pretty much full time, I found I used it less and less. I converted the attic of our house to a kind of studio space, but you know we are having to get the place ready to put on the market, so I've been, ahem, clearing it out and packing a lot of stuff away."

"Oh Peter, you have to sell your home? I am sorry I didn't know."

"Well, yes. The divorce is going through and that is what happens, I'm afraid. We have the house at the Angel, it is a big house, on three floors, but is a bit run down. I'm afraid we let things go a bit, so it is taking a bit of work to get it in a fit state to sell. Then we have the little place in Suffolk, which is just a little cottage. Anyway, between the two, Wendy and I should have enough for us each to be able to buy somewhere, you know, and start again."

Peter falls silent. Maggie is unsure what to say. She thinks about the home she lost herself but finds no regrets. But it is different for Peter, their home must be filled with many years of happy family memories. Peter continues, as though thinking out loud.

"Well, I'm thinking I will probably rent for a while. Maybe I'll get a flat in the same area, it sounds simple enough, but of course, there is always Stan and Ollie. Technically we have agreed to joint custody of them, but Wendy travels such a lot these days, so I'll need somewhere where they can be safe." Maggie looks baffled for a moment and then recalls their conversation from the previous morning.

"Who knows, I might end up buying a place out of London. Cornwall perhaps. I always loved the sea. There is the whole artist community thing in St Ives and it is only a couple of years now until I can retire...."

Maggie grasps his hand. She cannot imagine London without a Peter. Peter feels the tug and smiles wistfully.

"Well, it is all up in the air." Then brightening, he adds; "Perhaps you can help me with the flat hunting Maggie, women are so much more practical than us men, and to tell the truth it is a depressing, lonely business, on your own".

"I'd love to Peter, of course. You let me know when. But you know what I would like to do now?"

Peter shakes his head.

"If it is okay with you, I'd love to see your house, so I would, and your paintings, and the famous Stan and Ollie, if they will have me. They must all be such a big part of you, sure it would be grand to see them while I can."

Peter puts her hand to his lips and kisses it. *Her wish is his command.*

Suddenly the light glinting off a camera lens dazzles Maggie's vision. She shades her eyes with a hand and squints in the direction of the unwelcome brightness. The tall dark man is standing on the adjacent side of the square. He faces Nelson's Column and is engrossed in taking photographs, carefully taking readings with a light meter and meticulously framing his composition. He appears completely oblivious to Peter and Maggie's presence, yet the flash of reflected sunlight had betrayed a quite different focus. Maggie springs to her feet and pulls Peter up along with her. She heads at speed to the entrance of the tube station, half dragging poor Peter in her wake. He tries to read the look on her face, but it is a puzzling mix of anxiety and grim determination.

Once on the tube train, she relaxes a little and tries to make light of her haste. *She had a sudden headache, too much sun perhaps.* They chat on, but Peter can tell that she does not truly relax until they are safe inside his front door.

"Oh, Peter, you have such a lovely home. And you two are gorgeous, so you are." Maggie leans forward in the armchair to make a fuss of Stan and Ollie, with whom she is an instant hit. They rub against her shins, purring and trilling their speeches of welcome. Peter smiles. For two cats who are usually so diffident with strangers, they are being uncharacteristically civil. They clearly have excellent taste in women.

He hands Maggie a glass of wine. They have spent an hour wandering through the house and garden, and finally the attic. Maggie had examined Peter's painting for ages without saying a word until he had begun to suspect that she must hate them. But at last, she had clasped his arm and looked into his face, her eyes shining.

"Oh Peter, they are exquisite. I had no idea." Then she jokes, "Sure I'm going to have to treat you with a bit more respect now, so I am."

On the way back down to the living room, Peter had seen the sadness in Maggie's eyes as they passed rows of half-packed cardboard boxes of books, some bearing Peter's name, and others, Wendy's. *How on Earth did they decide, what belonged to whom?* She had wanted to know. It was a good point. Up until now, the divorce settlement had been largely amicable, but recently, making decisions about their treasured possessions, so full of memories, even Wendy and Peter had found it impossible to avoid a little acrimony. *Sometimes we toss a coin,* he conceded. Maggie had tried her hardest to look sympathetic, but all she could think about was the ludicrous coin-tossing scene in Stoppard's Rosencrantz and Guildenstern. Halfway down the stairs she had lost the battle and dissolved into giggles. Peter had had no idea what it was all about, as every time she had tried to explain, she had just become helpless with laughter. Instead, he had just scratched his head and enjoyed the eccentricity that was his Maggie Doyle. Eventually, she calmed down and was able to tell him the joke, though it no longer seemed funny to her. Peter nodded; he knew the play well enough. One or other of the characters, (no one can ever remember which is which), tosses a coin and it lands on heads ninety-two times in a row. He smiles to himself. *Now if Wendy were there, she really would have enjoyed the joke.*

"So, my Maggie, how do you fancy dinner and a movie? There is a great cinema up the road on Islington Green and any number of great restaurants. I think we should paint the town red on our first proper date, don't you?"

Maggie's face falls. She had quite forgotten her anxiety about the tall dark man, but now the idea of leaving the sanctuary of Peter's home revives it afresh.

"Well now, Peter, I was thinking, could we not just have a night in, just the two of us. Sure, that would be celebration enough for me and that way I get to keep you all to myself!"

Peter sighs, there is certainly much that appeals in the idea.

"I tell you what, how about dinner and a movie at home then? You help yourself to another glass of wine and make yourself at home. I'll pop out and get some stuff to knock-up something tasty and nip into the video rental shop on the way back. They have a great world movie selection, and you'll never guess what they had last time I looked? The film version of Joyce's Ulysses starring Milo O'Shea as Leopold Bloom. Am I tempting you?"

Maggie squeals in delight.

"Do you mean to tell me, Peter Carmichael, that not only can you cook, but you can read my mind as well?"

"Well, let's say I know my way around the kitchen," replies Peter modesty, "and I know a little about you by now."

"Tis decided then. You are without a doubt the only man in the world for me, so you are. And we'll be having no argument about it."

And with that, she clasps her arms around his neck and they kiss with an ardour so tender, that it will be a wonder if any dinner gets cooked at all.

It is strange the way things can have a way of working out. It is Tuesday evening and The Gang has arranged to meet up at the Louise. All afternoon Maggie has been fretting, anxiously trying to anticipate Sarah's reaction and how to soften the blow, she must inevitably feel. She has not told anyone about Peter yet, although part of her is bursting to do so. But the truth is, she likes Sarah *and* her pretty little nose, and neither wishes to put it out of joint nor rub it in her triumph. How can she be happy about something that is going to make her friend so miserable?

But she need not have worried. She stiffens as Sarah and Tony enter the lounge through the great swing doors, conscious suddenly of Peter's arm across her shoulders. But not for long, for Sarah hangs on Tony's arm and smiles into his eyes, even as they make their way towards them. Tony wears a smile that puts one in mind of the cat that has got the milk, the cream, and the rest of the dairy-rations for the year. It is obvious to anyone who cares to pay attention that this is a couple in the throes of first love.

"Ahh, isn't it sweet?" trills Summer, as if to make the point. Roger kicks her under the table. Sarah smiles sweetly and stoops to embrace Maggie as though she has not seen her for many weeks. She notices Peter's arm, still wrapped around Maggie's shoulders, and raises an eyebrow in delight. The world is indeed a marvellous place when you are young and in love. Peter gets up and goes to get the drinks in with Tony, and Maggie notices that he shakes Tony by the hand on the way to the bar.

Roger leans across the table to Sarah and mouths- "So, what happened to the great Peter passion?"

"Oh, that?" replies Sarah airily, her eyes shining as they follow Tony across the room. "That was just some adolescent crush, oedipal or something, I shouldn't wonder." She brushes a stray hair back from her face, then catching Maggie's eye, she adds;

"Not that he isn't a real catch though, for someone his own age, I mean!"

Maggie opens her mouth, then closes it with a shake of her head. It is not often she finds herself speechless. Peter and Tony return with the drinks. Roger raises his glass and declares the toast-

"Butter and parsnips!"

The others shake their heads in despair and laugh in unison.

"What?" asks Roger mystified.

"Butter and parsnips, it is then," sings Maggie, raising her glass and trying to keep a straight face. They all clink glasses.

"Butter and parsnips!"

Bethnal Green

Things are going well for Jack. Better than he could have dreamed possible only eighteen months ago. He is finding his feet as a schoolmaster and has been teaching "A" level classes in both Latin and Religious Studies since September. Of course, the success of the Boxing Club may have had a lot to do with the sudden rise in interest in these subjects, which had previously proved woefully unpopular, but that was just another win for Jim and himself, and the whole pugilist venture.

Even the lads who did not attend the club had started to treat Jack with a respect that had been hitherto lacking. Furthermore, that respect had only increased, once the accounts of his flooring of Jim became widespread, for Jim had long held the role of alpha male in the unwritten school hierarchy. Moreover, the lads who did attend the club were developing into confident and disciplined young men, for whom academic achievement and physical prowess were no longer mutually incompatible. Not surprisingly, the club still had its detractors, mostly, although not exclusively, amongst the female members of staff and board of governors, but the results were speaking for themselves.

Then one Saturday morning, Jack and Jim and the pretty well all the lads in the club had received the surprise of their lives. Despite the fact that Jack had kissed Janet goodbye and made his way to the gym, believing her to be enjoying her usual weekend lie-in, Janet had turned up at the club half an hour later, in tracksuit and trainers. Then, bold-as-brass, she had walked up to Jim and declared that she had come to learn the basic boxing skills, and to save time in arguing, he had better understand that she was not going to take no for an answer. The whole gymnasium had fallen into a stunned silence. All eyes had turned to Jim. What they were anticipating was probably some sort of rant or explosion, but it was certainly not what they got. Jim had beamed warmly. *Females were most certainly welcome, though she might find it awkward being the only one, for the time being at least.* After that, he had personally led the new pupil through the induction programme, sorting out some equipment for her and making a point of introducing her to all the lads by name.

Jack meanwhile had hovered in the background, struggling to recover his equilibrium. Given Jim's reception, Jack's immediate suspicion was that he had played no little part in the stunt. Try as he might, Jack could not work out the rationale for it, yet it bore none of the hallmarks of a mere prank. Janet was insistently serious. She could admit it; she had been wrong about boxing encouraging loutish behaviour. She had been in training, jogging every evening around Victoria Park Square and Bethnal Green Gardens where they lived, and she was as fit now as ever she had been. Jack had been forced to concur, sheepishly admitting that he struggled to keep up with her when they had been out running together.

"C'mon then, Lass. Show us what you've got." Jim had winked at her, ignoring any protest from Jack. Then throwing her a pair of practice gloves, he had led her over to the nearest punchbag. He had signalled a rather unhappy Jack to hold the bag and then extended his arm towards Janet in invitation. Janet had dropped her hold-all, shrugged off her tracksuit jacket and pulled on the gloves, planting herself squarely before the battered old punchbag. Avoiding the disapproval in Jack's eyes, she had let fly an undercut punch of such force that it had almost toppled Jack off his balance, and he had found himself staggering backwards in no small measure of astonishment. Jim, meanwhile, had clapped his hands together with decided relish and the whole gym had broken out in a round of spontaneous applause and whistles of delight. Jim had looked at Jack and cocked his eyebrow. Jim had had no answer for him. Janet, pink with self-consciousness and exertion, had smiled a little smile of triumph.

"I reckon that settles, it then," Jim had announced, "but no concessions for being a girlie. If you want to train with the boys, you have to work like one of them."

Janet had grinned. No concessions needed. Indeed, by the time the session was over, she was sweating as heavily as any of the lads there, completely dispelling any allusions that her function might be purely decorative.

Nonetheless, after the session, when the lads had departed, Jack had expressed his grave reservations about the place of a woman in such a testosterone-infused environment. Suffice it to say, he could hardly believe his ears when Jim accused *him* of chauvinism. As it turned out, the lads in the club had seemed especially respectful and on their best behaviour, and if ribald remarks were uttered in the showers after, or on the way home, they were made out of earshot and had certainly won their author no favours.

Jack had tried to maintain his opposition for the following few weeks but was stoutly out-argued by Jim and Janet. And since Janet's enthusiasm was more than the flash in the pan, he had half-hoped it would be, he was forced to concede, with the caveat that Janet would be excluded from sparring. Janet acquiesced, that is until a month or so later when she brought Jill Tuffin along with her. Jack had shaken his head in abject defeat. At least he could now see the method in Jim's madness. Jim's face had lit up when Jill walked in. Oddly enough, it had not been too long before the two of them had started dating.

What pleasure it gives Jack, that Janet and Jim had become allies and friends, and that Jim has at last found a woman he can get serious about. And to say he seems a changed man would be an understatement. Gone are the boastful accounts of his sexual exploits and unflagging virility, though his sense of humour remains as wicked as ever it was. In its place, Jack has the pleasure of seeing a man who, sure of his self-worth, needs only to see that worth reflected in the eyes of *one* woman. Jill, in turn, a demure young woman, who had always felt physically attracted to Jim, yet at the same time, repulsed by his overwrought machismo, is fairly blossoming beneath the gentle sunshine of his attentive and patient wooing.

Yet Jack is not completely at ease. For some time, he has felt as though he is watching over his shoulder; waiting for someone or some *thing*. After all, it is written in the scriptures clearly enough, *the wicked shall not go unpunished*, and, for all his scepticism, the words remain encoded in the very marrow of his bones. Thus, the better his life goes, the stronger the gnawing conviction that one day he will have to pay, grows.

Matters come to a head one evening towards the middle of October, a time of year that brings back the most sorrowful of remembrances. But Jack has locked that grief within his heart and is reconciled to the fact that he must bear it all alone. All Jim knows is that his friend has been out of sorts all week, so he proposes a night out at their favourite Indian restaurant down Brick Lane. After all, there is nothing quite like a good hot Madras and lager to raise the spirits. Jack agrees to the plan; sure, he'd never been known to say no to a decent curry and he is certainly not going to start now. Perhaps it is just what he needs, though a part of him wonders who he is fooling.

The evenings gets off to a slightly strained start. The pappadums and chutneys have been polished off and washed down by a Cobra beer and Jack is managing to maintain a veneer of good cheer, though he is more quiet than usual. The fact escapes the notice of neither Jim nor Janet, who are both trying too hard to make amusing conversation. Jim brings her up to speed on staffroom gossip and teases her about her fortune in having made her escape to the outside world. Sitting next to Jim, Jill finds it difficult to squeeze a word in edgeways and wonders what she is missing. For the briefest moment, she feels excluded. Then she looks across at Jack and notices a sadness around his eyes, a sadness she has not seen before. It would be just like Jim to do his level best to cheer him up. She smiles to herself and places her hand lightly on his arm for a moment. Aware of her touch he turns and winks the warmest of winks. Such a man. Such a heart. She wonders how she had never seen it before. She must make sure she never lets him go.

As the main dishes are placed on the table in their sizzling platters, Jim and Janet are sharing a joke about the role of confession, and Janet admits it has been over three years since she lasted entered the confessional. Jim is saying that, were it not for the confessional, he would have no hope of getting to heaven, and that is for sure. Suddenly, as though pricked by the same consciousness, both recall that one amongst them was once a priest. They exchange looks and fall into an awkward silence, turning their focus to spooning the fragrant basmati rice and curries onto their plates. Jack, however, shakes his head with a smile, waving the discomfort away. He can assure them that confession with contrition is sufficient, even if it is postponed until the death-bed. *After all,* he jokes, *isn't it better to be safe than sorry?* Jill, Janet and Jim all laugh together, there does indeed seem to be something to be said in favour of taking out the insurance policy, just in case. They raise their glasses and start to eat, sharing comments of appreciation for each dish, and passing around the raita and nan bread.

Jack's mood, however, takes an odd turn. All at once, he seems virtually unaware of the delicious fare before him and starts to talk, almost to himself. He wonders whether atonement through a few mumbled Hail Marys or Our Fathers can truly be enough. Feeling a little disconcerted, Janet tries to distract Jack away from the morbidity of his reflection, encouraging him to try the pawn Bhuna, which she knows is his favourite. However, Jill chips in, here. She had a friend who had been through the AA twelve steps programme. For them, saying sorry to God is not good enough. You have to seek out those against whom you have transgressed and make real amends.

Jill comments that in her opinion, this surely demonstrates more sincere remorse and is ultimately more productive. Jim pulls a face and jokes that it might become a full-time job for him. *He will stick to the Hail Marys, thank you, very much.* Janet smiles quietly, wondering to what extent her therapy is a form of confession. Bernard certainly exacts his own brand of atonement in the steepness of his fees. Jim continues to make fun of such a scheme and Jill berates him for not taking her seriously. The others laugh. But Jack falls silent. He wonders if Jill has a point. What value is atonement if it does not heal the pain of those against whom we have transgressed? Perhaps it is in their absolution, and not God's, that we can truly find peace.

Jim notices that his friend has withdrawn a little and seamlessly changes the subject. Janet glances at over at him gratefully. Any talk of his beloved Boxing Club seems to act as an antidote to her lover's low spirits, and soon he and Jim are reliving last week's junior sparring contest, blow by blow until she and Jill are fearing for the glassware and dishes beneath their flailing arms.

The two couples end their meal in the happy contentment that befits fine food and good company. The coffee arrives. Jill sits with her head on Jim's shoulder, her eyes closed for a moment. Jim drops numerous chunks of brown sugar into his coffee and smothers a satisfied yawn. Janet squeezes Jack's hand and whispering into his ear, reminds him that they had promised each other an early night. Jack places his hand on her thigh under the table and gives her a gentle wink. He is a lucky man and he knows it. He just wishes he could feel as though it was deserved.

Later that night, or rather in the early hours of the next morning, whilst Janet is slumbering peacefully in the next room, Jack takes out his fountain pen and paper and writes to Father Frank. He sighs as he pens the date then pauses, momentarily unable to continue. The silence in the little flat he shares with Janet hangs heavy around him. He sniffs quietly and pushes on. He shares the details of his life and how things have been since they last exchanged letters, but most importantly, he has a favour to ask.

When it is finished and signed, he lays down the epistle and sits a while before sealing it into an envelope and scribbling the familiar address. He finds a stamp in the little box on the sideboard, sticks it down, then places the letter in his jacket pocket before retiring to bed. Janet moans gently, as he climbs into the bed next to her, and instinctively reaches out for him. Jack wraps his arms around her and lays his head close to hers. But sleep will not come.

In the morning Janet remarks about the heavy bags under his eyes. It is not the first time she has seen them. Jack shrugs and jokes that if he falls asleep during double Latin, at least he will not be alone. Janet ruffles his hair with her fingers, then gasps as she notices the time. She is still not yet quite used to the twenty-minute rush-hour crush of the Central Line journey into Holborn. Slice of toast in hand, she drops a kiss on his brow and heads for the tube station, savouring what fresh air there is around her, whilst she can.

Thirty minutes later, Jack pauses at the red pillar box outside St James'. He takes out his letter and holds it up to the waiting slot, then hesitates. *Perhaps, in the end, we can only forgive ourselves.* He chews his lips. Perhaps, but surely, we must first *deserve* to forgive ourselves. Yet, how shall we forgive ourselves if those we have hurt cannot? He makes a determined nod, slips the envelope through the slot and heads for the main entrance.

October 18th. Islington

The little black alarm clock ticks loudly on the bedside table. Peter stares groggily at its fluorescent hands and wonders what can have awoken him at two o'clock in the morning. Thinking it might be either Stan or Ollie with a small hours' gift of a mouse or some other unlucky nocturnal animal, he listens out for the tell-tale mew but hears instead a muffled whimper. He turns to Maggie who is sleeping, yet seems to be crying in her dreams. He rolls carefully onto his side and folds his body around hers, not wishing to wake her, but the whimper is turning to sobs, and now her body begins to heave and shake with the force of them.

Peter carefully lifts his arm and stretches it across to turn on the bedside lamp. Stan and Ollie, who have been asleep at the end of the bed, are looking up in alarm, poised to leap to safety. Stan cocks his head and lets out a plaintive meow. Peter instinctively places a finger to his lips, then turns to Maggie. Tears stream down her sleeping face and the sobs have becomes moans of abject misery. He places a gentle hand upon her naked shoulder.

"Maggie, Love. Wake up. You are having a bad dream."

Peter recalls the old wives' tale that it is dangerous to wake a sleepwalker, but she is not walking, she is sobbing her heart out and he cannot bear it.

"Maggie, my Love, please wake up. It is just a dream."

Maggie opens her eyes and comes to with a jolt. But Peter has never seen so much pain in those eyes, or in anybody else's for that matter, and although she wraps her arms around him, and holds him tightly, her warm body continues to shudder with distress. Peter strokes her hair and whispers sounds of comfort, feeling suddenly helpless. Stan and Ollie stand and stretch and make their way up the bed, pushing their little damp noses up against Maggie's back and mewing in sympathy. Peter cannot help smiling, despite his concern and gives their heads a grateful rub.

When the outpouring of grief eventually subsides, Peter draws away and, raising himself on his elbow, gazes down into his lover's face. Maggie's eyes are closed and she has slipped back into the refuge of a dreamless sleep.

Peter herds Stan and Ollie back down to the foot of the bed, turns out the light then lies awake for some time, listening to the regular sigh of Maggie breathing and wondering what heartache must lie behind such troubled dreaming. It is some time before he eventually drifts off to his own dreams, and they too are uneasy.

Sometime later he is awakened again, this time by the sound of running water in the ensuite bathroom. The bed next to him is empty and feels quite cool. It is still very dark without and the hands on the clock tell him it is only three-thirty. He switches on the bedside lamp. Then listening intently, waits for the cessation of the water flow. But it does not come.

He calls out Maggie's name. There is no response. Doubtless, she cannot hear above the sound of the open taps. He waits a couple of minutes. He is beginning to feel anxious. He recalls how red and chapped Maggie's hands had been when they first met. Her occasional need to wash and re-wash her hands when she is upset or anxious has not escaped his notice, either. He gets out of bed, pulls on his towelling robe and knocks gently on the bathroom door. No response. He taps again, more firmly this time. The noise wakens Ollie and Stan who scamper off the bed and away out of the bedroom, startled by the rude disruption at this untimely hour. But there is no reaction from within. This time the knock is loud and urgent and Peter calls her name again. The sound of running water stops. Peter presses his ear to the door. All he can hear is a kind of urgent muttering. He strains to make it out.

"And moving through a mirror clear, that hangs - that hangs, and moving through a mirror clear - no, no - it's gone, it's gone…"

And then he hears a thumping, but it is only the sound of his heart racing. There is no lock on the door, Peter and Wendy had never entertained such modesty. Peter jiggles the handle without pushing open the door, somehow intuiting that he must not invade her privacy without negotiation. The muttering stops. Maggie responds in a quavering voice:

"Don't come in, Peter, please I beg you. I am okay."

"But Maggie, I don't think you are, so I am going to come in - now."

So, maybe it was not much of a negotiation after all, but at least it was the courtesy of a forewarning. Maggie lets out a cry of protest, but Peter has already pushed the door half open and is standing frozen in the doorway. Maggie is at the sink, soap and nailbrush in hands that are red raw from washing, and she has soap-suds around her face and mouth.

"Oh, Peter," she cries "I cannot remember the next line, I can't think, all I can see…"

She takes one look at his face and can tell that Peter is horrified. She slumps abjectly to the bathroom floor, her face contorted by distress, and wails an apology. How she must disgust him. The moment of paralysis passes. Peter gathers her up in his arms and holds her as though he might never see her again.

"It's alright, Love, I was just worried. I just didn't know what to think. I am here now, everything is okay."

Maggie sniffs and holds onto him, her hands and face still slippery with soapy water. Peter takes a towel from the rail and carefully dries them, making soothing noises as he does so. He helps her back onto her feet, fills a glass with water, then coaxes Maggie to rinse out her mouth. Then he takes a hairbrush off the vanity unit shelf and gently draws it through the tangles of her long hair. She offers no resistance, no opposition. She is like an obedient child in his care. When he has finished, he feels the gentle touch of her lips on his cheek as she reaches up to thank him. Peter breathes a sigh of grateful relief.

"Do you think you could, um - stop all this now, Maggie?" he says with the utmost tenderness. "Come back to bed, or we could get up and have a cup of tea?"

Maggie looks into his kind eyes and finds her smile.

"Tea?" She half snorts. "Sure, isn't that the English answer to everything?"

"Well, it seems a little early for whisky and butter, my Maggie," jokes Peter, touching his forehead to hers, "though in this case, I think we could make an exception."

Maggie nods, then swallows hard to stop her tears and allows Peter to usher her back to bed, where she waits patiently whilst he pads into the little kitchenette and pours out a couple of glasses of Irish whiskey.

Peter hands her one of the glasses, then climbs back into the bed next to her with the other. They clink glasses and Peter winks. They sit in bed and relish the reviving heat of the fine malt in silence. By and by Peter takes a deep breath and says:

"Now, Maggie Love, I want you to tell me what this is all about. I don't mean to pry and I may be an old fart, but even I can tell there is something very wrong. And I really think you have to tell someone. And I want to hear, to be there for you. I want to be that person in your life, Maggie. Truly, I do".

Maggie stares down into her glass. She is quiet for a moment but then starts speaking in a faltering voice.

"I don't think I can tell you all of it, Peter. Not - not yet. But today is, well, it would - should have been me little boy's third birthday, so it should, but - he died not long after he was born." She closes her eyes. Peter cradles her shoulders with his arm.

"I can't imagine what that must have been like. I remember when Annie was born, how precious she was. How I felt this intense wave of love, like a punch in the stomach almost. I had never felt anything so strong in my life..."

Maggie looks up into his face and nods her head with tears in her eyes. She continues through clenched teeth, her eyes closed again.

"I thought - I thought I was beginning to get over it, you know, get on with life, but it was like I was back there again, in my dream..." She shudders and puts her hand to her brow.

"But Maggie, Sweetheart, you are expecting too much of yourself. You will probably never 'get over it.' How could you expect that of yourself? I don't believe a mother ever really does. I wouldn't think so. Not ever, not really."

Maggie eyes him with curious gratitude. *Could he truly understand?*

"There is one thing, I do know," adds Peter. "You don't get through this kind of grief, by bottling it up, and if you don't feel ready to talk to me, you might find it easier to talk someone with experience with this stuff, a counsellor, I mean. We have a new student counsellor, everyone says she is good, very warm, and sometimes it helps to talk to someone outside..." Peter falls silent, aware that he might be starting to sound pushy, or as though he does not sincerely want to be the one who is there for her.

"It's just a suggestion - and I will always be here to listen if you need to talk." *God, why can't he keep his mouth shut?*

The two of them sit in silence for a minute or two.

"Peter, can I ask you something?"

"Of course, you can, my Love – anything."

"Now tell me, how is it that a man like yourself can be so wise?" Maggie's playful tone is returning, yet her question is real enough.

"It is the one, and I might say, only advantage of old age, my Dear."

"You're not in your dotage yet, so you're aren't," Maggie says planting kiss on his forehead. "I'd say you are mature and mellow - like this whiskey. And like this whiskey, you somehow take the sting away," she adds with a wistful smile.

Peter holds up his glass. "To butter and whiskey, then."

Vatican City. October 18th.

His Eminence Anatole Salvatore wakes from his sleep with a start. He waves his hand across his face, breathlessly trying to bat away the wings that are beating around his face. He opens his eyes. It was just a dream. Yet still, he seems to hear a distant flap and flutter. And still, he seems to feel the breeze and faintest sweep of downy feathers upon his skin. He stretches his arm out to the reading light on his nightstand and picks up his Rolex wristwatch. It is twenty minutes past four in the morning. A deep silence fills the room like undisturbed dust. He wonders why he cannot hear the familiar sound of car horns that are wont to punctuate the Roman night, even in the smallest of hours. Perhaps even now he is still asleep, or more likely, that stupid chambermaid has completely closed the window casement again. He abhors sleeping in a room without fresh air. It is no wonder he is having troubling dreams. He will see that she is chastised first thing in the morning. Then he recalls the date and sighs. He thumps his pillow and tosses over onto his side.

After an early breakfast and morning mass, The Cardinal summons a certain officer of the Vatican's most clandestine division to his office. Anonymous and sworn to utmost loyalty to the Holy See since the Medici dynasty, these agents tread unseen and in silent stealth wherever their mission takes them. They are the eyes and ears of the Holy

Roman Church around the globe and if at times they have served a darker purpose, then none shall ever learn of it from their lips whilst an immortal soul inhabits their mortal body.

A tall man in a dark suit enters the opulence of the Cardinal's office and stands before the great mahogany desk. The pallor of his skin suggests he has not spent the summer in his native city. They exchange no pleasantries or greeting, save for a formal nod of acknowledgement. The Cardinal unlocks the top desk-drawer and takes out a manila file. Without speaking a word, he opens it and thumbs through its pages. For a while, he seems lost in concentration and oblivious to the passage of time or the attendance of any other living being.

Signor Vecellio, meanwhile, remains impassive. His looks suggest neither impatience nor any peculiar interest. His role is merely to serve. The Signor hails from an unbroken bloodline of Vecellios, bound in service to the covert fraternity since Pope Pius IV himself. Discretion and unquestioning obedience have been selected into his very genes. He is a shadow that melts into the shadows, a whisper lost on the wind.

Finally, the Cardinal stirs. He looks directly into the eyes of his silent minion then, returning to the file, takes out a number of photographs and spreads them across his desk. Vecellio nods. These are the photographs he took with his own camera; Snapshots of a woman in dungarees and Doc Marten boots, a voluminous bag over her shoulder; the same woman entering a shop, standing at a bus stop, laughing with a group of young people outside a London Pub, cigarette in hand. There is an intimacy about the informality of the portraits that, in any other circumstances, might render them charming. Yet if the photographer has any personal interest in his subject, his demeanour does not betray it.

When the desk is all but covered by such records of one woman's life, Vecellio reaches inside his jacket, removes an envelope from his inside pocket and produces still one more, the most recent: Margaret Doyle sitting on the steps of the National Gallery exchanging a kiss with a rangy looking grey-haired man. Cardinal Salvatore's lip curls in contempt. *Why the woman is little better than a "puttana"- a harlot.*

"The Signora is fully recovered, then?" he mutters almost to himself.

"It would seem so. She has embarked on a degree in Fine Arts."

"Fine Art?"

"Painting, Your Eminence."

The Cardinal curls his lip again. It is worse than he thought.

"And the sister? They still live together?"

"Not exactly, Your Eminence. The sister seems to spend most of her time in a little town called St Albans, to the north of London, but continues to work at the hospital, at the weekends."

The Cardinal pushes his lower teeth into his top lip.

"And this - this senor? Who is he?"

"He is a lecturer at the Art School, Your Eminence, recently separated from his wife. We can find out more if you wish?"

The Cardinal meets his eyes with a glance of assent.

"And what of Father John O'Donnell?" There is a tightness in his voice and he speaks the name as though the very syllables are pollution to his lips.

"We know he took the crossing to Liverpool, but from there we lost the scent." Vecellio flares his nostrils, as though unconsciously sniffing the air. "There must have been someone hiding him, someone who understands these matters and knew how to cover his tracks. Our guess is that he is in London also, it is easy to lose yourself in such a city.

We have people searching. It is only a matter of time, Your Eminence."

"But you are certain he has not been seen with *her*?" He cannot bring himself to speak her name, even now, after all this time.

"No, there has been no contact as far as we know. Certainly, no meeting, we are sure of that."

The Cardinal nods. Vecellio hovers, uncertainty disturbing the customary equanimity of his poise. He is deciding the best way to frame a question. He clears his throat:

"And the Signora, Your Eminence? We have all the intelligence we need and I suspect she is aware that she has been under surveillance.

The Cardinal curls his lips and stokes the underneath of his chin with his fingers.

"Drop by and keep an eye on her every once in a while, and if you are less than discreet about it, then so much the better. We wouldn't want her to think we have forgotten about her, now would we?"

Vecellio almost, but only almost, raises an eyebrow, then remembers himself. He nods then stands to attention in silent obeyance and awaits The Cardinals further pleasure. The Cardinal stares at his folded hands for a few moments, then dismisses Vecellio with a wave of his hand. *Bene*, he has time. He has plenty of time.

Liverpool,
November 30th 1981

My Dearest Jack,

It was such a pleasure to hear from you and catch up with your news.

It sounds as though you were cut out for teaching after all, despite your misgivings, and I am pleased that I encouraged you so strongly to stay with it. I would love to meet this Jim of yours, someday. It sounds as though he is exactly the right person for you to be around at this time in your life. I used to be a bit of a pugilist in my seminary days, as well you know, and I won't be pretending I don't miss it. My poor old hips would not permit such shenanigans at my age, but I can't forget that particular rush of adrenalin, even now. It is good to be reminded that we are body as well as soul, at times, and I'm thinking we should not always be atoning for it, for it was the Good Lord whose gave us these mortal shells, in common with the other beasts, and sometimes a little celebration of that side of us does us a power of good.

I feel such happiness that you have found your heart again, Jack, for I was thinking it irreparable for a time. It is life, not women that truly breaks our hearts, yet the love of good women may do much to mend them. And I may be getting ahead of myself, but I hope I live to conduct any baptisms that might follow, for I cannot think of any service I would find more pleasure in taking. I know you will forgive your old mentor his impertinence and will know it is well-intentioned.

Things here go on in the same old routine. Our flock seems to dwindle monthly and the message seems to be losing its relevance to a generation raised to believe in the atom and the Big Bang. They ask questions which we can only struggle to answer. Sometimes I fear I am completely redundant, like a fossil or relic from a former age, and then I hold an infant in my arms and I feel my faith as sure and strong as ever it was. I pray that God saves me from outliving my usefulness completely, but it was ever his way to test us, and perhaps it is his will that we live through such trying times.

As for the other matter. As you requested, I have made extensive and very tactful enquiries as to the whereabouts of Margaret Doyle, but the trail appears to have gone cold. She was transferred to a hospital in the U.K not long after she had been admitted to the Central Mental Hospital outside Dundrum. I have been in touch with a trusted colleague Father Wynn who works in that same parish and knows many of the staff from the institution, but if anyone knows where Margaret Doyle went, they are not saying, and that is not surprising. The level of hostility around the whole sad incident makes me despair that there is truly such a thing as Christian Love. If they could bring back the Spanish Inquisition, they would do it, of that, I have no doubt. That poor wretch has suffered enough, yet the local clergy and parishioners are still braying for blood.

The husband was forced to flee, himself. He copped an unmerciful badgering from the newspapers as well as the good Christian people of County Clare. And I have it on reliable information that the Vatican bloodhounds have been let off the leash. Indeed, it pains me to say, but I received a visitor myself, not long before I received your letter, as it goes. Now, do not be worrying yourself, if they had any idea of your being on the mainland, they certainly got no hint from me, and never would. I rather think from the clues they dropped, that they believe you to have fled to the USA, and it is best it stays that way. Though at the same time, I do not believe them incapable of employing deliberate misinformation as a ruse to set us off our guard. They did also mention a sister of Margaret's, but as I recall there was some scandal around her and nobody had lain eyes on her or heard of her for close on twenty years. Yet the Vatican has many skilful and determined spies and I fear it cannot be long before they discover the poor woman. I counsel you to take care. I had an uncomfortable feeling that my own moves were being watched for a few days after their visit.

In any case, I am sorry that I cannot help you locate Margaret, but perhaps it is after all for the best.

We must both trust that she is in God's loving care, wherever she may be.

I shall mention one further matter before I close. I am sad to report that Father McCarthy, who was such an inspiration to the both of us in former, happier times, sadly passed away last month. He was the most genuinely pious man I ever knew. He once told me that we should look for the evidence of God's love in a man's failings and how he recovers from them, rather than in his successes. Sin gives us the opportunity for redemption, it is up to us to take that opportunity and use it. Perhaps you will think me a sentimental old fool, but I can't help but feel proud of you, whenever I recall his words.

Yours in deepest friendship,

Frank.

December, Bethnal Green.

Tonight, it is Janet who falls prey to the subtle tortures of insomnia. She has turned onto her side then onto her back, and then onto her side again several times but, as tired as she feels, sleep eludes her. She knows it is useless now, as once you start to worry about getting off to sleep you have already lost the battle. She has spent a good fifteen minutes lying still, focusing on the tick of the alarm clock in a feeble attempt at self-hypnosis. To be fair, this generally does the trick, but on this occasion, her thoughts will not cooperate by settling into the background.

She is aware of Jack sleeping peacefully beside her, even so, the slight irregularity that is creeping into the rhythm of his breathing tells her that her fidgeting is beginning to disturb him. She longs to wake him but knows this would be a bit selfish, so fights the urge to nudge him gently into consciousness.

She supposes she should get up and read, or make a hot drink, but the idea of this seems very unappealing, especially as the central heating would have gone off hours ago and the flat will be freezing in the December night. At least she is warm and cosy in bed, and just having the heat of Jack's body next to her is a comfort she is yet to take for granted. She snuggles closer to him. The luminous hands of the clock are telling her it is just past two in the morning. She will have to be up at six-thirty as she has a session with Bernard this morning. At least she will be able to talk to him. She had thought about cutting down the frequency of the sessions, or even, God knows how she could contemplate it, finishing her therapy now that she had completed her training, but Bernard was not having any of it. There was, he had declared, still work to be done, and to leave now just because her new relationship was in the honeymoon stage, (yes, he had actually used those words), would be recklessly premature. Janet knew he was right. She would never admit it to him as such, but he was. As it happens, since she had qualified, Bernard had become open to using the sessions in a semi-supervisory fashion, if Janet was struggling with a client. This alone made it worth continuing and it is, in truth, a counselling client that preoccupies her thoughts in these wee small hours.

She is thinking about the session today, wait, it is yesterday already, with Maggie Doyle. This was the fifth, no sixth, session they had had since Maggie's name had appeared for the first time on her self-booking appointment list. Since that initial meeting, Janet reckons she must have been through as wide a gamut of emotions as one could reasonably expect to feel in a lifetime's experience as a counsellor, and she is a mere novice. Over the last six weeks, she had found herself intrigued, puzzled, and then, frankly, shocked. And now she is feeling puzzled again, puzzled and concerned. Indeed, if she is being honest, she has to concede that her current insomnia is almost certainly due to a niggling worry that she may be way out of her depth.

Maggie seems together enough in herself. Indeed, she regularly demonstrates a strength of mind that makes Janet feel more than slightly envious. Yet, according to Maggie, it was not that long ago that she had been discharged from a mental health unit, where she had been given a diagnosis of postpartum psychosis. Maggie had been quite open with Janet about this at their first meeting, though quite what this really meant was another matter. Indeed, it had taken a good, few sessions to establish sufficient trust for Maggie to be able to talk about this in any detail. *And small wonder*, thinks Janet with a shudder, for yesterday Maggie, had shared her remembrance of the events around the birth and death of her child.

Janet could have little doubt of Maggie's truthfulness in relating the details; the level of her distress during the telling was proof enough that the trauma she recounted had been genuine; goodness knows it had left Janet herself feeling decidedly shaken. And yet it must surely have been a trauma born of psychosis. Something so real to Maggie at the time that it was indistinguishable in memory. But could any part of it be real?

Well, obviously her baby was not an angel but something may have triggered such an idea. The poor thing had certainly not been destined to live long. Maggie's retreat into a fantasy that her baby was an angel was, most likely, the desperate compensation of a bereaved mother's mind trying to cope with the intolerable pain of loss. But then, there are some people who truly believe in angels and miracles; goodness knows this man sleeping next to her must have some beliefs she would find very difficult to accept. And hadn't she, herself, been bought up to believe in transubstantiation, the tenant that the communion wafer and wine *actually* become the body and blood of Jesus during the Holy Eucharist. It seems equally ridiculous to her now, but millions of people all over the world still accept the veracity of this commonplace miracle. She is pretty certain Bernard would not, but then he is Jewish, and a rationalist at that.

And why would a cardinal from the Vatican be at a little hospital in Ireland? Well, of course, that was probably another part of the delusional system; it had probably just been a local priest who took on some overvalued significance.

But what of the rest? Janet starts to feel a little nauseated just thinking about what Maggie had told her, as much as she had skirted around any real detail. But the idea was horrific enough, but could someone actually do that? Is it even physically possible to consume a baby?

Janet is starting to feel upset. That must be part of the delusion as well, mustn't it? But then again, she knows full well that a truly disturbed mind is capable of acts wholly unimaginable to the rest of us. She had once read a case study of a woman who had plucked out her own eyes because she believed that they were not her own. Such things seem unimaginable to the sane, yet happen all the same. So, could there be a reality in this part of Maggie's account, be it ever so macabre and shocking?

And what about the fact that Maggie had been transferred to a hospital in London from Ireland, surely that was highly unusual? It did seem to support the notion that Maggie's case was in some way remarkable, the things she has done whilst in a psychotic state particularly disturbing.

Janet can feel her levels of distress rising. She is on the edge of wanting to sob. She needs to close these thoughts down but finds she cannot. She earnestly wishes that she could talk to Jack about all this, but of course, that is out of the question. The inviolable constraints of client counsellor confidentiality are the fundamental tenants of her practice.

The fact that Jack hails from Ireland and had been in the church suggests that there would be a fair chance that he would have heard of the incident, in which case, even the most oblique hint about her client's history might prove sufficient to compromise that confidentiality. She turns over again and pummels her pillow, and this time Jack stirs and awakens.

"I am so sorry," breathes Janet. "I didn't mean to wake you, go back to sleep."

"Urrghhh," yawns Jack scratching his head, "what time is it anyway?"

"Nearly three thirty..."

"Can't sleep, Love?" He pulls her close and closing his eyes, starts to drift back into slumber.

"Jack?"

"Hmmmmmm?"

"Do you believe in angels, I mean, actual angelic beings?"

Janet feels Jack's body tense next to hers. His eyes remain closed. There is a moment of silence, but Janet can sense he is fully awake now.

"Of course, I do," he whispers tenderly. "You are my guardian angel right enough, so you are."
He holds her closer.

"I thought Angels were generally male ..." says Janet remembering her Sunday School lessons and, right away, wants to kick herself for spoiling the moment.

"Hmmm - well now, I guess it must be Jim then," he slurs sleepily. With that, he yawns, rolls over onto his other side and falls into silence once more. But Janet can tell from his breathing that he is not asleep.

She lies awake feeling utterly alone. Thank God Bernard had talked her out of ending therapy. He is certainly going to have his work cut out for him in the morning.

Holborn, December.

The academic year is drawing to its end. Someone has made a half-hearted attempt to hang some festive decorations in the main corridor, but the paper garlands lend little brightness to the gloom of the afternoon.

Maggie is sitting patiently on one of the chairs outside her room when Janet opens her door for her three o'clock appointment. She smiles fleetingly, then picks up a large canvas satchel full of sketchbooks and rolled up drawings and follows Janet into the little counselling room.

Maggie takes her usual armchair and Janet seats herself across from her, whilst Maggie leans forward and places her bag on the table between them. Janet smiles and nods to indicate that their session has started. Maggie, as if waiting for the signal, slips her hand deep into the voluminous bag and brings out a small book, which she holds between her delicate fingers. The first thing that strikes Janet is how much less red those poor fingers appear now. It is only then that it registers that the little volume is a bible. She raises a questioning eyebrow.

Maggie's tone is hushed and tinged with the conspiratorial, as though she fears they may be overheard, though the corridors outside had been empty and there is generally no one around at this time of the day.

"I know you find it difficult to believe my story," she begins, "and who would not? Indeed, tis enough difficult for me at times, and I was there."

She pauses as if to collect herself.

"The thing is, I spent months in that unit, with all those psychiatrists and psychologists trying to tell me that it never happened, that it was a break-down, and, believe me, I know they were trying to help. I really believe that, so I do. But they were not there, and I - I was."

Her voice falters. She swallows then gathers herself.

"And I had to work so hard to hold on to what was real. Because I knew what I had done *and* why I had done it and ...."

Maggie is looking at Janet with an earnestness in her eyes that Janet finds hard to meet. Janet recalls the discussion she had had with Bernard last week and chooses her words with care.

"Maggie, I can feel how true this is for you and I was not there either, so it is not for me to say. It seems to me that what is important for here, is what you felt happened."

But Maggie is not buying this.

"No, no. You need to understand. I don't expect you to believe it, so I don't. What I do need, is for you to understand how important it is for *me* to hold onto what *I* believe. You see, I only ever had one thing that helped me and helps me to this day, when I begin to doubt it myself."

Maggie's eyes shift to the little book in her hands. Oh, so carefully, she opens the bible and from between its pages, lifts out a single small, yet perfectly formed white feather.

"Tis is all I have of my baby, so it is." She holds it up and gazes at it with a mixture of love and infinite sadness.

"It fell out of his – his wings when he was but a few hours old. I put in it my bible, which I had with me, and it has lain there ever since. I never showed it to anyone in the hospital. I was so frightened that they would take it away from me; take away the one thing I have left of him…"

Maggie sobs and rocks forward in her chair, holding the feather to her breast. Janet experiences a moment of rising hysteria, she wants to laugh or cry, or both. She is not sure she can cope with this.

She takes a breath; collects herself, giving Maggie a moment for her grief, then pushes the box of tissues across the little table towards her. Maggie reaches for one of them without glancing upwards and blows her nose.

"Maggie, I can feel how important it is for you to have this tangible connection with your Gabriel. I am very sensible of the trust you have shown by sharing this and, truly, I am not here to tell you what is real and what is not."

"I know," sniffs Maggie looking up and last, "and that is such a relief. It is such a freedom. And it is what I need, so it is." She strokes the shaft of the small quill with a finger then folds it tenderly back into the pages of the little bible then tucks it back into her satchel.

"You see, I have been given this second chance, and I'm thinking that perhaps God himself has forgiven me. And it is a life I could never have imagined. To be sure, sometimes I feel as though it belongs to another Maggie Doyle and that her old life must have been very different to mine. So, I feel guilty, as though I am trying to behave as though it never happened. And in some ways, it would be so easy, but if I do then..." her eyes fill with tears again.

"You will never forget him, Maggie," Janet has tears in her eyes herself now, "I do not believe a mother ever can. I do not think the loss ever diminishes, but rather our lives grow around it, as yours has done over the last year. So sometimes it may not be in our minds at all, and then at others, it is all we feel, as you do at this moment. Both are okay."

Maggie is looking at Janet her cheek on her hand, her elbow on the arm of the chair. She nods with a sad smile, then turns her eyes to the floor. Janet feels as though she has passed a test. But only by the skin of her teeth.

Camden Town. 8am.

"And how are things going with that client of yours, the little Irish woman?" Bernard asks, towards the end of the session, the following morning. Janet wonders if he is trying to change the subject but recalls how genuinely perplexed she had been about the situation with Maggie a couple of sessions back, and is, instead, pleased that Bernard has remembered.

"I don't know. We seem to have turned a corner. I - um, well she is still absolutely resolute about what happened." She cannot explain it, but it suddenly occurs to Janet that to tell Bernard about the feather would be some sort of gross betrayal of trust. She continues with guarded vagueness.

"So, we have agreed to just stay with her feelings about it and not focus on whether it really happened or not, and that seems to be going okay."

"Do you know if she is being followed up by the mental health team she was under?"

"I don't think so. She told me that she was not even on medication…"

"Have you picked up any other symptoms or thoughts that might suggest psychotic ideation?"

"No, not particularly. On the whole, she is very together. She has even reduced the OCD behaviours to almost zero. Just grieving and a little traumatised."

"Good. Well. If it is her memory of it, it is her memory of it. It won't change, I guess. It would be good to just keep an eye on it, though. You know how stressed these art students can get, a lot of them are quite fragile in the first place. She would not be the first to have a psychotic break. I guess you could always refer her to the local mental health services if you think there is a deterioration - What?" Bernard responds abruptly.

Janet is sucking her teeth.

"Nothing," grumbles Janet, "it is just that sometimes you can sound awfully…"

"Patronising?" suggests Bernard. "Condescending?"

"I was going to say, like a psychiatrist and not a psychoanalyst."

"Ouch! Touché," laughs Bernard. "Perhaps I deserved that. Old habits eh? Well, time's up."

"*Now*, you sound like a psychoanalyst."

Oxford Street.

It is the week before Christmas. Jack is struggling through the heaving throngs of Christmas shoppers that jam the pavements along Oxford Street. The darkness of the winter night is made bright by a million twinkling fairy lights and the jewel-like glow from every festive shop-window display all but drives away the bite of the icy cold. There seems to be a smile on every shining face around him, yet Jack finds himself distracted by the dazzle of the decorations and disoriented by the crowd that sweeps him along, like flotsam on the freezing rapids. He wonders what he can have been thinking, venturing into this part of town so late in the run-up for the Big Day. He had had it in his head that late-night opening would attract only a modest number of yule-tide gift hunters. Those who were otherwise unable to get to the shops in normal hours. How wrong can you be?

He marvels at where all the people can come from and why they have left it to the last minute, yet he is being unfair. There are still a good couple of shopping days in hand, and he is hardly one to talk. He guesses that they might be after that *special something*, too, for it is precisely that motivation that has driven him out of his usual comfort zone. He had wanted to find something *unique and thoughtful* for Janet, something that would *truly show* that he cared. Over the last few days, he had felt an undefined coolness between them that owed nothing to the onset of the winter frost. And he understood its origin well enough. Things had not been right since the night she had asked him about angels, of all things. How could he have been such an eejit? Fair enough, her question had completely thrown him, especially as he had been half asleep. Indeed, it had stirred up so many painful emotions for him, that it was all he could do to stay in the bed and act as though there was nothing wrong. But why on Earth did he have to go and make that ridiculous comment about Jim? If he had tried to make a suggestion list of all the most stupid things he could have said to Janet, that one would have been pretty near the top. But it was done, and he had no clue how to undo it, except by finding a way of making her feel special. *Really special.*

But his good intentions seem doomed to failure. He is now feeling so overwhelmed by the whole expedition that he wonders if he must return home empty-handed. He has to admit that he has not the faintest clue what a woman would like, let alone what would utterly delight Janet in particular. The whole notion of buying gifts for a lover, especially surprise ones, is completely alien to him. Sure, if he had thought it through a bit more, he would have realised a man needs to do his research before setting off on such an enterprise. He has no idea what perfume she likes, (although she always smells wonderful to him), whether she would indeed wear a silk scarf, or what dress-size she is. It had crossed his mind that he might buy her some fabulously glamorous nightgown, surely all women love such things, yet it might be too small or too big. Either way, that could go horribly wrong. Jack pulls a face at the very prospect. Besides which it is all so bloody clichéd. And cliché does not suggest special.

He is just about to give up and head on down to Marble Arch tube station when the throng of shoppers ahead of him appears to come almost to a halt, coalescing into little groups before the great stage-like windows that line the front of Selfridges department store. Jack grimaces in frustration. The crowd here seems to have become particularly dense, and small wonder. Unbeknownst to him, this old and revered Emporium of fine goods takes enormous pride in the fabulous spectacle of its festive window dressing which attracts visitors from all over the world. Just now some of those visitors press in towards the next window from behind him, sweeping Jack along with them in their wake. This year, each enormous display window has been styled as a sitting room from a different era, and every room is dressed in period Christmas splendour. It is quite a sight to behold.

Jack finds himself gazing in on a scene of Victorian charm and opulence, the like of which he could hardly have imagined. He finds he cannot help but feel enchanted. He sidles through the pack of excitedly chattering tourists to get a better view. He reaches the window and peers up, head craned back, his chin almost touching the glass. He has never seen such a beautiful Christmas Tree. And suddenly he sees it - the perfect gift.

Christmas Eve.

Janet is in the little kitchenette of their little flat preparing the vegetables for their Christmas lunch tomorrow. The skins from the spuds and carrots spiral into little festive garlands of their own beneath the careful blade of her vegetable parer. She places the last potato into a saucepan of salted water and reaches for the Brussel sprouts, frowning as she searches around for a place to set another pan. Every spare inch of the work surface is crammed with baking trays, bowls of whipped cream, jars full of mincemeat, cranberry jelly and every good thing.

They have invited Jim and Jill, and Janet is determined that it will be a Christmas meal to remember. She sings softly as she labours - O' Little Town of Bethlehem, Away in a Manger. She has had a glass or two of sherry and already seems to have thawed out a little since tea-time, when Jack had returned home from a last-minute shopping foray with an enormous real Christmas tree and all the trimmings, in tow.

A few weeks previously they had sensibly agreed not to go to the expense of a Christmas tree this year, but for all her pragmatism, Jack had seen the disappointment on Janet's face and, after all, it would be their first real Christmas together. Besides, there was the little matter of her present.

Jack puts the finishing touches to the tree decorations then calls Janet in to inspect his handiwork. Janet enters the living room, wiping her hands on her apron, and gives a little cry of delight. It looks so beautiful she could almost cry. She jumps up and down with delight and throws her arms around Jack's neck.

"Aye, but it is not properly finished yet," he smiles. "I've something for you, so I have. It is your Christmas present, but I'm thinking you should open it now."

He takes one of the parcels from under the tree and places it in Janet's hands.

"For you my lovely, lovely Janet," he whispers, brushing her cheek with his lips.

Janet stares down at the small beautifully wrapped parcel, her eyes as wide as any child's.

"Oh, Jack. Really? Open it now? You sure?"

He nods, they sit next to each other on the sofa and Janet reads the gift tag. Jack's eyes never leave her face.

"To Janet. To keep through all the years, I look forward to sharing with you."

Janet raises her eyebrows. Her heart leaps joyfully inside her chest. She carefully tears open the lovely paper, then gives a tiny gasp.

"Oh, Jack, she is wonderful, so beautiful…"

Janet seems entranced. She holds up the exquisitely modelled Victorian Christmas tree angel that had so captured Jack's attention only a few days ago. Her eyes sparkle with delight as she turns it this way and that, admiring every delicate detail. Jack smiles. His head had swum a little when the Selfridges shop assistant had told him the price, but she had assured him that it would become a family heirloom, in years to come. And if it made Janet happy, it was worth every penny.

"And you see she is undoubtedly a female angel, just like you," adds Jack, and if the lines sound a little over-rehearsed, Janet does not care.

"Oh Jack, I was never given anything half so beautiful in all my life. Help me put her on top of the tree."

Jack stretches up and sets the little angel amongst the very topmost of the fragrant pine-needled branches. He steps back and places his arm around Janet's shoulders and they both gaze up at her together.

Jack's investment has paid off. Her coolness towards Jack all forgotten, Janet is scarcely able to take her eyes off the angelic figurine for the rest of the evening.

The following day, Christmas dawns. Friends and family all over the country meet to share presents, good food and good cheer. Once the lunch table is cleared away, Jack, Jim and Jill unanimously declare that this had had to be the best Christmas dinner they have ever eaten, and the four of them sink happily full and more than a little tipsy into the comfort of the three-piece suite, in time for the Queen's Christmas day address. Jack, not over keen on the notion, is bamboozled by his three companions who insist that tradition is tradition, and it does not come more traditional than the familiar "My husband and I..." *Whilst in Rome thinks* Jack, then apologises silently to his late Grand-daddy and his staunchly anti -loyalist forebears.

Once the speech is over, Jim refills their glasses and proposes a toast.

"You have heard of the O'Jays," he pronounces with a slight slur, "well, here is to that other famous group The Four Jays. Riding on that old Love Train, keeping the groove alive, sisters."

Janet and Jill collapse into giggles, but the joke is lost on Jack, who immediately thinks of a fourth form class he finds particularly trying.

"The O'Jays, man," cries Jim. "You know, soul music, brother. You must know it." And with that he leaps to his feet and starts gyrating around the floor. Singing the words in a voice that would do more justice to Bob Dylan than to Motown, he grinds his pelvis and beckons to the girls to join onto the "Love Train". Jill and Janet, helpless with laughter and too full to move, wave him away. Jill comments that *it is news to her that he was the new John Travolta.* Jim snorts in derision. *What did that fairy know about dancing?*

"Man! When I grew up it was all Northern Soul. Now *that* is how *real* men dance!"

Jack, meanwhile, is staring at Jim with a face as blank as an unwritten cheque. He is starting to wonder whether they are all speaking an entirely different language.

"Northern Soul," grins Jim, as though repeating it more loudly will bring comprehension. Then, with an exclamation of - "Oh, what the Hell!"- he drops to the floor in a backward flop, hands beneath him. Kicking up his feet, he flips over onto his right knee and elbow, then back onto his left hip and spins on the spot, throwing his right leg around like a windmill sale. Jill and Janet clap and shriek with laughter. Jack starts to laugh too, shaking his head in utter disbelief.

Suddenly there is a loud crack. In the confined space of the little sitting-room, the toe of Jim's shoe makes contact with the base of the Christmas tree. Jim stops short and pulls himself back to his feet, but the huge tree is already toppling. Janet lets out a cry of alarm. Jack lurches forward to try and save it. But it is too late. The whole Christmas tree comes crashing down. Its branches sprawl across the carpet, strewing baubles and pine needles in all directions. The little angel hits the ground last. Noiselessly, and almost in slow motion, the delicate neck snaps and the beautiful head parts company from the fragile white-winged body.

For a moment there is a stunned silence. Jim starts to apologise profusely. Jack glances at Janet. Her face looks as though she has just witnessed a fatal accident. She does not even hear Jim's words. Jack darts forward and scoops up the parts of the body. The break is clean, and when he presses the two parts back together, there is only the tiniest hairline crack.

"It's okay Love, look."

He holds the broken pieces together and tries to show her.
> "All you need is a dab of that super glue stuff and no one will even know it was ever broken".

But Janet looks away, her face crumpled into heartbreak.
> "*I will*." She whispers almost inaudibly. "*I will*".

A little further north of London, in a neat little cul-de-sac near the centre of St Albans, things are going rather better. Kathleen and Vonnie had invited Maggie and Peter to theirs for Christmas lunch, and the four of them have been getting on like a house on fire. Peter had insisted on helping Vonnie with the washing up and the two of them are joking together, out in the little scullery that backs onto the kitchen, the merry clinking of the crockery and glasses creating a pleasing counterpoint to their chatter and laughter.

Kathleen is fussing around the kitchen, insisting that she make up a 'doggy bag' for Stan and Ollie. She calls to Peter to ask whether they might prefer red or white meat. There is so much turkey left, sure she and Vonnie will be eating it until Easter at this rate. Peter laughs, he can't say that they have ever expressed a preference. Kathleen will put together a bit of both then.

Maggie sits momentarily alone in the front parlour, basking in the glow of the real coal fire that flickers in the old chimney place, brightening the already darkening afternoon. But it is not only the fire that warms her heart. Her sister seems to have found genuine happiness and peace of mind and Maggie cannot help but be infused with a sense of wellbeing she had thought beyond her reach. And then there is Peter. Both Kathleen and Vonnie seem to have half fallen in love with him themselves, and Maggie reflects that this is the first time in her life that she has truly understood how it feels to be part of a happy loving family.

She sighs. Peter has to leave tomorrow morning, to see to Stan and Ollie and drop in to see Annie and his son-in-law for Boxing day lunch. Peter had wanted to take Maggie with him, but she does not feel quite ready for that, with Annie's parents only just finalising their divorce. Peter had understood, without the need for any lengthy explanation or discussion. He always does. She smiles to herself. Perhaps that is what she loves about him most of all.

They had driven up to St Albans in his old Ford escort last night and he will leave early in the morning. That had been an adventure in itself. Peter, like most Londoners, hardly ever uses his old car and the busy North Circular had proved testing, to say the least. It must have been one of the only times Maggie had heard Peter use a double expletive. Maggie had felt secretly glad she had never taken driving lessons. She would prefer to take the train or tube any day.

Maggie is going to stay with Kath and Vonnie for a few more days, then catch the train down to London for New Year's Eve. And what a New Year it promises to be. Maggie can hardly believe how blessed she has been. She has so much for which to feel thankful. Her first term at Central has been a great start to her future and she has not had the feeling that she is being followed for several weeks. Talking to Janet seems to have helped. Maybe it really had been her imagination, after all. That feels entirely possible now. She looks deep into the glimmering red heat of the coals and sighs. They always say that you can see the future in the embers of a fire if you stare for long enough. Yet for the first time in her life, the journey and not the destination is quite enough.

She puts her fingers to her hair and touches the antique silver and amber art nouveau hair slide Peter had surprised her with this morning. He had said that only something so beautiful would do for those auburn locks and had known it was right for her as soon as he had lain eyes on it. Maggie feels herself surrendering. She might as well accept defeat. It is impossible to sustain the belief that romance is dead, in the face of such opposition. Sure, and at their age too.

Maggie glances out of the window. The first white flakes of snow are beginning to fall like down from God's pillow. She jumps up and runs into the kitchen to find the others.

"Kathleen, Vonnie, Peter. Look outside. It is starting to snow!"

Kathleen flings open the back door and the four of them tumble outside into the back yard where the snow is already beginning to blanket the lawn like a soft white eiderdown. They spin giddily around, faces turned upwards relishing the delicate wetness of the icy particles on their cheeks and lashes, then embrace each other in turn.

"A Happy Christmas to all of us!" cries Maggie. And it truly is.

Spring 1982

Maggie perches on an upturned milk crate in the first-year studio, idly flicking through her notebooks. The year seems to be flying past. There is already a large number of canvases stacked against walls and in the drying racks, and this term they have all started to work on projects of their own choosing. Maggie and her peers have each established their respective little territories in the large high windowed atelier and have fallen seamlessly into the rhythm and social drama of art school life.

Maggie has been fortunate enough to find her herself somehow removed from the politics of shifting student alliances. As a mature scholar, she finds she receives unexpected respect from her peers, who appear to hold her in some sort of reverence. Yet, while Maggie's modesty permits her to attribute this purely to her advancing years, anyone else can tell you it as much to do with the talent that shines out from every one of the images she produces.

She gets up and stirs a bucket of rabbit skin size that she has prepared for a canvas she stretched this morning. She wrinkles her nose in faint disgust at the sickly smell and taking a brush, coats the canvas, carefully following the direction of the weave. Despite her objection to the odour, Maggie enjoys the workmanship of constructing the frame then stretching the heavy canvas and sizing it in the traditional way that painters have followed for perhaps centuries past. It lends a sense of continuity that she finds curiously comforting, and helps her in the incubation of her ideas. The whole process has a kind of reverence and devotion about it, a kind of spirituality almost. If only there was a better synthetic alternative to rabbit skin glue. And later, as the size begins to congeal and dry out, Maggie thrills at the almost miraculous tightening of the canvas, as if the very fabric is readying itself for the act of creation.

Maggie glances around. The studio is emptying. Big Rob calls across from the other end of the studio and asks if she is coming down to the student café for the afternoon break. Maggie shakes her head in grateful refusal, raising the sizing brush by way of explanation. Rob grins and nods. First lesson in canvas sizing: You have to finish sizing once you have started. Maggie completes the first coat and moves on to her next stretcher. She is thinking that perhaps she will not use a white primer for this one. An Umbrian base might be more effective. Yet there is no time for distraction. It is warm in the studio and the size is already thickening. She has to work hard now to spread it evenly across the coarse weave of the canvas, and there are still three other stretchers waiting. Half an hour flies by without her notice. There is something about the physicality of the task that is wholly absorbing and Maggie works on, oblivious to all other thoughts, as though under some rabbit wrought enchantment.

Her reverie is broken by the appearance of Roger, who has an excited grin on his face. *Is she ready? He is. It is all set up in his studio space. And the light is just perfect.* He holds some folded fabric over his arm; a swath of rich tourmaline-green satin and a chemise of pure white cotton. *Just a tick.*

She just needs to finish up then wash this disgusting stuff off her hands. Roger wrinkles his nose in distaste. *He refuses to use it, he is a vegetarian, so you won't catch him smearing dead bunnies all over his canvases. Even if it does mean his canvases sag more than they might.* Maggie laughs. At least he is trying to be consistent in his convictions, although she observes that he wears leather workman's boots. Idealism and youth. Such a heady, confused mix. She decides to let it go. She tells him to leave the costume over a nearby chair. She will change and meet him in his studio space just as soon as she is done. Roger beams, he is so looking forward to this.

Maggie shakes her head; Roger's enthusiasm is nothing if not endearing. She makes sure the canvas is nicely soaked, stands the brush back in the pail, wipes her hands on a piece of leftover canvas, then seizes the bundle and heads for the Ladies' cloakroom.

In the washroom, she rinses the last of the rabbity-smell from her fingers, then unrolls the cloth. She glances at herself in the full-length mirror on the wall next to the sinks and shakes her head. Who would have thought she would be dressing up like a kid in a Christmas play at her age? She lets down her hair, removes her dungarees and T-shirt and changes into the delicate white shift. Roger has certainly done her proud. She is not sure how he came by the outfit, but it looks pretty authentic. The long white chemise is finely pleated and fits as though made to measure. She arranges her long curls around her neck and pulls the long green drape of the overdress up over her head, like a hood.

She wonders a moment at his choice of colour, for surely blue is more traditional for The Holy Mother, yet when she catches her reflection in the mirror, for a second time, with the jewel-like green next to the fiery auburn of her hair, it all makes perfect sense. Roger's aesthetic instincts are spot on, as always. And to be sure, this afternoon, she truly does look like The Madonna.

Maggie peeps outside into the empty corridor and trips self-consciously across to Roger's studio. She has not removed her Doc Martens and cannot recall ever having seen the Holy Mother's feet in a painting, although she can be pretty sure they would not be shod in lace-up boots. Roger, however, is completely delighted and not the least bit perturbed by his Madonna's footwear.

Maggie's Madonna is everything he dreamed of. It is like all his birthdays at once. He directs her to the corner of his booth, where he has set up a throne-like structure, with a high steeple shaped wooden back, and scalloped edging. Maggie seats herself regally, and Roger arranges the cloth of her robe and drape around her, stepping back to admire his creation. *If they could just do one hour this afternoon, that would be a brilliant start. Oh, and of course, he had nearly forgotten, what an idiot!* He makes to the other corner of the alcove and ferrets about in a large bag, then lifting out a swaddled bundle, stoops to place it in Maggie's arms. Maggie pulls back with a cry of pain, as though singed by fire. There is a look of terror on her face. He had never mentioned a baby. Maggie is trembling. *But there has to be a baby, the baby Jesus, right?* Maggie looks stricken. She had seen many an image of the Madonna without a baby. This was not what they had agreed. Roger peers at Maggie mystified. He offers the bundle again. *It is just a doll.* How can that be a problem? But Maggie is by now beyond the reach of his words or reassurance. She hurls herself from the seat of her throne and runs wailing back to the washroom.

"What on Earth?" cries Sarah, nearly dropping her cardboard tray of takeaway coffees, as she passes the fleeing Maggie at the door.

"Roger, what in Hell's name have you done to Maggie?"

Roger stands helplessly with his hands held open. The baby Jesus lies at his feet, discarded and forgotten.

"Fetch Summer - I'll go and see if I can help," and with that she dashes after Maggie into the female toilets.

Inside Sarah can hardly believe what her eyes behold. Maggie, still in the fine linen shift, is hunched over the washbasins, mouth and hands covered in suds, sobbing. Sarah says her name and gently tries to pull her hands away from her face. She knows that Maggie sometimes has handwashing issues, but she has never seen her like this. Maggie looks at Sarah unseeingly. There is such torture in her eyes that Sarah feels suddenly frightened.

"Maggie, it is Sarah. It is okay. You are alright." But it is to no avail.

Summer comes bursting through the door. Sarah looks at her with an expression of relief and desperation, grateful for her friend's cool head. Summer takes Maggie and gently but firmly pushes her away from the washbasin and up against the wall. She looks at Sarah and whispers urgently:

"Go and find the student counsellor, tell her - it's an emergency, quickly. Go!"

Maggie groans and slumps to the floor, eyes tightly closed. She seems lost to them. Summer continues to call Maggie's name and hold her hand. It seems an aeon before Sarah arrives back with a tall dark-haired woman, whom Summer has never seen, but who obviously knows Maggie.

The woman drops to her knees and takes Maggie by the shoulders and speaking her name, very gently shakes her, as though trying to rouse her from a dream. Maggie opens her eyes for a moment, then places her forearm across them, as though trying to block out the terror. Janet feels lost. This is not at all something her counselling training has equipped her for. She sees the expectation of the frightened young girls standing next to her and feels all at once helpless and something of a charlatan. But she *does know* Maggie and is almost certainly the only person there who has some understanding of what this woman has been through.

She recalls that Maggie had described experiencing attacks similar to this, from which she eventually recovers. Breathing more slowly she finds her thoughts becoming clearer and less panicked. She is pretty sure that Maggie had mentioned that Peter, the man she was seeing, was a member of staff here. Indeed, if her memory serves her right, Maggie had experienced a similar episode at his place and it was he who had prompted Maggie to seek Janet out. She asks the girls if they know where Peter is. Sarah nods and makes off to the life drawing studio to find him, but almost collides with Roger, who is pacing around in the corridor, beside himself with mortification.

"Fetch Peter, now. Hurry," she hisses, and Roger, glad to be of some uses, sprints off in the direction of the life drawing studio on his errand of mercy.

Sarah returns to the scene where Janet is sitting, her arms around Maggie, rocking her and rubbing her arms and all the time talking quietly to her. The worst seems over. Peter arrives, out of breath, his brows furrowed by concern. He mumbles a greeting to Janet, then drops to his knees and holds Maggie's face between his hands.

"Maggie Love, I want you to open your eyes. Come on, now. Look at me, it's Peter."

Maggie forces her eyes to open and looks into his face, bewildered.

"That's my Maggie," continues Peter. "Now, I want you to keep them wide open, okay, and look around you. Look very carefully, Maggie."

Maggie is reluctant but obeys.

"You see where we are Maggie, we are in the washroom at Central - and here is Janet, and Summer and Sarah. You see them?"
Maggie nods slowly.

"Now, look at your hands and dress Maggie." Peter's voice is firm but kind.
Maggie shakes her head; she cannot bear to look.

"Look at them, Maggie," Peter holds up one of her hands. "You see all clean. Look how beautiful and white this lovely gown is, not a mark on it - you see?"
Maggie shifts her eyes and nods.

"Good girl," coos Peter. "Now, keep those eyes open. You are doing great." Then reaching up for one of the polystyrene cups of coffee which still sit on the sink where Sarah had left them, he sniffs it and holds it out to Maggie.

"What do you smell?"
Maggie pulls a face of revulsion. She screws closed her eyes and lets out a groan of distress.

"No, eyes open, please. Look, here, right here. What can you *actually smell*?"

Maggie forces open her eyes again, sniffs, then blinks in surprise.

"Yeah, coffee - and still warm. Take a sip Maggie, go on, you know how much you like your coffee."

Maggie takes a tentative sip. Then pulls another face.

"It is coffee, Maggie. Really. Try to focus on the flavour." Peter puts his head to one side
Maggie shakes her head.

"Eurgh, no sugar!"
Peter laughs and folds his arms around her.

"Keep those eyes open. Now, what can you feel?"

"I feel *you,* Peter, and I smell you, and the floor is cold and I want that coffee, with sugar, now."

The little group all smile with relief. Peter helps Maggie to her feet and hugs her.

"Now, let's get you changed and go and get you a fresh hot coffee with sugar and then…"

"You should probably go home to bed…" suggests Janet, trying to be helpful. But Peter speaks over her hurriedly, with an emphatic shake of his head in her direction.

"And then you are going to come to the evening life class and draw me the most detailed study of your life."

Janet looks mystified. Peter gives her a look that indicates he knows what he is doing, and assuring Maggie he is just out in the corridor, leaves Sarah and Summer to help Maggie back into her dungarees, which are still in a pile on top of her bag on the washroom floor.

Out in the corridor, Peter questions Roger sternly. What had happened? What had he done to upset Maggie like that? Roger has never seen Peter so serious. He is at a loss. She had agreed to model for him, it was all fine, and then he gave her the baby Jesus to hold. She had just lost it. Peter rolls his eyes and puts his face in his hands. For a moment Roger wonders if he is going to hit him. Then Peter drops his hands and reaches out to ruffle Roger's hair, but Roger is flinching away from him. Peter's chagrin is palpable. He apologises profusely. *Of course, Roger was not to know. It has all been a bit difficult.* At that moment, the doors to the washroom open and Maggie steps out with Sarah and Summer. She looks at Roger, who returns the look with a sheepish grin.

"Not much of a Madonna, am I now?" she smiles sadly, handing him back the clothes.

"Maggie, you are the only Madonna there will ever be for me," he replies with gentle gallantry, "even if I never do get to immortalise that face in paint."

"How did you do that, the other day?" Janet spots Peter sitting in the Staff club the following Monday, and decides not to beat around the bush. She is mindful of her client's confidentiality, so has given a lot of thought to how she will approach Peter about what happened, without inadvertently betraying Maggie's confidence.

Peter looks up from his crossword. He purses his lips and invites Janet to join him. The lunchtime crush has cleared, and there is no one sitting close enough to overhear their conversation. Peter chooses his words carefully.

"She has not told me the particulars, but this isn't the first time that this has happened to Maggie and I recognise trauma flashbacks when I see them. You might say I have some experience in the area."

Janet looks into his face searchingly. She does not want to be intrusive, yet she is itching to understand what Peter did and the rationale behind it.

"The way you dealt with it was very impressive, demonstrated expertise, even," she says slowly. "I attended a seminar on trauma as part of my counselling training, but I didn't have a clue what to do."

Peter places his elbows on the table, clasps his hands together and chews his thumbs in thought.

"As you may have guessed, I am old enough to have had the dubious honour of having served in World War II. I had won a scholarship to the Royal College of Art and was called up at the start of the second year. I was offered a commission as a war artist, as were many of my colleagues at the time. People don't often realise, but we were often right on the front line. We were the witnesses. A good few of us paid with our lives or limbs for the privilege. I guess I was one of the lucky ones. My injuries were only psychological."

He glances at Janet. She nods, she wants to hear more.

"I was at Anzio towards the end of the war. I wasn't prepared for the sheer horror – none of us were. But it's not just the sights; it's the smells, the sounds, what you feel in your body. It all comes back in a flashback and feels just as real and vivid as it did at the time. I guess a bit was understood about Shell Shock, or Post Traumatic Stress as it is known now, from the Great War. But most of us had to work it out for ourselves and support each other, as best we could. The flashbacks are memories but are experienced as happening in the moment. Closing your eyes, blocking your ears and shutting out the world only makes them all the more powerful. You have to concentrate on what is currently going on and register where you really are, using all your senses. If you can manage that, you can recognise that, as real as they seem, they are just memory. Easier said than done, I know. Even the recall of injury and terrible pain can feel very real and immediate in a flashback."

Janet looks thoughtful.

"So, you got her to focus on her senses to pull Maggie back into the here and now?"

"Something like that. All people want to do is curl up, screw up their eyes - naturally, but it is the worst thing you can do. It helps if there is someone who can encourage you though. Much more difficult when you are alone, and in your sleep, of course…"

Peter falls silent. Janet gives it a moment, then asks,

"And I guess talking about it can trigger it off?"

"Sure," replies Peter," but more often it is the unexpected things, smells, noises. The truth of it is, talking helps. It helps you feel less alone with it, which is why I suggested Maggie came to see you. But you need someone who is outside of your life, or who has been through a similar thing. I don't know the details with Maggie, and I don't need to know, unless or until she particularly wants me to. We, people of my generation who went through the war, we rarely talk of it to others who did not. It is a way of keeping it separate, but when I was recovering, talking to each other was how we learned to manage it."

Janet smiles a little smile. Peter had quite skilfully let her know that she might be the only person who currently knew what Maggie had been through.

"Maggie's a remarkable woman," she says.

"I guess I had already figured that one out."

"Well, I had better get going now". Janet looks at her watch and rises to her feet.

"Janet?"

"Hmmm?"

"Maybe it is not my place to say, but well, I think your support is making a real difference, don't think it isn't."

"Thank you, Peter. I do appreciate that. And I sincerely appreciate what you have shared with me, today."

Peter watches Janet as she leaves, then turns back to his crossword. He is in no hurry to move. Old scars can smart, even when they appear, to all the world, to have fully healed.

July 1982

It is the long-awaited night of the opening of the third years' final show. Two weeks earlier, Maggie and her fellow first years, had found themselves unceremoniously evicted from their usual workspaces, so that the third years can take over the whole of the fourth-floor to set up their degree examination exhibitions. Not that their study was to be interrupted. Far from it. All sixteen of the first years had been exiled to an enormous and vacant studio space in a disused warehouse in Wapping. It was an area that had become increasingly popular with down-at-heels artists in recent years, for rents were cheap and availability of floorspace seemingly endless.

When they had heard the news, Maggie and her peers had felt a thrill of excitement and had congratulated themselves on having the opportunity to be out in the real world, amongst real artists. But for Maggie at least, the feeling was to be short-lived.

The first years had been gathered together that first morning and briefed about the expectations and ground rules for the next two weeks. The assignment, as one might imagine, had been to capture the flavour and spirit of the local area in charcoal and paint. The students were to make studies in situ and produce a painting by the end of the fortnight. It was an opportunity to work *en plein air,* with all the challenges that might bring.

It had been with her characteristic enthusiasm that Maggie set out for the day with her fold-up stool and sketching materials, in search of inspiration. To begin with, she had made her way upriver along the embankment, eyes wide with fascination. Thirty minutes later, however, the alacrity was already beginning to drain from her step. She began to feel increasingly appalled by the bleakness of the disused docks and run-down wharves that dominate a wasteland so fallen into neglect, she could smell only hopelessness in the decay of rusting oil drums and rotting garbage that pervaded the river air.

Little by little, as she trudged on, she felt the bleakness of the place begin to oppress her very soul. For the first time since she had left Ireland, she found herself yearning for the greenness of the trees and meadows of her homeland and longing for the scent of the spring rain on the peaty soil. She told herself that there was plenty to find of visual interest, even if she did not find it attractive personally, but she was not convincing anyone. Eventually, she had settled on a spot that seemed as good, or as awful, as any other and opened her sketchbook.

The first day had dragged past and she had not looked forward to the next day, let alone an entire fortnight. The weather had not helped, unusually damp and cold for the last two weeks in June, she had seemed to spend an infinity huddled uncomfortably over her sketchbook, with very little to show for it.

She had even started to feel apprehensive of the denizens that roamed that forsaken place, rattled by the blankness in their looks and roughness in their voices. Soon, even the dereliction of the deserted structures seemed to menace her with the vacant eyes of their long-shattered windows. She felt herself an unwelcome voyeur, a pretentious poseur with her paintbrushes and fancy ideas; a tourist in the badlands of despair.

Every evening for the last two weeks, she had breathed a sigh of relief when, at last, she has been able to shut her front door in the Peabody building or let herself into Peter's new flat and the welcoming attentions of Stan and Ollie, and of course Peter. Then every morning, she had had to steel herself anew for the day to come, to battle with a slowly growing conviction that her new life was nothing but a sham, a fake. She may have thought she had found a purpose, some self-belief, but it was just a shiny trinket in a mire of meaninglessness. It had looked real enough, but it was worthless.

For the last week, Maggie had struggled desperately to counter the increasing negativity of her thoughts, yet had seen an expression of concern forming in Peter' eyes. She wondered if despondency might be contagious? A cancer that feeds on misfortune and futility. Perhaps she was not, after all, as immune to its ravages as she had started to believe.

But, tonight is different. And what a relief. To Maggie, it seems as though she has emerged from some underworld labyrinth to find herself in daylight once more. She relishes the excitement of sharing her friends' graduation celebration, and besides, they have all dressed up for the occasion. Sarah dazzles in a beaded and sequinned 1960s top and slacks with a beehive hairdo. Summer wears a floating chiffon gown that might have come straight out of Biba, complete with a feather boa. Roger and Tony have both managed to get their hands on dinner jackets and bow ties. Maggie cannot help but smile with delight. Sure, they look like a pair of young film stars. Even Peter has forsaken his beloved fisherman's jersey, for a Liberty print floral shirt and is looking just adorable. Maggie wears a tiered black velvet cocktail dress, a treasure that she discovered in the little second-hand shop in Sicilian Avenue. She has also splashed out on a pair of kitten-heeled slingbacks and paste diamante earrings, that remind her of little chandeliers. Peter can hardly take his eyes off her.

They greet each other with kisses and gasps of admiration when they all meet up in the Louise for a pre-show drink, and thankfully, Wapping suddenly seems a million miles away. Maggie has bought a corsage or buttonhole of lily of the valley and violets for each of her friends, which she solemnly presents, and they are ready. They all link arms and head off over the road to the exhibition.

Five minutes later, as they tumble out of the lift together with excited laughs, the fourth floor is already filling up. The exhibiting artists rush off to man their spaces, while Maggie and Peter make their way along the corridor, examining and admiring the paintings that line every spare section of wall. She knows many of these pieces of work well, having witnessed them perched on easels, taking form over the last year. Yet mounted in frames and hung on pristinely painted walls, they seem as fresh and new as any exhibition she has visited. The illumination from the overhead skylights seems just perfect. Maggie squeezes Peter's arm, feeling blessed just to be herself, right here, right now. Everything really is going to be alright.

Halfway down the corridor, they come to the room where Roger is exhibiting. A card on the door indicates his name and an acknowledgement that his work has been awarded a first-class honours degree. Maggie's heart turns a little somersault of euphoria on Roger's behalf. She steps in, drinking in the colours and forms that are almost as familiar to her as her own work. She raises an upright thumb in approval to Roger, who is talking to a small group of people, who have gathered around him, then stops open-mouthed. There, in the central position of his exhibition, a luminous Madonna looks out of the picture frame, from amid a bower of cornflowers. In her arms, where the infant Christ should lie, she cradles instead a bouquet of pale peonies, whilst about her eyes and lips there dances an expression of exquisite sadness. The colours are as rich and soft as petals, and the face, as lovely as any flower, is unmistakably Maggie's; the almond green eyes and thin soft lips, the soft waves of auburn hair.

Maggie squints at the painting and shakes her head in puzzlement. She glances at Peter, then back at the painting. Roger, having registered her arrival, rushes to her side. His face is its very own picture of apprehension. But his fears are ungrounded. Maggie is thrilled to bits. A glistening tear trickles down her face, and she kisses Roger on the cheek. Roger turns crimson. *He had not needed to have Maggie in front of him, to paint her, for her image is as familiar to him as his reflection.* This time, it is Maggie's turn to blush. Roger takes her hand and kisses it. He looks as though he will burst with pride. Peter winks at him. He notices out loud that there is a red spot beneath the painting: it has already found a buyer. Maggie, a little sad, embraces Roger in congratulation. Roger nudges her and nods his head towards Peter. The penny drops. Maggie flings her arms around Peter. How can one woman contain so much happiness?

Peter looks into Maggie's face and shakes his head. If there was never such a moment like this in all the rest of his life, you would not hear him complain, for this would be enough.

Dusk begins to fall, subtly deepening the hues of the paintings all around so that the colours glow richer still in the failing light. Maggie and Peter complete the tour, spending time with Summer, Sarah and Tony, whose parents proudly introduce themselves, shaking hands and handing out glasses of champagne.

Maggie watches the joy of these little family interactions and all at once realises how young her friends are still. She feels a sudden stab of loss for her own dear Daddy. She consoles herself with the thought that she will at least have Kathleen and Yvonne and, God willing, her own Peter to share her achievement when it is her turn in another two years. But how she would have loved for him to be there. She wonders if he is watching from Heaven and smiles ruefully.

Such bitter-sweet reflections already, and the evening is by no means over. Once the initial bustle has died down a little, Peter whispers something in Maggie's ear and guides her down along the corridor towards the door of a broom cupboard, near the service-lift foyer. Maggie looks at Peter askance, but he just places his finger on his lips, furtively opens the door and pulls her in behind him, fumbling for the light switch as he closes the door behind them. The brightness of the naked lightbulb illuminates the front of the storeroom, throwing into relief a collection of mops and buckets, brooms and replacement rolls of paper towelling. Maggie giggles, despite some measure of puzzlement; she had not thought Peter in a particularly amorous mood this evening, and without wanting to be a killjoy is never-the-less thinking they are a little too old for this kind of thing. Peter looks earnestly into her eyes and winks.

"Maggie, there is something I want to show you."

In the meantime, down on the floor below, Fate is up to mischief of its own. Looking at her watch in dismay, Janet is tugging impatiently at Jack's arm. He has been waylaid by the attraction of the industrial design exhibition on the third floor. Not naturally interested in the fine arts, the precision draughtsmanship of blueprints, mock-up models and prototypes for ingenious gadgets that he might well see in his vacuum cleaner or fridge next year, is much more his cup of tea. They have dinner reservations for 7.30 pm and still have to get around the Painting and Print exhibition upstairs. She reminds him that the exhibition will be on all week if he is genuinely that interested, but right now she needs to show her face in the painting department, even if it is only for ten minutes. Jack complies obediently, he understands the call of duty. He has already taken in as many sculptures, ceramics and textile exhibits as one man can reasonably be expected to cope with in one evening, but if this is important to Janet then it is important to him, too.

The pair ascend the stairs up to the fourth floor, to be greeted by one of the senior lecturers, who nods at Janet and thanks her for her support for the students over the last twelve months. Janet receives the thanks with an appreciative smile. The role of college counsellor can feel rather solitary at times and though there is plenty of interest and variety in the work, she misses the collegial environment of a school staff room. The staff at Central are friendly enough, but the singularity of her occupation inevitably sets her a little apart from the other academic staff. Yet it is clear how popular she is with the students, who have almost all had cause to visit her little office at some time over the last twelve months. Jack notices that she is greeted with happy nods of acknowledgement at nearly every exhibition space they pass through, as Janet calls out her congratulations, and occasionally warmly shakes the hands of parents, to whom she is enthusiastically introduced. Jack finds himself wandering around in a bit of a daze. Modern art has never made much sense to him, and he is left feeling like someone who has not "got the joke."

The canvases are all starting to become a bit of blur to him when suddenly he turns into a studio halfway up the corridor. His heart almost stops inside his chest. Directly before him hangs a stunning painting of The Madonna. His head starts to swim. There is something about the face, so beatific, so sad, and yet so familiar. Even the colours put him in mind of Ireland. He notes the peonies in her empty arms and feels a pang of grief deep within his heart. He peers more closely at the delicate features. All at once, the room seems very small and stuffy in heat of the summer evening, yet his hands and feet feel icy cold. Janet appears by his side and takes his arm.

"Why Jack, whatever is the matter? You look as though you have just seen a ghost."

Jack rubs his brow and asks if they can just get out of there now; *maybe it is the heat, maybe it is his blood sugar, he skipped lunch today.* Janet is all understanding and apologies. *Of course, they can go now. She has done her bit.* Then the painting catches her eye. She recognises the face instantly, but cannot make the connection. She looks at Jack anxiously. The Madonna. That might be it. Perhaps the painting serves as an uncomfortable reminder of his past. A past he still never really talks about or shares. She takes him by the arm.

"I don't know about you, but I could eat a horse."
Jack laughs. One of the things that he loves about Janet is that she never picks at her food, as some women do. Indeed, he sometimes wonders where she puts it all and often teases her that her legs must be hollow. They make their way down the great staircase, laughing as Jack ribs Janet about her famous appetite, but their hilarity is slightly forced. The truth is, both of them are struggling to push their thoughts about the painting to the back of their mind. Struggling and failing.

Back in the broom cupboard, Peter had grinned and indicated a small staircase, hidden in the shadow at the far end of the storeroom. Maggie's eyes had widened in surprise. It seemed, for all intents and purposes, to lead up through the very ceiling itself.

"This is very secret and strictly out of bounds," Peter had breathed, "but then, after all, this a very special night."
He had led Maggie up the little stairs then pushed down on the bar of the fire-escape door at the top, opening it outwards. Taking Maggie by the hand, he had ushered her onto the flat lead-lined roof of the old building and into the cool evening air. They had stood together in silence. Maggie had shaken her head in awe. From this high up they had a panoramic view of the lights of the City and beyond, and Maggie had felt as though she had truly seen London for the first time. She had walked its streets for nigh on three years

and had never really understood what all the fuss was about. Now, at last, she had got it. And suddenly it had felt like her home, her city.

A slight chill is descending. Peter removes his jacket and places it around Maggie's shoulders. She had remained planted to the spot like a statue, willing the moment to last forever. Now, she nods her thanks, lets out a long sigh and casts her eyes around. Ahead of her, the roof follows the singular quadrangle design with which she is so familiar from the interior. Clutching the jacket to her, she makes her way carefully to the edge, where a shallow parapet serves as the only guard to the lip. The air seems eerily still, despite the dampened sound of traffic and taxi horns below. Peering over, she can see the great glass dome of the ground floor exhibition hall below, lit up like some fairy-tale ballroom. She exclaims in delight. Peter laughs and beckons her over to the other side of the roof and points down towards the river. Maggie giggles in delight. From here the little boats and party cruisers appear like toys, while the glow of the red tail lights of the traffic, as it crosses the bridges, glow like rubies. Maggie recognises the neon signs of The Southbank and grins. It is all so pretty.

Peter places one arm around her waist then makes a sweeping gesture with his other hand.

"I know you have a couple of years to go before it is *your* night, Maggie. But I wanted to show you this, because, one day, I believe that you will have the world at your feet. I honestly do. You have a great talent Maggie, and well, I know the art world, and I can guide you through it. If you'll let me."

"And all I have to do is worship you, is that it?" smiles Maggie, her words half playful, half wistful.

"Well, I don't know about worship - just love me, I guess," jokes Peter, kissing her forehead.

"And I suppose if I was to be casting myself off the edge here, the angels would be gathering around to save me, now?" whispers Maggie. But the playfulness has gone from her voice leaving only a sadness that causes Peter to step back and draw her further away from the yawning drop.

He looks into her face, then holds her close.

"Let me be the one to catch you, Maggie, I'll always be there if you'll have me."

Maggie rouses herself to rescue the mood;

"Sure, there is an offer so tempting, 'tis impossible to resist, so it is."

Jack's peace of mind lies in shreds. The image of Roger's enigmatic Madonna hangs before his eyes for the rest of the evening and haunts his dreams throughout the broken sleep of his night.

Janet, too, finds herself tossing and turning and it is the same image that fills her head. She remembers all too well the trauma of the afternoon Roger had asked Maggie to sit for him. Surely, he had not gone ahead and painted the image without her knowledge? Maggie had certainly not mentioned it since. Janet is concerned. Now she comes to think of it, she had not seen Maggie at the Opening. She knows that the little group of friends are thick as thieves, even though Maggie is only in the first year. Could it be that Maggie had seen the painting and had had to leave? Yet Roger seemed in buoyant enough spirits, and she knows him sufficiently well to know he could not be so, if his friend was in distress. Janet plumps up her pillow, which is full of lumps tonight. She guesses she will get to the bottom of it soon enough.

In another corner of the city, Maggie also struggles to find sleep. She, Peter and the Gang had all repaired to the Louise for drinks after the show and now she is regretting having so thoughtlessly mixed the grape with the grain. But it is more than the alcohol that is keeping her awake. She keeps going over the things that Peter had said in her mind. Could it be true? Might she truly have such a bright future as a painter? She has the passion and commitment; she knows that well enough. Yet, is she truly deserving of success? Indeed, does she even deserve a man like Peter, for that matter? What might he really think if he knew what she was, what she had done? She struggles with the wish to confess all, but Peter neither is nor wishes to be, her confessor. He has made that very clear. But how can he ever really know her, if the secrets of her sorrows lie locked away?

The following Thursday, Jack has a free period at the end of the day, so slips away and takes the underground into Holborn. He knows he is taking a gamble and perhaps even a risk, but the question mark hanging over the Madonna will not let him be. The exhibition closes tomorrow. This will be his last chance. He looks distractedly around the tube carriage. So many faces, so many souls in this great metropolis. Perhaps it is just a coincidental resemblance. Yet Frank had been sure Maggie was probably still on the mainland, so he had. He simply cannot let it pass.

The entrance of the Art School is open to welcome visitors to the exhibition, so there is nothing amiss with a stranger wandering in off the street, indeed the doorman favours him with a polite nod and some comment on the weather, by way of a welcome. *What is with the English and the weather?* wonders Jack, still a stranger in a strange land.

He hastens up the great staircases, mouthing a silent prayer that he will not bump into Janet, although if he does, he has already rehearsed his excuse; he had been able to get away from school early, so had decided to surprise her with an offer of a movie in Leicester Square and was just taking another look at the exhibitions before the end of her working day. He is trembling never-the-less. What if the artist is not around, and he has to leave non-the-wiser? He is playing a long shot, at best. But he is in luck. He ambles, as nonchalantly as he can, towards the studio, in which he had seen the painting, then pauses. He hears voices. Peering around the door he sees the slight looking lad, whose name he recalls as Roger, gesturing to the wall of images, amongst which the Madonna hangs. He is talking with proud animation to a small group of visitors.

Jack tries to be patient. He waits a while until the little group shuffles off along to the next space. He takes a deep breath while Roger takes a seat and opens a little book, he has had in his pocket. Jack approaches and coughs quietly. Roger looks up from his notebook and smiles. Jack congratulates the artist on his achievement and work. Roger smiles still more. Jack tries to sound casually conversational. He is very interested in the beautiful painting of The Madonna, being Irish and all, and wonders where the artist might have found such a face, for surely this one was enough to make Raphael himself weep. Jack, of course, could not have more effectively hit the mark, if he had made a personal study of Roger, who grins with delight, and thus resolves to tell the whole story, as it had unfolded. He turns the pages of the little notebook he has been studying and holds up the sketch he had made of a complete stranger in a pub, just over the road, some two years ago. Jack stares at the little sketch transfixed. He fights his impatience to demand the woman's name, enquire where she is now, but knows he must maintain the façade of idle curiosity, lest he betray an interest that would take some explaining away. Roger has started to relate how the woman had confronted him about drawing her without her permission, when there is an exclamation from the doorway to the studio.

"Why, Jack! What on Earth are you doing here at this time of the day?"

Janet has popped up to the fourth floor in search of a third-year who had put their name on her appointment booking-sheet, then failed to show up. Her keen eyes cannot fail to notice the look on Jack's face as he turns to see her and it is not the look of pleasure she anticipated. Her stomach knots uncomfortably. Jack tries to cover his confusion with his rehearsed lines, but his manner is closed and falsely bright. He walks over to Janet with a nod to Roger who returns to flicking through the pages of his notebook, sorry for the loss of an audience for his story. Janet catches him glancing briefly over his shoulder to the painting. There is an expression in his eyes she cannot read. She pecks his cheek but knits her brows with a misgiving she is unable to name.

Janet chats cheerfully enough about which film they might choose to see as she leads him down to her little office on the ground floor, but her thoughts are far from carefree. And she would be unable to tell you the name of the film they do finally plump for, scarcely taking in the celluloid images that flicker across the screen. She barely responds when Jack's fingers search for her own. She is unable to stop herself ruminating upon some of her counselling sessions with Maggie. Dismissing it as paranoia herself, the poor woman had nevertheless struggled to let go of the idea that The Vatican might, even now, be keeping tabs on her.

Janet fidgets in her seat. What if she was right? The doubt bites at her like a persistent gnat. She tries to bat it away. Surely, she is being ridiculous. The whole idea is preposterous. But Jack is from Southern Ireland, just as Maggie is, and although no longer a priest, used to be one. And he does seem to be unusually interested in the painting. What exactly does she know about him, when she thinks about it? He has certainly never been very forthcoming about his past, but then, to be fair, she has never shown much curiosity about it. Not that she has not *felt* curious, quite the opposite, in fact; there has always been a million questions she would love to have asked, but there is a privateness about the life of a priest that demands respect. Perhaps it is her catholic upbringing. Then again, look at how she messed up when Jack had attempted to share something about his past. Janet blushes with the shame at the memory of it and if she could go back in time and change it, she would. As it is, something deep inside tells her that she failed some kind of test that day and it may be a long time before Jack is ready to trust her enough to try again. Perhaps it is easier to see him as part of a conspiracy, than admit to her own failings. Goodness, *there* is an insight. Bernard would be proud of her.

Jack meanwhile fairs no better. He feels angry with Janet, which he knows is wholly unfair. He senses she can feel it, though he is trying his best to conceal it. She all but withdraws her hand when he tries to hold it and seems preoccupied all the way home, although no more so than he is. They are hardly talking by the time they retire to bed, each bound by secrets and confidences that cannot be broken; each tortured by regret and self-doubt.

The next morning, when she sees Jack all bleary eyes and familiar in his little domestic routine, Janet wonders how she could have entertained such a catastrophic loss of perspective. Jack is no Vatican spy, even if he is a closed book when it comes to the past. Doubtless, her first instinct, that the painting had triggered painful or perhaps even cherished memories, was closer to the truth. Given the aloofness of her response to what may have been a difficult moment for him, small wonder the man cannot talk to her. She apologises for being such a grouch. Now, she is *sure* Bernard would be proud of her.

Jack too, despite his frustration at having been thwarted in his detective work, is all apology. He does sometimes wonder how Janet can put up with his taciturnity, yet, priests as confessors are habituated to bearing the burden of other people's secrets, and it sits naturally with him. And as a counsellor herself, Janet must surely have an appreciation of this. The story of Margaret Doyle and her angelic infant is not truly his to share, though he had his part in it right enough. There is no escaping it. Yet, he cannot deny that shame plays a large part in his silence. He failed her back then, the least he can do now is to protect her from judgement and speculation now. And who would believe it anyway? Wherever she might be, Jack is pretty sure that the authority of rational secularism will have stamped its scepticism on Margaret's fate. And would Janet's reaction be so very different, even if he were at liberty to tell her? She would likely put it down to some manifestation of hysteria or some other mental aberration. But he had been there and he knew the truth. It was no good. Jack had made his bed when he left for Liverpool. Perhaps, in the end, his penance is having the leisure to acknowledge the enormity of his failings, with no prospect of any opportunity to make reparation. The painting has proved to be a timely tormentor, a tantalising reminder that there will be no absolution for him. Perhaps Frank is right, absolved or not, he has a new life, he just has to get on with it.

Term is nearly over. Perhaps the summer holidays will be as good a place to start as any.

September 1982

Monday morning. The little clock on the bedside cabinet sounds its discourteous alarm. Summer, it seems, is over. Janet nudges Jack and gently reminds him that they have to get up for work. He laughs. *No more lie-ins then*? Janet rubs his back as he sits on the edge of the mattress and stretches. He turns and smiles into her eyes. There! There it is. The closeness for which she had so long yearned. Who would have thought it?

Six months ago, if you had suggested a two-week camping holiday in Cornwall with Jill and Jim, Janet would have laughed in your face. Even as recently as Easter, she would have predicted that it would more than likely end in a falling out of seismic proportions. As it was, it had taken a vast quantity of alcohol and friendly persuasion to get her to agree to the scheme at all, with Jim promising to be on his absolute best behaviour and Jack offering to do all the cooking. Yet, Janet could hardly remember a happier fortnight in her whole life. In her childhood, family holidays had been fraught with her parent's marital tensions and Janet had spent most of the time alone, trying to keep out of the line of fire. She had loathed the idea of holidays ever since. But they had had such fun, riding bicycles, messing around in rock pools, lazing on the beach eating ice-cream, and sitting up late singing songs around a campfire. She had felt like a kid out of an Enid Blyton book and joked happily that The 4Js had now become the Famous Four. She had also had the pleasure of seeing another more playful side of Jack. Like it or not, she had to admit that Jim brought out the best in him, and the best in Jack brings out the best in her.

Janet yawns, reluctant to let go of the warmness of the memory just yet, but the clock is ticking.

"How about we eat out tonight, to commiserate?" suggests Jack, as he returns from the shower. He is still deeply tanned, and if nothing else the weekly training at the Boxing Club has rewarded him with a physique of a man ten years his junior. How handsome he looks, thinks Janet with a little thrill that not even the prospect of the underground commute to work can diminish. A meal out does indeed sound likes the perfect antidote to the back to work blues.

"I was wondering whether, well - if we should, you know, buy a flat, or even a little house, together?"

Jack has taken Janet's hand from across the table as they wait for coffee after the meal at their favourite Curry House. Janet does not reply. The proposition has taken her by surprise. She should be feeling over the moon, yet she wrestles with her own reaction.

"Well, we both have a steady income now," Jack continues. "My contract is permanent and the prospects seem pretty positive for me at St James's. Especially with the

Boxing Club and everything - Why Janet, whatever is the matter?"

There are tears pooling in the corner of Janet's eyes and she is holding her free hand to her mouth.

"I'm so sorry Jack. I know you will think I am pathetic..." She turns her head away.

Jack squeezes her hand.

"No, please, tell me what it is. I thought you would want..."

"It's not that, Jack. Of course, I do, of course, I have dreamt of making a home with you. It's just that - oh, to Hell with it. I just always wanted to get, well, married. There - I have said it. The thing that women are not meant to say until they are asked. I am so sorry. No wait, actually I'm not. I did, I mean, I do. Want us to get married, I mean. It is nothing to be ashamed of."

There is a pause. The waiter sets down two cups of coffee, bows his head and departs.

"Say something, please!" Janet pleads.

Jack scratches his head. He tries to make her understand. *It is not that simple. He was a priest and under canon law, a man who has been ordained remains so, even if he has been laicized. Technically he is supposed to remain celibate, but more specifically he cannot be married - ever, or if he is, the marriage can never be recognised by the Holy Roman Church. Once a priest always a priest.*

Janet meets his eyes, shakes her head. "But what about applying for a special dispensation from the Pope? Surely you can do that?"

"Janet, Darling. Sure, it is not that I do not want to. But it is not possible and that is a fact. That kind of dispensation is extremely rare. And besides...'"

Jack falls silent and stares into his coffee.

"Besides what...?"

"Besides, I have never formally applied to renounce my clerical state." He speaks the last words so quietly that Janet has to strain to catch them.

"Jack, you have lost me. What does that mean?"

"It means - officially I am still a member of the clergy. I am still a priest."

Jack covers his eyes. He cannot look at Janet.

Janet's head is swimming. She struggles to withstand the tidal wave of thoughts and emotions that is crashing through her mind from all sides. She does not know whether to laugh, shout, cry or just run out of the restaurant. In the end, she just pulls away her hand and stares mutely into her coffee.

"I wouldn't blame you if you never wanted to see me again, so I wouldn't," says Jack in a small voice, "it is just that I, well it was all such a Goddamn mess. I never meant to hurt you. Christ, I never meant to *fall in love…*"

"Oh, Jack!" Janet's face lights up and this time it is *she* who reaches across the white linen tablecloth to squeeze *his* fingers. "You've never said …" She stops herself and dabs her eyes with her napkin. "Look, if I love you and you love me, then so long as we can just be together, I don't care about the rest of it. Truly I don't."

Autumn

It has been a glorious summer for Maggie, too. Peter had taken her to stay at his friends' old farmhouse in Provence for the summer, where they had both received the warmest of welcomes. The days had been filled with bread, olives, sunshine and wine, and there were moments, lying on her back beneath the poplars and immense cerulean vault of southern French skies, Peter's head cradled in her lap, when Maggie believed she might truly be in heaven. *It reminded her of Ireland, only without the rain,* she had joked. Jest or not, the sparkling luminosity of the countryside seemed at times almost to infuse her very being, brightening her eyes and finding its way into the colours of her paintings.

Midway through their stay, Annie and Neil, Peter's daughter and son-in-law had turned up. With flushed cheeks, Annie announced that she was expecting a Christmas baby. Peter had been thrilled at the prospect of becoming a grandfather and had laughed soundly at the prospect of being called 'Grandpa'. Annie had adored Maggie from the moment they met. She had accepted the break-up of her parents' marriage with sad resignation, it seemed hardly unexpected and Maggie could scarcely be held to blame. Besides, this gentle little Irish woman had made her father happier than she had seen him for many a year. She opened her already overflowing heart to Maggie, for you can always find room for a little more love. Maggie, in turn, had positively glowed with pleasure at the prospect of becoming a step-mother, be it ever so late in life. She had a feeling that Annie and she would become fast friends, and her intuition in such matters seldom led her astray.

Yet, day by day, Maggie's uneasiness and sense of unworthiness had seemed almost to increase in proportion to her happiness. It would catch up with her at the most unlikely moments and all but snatch the breath from her lungs.

Choosing a baguette from the local boulangerie or laughing at a joke over a long and lazy dinner, the accusing voices in her head would start to whisper, questioning her right even to sit amongst such virtuous people. She had blood on her hands. She was a tarred black sheep among the snow-white lambs, and the truth will always out. At such times, Maggie began to slip away and wash her hands repeatedly in a bid to still the clamour of her self-accusations, until she was obliged to renew her acquaintance with the Lady of Shalott, a lady she had hoped to have left behind. At such times, Peter would notice her absence and the redness of fingers, and she, in turn, could see the helpless sadness written all over his face. Maggie would brush it off as a momentary setback, but her past was becoming an unacknowledged chasm between. It was a chasm that yawned wider every day.

Back in London, at the start of a new term and her second year, Maggie places her name on Janet's appointment booking list. She is already missing The Gang and feels all at once alone. She reminds herself that she can easily pop in and see Roger down the Road at the Royal Academy of Art, where he is commencing his MA. But it won't be the same. The problem is, bereft of the shared concerns that used to preoccupy them all, she has too much time to think.

"I am thinking that I ought to tell Peter the whole story, so I am ..." Maggie looks into Janet's face to read the reaction, but Janet is well practised in maintaining neutrality. Maggie looks away, examining her hands in sorrow. Janet's eyes flick to the clock. It is getting close to the end of the session. Janet feels a momentary concern that Maggie has left it so late to broach such a major consideration.

"Could we think about that for a moment, Maggie? Do you mean that you feel morally obligated, or is it an emotional need, or do you feel, for that matter, that Peter somehow needs you to?"

She has hit the nail, partially if not squarely, on the head.

"Peter does not need me to, but I think he needs me to feel happy."

"And you don't?"

"Yes, yes, I do. That is the problem". Maggie is suddenly tearful. "I am happy, but I'm not at all sure that I deserve to be."

"And how will telling Peter change that?" Janet's tone is measured, curious, but making no demands.

Maggie shakes her head in confusion. "I don't know. I know Peter would understand, so he would, and he wouldn't think I owe him any explanation. But he wants to know me, I mean *really know* me, and, there's no denying, it is a big part of who I am."

"Maggie," Janet chooses her words with care, "It may be true that you *are* the person you are, because of the things you have been through. But that *is* the person Peter knows and that *is* the person he loves. Knowing your history will not change *you*."

Maggie looks at her hands. Janet must have noticed how red they have become again. She folds them together and shifts uneasily in her chair. She is still shaking her head.

"I think he deserves the truth," she says in a low voice.

The two of them sit completely quiet for a minute, each struggling with their private thoughts. It is Janet who breaks the silence.

"Maggie, can I just check this out with you? I think that you are still having difficulty forgiving yourself..." she holds up her hand, as Maggie starts to speak. "Please, let me finish. It is not up to me to tell you whether to share your past with Peter or not, but if you are thinking that you should do such a thing before *you* have forgiven *yourself*, then, well, I do have to wonder about the motive".

Maggie stares at Janet a moment. She squeezes her forehead between her fingers.

"You think I am looking to be punished - that I *want* him to reject me?"

Janet shrugs her shoulders questioningly.

"Do you think that could be part of it, Maggie?"

Maggie's eyes fill with tears.

"Isn't it better to make the worst happen, rather than to live your life fearing it?"

"It seems a rather self-defeating way of maintaining control over what cannot be controlled, if you ask me," sighs Janet. "I guess it is one way. But then so is throwing yourself under a bus!"

She cringes at her unintended flippancy, but Maggie laughs.

"I see what you mean. I guess I do want to feel more in control. Waiting for some kind of retribution is giving me a feeling that my life is like a tower of cards, so it is. Liable to collapse around my ears at any moment. Yet I think you are right, there is a part of me that thinks it is retribution I deserve, and so in some ways, it is a purgatory of my own making."

Janet glances at the time. She hopes she has done enough. She has a sudden sick feeling in her stomach that Maggie may have set herself on a path from which there is no turning back.

"Perhaps we can think a bit more about how to start to forgive yourself, next time?"

Maggie nods. Janet meets her eyes and returns an unspoken acknowledgement. She sighs as Maggie closes the door behind her. She can only do her best, but sometimes it seems to count for so little.

Three weeks later, despite Janet's caution and support, as the anniversary of her loss draws near, Maggie can bear it no longer and tells all to Peter, blurting out the secrets of her past to her lover over lasagne and too much red wine. Peter cannot pretend that he is not shocked. He had of course suspected some bloody trauma lay at the root of Maggie's malaise, but the horror of her act lies outside all imagination and experience. Still, his instinct is to comfort her and offer love and reassurance. He does not judge, he has seen too much of life to see people's motives in terms of black and white, or right and wrong. Neither is he phased by the possibility of her post-partum psychosis. In reality, his vasectomy had been the response to the severity of the post-natal depression Wendy had endured after Annie's birth and his acquaintance with mental illness in those he had called friends during the war had been all too common.

Yet something changes. Something visceral. He sees the masticated body of Maggie's infant in his dreams and the tint of blood on her hands and arms, where he had once only seen paint. Increasingly, he tastes the metallic tang of blood on her lips as he goes to kiss her and draws away despite himself. Though his mind and judgement remain as constant and devoted as ever, it is as if a revulsion, almost independent of conscious thought, has seized his body, like a febrile infection. He is beside himself with sorrow. Maggie hears his expressions of reassurance, but his body language screams at her with a voice louder than any spoken word. She retreats into hurt confusion and ruined heartbreak. The Provence light that had begun to suffuse the darkness of her paintings seems all at once extinguished, and her fellow students feel an involuntary chill whenever they stray into her studio space to ask advice or beg some turpentine or linseed oil.

Peter and Maggie limp on in a miserable imitation of intimacy. Maggie spends increasingly fewer nights at Peter's flat at the Angel, though in fact, the only comfort she finds nowadays is in the unalloyed affection of Stan and Ollie, whose insistent demands for her attention seem driven by a need to offer comfort, where they see none. Peter, in turn, seems to find increasingly frequent reasons not to stay over at Maggie's, though time apart brings no respite. He finds it hard to settle beneath the gaze of the framed Madonna in his sitting room and begins to imagine a look of hurt reproach in the sadness of her painted green eyes. It crosses his mind to take the painting down, but what kind of admission would that be? The world keeps turning, yet the days have become long and joyless. He no longer recognises himself, when he looks at himself in the shaving mirror, each morning. He is not the man he thought he was, and he is beginning to resent Maggie for reflecting this back to him. Yet if he leaves her, what kind of a man does *that* make him?

Finally, Maggie puts them out of their mutual torment and breaks it off. There are no tears, no angry words, just a numb sense of inevitability and relief. Maggie saves her grief for the following morning when she sees Janet.

"I let him go," she states mournfully, "it was the only thing to do, so it was."

Janet feels a pang of anguish she struggles to contain. She feels for Maggie, but there is more to it than just that. It is as though all the Happy Ever Afters from her favourite childhood stories have been revealed as bogus propaganda. *And we just keep buying into it,* she thinks with bitterness, then realises she needs to focus.

"And how are you, Maggie? Is there anyone around for you?"

Maggie blinks back her tears.

"Kathleen insists I go up and stay with them at the weekend, and Roger, you know, he is always there if I need a bit of cheering up, but…"

"But what?"

"I was wondering how I can – that is to say, if I should, transfer to another course? St Martins' or Chelsea maybe?"

Janet is suddenly angry. She reminds herself to take a breath before she speaks. *I should think he is the one who should go* - is what she wants to say, but she catches herself in time.

"No, Maggie, no. I don't think that would be such a good idea. Another big change on top of what you have been through, would certainly not help matters. I know I am not supposed to give advice, but you belong here and you worked so hard to get here, and you have already lost enough. I should think Peter must be due to retire soon anyway. Do you think he might?"

Maggie shrugs. What can she know of Peter's wants and wishes, now?

"Well, I think we can keep out of each other's way. Not that there is any animosity, I almost wish there were. It's just so..." She falters, unable to continue.

"Look Maggie," says Janet firmly," I know that some days I get fully booked up, but anytime you need to talk to me, I can always make a space for you. You just let me know. I mean it."

Maggie nods gratefully. She sighs wistfully.

"Why didn't I listen to you, Janet?"

"Oh Maggie, it is easy to see things more clearly from the outside. Believe me, it is quite another thing when it is your own heart and life. Please, don't beat yourself up about that as well."

A week later, Maggie decides it is time she reached out to a friend.

Roger returns from the bar and places a glass of Irish Whiskey on the coaster in front of Maggie. Their favourite pub is crowded and they were lucky to find a free spot. The grand old Louise seems to become more popular with every passing year. He plumps himself down on the padded velvet stool on the other side of the little round table and sucks the top off his pint of Guinness. Maggie smiles then producing a pocket-handkerchief leans over and dabs away his creamy moustache. Roger submits with the meekness of a child then reddens and starts to wave her away in protest. He wipes his mouth on his sleeve then smooths back his long fringe, glancing around to ensure no one had been observing.

Maggie raises her glass but cannot bring herself to make the familiar toast. She takes a sip then stares down into the fiery depths of the sparkling spirits.

"Is it really over then, Maggs? I always thought the two of you made the perfect couple."

Roger's question might be construed as insensitive coming from anyone but he, but it has always been his directness Maggie finds endearing. Maggie nods sadly. *Perhaps, it was never really meant to be.* Roger screws up his face. He is not of a generation to buy into such fatalist sentiments. Yet, anything he can think of to say seems just as clichéd. They sit in silence until, at last, he finds some words.

"Maggs, I can't tell you how sorry I am."

Not exactly original but spoken from the heart. Maggie smiles sadly and blinks back a tear. Roger wants to know more, but he has known Maggie long enough to respect her privacy. She will talk when she is ready. What she needs now is distraction. He starts to tell her all about his new painting. It is causing quite a stir over at the Royal Academy. Maggie folds her arms and listens to him in quiet enjoyment. As always, his company is just what she needs.

Just behind them, screened by the etched glass of a wall booth, a certain Italian gentleman sits and strains to catch their words. He has dropped by for a flying visit as he is passing through London en-route to Rome from the near-pagan Isles of Scotland. Some joker had claimed to have unearthed the remains of St Oran beneath the foundations of an ancient chapel on Iona. A clumsy bid to attract tourism, no doubt. Cardinal Salvatore had rolled his eyes and sent Vecellio, more as a matter of courtesy than out of any scholarly curiosity. The Vatican's vault already boasts bones enough to reconstruct the hapless Oran three times over, should it so wish. And it harbours not the slightest wish. Besides, it had taken but a cursory glance to determine that the discovery was a fake. Meanwhile, it had been three bleak days out of Vecellio's life, he would never get back. Unsurprisingly, he is not in the most sanguine of moods.

This afternoon, he is the lone occupant of the booth and seems likely to stay that way, even though there are folk enough searching around for seats, drinks in hands. One or two of The Louise's regulars draw near, hover a moment than seem to change their minds, driven away as though by some invisible repellent. Vecellio may possess the skill to lose himself in the shadows but when he wishes to be seen, his brooding presence is more than sufficient to discourage unwelcome company.

He takes a chance and peers around the corner of his hiding place. He catches a full view of Maggie's profile as she follows Roger's exploits, nodding and shaking her head in response to the narrative. Vecellio ducks back and leans heavily against the dimpled leather back of the bench. How thin and sad she looks. She seems half the woman she was the last time he had seen her. The snippets of conversation and her appearance tell it all. She is a woman disappointed in Love.

He sighs. The Cardinal will find gratification in the news, even if no one else will. As for himself – well, what he thinks or feels is of no importance. And yet - and yet, try as he may, Vecellio cannot suppress a simple wish to see that face lit up once again by a smile of happiness.

He shrugs, empties his glass and slips back out into the anonymity of the crowded street. The Cardinal will have to find his pleasure elsewhere. He is in no mood to torment Margaret Doyle today.

December 1982

This will be Janet's second Christmas at Central. She misses the hectic bustle of nativity plays and carol concerts that pervade school life at this time of year but consoles herself with the thought that here at least, her skills are valued. She has made some fledgeling friendships with the teaching staff, who are often glad to bend her ear whenever they become concerned that the inevitable exposure to 'objective criticism' is beginning to take its toll on the more sensitive students. The tearful conclusion to a 'class crit', as it is termed, is no isolated an occurrence and many a personal tutor has had to re-bolster a shattered self-esteem in the aftermath of a disappointing peer review.

Janet, who battles with mild social anxiety at the best of times, has consequently made the effort to attend the staff party in the Central Club on the last Friday of term and is ever so slightly tipsier than she intended, relying a little too heavily upon the liberally provided alcoholic beverages.

Just as she is thinking about taking her leave and heading for home, she spies Peter sidle into the room. She has not seen him for ages and wonders if he has been purposely keeping a low profile since the break-up with Maggie. She notices that he looks gaunt and somewhat older than she remembers. He has lost his characteristic ease and aura of self-possession. She recalls how she had admired his poise that day in the washroom with Maggie, and suddenly she can feel her body tense with indignation. She makes her way through the little groups of affably inebriated staff to where he stands then faces him with a forced smile.

Peter greets her cordially, as though nothing is amiss. He shares the news that he has become just become a grandfather. Janet rewards him with a tight congratulations, then contrary to every sensible promise she has made to herself in the last few weeks, says coldly;

"It's funny, I didn't take you for a coward. And I am usually such a good judge of character."

Peter's face drops like an elevator with a broken cable. For a moment he is unable to speak, or even think. Then he gathers himself and whispers angrily;

"Janet, I think you may have had a little too much to drink."

"On the contrary," retorts Janet, her voice still as cold as the ice on the puddles outside in the frosty night. "I rather think I have had just the right amount."

Peter takes her gently, but firmly, by the elbow and steers her to a quiet corner.

"I think you may be in danger of overstepping your professional boundaries," he hisses angrily, "and I caution you to stop before you go too far…"

Janet is mortified. Even slightly drunk she knows that he is in the right. But there is no turning back.

"I have not revealed any confidences. I - I just..." She bursts into tears. "How could you, Peter? How could you do that to Maggie?"

Peter is suddenly on the verge of tears himself. He places his arms around Janet and holds her tightly to him. Then gently pushing her away from him again, he looks into her face. Janet meets his gaze, sniffling. She does not need an explanation. The anguish of his disappointment in himself is written across Peter's face and needs no translation, no interpretation. There is no bad guy here. Placing a damp cheek to his, she mumbles a seasonal greeting and heads for home.

December 31st 1982

It is New Year's Eve in the country town of St. Albans. The snow that started to fall just before Christmas cloaks the ground like an ermine mantel. The noise from the last few cars and taxis heading to celebrations in the town-centre is dampened by the softness of the sparkling icy carpet underfoot, and the stars above the town wink brightly in the inky winter sky.

Kathleen and Yvonne sit with Maggie in the snug little parlour of their semi-detached house, watching the countdown to the New year on their little colour television set. Yvonne stands with a bottle of champagne wrapped in a tea towel, in readiness for the chimes of Big Ben. The laughter lines around her eyes gather from frequent employment and tonight they crease still more deeply in hopeful anticipation of the New Year.

Kathleen leans across the sofa to hug her little sister, her *little Maggie May,* and Maggie smiles a teary smile. There is something in the happiness of these two women, whose mutual adoration is so obvious, that has been a balm for the sores of her heart, these past two weeks. Maggie almost wishes that she might never have to leave this world of warmth but knows she will soon have to go back out into the cold. The famous old clock strikes mid-night and Yvonne fumbles with the neck of a bottle of champagne, whilst the voices from the T.V sing out Auld Lang Syne. The cork pops joyfully. She fills their glasses and the three of them exchange kisses and Happy New Years' salutations. The bubbles tickle Maggie's nose and she laughs then laughs again to discover that she *can* still laugh. On the TV the dancers of the White Heather club execute an enthusiastic Highland Reel and Vonnie and Kathleen take one another's hands, tapping their feet in time to the music. Maggie smiles and suppresses a yawn. She wonders how long she can reasonably leave it until she can slope off to her bed.

At about ten minutes past midnight, the doorbell rings. Yvonne pulls a face of mystification, but Kathleen exclaims - "First footing!" and totters a little unsteadily to the door. After an exchange of low voices, she returns and announces that the visitor is for Maggie. Maggie looks bewildered. She puts down her glass, smooths her hair then rises from the sofa and makes her way into the little hallway. Huddled on the doorstep, a bottle of whiskey in one hand and a pound of butter in the other, stands Peter.

"I know it supposed to be coal," he begins, "but well this seemed more "us". I am so sorry my darling, darling Maggie. But if you can forgive me, could we please make a new start with a New Year?"

Maggie flings her arms around his neck and bursts into tears. They kiss and Peter does not draw himself back. She kisses him more deeply and feels his body fold hungrily into hers.

"How?" is all she can say.

"It was Annie," whispers Peter. "She has had the baby, Maggie, a little girl, Poppy. She is so beautiful, just like her mother. And it was something she said to me when I went to visit her in the hospital. She told me that becoming a mother had completely changed her. Annie has always been so meek, so mild, but she said that, from the very first moment she had held Poppy in her arms, she had felt as fiercely protective as a *tigress,* a tigress that would do *anything* to save her cub from harm. And I remembered how I had felt when she had been born. That instinctual rush to want to defend this tiny creature, at all costs. And suddenly I understood. I mean, really understood. Please tell me it is not too late."

Just then a jovial exclamation sounds out from within the parlour. It is Kathleen.

"For the love of God, Maggie May, will you not bring the poor man indoors. He'll be catching his death of cold on that doorstep, so he will."

Maggie winks at Peter.

"You'd better be coming in then. That bottle of whiskey'll not be opening itself, now will it, Peter Carmichael?"

Verse 4

Autumn 1983

The glittering days of another Provence summer had slipped through Maggie's fingers like rain dripping from the trembling poplars. It had seemed over, all too soon, and October has come round again, as it inevitably must. Maggie leans back in the battered old armchair she has recently acquired from a local junk shop and draws thoughtfully on her roll-up. Though it is barely five o'clock, the mellow light of the shortening day is already dying, casting indolent shadows across the canvases that cover the walls of her little studio space and causing the oil pigments to gleam with a distinctly autumnal warmth.

Her final year. The time has melted away like the morning mist on the meadows over which she had wandered in her youth. Not for the first time, Maggie wonders if the old life was truly real, yet the pain of her loss remains an ever-constant reminder; a dark sphere of sorrow that threatens to eclipse the brightness of her present happiness.

Even now the butterflies gather in her stomach, for the anniversaries of her Gabriel's birth and death loom on the horizon, immovable and pitiless milestones along the road of passing time; a road she must navigate at her peril. She wonders what he would have been like at five years old, but then pushes the thoughts away. They can bring nothing but pain. This year, at least she will not have to struggle alone with her grief. Peter will be there for her. Funny things anniversaries. In so many ways just another day, yet without our even being aware of it, Grief takes a thick black marker, circles the date on a calendar deep within the psyche, and defies us to overlook it.

Maggie sighs; the moments of happiness she enjoys are the best antidote for enduring sorrows. And the satisfaction of a roll-up at the end of the day always makes it even better.

There are stirrings in the wider space of the room. The inhabitants of the little sectioned off cubicles lay down brushes and charcoal, and prepare to call it a day. Half a dozen of them stop by to make their farewells or to sit awhile, cross-legged in Maggie's space and talk well into the evening, as has become their wont. Maggie cannot deny she has become grateful for the company, though she misses The Gang all the same.

They talk of art, and of painters they admire or detest. They talk of society and its ills and the role of the artist, poet and philosopher. Most of them have hardly outgrown their childhood school uniforms, yet their passion burns with a fierceness that makes Maggie tremble at times, and all too often she finds herself in the role of arbiter and referee. She feels amused by the status to which they appear to have tacitly elected her; a status due, she supposes, to the assumed wisdom of her years. Her modesty certainly forbids that it can be anything else as, for all the catching up of the last three years, most of them have an education that puts her own to shame. Yet she is mistaken, for it is neither her maturity nor her knowledge that sets her apart. Her peers gaze up at the images and canvases around them and shake their heads in admiring submission. Whether they like her paintings or loathe them, Maggie has set the benchmark to which they aspire.

This evening the topic turns, as often it does, to representation versus abstraction. Mark, a Cheshire-cat faced young man with bohemian moustaches and fashionable stubble, is insisting that mere representation, as Plato so persuasively asserts, is pointless, since what we represent is already but a weak copy of an ideal. Nicola, a pretty young woman who wears her hair geisha-style, pinned up by two paintbrushes, accuses him of missing the point. *Artistic representation has nothing to do with copying, it is the use of paint, and the rendering of the three dimensional into the two dimensions of the canvas.* Mark throws up his hands in a gesture of despair. He had heard it all many times before.

"Well, what about Maggie's paintings, then?" Big Rob, the shy Mancunian with a gentle voice and heart, speaks up. His plump face turns the colour of beetroot as he realises Nicola's gaze is upon him.

"I - I mean to say," he stammers, "Maggie dun't depict owt that is in the *real* world, does she, like?"

All eyes now scan the canvases around them, anew. For a moment, Maggie feels more naked than ever she did in the life drawing studio. She blanches slightly. Her peers gaze as though seeing for the first time the fractured revelations of an inner landscape, populated by winged beings of terrible beauty; a conflation of the angelic and demonic, the perennial battleground between good and evil.

A hush falls over the little gathering, a hush of anticipation and expectation. Nicola, perhaps sensing her discomfort, jumps to her rescue;

"I would say that Maggie's paintings are representational, though they may not depict what can be seen with any earthly eye. They are at the same time, however, painterly almost to the point of abstraction. Strokes of paint that individually speak of themselves and for themselves, yet together conjure the illusion of shape and form." She winks at Maggie, who smiles appreciatively.

"That's all very eloquent," snorts Mark, "but what might the artist herself have to say about it?"

There is a sudden silence. Is he throwing down the gauntlet of a challenge? Perhaps he had sensed her moment of fragility and sees an opportunity to assert his dominance in the unspoken hierarchy. Well, Maggie has no interest in such politics and this time she has recovered her composure.

"I don't know," she says slowly. "It is not an intellectual process for me. I just know that I have to paint and that in those moments when I give myself up to it, the painting paints itself."

There is further awed silence.

"But you know, I like Mondrian as well," grins Maggie, tiring of all this earnestness.

Mark looks at her with quizzical disapproval. Maggie shrugs. Why do some people always seem to need to pin another person down? Well, she had lived her life as securely pinioned as a butterfly in a glass case, and now she is free. Mark will have to stick his pins elsewhere.

Sensing that the audience has run its course for the day, the little meeting breaks up and its members drift out of the studio. Nicola lays a hand on the little Irish woman's shoulder on her way out, and Maggie pats it, shaking her head. She relights her roll-up and slowly exhales an arabesque curl of smoke then looks up at her canvases which glower ever more deeply in the late evening gloom. Maggie shakes her head. *'Tis a strange business at the end of the day and that is for sure.*

"You really should try making up your own pigment, it is easy enough, and the colour refraction is just so much deeper than ready-mixed," suggests Roger. He leans over from his easel and hands Maggie his palette. The little blobs of pigment do indeed seem especially intense in their hue. Maggie looks around Roger's little space and marvels at the vibrancy in his latest paintings, paintings that look completely at home against the backdrop of the antiquated architecture of the Academy. Maggie smiles to herself. She still gets goose bumps every time she visits, wandering through its hallowed corridors and running her hand over the casually discarded sculptures and plaster casts of random body parts; the very same casts that deities such as Turner, Constable and William Blake might well have used to make studies, since back in the eighteenth century when The Academy has first opened its door to students.

She is truly happy for Roger that he has found his home there, yet misses him terribly and today, as the middle of October approaches, she feels especially comfortable to find herself back in the familiar role of apprentice to his master.

Maggie rouses herself and returns her attention to Roger, *where would one find the raw pigment?*

"Well, Cornelissen and Son, silly. You know, you must have been there."

Maggie's face is a blank.

"Surely, one of us at least must have told you about it? No? Well then, we have been remiss in your education, Mrs Doyle. No one in London can call themselves a *bona fide* painter until they have been to Cornelissen's. Rossetti and Ford Madox-Brown bought their materials there. Imagine! But you must have seen it, it is this amazing little old shopfront in Bloomsbury, looks like something out of Dickens. I can't quite remember the address, but you can't miss it. Anyway, you have to go. It is like an initiation. Perhaps I could show you next week sometime?"

Maggie's face is lightening with a dawning recollection.

"No, you are alright Roger, thank you for the offer. But now you mention it, I'm thinking I have seen it, so I have. It's almost on my way home, I'll drop in on my way back."

"Really? That would be marvellous." Roger beams with delight. "And make sure you don't get carried away - those pigments are to die for, but don't come cheap, I warn you. Which is why we poor penniless undergraduates did not make more use of them, I guess. Now, what is the news with Sarah and Tony? I haven't heard from them for an age."

"Oh, yes. Bless me, but I find this place so distracting. I had meant to tell you as soon as I saw you. I spoke to Summer last night. They are getting engaged. Our little Sarah and Tony. Imagine. Isn't it wonderful?"

"Oh, yeah. Great." But Roger does not seem exactly thrilled. On the contrary, he looks away, a sudden flash of pain dulling the usual brightness of his eyes.

"Oh, Roger, I never knew you were carrying a torch for Sarah," cries Maggie sympathetically, reaching for his hand.

"I wasn't," replies Roger with meaning.

Maggie knits her brows, then asks slowly. "Tony?"

Roger rolls his eyes then looks at her through half-closed lids.

"Oh, Roger, me darling boy. I had no idea."

"No, neither did I till that night in The Louise when she was all over him like a rash. And by then it was a bit too late, apparently." Roger may be trying his best to make a joke out of it, but Maggie is not laughing. She takes his hand and pressing it to her lips, kisses it, then holds it to her cheek.

"You're not disgusted? That, you know - I'm batting for the other side."

"Now, Roger Matthews, whatever do you take me for?" retorts Maggie with a smile, returning his hand. "I'll tell you one thing, if you are batting for the other side, then it'll be that side I'll be placing me money on, so it will. And if I'd have had a son as wonderful as you, Roger…", but she cannot continue, her eyes are filling. She clears her throat, "If you had been my son, I would have felt myself truly blessed by God, so I would, and I would have counted those blessings every day." And she can say no more.

Outside the air tingles with the promise of Winter around the corner, and Maggie, still feeling a little flushed with emotion, decides to walk. Physical activity is often the best remedy for morbid speculation.

Sure enough, making her way up from Piccadilly via Shaftsbury Avenue, Maggie soon feels her spirits begin to rally. Ever since that wonderful night of the roof, she has heartily savoured the thrill of life in London. She studies the billboards of the theatres and makes a mental note of the plays that catch her attention, with student stand-by deals in mind.

Yet, this afternoon, she becomes conscious of a chill that has nothing to do with the season. She stops midway through her perusal of the critic's notices outside the Queen's Theatre and looks furtively over her shoulder. She would swear that the bearded gentleman in the dark suit and sunglasses who is gazing in through the windows of the Trocadero had been loitering at the entrance of the Royal Academy when she came out. *Please God, not this again.* Perhaps she is just a little on edge, she needs to get a grip of herself.

She takes a look around. It is true, that there are many gentlemen in suits and dark glasses out this afternoon, as the sun is bright, yet there is an awful familiarity about this particular specimen, and she feels a crawling at the back of her neck.

Maggie pauses on the pavement and considers her options. The street is crowded and the traffic, heavy and slow-moving. She could duck into a shop, but she just wants to get as far away from this place as she can. Spotting a passing Route-master bus, she springs onto its entry-platform. Keeping her head low, she creeps along the bus aisle then slips into the front sea and rifles through her bag for her travel pass. Peering anxiously through the bus window, she sees the dark gentleman turn then swivel his gaze like a searchlight when he notices that she is no longer on the opposite side of the road. The shaded eyes fix onto the back of the bus and he begins to walk apace. The bus labours slowly up the road as the traffic light turns red at the crossing ahead. Honestly, it would be quicker to walk. Maggie's heart begins to thump about in her chest like a rabbit in a sack.

She looks about her, in search of someplace to hide. The blood throbs in her ears. The bus conductor, a somewhat swarthy man of no little corporality, with moist armpits and puffy features, is saying something, but she cannot focus. The incongruous notion that he looks like the film star Victor Mature pops unbidden into her head. Saturday matinee-idol or not, he is becoming impatient. He points at her travel-pass, she nods and clumsily fumbles to open it. He grunts an acknowledgement and moves on to the seat behind her, where an old lady appears to have fallen asleep, her head resting against the window. He grunts again. It is turning out to be one of those days.

Just as the conductor leans over to nudge the old woman's shoulder, the dark gentleman jumps onto the platform and looks up the bus. He does not see Maggie, concealed as she is behind the considerable bulk of the uniformed Clippy. Maggie's stalker peers up the winding stairwell and into the concave circular mirror at the top, searching the upper deck. The upstairs seats are all but empty. Maggie holds her breath. By some stroke of fortune, the conductor is having difficulty rousing the woman behind her, and when he does succeed, she is very hard of hearing. The dark man shoots another look up the aisle, then turns on his heal and skips lightly back onto the pavement.

Maggie exhales, her chest heaving. The transaction between the ticket collector and old woman at last complete, she sidles past and hovers at the end of the lower deck, half hanging from the ceiling handrail, as the bus lurches forward on a green light and rounds the corner into Charing Cross Road. A couple of stops further on, she alights from the bus, looking up and down the street as she does. There is no sign of her shadow. She makes her way home. Cornelissen and Son's will have to wait. She will only be happy once she is back in the sanctuary of the little flat in the Peabody buildings, with the kettle on.

She ponders the meaning of the dark bearded man. She has become a little jaded by this sense of surveillance and is almost ready to admit it is all in her mind. But this afternoon's escapade felt all too real and all too threatening. She wonders whether she should mention it to Peter, or perhaps Janet, but thinks better of it. After all, they would most likely just worry about her mental state, and how is that going to help anyone? If The Vatican want her, she thinks, well, they must know where they can find her by now. But for all her stoicism, the memory of Cardinal Salvatore still makes her blood run cold. *If he is watching her, what is he waiting for?*

Later that evening, Peter comes over with an Indian takeaway. Maggie feels instantly safer and almost back to her cheerful self. She had stolen an anxious glance out of the window, as she awaited his ring on the flat buzzer and had been reassured to find the street below quite empty. All the same, she cannot help but creep out of bed, as quiet as a mouse, to peep behind the curtains a couple of times during the night, whilst Peter slumbers on in blissful unawareness. Back beneath the covers she snuggles up to him and allows herself to be lulled to sleep by the comforting rhythm of his breathing.

The next morning Maggie rises and checks one last time, before drawing back the drapes. The street is still clear - of suspicious-looking gentlemen, at least. She fixes breakfast for them both and as they chatter about the day, her fears, at last, seem to dissolve like the sugar in her coffee. Maggie tells Peter that she is off to Cornelissen's later. He applauds her, knowing how much she will love it, then wonders why he has never thought to recommend it to her himself.

They walk over to Holborn together, arm in arm, and exchange a discreet kiss as they part ways. Maggie is already relishing the idea of mixing up the raw pigments and races up all four flights of stairs to her studio space with the excitement of a child who has been promised a visit to Hamleys toyshop.

The front of Cornelissen and Son's is all that it had promised to be. Enchanted, Maggie makes her way inside, smiling at the sound of the old brass bell that tinkles as she opens the door. She stares around in rapture. The little shop is crammed with tiered banks of little wooden drawers, and shelves packed with great glass jars of powdered pigment, in every imaginable colour, line every wall.

She wanders around, craning her neck to read the copperplate handwritten labels. There is a quiet but polite cough from the far end of the shop. Maggie looks over and sees a figure, standing behind a long old-fashioned wooden counter. She smiles. The figure beckons her over.

Maggie approaches and tries to disguise her sense of bewilderment as she draws near. This must surely be the most extraordinary person she has ever seen in her life - and living in the heart of Covent Garden in the last part of the twentieth century, she has seen her share of interesting looking people. She is uncertain whether it is a man or a woman who addresses her, and given the paleness of the skin, the almost white-blonde shoulder-length hair and the whiteness of the eyelashes, she wonders for a moment whether the unusual individual might perhaps be an albino.

She smiles cheerfully, trying not to stare. The figure speaks. The voice is deep but strangely sweet. Maggie is still unable to decide entirely about its gender, but decides on balance, that he is probably male. As she draws closer, she is taken aback by a pair of the palest blue eyes, she has ever seen. Almost like the eyes of a wolf. Do albinos have blue eyes, or could they be red? She is not at all certain, but in any case, her astonishment at his words soon eclipses all other thought.

"Why, Maggie, isn't it? We have been waiting rather a long time for you to visit us. But you are very welcome now that you are here. How can we help?"

"How do you know my name...?" she falters.

The pale figure is unphased by the directness of the question.

"Why of course, everybody knows The Madonna of Southampton Row. It is an honour to meet you at last, in the flesh, as it were, if I am not being indelicate."

Maggie is stumped for words. For a moment she is at a loss as to how a complete stranger could know her. Then she recalls Roger's painting. It had, after all, been on public exhibition. There seems no other explanation, yet how odd that he should refer to her using Roger's pet name. Surely that had remained a private joke? The figure is regarding her intently. She collects herself and enquires politely about pigment.

"You do us a great honour," he nods, almost in a purr. "Allow me to show you our merchandise."

A quarter of an hour later Maggie has amassed a not inconsiderable collection of little brown folded paper bags, which sit in front of her on the countertop, each carefully filled with the fine powder of a different raw pigment. The androgynous assistant enters the prices into an antiquated mechanical cash till and gives Maggie the bad news. Maggie pulls a face, knowing she has blown her budget for the month, but cheerfully hands over the notes from her wallet.

"Will there be anything else, Madame?"

"I don't think so, not today," replies Maggie placing the precious packages carefully into her bag, "but I am sure I will be back.".

"In that case," adds the singular shop-assistant, raising an eyebrow archly, "may we suggest you take the back door on your way out?"

"Now, why would I want to...?"

But before she can finish, he is indicating to her to look through the shop front window. Maggie turns and catches sight of the dark bearded gentleman outside in the street. She freezes. Her strange benefactor stalks out from behind the counter, takes her gently by the arm, then ushers her through to the back entrance of the shop with a reassuring smile.

"They can't hurt you, Maggie. Pay them no heed."

"Who *are* you?" breathes Maggie, as he opens the back door for her.

"Just a well-wisher, who is at your service."

The door closes behind her and Maggie is left blinking and shaking her head for a moment. No matter how strange this young person seems to her, she has the queerest feeling that she has met him somewhere before. Yet, it is not exactly a face you could forget. Maggie knits her brows and shakes her head. However, she is hardly at leisure to pursue the idea and it is soon driven out of her mind by the anxious recollection of the dark gentleman, which sends her hurrying on her way.

Camden Town

A fingerprint? No. It seems too big. More like a big toe, but that would be ludicrous. Janet is lying on the couch in Bernard's consulting room staring a mark on the ceiling. She cannot count the times she has stared at the same mark, over the years, but this morning, it seems to have taken on especial significance. The fact is, she is struggling to take in the reality. This really *is* her last session. Of course, she and Bernard had been discussing it for months. Sometimes it seemed as though they hardly talked about anything else but "the Ending". But now that the day has finally arrived, Janet is feeling oddly disconnected. Her attention wanders to an unfamiliar ache in her bones and she fidgets. She examines the mark above her again. How many times had she invented stories in her head about that innocuous smudge? *Goodbye, smudge*, she says to herself, a trial farewell. She wants to feel something but finds herself becalmed on an ocean of millpond indifference.

Bernard breathes out. He is being unhelpfully taciturn. Did they honestly have to wait it out until the last 'time is up'? Couldn't she just get up now, nod politely and make her exit. At length, Bernard speaks some words, but she misses the meaning, deafened by the clamour of her internal rumination. She props herself up on one elbow and turns to look at him. He smiles; just a little smile, the one she knows so well, and all at once she feels her heart breaking.

"I didn't think it would be this bad," she sighs.
Bernard shrugs,
"Can you put it into words?"

"No. Well, just that - there is going to be this gap, this void, where you used to be. And who am I going to turn to? No matter how much you drive me crazy, and no matter how beastly I have been, you are always there. And now you won't be." Janet lapses into a dismayed silence.

"A lot has changed since we first started working together, Janet. There are other people, who can be there for you now."

Bernard kicks himself mentally, *what in God's name had possessed him to say that*? He is not sure he truly wants to know the answer.

"You mean Jack? Well, it is true, we have a steady happy relationship and he *is* there for me, and I guess that really is progress, isn't it? I certainly could not seem to hold one down before, a relationship, I mean. Too insecure, too needy. And maybe it seems a bit too comfortable at times, but we both have demanding jobs, and to be honest I would rather do without the excitement of tempests and high passion at this time in my life. And you know what, I love him, I honestly do. There is no ambivalence, no inner conflict, he is a good, good man, and even if a part of him is closed off to me, that is okay. I no longer feel threatened by that; he has had his life and I have had mine. What matters is that we want to be together and we are. And that is enough."

Bernard makes a noise of acknowledgement.

"And our house. Okay, so perhaps it is more of a run-down ruin than a house at the moment, and I spend every free moment renovating it. But it is ours, and I love it. And it is the first time in my life that I have ever really felt I had a home. I'd say we did pretty good here, Bernard. And I'm not just saying that to please you, so there."

Janet laughs and Bernard permits himself a chuckle too.

"Seriously though," she adds, "you know something? I am even beginning to entertain the idea of motherhood, and God knows the very idea of it appalled me three years ago."

Bernard nods, impressed, though of course, Janet cannot see it.

There is that silence again.

Janet returns her gaze to the smudge on the ceiling, then asks tentatively;

"Bernard, if I needed to, can I, you know, contact you, come back? I know that technically it is a denial of the finality of the ending, but if I genuinely needed…"

Bernard is silent for a moment. Janet's heart sinks. She knows the official line on this, *why did she have to go and put him on the spot*?

Bernard takes a breath.

"Janet, my door would always be open, should you really feel you need it to be. I do not believe that that detracts from the ending here today, though I am aware that many of my colleagues might be in disagreement with me."

Janet hears the smile in his voice. She thanks him. Then has a thought.

"Of course, I am not sure who I can talk to now about Maggie."

"Ah, yes," replies Bernard. "Well, I can suggest a couple of people you might approach for supervision if you wish." He reaches for his fountain pen and scribbles a couple of names on a slip of paper, passing it to Janet as he continues. "I was under the impression that she was doing well, last time you mentioned her."

"And she is. (Thanks for that) And yet, only this week she was so positive that she is being followed. She had only really obliquely hinted at it before, but last week she had felt completely freaked out by this guy who, she claims, had followed her one day. She had struggled to keep it to herself but eventually blurted it out. The whole account sounded a bit odd, actually. Apparently, it has been going on, on and off, since she left the hospital. It does worry me sometimes that I have not encouraged her more actively to see a psychiatrist."

"And what would have happened, do you think if you had, I wonder?"

"I think she would have run a mile. I don't believe she would have trusted me as much as she does, that is for sure".

"Have you ever wondered if there *might* indeed be people following her?"

Janet is silent. As a matter of fact, she had. There was something so convincing about Maggie that she found it difficult to doubt anything she said.

"This woman seems very important to you, Janet, we have discussed her a great deal over the last two years or so, and here we are in your last session, and she is central to your concerns about finishing here."

"Hmmm, I guess she does seem important, more so than any other of my clients. I am not sure why. She has been through such obvious and terrible trauma, and yet she has this indomitable spirit, faith in life maybe. Perhaps I envy her, in a way. My troubles seem so - so pedestrian in comparison. I guess I see her as a kind of mythical heroine -

perhaps I am a like a sort of reliable sidekick, you know, the plodder."

Bernard cannot help but laugh, but then says in a serious voice.

"I wonder if she represents a side of you. Not the plodder, which is the persona that you hide behind, but the lost child who struggles between vulnerability and strength, heartbreak and hope, recklessness and courage?"

"Oh Bernard, I never heard you say anything so beautiful." Janet can feel the warm trickle of tears running down her cheeks, she wipes them away with her sleeve and sniffs.

"Well, it's time".

"One last thing," says Janet with the old mischief back in her voice,

"How *did* that smudge get up there on the ceiling?"

Bethnal Green

It is getting towards that time in the term when all anyone can think about is the approaching Christmas Holidays. There has been a cold snap and, whilst the frost has melted away with the December sunshine, the air stings with the chill of winter. The radiators are turned up to maximum and pump out welcome warmth into the main school corridor. Another lunchtime supervision for Jack and Jim. Jim breathes on the cold window, then draws a heart and two Js in the patch of condensation. Jack shakes his head and stares out through the plate glass pane. He cannot help but smile. Who would have thought it, this time two years ago the boys were hanging around the schoolyard looking for mischief and getting into fights, now many of them bring skipping ropes to school and make the most of the breaks to get in a spot of impromptu training. Some of them have formed little groups and jog around the yard or challenge each other to press-ups.

Jack grins and summons Jim to take a look at a kid they call "Chippy." Twelve months ago, he was a scrawny kid, unusually delayed in his adolescent growth spurt, afraid of his own shadow and easy prey for random bullies. Now, he demonstrates a fiendishly complex skipping routine to a little gaggle of lads from a couple of years above him. The rope gyrates faster than the eye can follow, but he never misses a step, as quick and nimble as Jack jumping over his candlestick could ever have hoped to be. The older lads stand and watch, eyes wide with admiration.

"I reckon Bantock has a real future ahead of him as a featherweight," remarks Jim following Jack's gaze.

"Ah, go on with you. Did you not know the lad wants to be a surgeon? He is already choosing his subjects for application to medical school, so he is. I have him in my GCSE Latin class. The lad means business, and that's the truth."

Jim shrugs.

"Seems a shame. Probably more money in Boxing if he goes all the way."

Jack rolls his eyes. Jim will be Jim.

"But sure now, doesn't it make you proud - all this I mean." He inclines his head towards the activity outside.

"Actually, you know something, it bloody does! I reckon we pulled off something quite special here, Jack, old sport."

They bump fists.

"And you know something else, for the first time in my life, someone else thinks I am more than a waste of space. You heard that Philips is going to retire at Easter, right?"

"Aye, now that I come to think about it, I did hear something like that on the grapevine," concedes Jack.

"Well, that means there is a vacancy for Head of Year, right? Well, you'll never guess who old man O'Leary has asked to apply for it. Yours truly. He reckons there is no-one in the school who has done more for improving discipline and motivation." Jim beams with unmistakable pride.

"Of course, I couldn't have done it without you, like, but well you know..."

Jack congratulates his best friend heartily. It is almost unheard of for a gym master to make it to such a position. He couldn't feel more pleased for him.

"It's been a real blast, hasn't it?" continues Jim. "Tell you what though, I miss the girls. I know I never really expected them to continue coming to the club after the novelty rubbed off, but they did add something."

"Eye candy, do you mean?" asks Jack with a wink.

"Well, that of course. There is nothing like a woman in gloves to get my sap rising, but no, actually I meant a bit of *finesse*, I suppose."

Jack almost snorts to hear such words from Jim's mouth, but then quite a few things about Jim surprise him at times.

"Aye, I was sorry when Jan dropped out, but you know since we got the house, she has wanted to spend every minute of her free time doing it up, so she has. I don't know where she gets the energy. Just as well I suppose, there is certainly enough to do. And to be sure, she has a real gift for it. She has usually got her head stuck in a Home and Gardens magazine and is always asking me if I think this border goes with these curtains as if I should know anything about it, for Heaven's sake. Truth is, I'm thinking I may have a touch of the colour blindness about me, so I leave her to it. And it's a grand job she is making of it. You must come over and see. Now, what am I thinking? Sure, didn't I mean to invite the two of you over for Christmas lunch. It had gone straight out of me head."

"Are you certain, mate? I am not sure Janet has forgiven me for last Christmas yet. You know, what with knocking the Christmas tree flying and all."

"Sure, you know Jan. The woman is not one to hold a grudge and she is fair dying to show off her efforts to someone. And besides our new living room has room enough for you, a tree and a troupe of dancers doing an Irish jig. Now, don't be telling me that you and Jill have made plans already?"

"Well, not so far as I know, although I know she is pretty keen for me to meet her family," adds Jim grimly.

"All the more reason to accept my invitation first then, I would say."

At that moment, a football slams into the great glass window causing both men to startle. Jim glowers out into the yard and gestures to the culprit. The lad picks up the ball and troops dejectedly up to the entrance. Jim pushes open the door, takes the offending item from him, and informs him that he can have it back at the end of the week. The lad, scowls, turns away and scuffing his shoes along the ground, heads sulkily back to his friends who greet him with jeers of derision.

Jim plants the ball in the crook of his arm and retraces his steps back towards Jim, his eye turned to the floor in thought. Jack wonders what is going on it in that head now. He does not have to wait long to find out.

"Well, the 'meet the parents' thing - if you want to know, Jill and I are thinking of getting hitched..."

Jack gapes a moment.

"Married? Jill and yourself, like?"

"Yeah, me! Hey man, it is not that impossible, is it? It is not like I have the pox or anything. I mean I know I've been a bit of a Casanova and all, but that's all in the past. And everyone has to settle down eventually..."

"Jim, mate. I couldn't be happier for you, and that's the truth. You and Jill seem just made for one another, so you do. It is just - a little unexpected. You've kept your cards close to your chest and no mistake. You never hinted - well, what does that matter?"

He seizes Jim's free hand and gives him a good old-fashioned handshake. "Congratulations! From the bottom of me heart, Jim."

Jim turns a little pink and then clears his throat, as though preparing a little speech.

"I would like you to stand up and be my best man Jack. I can't think of anyone I would rather have by my side. Will you do it, Jack?"

But Jack is unable to give the reply Jim is hoping. He shakes his head sadly.

"What the Fuck?" Jim claps his hand to his mouth, then looks around in mortification, all at once conscious of his lapse in professionalism. The corridor is clear. "Sorry, mate. But is that the best reply you can give me, really? I thought we were friends."

His tone is a mixture of anger and hurt. He starts to bounce the ball repeatedly, his eyes averted from Jack. Jack softly speaks his name and tries to get his attention, but Jack is fixed on the slapping rhythm of his game. Jack makes a grab for the ball, but Jim snatches it up and looks at Jack with the glare of a wounded animal. For a moment Jack thinks Jim is going to punch him. He holds both hands up before him then takes a deep breath.

"Forgive your friend's stupid selfishness, Jim. I had not thought to hurt your feeling, as I so plainly have. Sure, I was thinking only of my own feelings of unworthiness. I am thinking I'll not be deserving to be called a good man, let alone a best one, and that is the truth. But if by Best Man you mean best friend, I am your man. And it would be my very great honour."

"You know your trouble, mate," grins Jim, "sometimes you just talk a load of shite. But I like you anyway," and he gives him a friendly punch on the arm. "But, seeing how *I am* your best mate, suppose you tell me what this bullshit about not being worthy is all about. You had me worried for a moment there."

Jack shakes his head. In about three minutes the afternoon bell will ring. He chews his bottom lip and thinks. Jim waits, patient now.

"I am thinking I did someone a great wrong Jim. A woman. I put my own needs before hers, so I did, and left her in a terrible situation to face the consequences alone. I was a coward and weak-willed. I have tried to find out where she is, to make restitution if that were even possible, but she is nowhere to be found. Last year I thought I had got close, but it was not to be. I am not sure I can forgive meself, and I'm not sure I'd deserve to if I could."

"Mate, we've all done things we are not proud of. I've not exactly behaved like the perfect gentleman myself, at times..."

"Sure, this is a bit different. I can't really explain - it was very complicated"

"Have you spoken to Janet about it?"

"No, God, no! It's not something I could do. Believe me. She wouldn't understand."

"Are you sure about that, Jack mate? I mean, she earns her living by listening and understanding, doesn't she? And under that rather sexy primness, I get the feeling she is pretty broad-minded..."

"So she is. I'll not deny that. But take my word for it, Jim, this is not something she *could* understand. And I'll not be asking her to try."

Jim lets it go. He can see that Jack is in no mood to change his mind and the peeling of the afternoon bell saves them both any further awkwardness. All the same, Jim heads off to his next P.E lesson with Jack's unhappiness hanging about him like stale tobacco smoke.

January 1984

Maggie finds herself outside the Royal Academy feeling at a bit of a loss. She had been missing Roger, whom she had not seen since before Christmas, and had dropped in on spec. However, instead of finding Roger in his studio space as she had expected, all she had found was a scribbled note bearing the words - "Gone to the British Museum."

Maggie had smiled to herself. She might have known. The Print Room in the British Museum was perhaps Roger's favourite place on Earth. He would don the mandatory white cotton gloves and spend hours poring through the prints and original drawings of the greatest painters and draftsmen in European history. Membership of the Print Room had been a privilege afforded to all students of art for over a hundred years, yet Maggie doubts that anyone has valued it so highly as does her dearest friend. She thinks about going over to join him but is loath to intrude on his private time. Besides she is not in the mood.

She looks up at the clear blue January sky. Despite the chill, she decides that a walk will do her good and eschews the bus stop, even though she can see a number nineteen labouring up from Green Park. She checks around her first, however. It has been a while since she had a strong sense of being followed, and yet it never quite leaves her. There is no one around who arouses her suspicion, so she starts towards Piccadilly Circus. She pauses to gaze longingly into the shop fronts of Burlington Arcade but lacks the confidence to enter the high-end arcade, let alone its exquisite boutiques.

Across the road, she notices that Simpson's have a mid-season sale on. She shakes her head but then thinks, 'and why not?' Her money is as good as anyone else's. She has talked herself into it. She crosses over to the opposite pavement, weaving casually through the thick swarm of beetle-black cabs that swarm the Piccadilly streets. She hesitates momentarily outside the tastefully arranged display windows of the up-market department store then, with a boldness she scarcely recognizes in herself, makes her way in through the heavy glass doors, trying her best to look as though she shops there all the time. Nevertheless, she almost falters as she senses the perfectly lined eyes of the girls on the make-up counters widen in her wake. She must present quite a novelty in her Dungarees and Doc Martens.

Undaunted, she heads up the steel escalators to the women's department on the first floor and starts to browse, running her hand along the silky fabrics of the jewel-coloured evening dresses and peering at the price tags, which shock her even with their generous sale discounts. An elegantly dressed woman with poise that Maggie can only admire, approaches and asks if she can be of help. Maggie demurs, making a polite comment about the beautiful range of merchandise in her soft Irish lilt. Does she imagine it, or does a look of slight panic pass over the shop assistant's face? Whatever the case, the woman scurries off, her self-possession momentarily punctured.

Maggie stares after her. Over at the cash desk, the assistant huddles with a colleague. They appear to be in hushed conference. She cannot catch what they are saying, but Maggie is certain, from the way that they every now and then glance her way, that they are indeed discussing her. And then the penny drops. They are worried that she is some IRA operative, come to slip some explosive device into the pockets of a jacket, or perhaps leave a homemade bomb in the changing rooms. It seems so ridiculous that she is obliged to check a sudden desire to laugh out loud. But, perhaps it is no laughing matter.

Maggie quickly lowers her gaze and tries to think. She suspects she ought to feel affronted but feels only sympathy. Perhaps these women have good reason to be nervous. Barely a month has passed since the explosion in Harrods on that terrible day last December. Maggie had watched the news in tears. She understands well enough the grievances of her countrymen, what son or daughter of Ireland can forget the plight of the Irish under British rule, yet still, she cannot comprehend the soul twisting hatred that sets neighbour against neighbour and soaks the land in blood.

Maggie pauses, feeling clammy with self-consciousness. She could just turn on her heels and leave, but instead, she resolves to take the initiative. Putting on her sweetest smile she strolls over to the assistants and speaks;

"Excuse me, ladies, I could do with some advice, if you would be so kind. I am looking for something really special, and I'll not lie to you, I am feeling a little lost and would appreciate your opinion, so I would."

The two shop assistants beam in unison. Such affability hardly fits the profile of a would-be bomber. Their relief is almost palpable.

Thirty-minutes later Maggie emerges with a smart Simpson's cardboard carrier bag in hand. She feels as excited as a schoolgirl who has just bought a dress for her first formal dance. Phyllis, the elegant sales lady had looked Maggie up and down, noted her colouring and build and had then picked out an emerald green velvet trouser suit. It was not at all what Maggie had had in mind when she walked into the store, yet it had been Love at First Sight.

How Maggie had found the courage to take it into the changing rooms, she could hardly say, yet both Phyllis and her junior, Agnes, had been so encouraging. Then, when she emerged, to stand in front of the full-length mirror, both women had gasped in admiration. And Maggie could feel that the admiration had been genuine. She had gazed at her reflection with surprise verging on amazement. The suit fitted her slender frame perfectly, and the green brought out the colour of her eyes and auburn hair. She looked like a catwalk model, if she said so herself, though admittedly a little on the old side and with not nearly so much make-up.

She had peeked at the price tag that hung from the sleeve and blanched. True enough, it was half price, but it was still more money than she had spent on clothes in her entire lifetime. Still, she had worked hard, and she was going to need something really special for her final year exhibition. *She would take it.* Agnes had almost squealed with delight herself and Phyllis could not have looked happier. Indeed, it would not be going too far to add that the three women had exchanged hugs, by the time Maggie had completed the transaction.

Back in the street, Maggie smiles to herself. To think they had been entertaining the idea she might be a terrorist. And then she has another thought. There is no doubting the intensifying of the security measures since the escalation of the mainland bombing campaign. Could it be that she is under surveillance?

She is sure it is not just her imagination, and perhaps this explanation would not be as far-fetched, after all. British Intelligence may have mistaken her for someone else. Maggie shrugs her shoulders, somehow comforted by this thought, for it seems more benign than the alternative. If this is the case, someone is indeed barking up the wrong tree. She wonders again about discussing the idea with Peter but thinks better of it. Sure, there is only so much crazy a man can take, even when he is in love.

Once back home, Maggie tries on the suit again, striking poses before the mirror, placing her hair high on her head, and now loose around her shoulders, turning this way and that. She caresses the softness of the silk velvet sleeves as though embracing herself and laughs softly with relish. She can hardly wait for Peter to see her in it and imagines his face when he does. But for all the delight in the prospect of his reaction, she is determined to keep it as a surprise. She changes back into her dungarees then carefully conceals the suit at the back of the wardrobe, re-arranging the few dresses she owns to hide the rich green of the fabric.

Of course, she must now find the right shoes, for her habitual Doc Martens simply will not do. She will need heels for maximum effect, she wants her legs to look as long as possible. But her credit card is maxed out, for now, so she will have to wait for the Spring sales. Maggie shakes her head and winks at herself in the mirror as she closes the closet door. When on Earth had she become so vain? "Margaret Doyle, I would hardly know you, and that is the truth, so it is."

She shakes her head with a smile, but then for a few horrible seconds, she is gripped by the old compulsion to wash her hands. She stands firm and allows the wave of anxiety to wash over her like a crashing breaker. Her heartbeat peaks, then starts to drop again. She breathes out. The threat has passed.

Maundy Thursday 1984

Cardinal Salvatore sits at the great leather-topped desk in his private office. All about him, in the halls and corridors of the Vatican Palace and the Square below, frenetic preparations are afoot for the most important date in the Holy Roman Church's calendar, yet the Cardinal seems all but oblivious to the hive of activity that surrounds him.

The golden light of the Roman Eastertide filters in through the great window casement, illuminating the ancient and rare tomes that line the lofty bookcases. The very parchment of these priceless books seems to exude an odour of antiquity and learning, while the dry pages, if turned, could whisper of mysteries far beyond the ken of the common Catholic Church's congregation. They are, however, the bread and butter for The Cardinal and his forbears in the Vatican Commission, who have dedicated their lives to their investigation. Yet, whilst the library might lull you into an assumption that the aforesaid investigation is of a purely scholastic nature, you would be mistaken. The current curator, like those before him, is a ruthless pragmatist, prepared to establish material fact with a rigour undreamt of outside the Vatican walls.

The Cardinal contemplates the red embossed seal on a plain flat wooden box, lately bought up from the vaults, that now lies waiting before him. His hands tremor a little as he adjusts the desk lamp then runs his fingers over the letters *NC*, which have been scrawled across its side in red chalk. He takes a sharp breath, then rips open the waxy disk and lifts the lid. It is five years and many months since the contents were sealed within then stored deep within the temperature and moisture regulated cellars beneath the Vatican Palace. Five years it has languished in the company of relics such as the hand of Saint Teresa of Avila and the finger of St Thomas, the father of all sceptics, to name but a tiny fraction of the collection of body parts, phials of blood and holy objects which lie carefully stored on the endless racks that line the repository's ancient walls.

To the right proudly sit those items catalogued and classified as *constat de supernaturalite,"* (established as supernatural); those hallowed objects upon which the very mystery of the church is built. To the left, and classified as *"non-constat,"* (not established as supernatural and awaiting further verification), are stored those relics and artefacts whose authenticity is yet to be proven. Waiting in patient anticipation of the day when they will be transferred across to the right, or discarded, some of these objects have remained undisturbed for hundreds of years, and indeed seem doomed so to remain in perpetuity.

Cardinal Salvatore's thoughts stray to one particular specimen amongst them, not least in importance - the alleged head of John the Baptiste, one of at least six around the world for which the same claim has been made. As uncomplaining as the saint may be, the Cardinal has always felt saddened by the prospect that final verification is likely to remain forever elusive. Yet the very box before him now, reminds him that hope may not be lost whilst science breaks new frontiers every day.

Sealed within airtight plastic covers lie the articles he remembers, as though he had only laid them there yesterday. A tiny ball of feathery down tinged brown but once pure white; a blood-soaked and stained linen hospital sheet, carefully folded in tissue to keep the layers of fabric from adhering together; three tiny splintered shards of bone and finally two long auburn strands of hair. With infinite care, he removes the items from the box, holds them up for closer scrutiny. His plump lips curl into a smile of triumph.

What God and Margaret Doyle had tricked him out of, over five years ago, is now within his grasp. And the science never lies.

The previous day Cardinal Salvatore had sat through the final day of the week-long Pontifical Academy of Sciences special meeting on genetics and ethics. As it had done since the founding of the first Accademia dei Lincei, (Academy of Lynxes), as it was titled in 1603, the Catholic Church had demonstrated a keen interest in the developing fields of mathematics, physics and the natural sciences. The road had not always been smooth. Galileo, its first president, had famously fallen foul of the dangers of highlighting the discrepancy between scientific observation and doctrinal edict, and he would not be the last. Not surprisingly, the enthusiasm of the whole beleaguered endeavour had slowly petered out under the threat of heresy, until being formally resurrected in 1847 by pope Pius IX and the establishment of an academy of the New Lynxes.

The Academy had been re-founded, divested of its archaic title and bought into the twentieth century under another Pope Pius, this time XI. Its new brief had been to gather scientists from all over the world with no restriction on its research. And it had new and ambitious aims - to oversee the progress of the mathematical, physical and natural sciences and the study of related epistemological questions and issues. The Academy, whose members still chose to refer to themselves as "The Lynxes", had prided itself on attracting the most brilliant and promising members of the scientific community, both from within its church and from without.

Young Father Anatole Salvatore had been one such prodigy. Trained in forensic pathology and bio-chemistry, he had found himself firmly established within The Vatican City with direct access to the papal ear, after his talent for exposing fakery in cases of alleged medical miracles earned him a prized position on the Vatican Commission.

If knowledge is power, the Holy Roman Church is all about Power and it needed Knowledge. Or at the very least, it needed to know what the opposition was up to. 'Related issues,' therefore, continued to cover the pursuit of matters miraculous and supernatural. A Lynx can no more change its spots than can a leopard.

In this capacity, the ambitious Cardinal had kept a weather eye to the emerging field of genetics and never, since Crick and Watson's discovery of the double helix in 1953, had that field become so energised. Hence, although much of the preoccupation of the Holy Roman Church with genetics was focused on keeping a place for the Creator within the increasingly dominant Darwinian narrative, the Cardinal's interest was driven by motivations quite his own. He was not interested in evolution, but he *was* interested in establishing identity and changes in DNA structures that could not be medically explained.

In 1978 when he had torn the bloodied sheets from Margaret Doyle's hospital bed and gathered what evidence remained, DNA sequencing had only been in its earliest infancy. Large samples, uncontaminated and fresh, were required. Meanwhile, the process was laborious and the chances of conclusive results remained, at best, tenuous. This week he had heard of the work of Kary Mullis whose development of a process called PCR (polymerase chain reaction) was revolutionising the ability to recover information from the tiniest and degraded of samples. Information that could pinpoint identity, species and family relationships with undreamed of accuracy. He had sat through the presentations in studied silence until the final plenary.

"And are you saying," he had asked for the sake of absolute clarity, "that if you take even the tiniest sample of material, no matter how old, you can tell me within 98% accuracy, to which species the sample belongs and what family relationship it bears to another discrete sample?"

"Indeed, your Eminence. It is going to be a whole new world. We predict that DNA sequencing using this method is eventually going to be able to solve crimes where there appears to be no evidence at all to the naked eye..."

"A worthy endeavour, I am sure," the Cardinal had nodded. "I wonder, would it be possible to organise a little demonstration for me; for me to set you a challenge so to speak?"

The Cardinal, carefully lays out the contents of the box, spreading them in an ordered fashion across his desk. He nods his head with satisfaction, presses the intercom and speaks.

"Have the representative from Doctor Mullis' team sent in will you, I am ready for them now."

He clasps his hands together and rests his chin, a placid smile of welcome disguising the febrile agitation of his inner cogitation. *Soon, very soon now, the wait will be over and this damned box will be consigned to its rightful final resting place. The Vatican waste incinerator!*

Easter Sunday 1984

A cheerful clinking of dishes and glasses emanates from the kitchen, where Jack and Jim are washing and drying up after their Easter lunch. Janet had gone to town with a prawn cocktail for starters, rack of lamb with all the trimmings and an enormous homemade Kirsch-soaked Black-Forest gateaux for afters, washed down with a bottle of Blue Nun, and a good dessert wine to follow.

Janet and Jill have repaired to the little lean-to sunroom with their coffee and Cointreau and have left the lads to their work. Janet is a little disappointed that the weather has not seen fit to allow them to sit in the garden of their Victorian terraced villa, but that is Easter for you. In any case, she and Jill are soon absorbed in the task of flicking through bridal magazines in search of 'The Dress.' The wedding is booked for the end of July, and the clock is ticking.

"For goodness sake, I'd look like a cream puff in this, and they all look the same." laments Jill holding up a full-page photograph of an impossibly overblown gown, with inflated puffed sleeves and a hooped under-skirt.

"I blame those bloody Emmanuels," sympathises Janet. "Ever since they dressed up Diana like a Disney princess, the concept of classic elegance has simply flown out of the window, when it comes to wedding dresses. But there has got to be something more "you" in one of these magazines somewhere. Did you have anything particular in mind?"

"I don't know. It's not going to be a huge wedding. I suppose I had always dreamt of something a bit like Dior, you know, the sort of thing Grace Kelly wore in High Society, wide neckline, fitted bodice, maybe lace, but plain, and you know, chic. But I haven't seen anything like that anywhere." Her face falls.

Janet has a sudden thought.

"What about having one made? I'll bet a hundred quid Vogue still do a pattern along those lines. You know, my Aunty Linda is an incredible seamstress, she has made dozens of bridal gowns. She only lives just up the M1 in Luton. And you can get the most amazing fabrics in John Lewis. We can go up to Oxford Street on Tuesday if you like. I can give her a call beforehand, just to be sure."

"Really? God, you would be saving my life! I was beginning to feel a bit desperate. I know this is the era of the new Romantics and all, but I've got a feeling people are going to feel dreadfully embarrassed when they look back on their wedding photos in twenty years' time. It will all look so dated."

The girls laugh. The merriment in their voices carries through to the little kitchen, where Jim and Jack are putting away the last of the dinner service and polishing the wine glasses.

"Hey, what are we missing out on?" yells Jim, winking at Jack.

"Nothing that need concern you," trills Jill, calling over her shoulder and winking conspiratorially.

Jim shakes his head.

"Wedding talk. It's all she can think about these days." But his eyes shine with happiness. Jack returns the smile, then looks away. But Jim, never the one to take the hint, ploughs on regardless.

"You know, I never had Janet pegged for the domestic type. But look at this place of yours. And that lunch. She is some cook. I think you are a lucky man, my friend. And you know the old saying, one wedding brings on another. Nudge, nudge, wink, wink..."

"Yeah, I think I get the drift. But it is not that simple, as you well know, Jim."

"Isn't it?" asks Jim. "Aren't things just as simple or complicated as we make them, in the end?"

Jack stares at Jim. Jim cannot read his face. Then Jack speaks.

"I think it is time we all went for a postprandial walk, don't you?"

Jim sighs. Well, it had been worth a try.

Across the way in Islington, an exhausted Maggie is reflecting upon her own Easter Day; it had been a proper family Easter, the like of which she would be hard-pressed to remember.

Peter had invited Annie and her husband Neil over, along with little Poppy, of course, who was old enough to get excited about Easter eggs and getting spoilt rotten by Grandpa Peter. As it turned out, she was also old enough to suffer the inevitable consequences of a surfeit of chocolate. She had ended an afternoon of sugar fuelled crawling, by climbing worn out into Aunty Magg's lap and falling asleep, before being driven home still drunk on cocoa butter.

Maggie had been delighted. It was not so long ago she had a terror of even touching the tiny infant, never mind cuddling her, yet Poppy had never held her aloofness against her. On the contrary, rather like a cat who will single out the one person in the room who is most nervous about felines, she would hold her little arms out and make a beeline for Maggie, from the moment she could shuffle her bottom along the floor. It could not be long before she had succeeded in winning her over.

Now, of course, Maggie could not love her more if she had been her natural grand-daughter. She counts her blessings. Tinged with sadness they may be, but they are blessings nonetheless.

"Come and sit next to me, my Love." Peter is lounging on the sofa, exhausted, feeling slightly over full, but content. Maggie sinks into the cushions next to him and snuggles up against his side with a -

"Now Pete, you know I can't sit long, I have to get back to my thesis, so I do."

He takes her hands and kisses her fingers.

"Now, Maggie you can spare me another five minutes. I've hardly had you to myself for a whole minute today. Did you have a lovely day?"

"Aye, Peter. Indeed, I did. Though heaven knows, I never want to look at another Easter egg again! Sure, I never ate so much chocolate in me whole life, and that's the truth."

"As if you weren't sweet enough already," laughs Peter. "But Maggie, there is something I wanted to talk to you about. And now seems as good a time as any. Now, tell me, do you ever think about the future? After your final show, I mean?"

Maggie looks serious.

"Peter, Sweetheart, to be honest, you know my whole focus is on that show at the moment, so no, I suppose I haven't. You know how much it means to me. I can't even imagine beyond it at the moment…"

"No, I mean yeah, I get that. But you see, *I have* been thinking about it. I am planning to retire at the end of the academic year - no, let me finish. You know we have had such wonderful summers in France, and I was just thinking, you know, whether I could use the money from the house to buy us a place there, with a studio for you, and well, you could just paint. Would you like that, my Maggie?"

Maggie's eyes shine with surprise, but before she can even gather her thoughts to make a response he continues.

"You remember how we loved the little hamlet of Goult, not far from Rousillon? The one on the hill, with the pretty old mill? Well, a place has just come onto the market; it needs a bit of work, but I think it would suit us perfectly, so I am thinking about making an offer. What do you reckon?"

Maggie shakes her head, as though trying to grasp what Peter is saying, and Peter feels suddenly anxious.

"Of course, you can have Kathleen and Yvonne over to stay, as long and often as they liked, and I know Annie and Neil would come over with Poppy and - well? Please say you will at least think about it."

Maggie puts a finger to his lips to quiet him and smiles her warmest smile.

"Peter, I can't think of a place on earth where I could feel happier. Truly I cannot. I seem to find a sense of peace there, that I cannot anywhere else, so I do. So, if you are sure it is what you want, you'll not hear me refusing."

She pulls his face to her and kisses him. She smiles. His lips still taste of chocolate.

"But Peter. What about Stan and Ollie?"

"Maggie, Maggie. You may find this difficult to believe but Wendy loves them almost as much as you do! We have nearly had a custody battle over them as it is. Believe me, she will be only too happy to offer them a home, now she is settled herself, and since she and I have managed to come through all this on amicable terms, I don't see any reason we can't negotiate visiting rights."

"Sure, but we'll miss the little rascals, all the same."

"That we will. But you know, they do have cats in France, and perhaps we could have a couple of our own."

"Oh, Peter. You really mean it?"

"Maggie, I would build you a menagerie to rival London Zoo, if that's what it takes to make you happy."

Back in Bethnal Green, in the small hours of the morning, Jack finds he is unable to dismiss Jim's words of wisdom quite so easily. Perhaps he is right. He is still mulling it over in his mind when he wakes, groggy and tired, on Easter Monday and is relieved to recall that it is still the school holidays. The day passes pleasantly enough, he and Janet go for a walk in Vic Park in the spring sunshine. The leaves on the trees are fizzling into life while the birds build nests and tweet their joyful version of The Hallelujah Chorus, as they work. He regards Janet from the corner of his eye as they wander hand-in-hand, content to drift without direction or the need for haste. *They are happy enough, so why upset the apple- cart?*

Yet, despite his best efforts to shake it off, the conundrum follows him to the bed once again, as the day draws to a close.

"Janet?" He knows she is sleeping, but he shakes her gently by the shoulder.

"Waa...?" Janet opens her eyes and yawns sleepily. "What time is it? Is everything alright?"

"Yes, yes - of course. I am sorry if I woke you."

"S'alright...," lisps Janet, beginning to fall back into the drowsiness of slumber.

"Janet. You know I said I could not be married? Well, I guess that is only the case for a religious ceremony. I suppose there would be nothing to stop us having a civil ceremony, being legally married, that is to say. It's just that the marriage would not be recognised by The Church."

Janet is wide awake now. She stares up into Jack's face.

"Jack O'Donnell. Are you asking me to marry you?"

Jack is caught wrongfooted. He tries to stutter a response but flounders hopelessly.

"It's – that is, I was just thinking. You know, if that- well, if that was what you wanted?"

Janet tilts her head to one side and screws up her eyes in thought. Something tells her that Jim had something to do with this. Which is fine, but not really how it is supposed to go.

"Jack, Darling," she places her arms around his neck. "I never thought I would hear myself saying this, but the answer has to be no. I appreciate you suggesting it, truly I do. And it would be so easy to do. But it wouldn't be right. No, no, hear me out." She places a finger against Jack's lips. "Even if *I* felt married, I know that deep in your heart, *you* would not feel you were, not really, because, for you, marriage is about the solemn vows taken in the sight of God. And perhaps it always will be. And if only one of us feels married, what sort of marriage would that be?"

Jack is stumped for words. He thinks a while then proceeds in a sad voice.

"I am sorry, Janet. I can't argue with your reasoning. You are right. But it always seems so much about me and I just wanted to make it about you, for once. Yet, there seems to be no way I can make it right."

Janet strokes his hair.

"And I love you for it, Jack, truly I do. Now let's leave it. I have to be up bright and early to meet Jill in Oxford Street. We have a wedding dress to organise."

Jack kisses her goodnight and wraps his arms around her, as she turns onto her side. But this time, it is Janet who struggles to drift off. As rationally as she has coped with it, she cannot entirely let go of her a lingering wish for a white wedding in a quaint old church, with all her friends and family and that band of gold on her finger. Janet dislikes envy, yet how envious she feels of Jill.

The sad truth is, she had dreamed of the day when she would ask Aunty Linda to make her own dress since she had been a little girl and Linda, who had no daughters of her own, had used to promise her that it would be the most special dress of all. Now, the closest she would come to it was the rose-pink organza bridesmaid's dress, Jill had in mind for her. *How ridiculous*, she thinks *it is just one day. What is the matter with us all? It is almost as though the whole female species undergo massive brain-washing. And it starts with all those bloody silly fairy tales. After all, being with the person you love is what really matters, and surely, she already has her happy-ever-after?*

Still, the sadness she feels is real enough and Janet would be the last person in the world to deny emotions, no matter how unreasonable. She will just make have to make it her business to see that Jill has the best-damned dress ever.

June 1984

Maggie has just popped in to see Roger at the Royal Academy. The end of her course looms before her and the mountain of tasks associated with selecting and mounting works for the final show is beginning to get a bit out of proportion. She is in need of refuge, a cool head and the benefit of experience.

On the way into his studio-space, she hears raised voices. She pauses and is almost mown down by a tall boilersuit-clad figure who is exiting at some speed. She steps back and gasps. It is the strange shop assistant from Cornelissen's. The figure concedes a curt nod of acknowledgement but hurries past, in no mood, apparently, for pleasantries. Maggie stares after him, scratching her head, then makes her way into Rogers cubicle, her eyes all agog.

"Who *was* that?" asks Maggie, by way of a greeting.

Roger is in the middle of scraping off the paint from a ruined canvas and if the air about him is turning blue, it is not from any flying pigment. He sees Maggie but continues without answering so that Maggie finds herself obliged to repeat her enquiry. Roger tosses down his palette knife, pouts his lips then replies.

"Yeah, right. You as well, eh? Everyone wants to know about Lars, don't they? Oh, Lars, he is sooo unusual looking, Roger. He is such a nice guy, Roger. Why don't you introduce us, Roger? Well, I tell you what - Lars can go fuck *himself*, as he obviously doesn't want to…"

All at once, Roger sees the look of distress on Maggie's face. He hastily cleans off his hands on a rag and reaches towards her, as though fearing she will just turn and run.

"Oh Christ, Maggs. I am so sorry. He just does my head in. I just don't know where I stand with that guy. Just forget you heard any of that. Can you? Please."

Maggie nods.

"I just wondered who he was, was all. I met him that time I went to Cornelissen's. He seemed to know me and I had a vague impression that I knew him, but I have no idea from where, and I hardly think he is a face one can forget, because, yes, he is rather unusual…" Maggie grimaces an apology. Roger laughs now.

"He is, isn't he? Pretty amazing actually. I get weak knees just looking at him. His parents are from Lapland, of all places. He is studying sculpture here but does an occasional day at Cornelissen's to help make ends meet. Family friends, I think. And he *should* know you, I've told him enough about you. I showed him that sketch, and…" Roger blushes. He tilts his head to one side. "I've got it pretty bad, Maggs. But he is just heavenly, don't you think? Whatever am I going to do?"

Maggie places her arm around Roger's waist and squeezes him.

"Sure now, I have to admit, he did have me wondering, meself, whether he hadn't been sent from Heaven, the first time I saw him," jokes Maggie. "And if you want to know what I think, I think that if he gets to know you as well as I do Roger, he won't be able to resist you. You mark my words. Just you give it a little time." She winks. "Now, why don't we go and get a coffee in your refectory, you know what a thrill it gives me. Why I might be sitting on the very bench that William Turner used to park his backside on."

Maggie bites her lips and widens her eyes in excitement. Roger grins, shakes his head and donning his duffle coat, takes Maggie's arm. *How is it that Maggie can always make him feel better?*

Thirty minutes later, feeling buoyed up by a decent cup of coffee and her close encounter with art history, Maggie heads back for Southampton Row, leaving Roger to salvage what he can from the ruin of his painting.

Maggie makes her way back out through the winding maze of stone pillared corridors that run beneath the main galleries of the Academy. All at once, her glance is arrested by a glimpse of blue boilersuit through an archway that opens onto a studio to the left of her. She stops and peers around the column. Directly before her, in the middle of the floor, the very same Lars, of whom she was so recently speaking, stands statue-like next to an enormous block of pale stone, gazing at it in rapt contemplation.

To Maggie's eyes, he appears as cool and static as the very rock itself. She finds herself holding her breath as if time itself has somehow has frozen with him. She notices that his long silvery locks are tied back in a ponytail, highlighting the impossible smoothness of the almost translucent skin that stretches tautly over his cheek and jawbones. That must surely be a chin upon which no hair could ever hope to grow. Protective goggles conceal the upper portion of his face and, in his hands, he holds a mallet and chisel. *Strong hands*, thinks Maggie, *strong yet sensitive* and she is surprised by her own appraisal.

She coughs quietly, fearful to break the spell yet driven by her need for answers. The figure does not move. Perhaps he does not hear. Maggie moves forward into the room and speaks his name and is alarmed at how loudly the word reverberates around the studio space.

"Lars."

Lars, snaps out of his reverie, like one awaking from a sleep. He turns face eyes towards her. Through the distorting lenses of the goggles, his eyes appear even more opaque and oddly blue than before. Maggie feels the hairs stand up along the back of her neck. Lars tilts his head to one side questioningly then pushes the goggles up onto his forehead.

"Why Maggie. I beg your pardon. I did not see you there. What can I do for you? Please be so kind as to overlook the rudeness of my behaviour earlier. I was not *myself.*"

He carefully lays his tools down on a small workbench then turns back to her.

Maggie mutters a polite response, thrown a little, by the unusual formality of his address. It takes a moment to organise her thoughts. Lars is all attentive patience. She swallows then chooses her words with care.

"Lars, I had wanted to ask you something. It may sound a bit foolish, but it has been troubling my mind, so it has."

Lars regards her intently. He folds his arms across the top of the stone block and rests his chin, his face still turned towards her, as if in preparation to hear a story. Maggie continues, trying to keep her nerve.

"That day I came into your shop, last year. Do you recall?"

Lars responds with a simple blink of his eyes.

"Well, I would like to thank you, so I would…"

Lars accepts her thanks with a further movement of his eyelids and a curl of his exquisitely fine lips.

"But I would also like to know, I mean - to ask, how you knew I was being followed and that I needed to get away?"

Maggie's heart is beating so fast that she can hardly hear her own words now. She searches the strange and beautiful face for a reaction. But there is no disturbance to the striking regularity of those features. For a moment Maggie wonders whether he heard, or understood, but presently Lars raises his head, straightens up and stretching languidly, knits his fingers behind his ponytail.

"Well, it seemed quite straightforward to me…"

His voice is monotone and again he tilts his head to one side, as though in search of the correct explanation.

"I noticed that there was a gentleman, shall we say of 'Mediterranean' appearance, standing outside our shop-window. He was patently observing your movements and, as he did not enter the shop, I deduced that he was neither a friend nor an acquaintance. I am cognizant that some of our continental cousins, who are wont to pride themselves as being regular Latin Lovers, can at times make quite persistent pests of themselves on our City's streets. I, therefore, surmised that as a lone attractive woman, you might have fallen prey to such a person's unwanted attentions. Such a thing would never be tolerated in Lapland, of course. And besides, I knew that my friend Roger would want me to watch out for you. He holds you in particularly high regard. Was I correct in my thinking?"

Maggie is so thrown by the peculiarity of Lars's words and manner that she is hardly able to think. She stammers to make an answer. Lars regards her dispassionately.

"Well - I - that is, you were probably right. In any case, I appreciated your help, so I did..." Maggie is now feeling anxious to make her excuses. She gestures over her shoulders, as if that could mean anything comprehensible, looks at her watch, then mumbles her Goodbye. Lars blinks his eyes in acknowledgement and turns back to his stone carving tools.

Why, what an extraordinary person! It's no wonder Roger does not know whether he is coming or going, and that's for sure, thinks Maggie on her way home. *And Bless me if I haven't let me imagination run completely away with me. 'Tis a miracle I have not gotten meself taken away by the men in white coat again, so it is.*

Yet, for all her light-heartedness, Maggie's imagination is not quite done with her. That night she awakes from a vivid dream with a start. The pale image of Lar's face floats in wisps before her eyes, yet it is not the dream that makes her feel suddenly anxious. It is the sudden and unmistakable sense of déjà vu. She has dreamt of that face before. Many times. It might sound crazy, but she is positive of it. Small wonder he had seemed so oddly familiar.

Maggie lies awake, listening to the familiar noises of the old Peabody Buildings unable to make sense of her thoughts. Peter had not stayed over this evening and now she wishes that he had. Suddenly, there is a sound in the hallway and Maggie freezes in her bed. Then exhales in relief. It is only Kathleen's key in the door. She had worked the late shift and tiptoes in, oblivious to the heart attack she has nearly given her younger sister. She heads to the kitchenette and quietly fills the kettle. Maggie slips out of bed and pulls her dressing gown around her. A nice cup of tea and a chat about Kathleen's evening will go down very well, just now. Things will make much more sense in the morning. They always do.

The Vatican, Rome.

Cardinal Salvatore, too, is having another restless night. Perhaps it is the suffocating heat of the early Roman summer or perhaps he ate too much of his favourite zabaglione at dinner. Rich cream is beginning to disagree with him and he wonders whether he might be developing an ulcer. He is getting older, what can he expect? He listens to his physician's advice, then ignores it completely. His life and health are in God's hand. And the Lord looks after his own.

Besides, he knows there are more likely reasons for this unwelcome insomnia. He has been experiencing a kind of anxious disquiet since the afternoon he handed the samples to one of Dr Mullis' assistants. He had failed to tell the truth when he had casually assured them there was no urgency in the matter. Perhaps he had felt instinctively afraid of betraying a note of desperation in his enquiry. And now he is half-wild with impatience for some news of the results. He bridles at the thought of the samples languishing at the bottom of some lab assistant's in-tray. Do they not understand who he is? At the same time, he is uncomfortably aware that the results in themselves may place him in a potentially compromising position, and it is not a situation towards which he should proceed with undue haste. He knows, full well, that he should have discussed the course of action upon which he has embarked with the other members of Commission, yet hardly knows why he did not. Strangely enough, he suspects that his motives remain opaque to him purely because he prefers not to think about them. If he is honest, and it becomes easier to be honest when you are lying awake at five o'clock in the morning, *it had become personal.*

In all his years on the Commission, he had never seen or come close to an authentic miracle. Oh, he had debunked enough of them on his watch; they were often unsophisticated hoaxes or genuine misinterpretations fostered by the hopes of an uneducated mind. He had seen stigmata and weeping statues of the Madonna and had been obliged to sit through tireless accounts of cure and recovery from complete paralysis by obvious hysterics, who seemed unaware of the plethora of recorded case histories of hysterical conversion syndrome and its tell-tale symptoms. He had certainly heard enough first-hand witness statements, but everyone is aware of the fallibility of such evidence. What *he* demands is scientific certainty.

What is a miracle anyway? He is no longer sure that he knows. From the root *mirari* - to be amazed. He had certainly been amazed that day he had beheld Margaret Doyle's baby, amazed and galvanised into an unexpected if temporary re-examination of a faith that was beginning to fail him. Yet the infant had been conceived in sin, so the amazement had quickly turned to outrage and puzzlement. If this was to be the only genuine miracle he would ever witness, what could God be about? That He should bless a sinner, was all very New Testament, but it would fly in the face of the teachings of The Holy Roman Church and undermine its very authority. An authority founded on the fear of eternal retribution and cowed conformity. Thus, it had always been and thus it must surely remain. And yet, Jesus had himself singled out The Magdalene as his most favoured consort. Could it be that The Lord had chosen him, Anatole Salvatore, as the earthly witness to his divine missive of reform? And then the infant had died and that ignorant and adulterous little housewife had cheated him of the only hope of certainty he would ever get.

He had been angry then, angry with her and angry with God himself for permitting such an atrocity; and for having toyed with his vanity and ambition. But mostly he had been angry with himself for having so wanted to believe, for having so needed to have that belief confirmed. Yet faith is not faith if it is predicated on evidence and confirmation, for then it is knowledge and the two are very different things. So perhaps it had been God's greatest test of him; a test he was never going to pass; a test which had found his faith lacking.

In the intervening months and years, that anger had simmered down into obsession, an obsession that neither sleeps nor weakens through want of sustenance. And now, through science, he has found a way to best God himself. A way to reveal the truth. The Cardinal tosses and turns in his bed. He is not sure which he wants more – the unveiling of a hoax or the revelation of a genuine miracle.

No. That is incorrect. He *does* know. He will not be made a fool of. He wants to reveal it for the sham it was. And when he has done so, he will find Margaret Doyle and reveal her paltry perfidiousness for all the world to see. His memory flicks back to the last meeting with Vecellio. The photographs spread across his desk had seared his brain like a white-hot filament. A woman, incandescent with life and energy. It was enough to make the blood simmer in his veins.

And then, as he was leaving, his spy had cast the final grenade.

"One more thing, Monseigneur, The Signora, she is known as The Madonna of Southampton Row."

"So, God insists on laughing at me still," muses the cardinal frowning darkly. "We will see who is laughing, once I get the results."

He looks at his bedside clock, reaches for the phone and dials.

"Pronto? Ah, Vecellio, you are awake. *Bene*. It cannot be long now. I want you to find an opportunity, some public arena where we can confront her with the truth and expose her, for the fake she is, before all the world."

Bethnal Green

Janet puts down her glass of wine and looks around her with a glow of pride. It has been hard work, these last few months, but it has been worth it. Definitely worth it. Jack sees the look on her face and reads her thoughts. He does not know the names of the pretty yellow and blue flowers that fill the tubs on the little paved patio, or the climbers with their extravagant blooms that wind around the trellis, Janet had fastened to the long garden wall, but he appreciates them all the same. And Janet *does* know their names and how to care for them, another thing he loves about her.

"Are you happy, Love?" he asks, knowing the answer.

"Oh, Jack, I couldn't be more so. I guess I had begun to think I'd never have a proper home, a house I mean, with a garden and - well, you know."

The early arrival of summer seems to have cemented Janet's felicity. What could be better than getting back from work and dining *al fresco* in your own back yard? And if Jack has no green thumb, well then, he certainly knows how to whip up a pasta carbonara fit to shame an Italian housewife.

"A penny for your thoughts, Jan?" he asks playfully.

"I was just thinking about Jill when we went up to Aunty Linda's for her dress fitting. Jack, she was a vision. Truly, she is going to be such a beautiful bride. I hope Jim knows how lucky he is."

"Believe you me, he does. He may play the fool, but when it comes to matters of the heart, he is deadly serious, so he is. And what about you?"

"How do you mean?" queries Janet, uncertain where the question is leading. She is quite unprepared for any deep emotional soul searching on this lovely June evening.

"Why, how did you look in your bridesmaid's dress?" Jack raises his eyebrows.

Janet laughs.

"It's actually rather better than I could have hoped. Very elegant. I think I will scrub up rather well."

"I bet you look drop-dead gorgeous. You'll be upstaging the bride, so you will."

Janet smiles at his gallantry, but a veil of wistfulness clouds her bright eyes. Jack wishes he had been a little more sensitive, yet saying anything more will only make it worse. They drink their wine in silence, listening to the twilight twittering of avian evensong. Janet is reconciling herself to the fact that a little soul searching may, after all, be unavoidable.

"Jack?"

"Hmmm?"

"You know that thing we talked about?"

"Which thing, Darling? We do talk about a few of them."

Janet thinks about accusing him of being deliberately obtuse but decides this is unfair.

"The thing about getting married, or rather, *not* getting married."

"Yes...?"

"Well, I still stand by what I said, but, well I have been thinking. If, say, just say, we decided we wanted to start a family, well I would want to be legally married, at least, you know, in a registry office. We both know how hard it can still be for kids born out of wedlock, even though it is much more common these days, and besides, it makes it so much easier - legally, I mean."

"Are you trying to tell me something, Jan?" Jack speaks slowly and cautiously.

"What? Oh, Christ no. No. I am on the pill, you know I am. I would never come off it without discussing it with you. I'm talking hypothetically." She searches Jack's face for his response.

"Aye now, that makes sense. But I never heard you say you wanted children before. I guess it is all this nest building." He smiles, gesturing to their house and garden and Janet feels on safe ground.

"The truth is, I never thought I really wanted children. But then I never knew *you*, Jack. And now I guess I do find myself thinking of it from time to time." She shrugs. "Don't get me wrong. I mean, I am in no hurry. In any case, neither of us know the first thing about babies, and neither of us has any family close at hand to help out or show us how it is done. I was rather thinking in the future, perhaps after Jim and Jill have had one. So then, they can show us how it is done."

She laughs, but there is some earnestness in her words. Jack laughs too.

"Now don't you be telling me you of all people would be wishing a mini-Jim on the world? I would think one wreaking havoc might be enough, so I would."

"Well, it might be a mini-Jill, and then she would just be the most beautiful, gentle child."

"Well, that would be in the hands of God to be sure. But, to tell you the truth, Jan, I think you have a point. But since we are in no hurry, perhaps we can think about it more seriously once Jim and Jill's nuptials are done and dusted."

Janet nods, happy with this response. She is quite content to be the pragmatist. It seems to be working for her so far. Jack, on the other hand, has quite different ideas. He has observed Janet's face whilst she and Jill have been conspiring over wedding plans. He is painfully aware of how many of her dreams Janet has sacrificed for him. If they are going to be married, in the sight of the law at least, then he is going to save up and buy her the most beautiful engagement ring his monthly salary will stretch to. Then he is going to go down on one knee and propose. *She may not have him body and soul, but she will have him body and heart. She deserves no less.*

The next day finds Janet running late. Janet may love her garden but, as is often the case in life, there seems to be an inevitable downside to all the prettiness of the blooms. The pollen count seems to be unusually high already this summer and she has been sneezing her way through sessions, to the point where she had made more use of the box of tissues than her clients. She had popped out at lunchtime to try and get to the chemists to pick up some anti-histamines, but clearly, she is not the only sufferer as the queue had been frustratingly long.

She is rushing along Southampton Row and is almost at the main entrance of the old Central building when she has a sudden panic that she has left her wallet on the counter in the pharmacy. She fumbles in her handbag, without letting up on her pace and rounds the corner into the great stone pillared doorway with eyes still cast downwards in search-mode.

"Scusami, Signora!"

The tall man in her path spins around and holds up both hands in dismay as Janet clips his shoulder, scarcely avoiding a full-on collision with him in her blind haste. He had been closely perusing the display boards on either side of the porchway and had had his back to her, so had been unable to step out of her way.

"I am so sorry," gasps Janet "How clumsy of me. I hope there is no damage done?"

The man, who is of continental appearance, smiles charmingly, shaking his head in the negative.

"How coulda such a, 'ow you say, delicate young woman, lika yourself cause any 'arm. Would be impossible!" He gestures extravagantly. Janet returns the smile, though it must appear a tad forced. She is still late and wants to rush away, but after such carelessness, surely that would be adding insult to injury.

"Might I aska, does the Signora work here?" he indicates the art school with a gesture of his hand, which Janet notices is immaculately manicured and adorned by an exquisite antique jet and gold signet-ring.

"Yes. In fact, I do. Why do you ask?" replies Janet, looking at the watch and hoping her interrogator will get the hint.

"Well, I am reading this, 'ow you say, poster, and it is telling me about an art show, that is 'appening next month."

"And?" Her tone is sounding a little impatient now.

"Well, am I correct in thinking it isa open to the public? I am in London for a while longer, I am thinking to myself I would lika to see this very much. Isa right?"

"Yes, yes. By all means. Please, you would be more than welcome. Come along to the opening night. You may even be offered a glass of wine then. But I am sorry, I really must rush now. It was a pleasure to have met you."

"*Benissimo!*"

The man thanks her and inclines his head in a formal bow. Janet shakes her head and sprints off and in through the revolving glass door, the dark gentleman and the wallet already forgotten. She looks up at the large clock in the foyer and cursing quietly, trots down the corridor towards her little office. A lone figure sits in the waiting area, hunched over a dog-eared paperback.

"Oh, Maggie! I am so sorry that I am late for our appointment. I got delayed and could not get away." She opens the door to the little counselling room, by way of invitation. Maggie looks up from her book and grins.

"Sure, I had not even noticed, I have been so engrossed." She holds up the paperback. *Gormenghast*. "He has such a wonderful imagination with him. And his illustrations are as beautiful as his prose."

Janet smiles. She has a soft spot for Mervyn Peake herself. She can almost believe that her client might not have noticed the time.

"So, Maggie, I haven't seen you for quite a while. I hope everything is going okay with the preparations for the final show?" Janet is not kidding. She can hardly keep track of the number of students who turn up at her office at this time of year, in a state of near hysteria about their final assessments. Yet Maggie looks far from distraught.

"Well, I have done me best, so I have. And what will be, will be. My tutor has high hopes for my final grade, and I'll not be pretending I don't care what it will be. But whatever happens, this has been the most wonderful experience of me life." She stops.

Janet, looks at her enquiringly.

"Well, that is the problem, I suppose. Everything is going so well. The painting, Peter - I have even rediscovered a sister, I had all but forgotten I had. I am coping much better with my handwashing and flash-backs, I have not even had the sense of being followed or watched in a little while. But, sure, you know how the saying goes. If it seems too good to be true, it probably is. I have just started to feel this kind of anxiety, dread really, that something is going to go wrong. Because it is going so right. What in the Mother of God's name is wrong with me?"

"Oh, Maggie. Perhaps that is understandable, given all that you have been through. But these good things have not just happened through blind luck. Most are down to you. The person you are, the effort you have made. Why even the hand washing. I never saw anyone so determined to overcome their symptoms, as you have been. It was no stroke of fate. And then, look at your relationship with Peter. You worked through the difficulties together, and Peter loves you because of the person you are, not despite it. Do you see what I mean?

"That I do, Janet. I guess it is that old self-protection thing again. If I prepare myself for it all to go wrong, it won't seem so bad when it does…"

"But you can spoil the happiness you feel with that preparation and it might be for something that never happens."

Maggie nods. She smiles warmly at Janet. She feels a connection with Janet that she has seldom experienced with another woman.

"And of course, I will miss this - you, Janet. I suddenly realised that moving on means leaving my safety net behind, so it does. I can't tell you how important this has been for me. I don't think I would ever have coped without you. Especially when Peter and I broke up."

Janet can feel her eyes watering and this time it is not the hay fever that stings them.

"Maggie, I know we touched on this a while back, but perhaps I have not given it the attention it deserves. It is important for us to acknowledge the ending of this relationship because that is what it is. Not like others perhaps, but just as real and important. One of the problems with an informal appointment system is that it can make working with the ending a bit haphazard. I am so pleased that you came in before the end of term. I know we will see each other around and at your final show, (which I wouldn't miss for the world), but we can only talk about the feelings about it, here."

Maggie casts her eyes down. She is struggling not to weep. Janet meanwhile silently remonstrates with herself. *How could she have handled the conclusion of their work together so poorly?* It is true enough that the first-come-first-served booking system can be unhelpful in this way; there is no agreed contract or number of sessions and sometimes a student might only attend a couple of sessions, after which their name never re-appears on her appointment sheet. The frequency of Maggie's session had varied greatly over her time at Central, yet they had been meeting for over two years. *Why hadn't she thought it through more thoroughly?* Janet wonders if she has been in some kind of denial about it but is rescued from the discomfort of her self-reflection by Maggie, who speaks at last.

"Janet, I wanted to give you something, but I am not sure if..."

"Well, I can't accept expensive gifts," Janet raises her eyebrows, "but if it is some small token of thanks, a sketch perhaps...."

Maggie shakes her head but continues to look downwards as though still uncertain.

"Maggie -tell me, what is vexing you?"

Maggie gives a deep sigh then fetches out a little book from her bag. It is the same little bible she had shown Janet all those months ago. She opens it at the centre and takes out the small folded scrap of silk, which she places on the table between them. She gently unfurls the flimsy fabric. It is the little white feather.

Janet cannot help but gasp.

"Maggie, surely - you cannot mean..." She hardly knows how to continue.

"Now, hold on for just a moment," replies Maggie, raising her eyes to meet Janet's. "I know you will say you can't accept it. But in a way, it is not a gift. I want to let it go. I don't need it to remember my son, for as God is my witness, I can never forget him, so I can't. I used to need it to remind me what was real, but I don't feel the need of it any longer. Can you understand? Janet, you have never questioned the truth of what happened, even if you couldn't believe it yourself and, because of that, you've helped me more than you can know. And don't you be thinking it isn't so. Entrusting this to you would somehow be close that chapter for me. I know you would keep it safe because you understand what it means. It's not that I would ever want to ask for it back, and that I believe I can promise you, but knowing it is with someone who cares, well – I need that. Perhaps it sounds silly. I can't explain it any better, so I can't."

"I think you just explained it rather well," smiles Janet. "I tell you what. You may leave it in my safekeeping and, believe me, I understand the deep confidence you place in me, in so doing, though I cannot accept it as a gift. I will hold it in trust, as it were, but it will still belong to you, and if you should ever need it, well…"

Maggie nods and smiles a grateful smile. She picks up the feather in its little fold of silk and holds it out. Janet extends her own hands. Maggie kisses the tiny bundle than presses it into Janet's palms. The two women meet eyes. Janet feels her heart lurch in her chest. Maggie rises without words, inclines her head in a gesture of farewell, then leaves the room. Janet sits for a few moments unmoving then rises and with the utmost care places the silk-wrapped feather between the pages of her diary.

That night she rummages through her the bottom drawer of her dressing table to find her little white leather-bound bible, which had been stowed away among her scarves and gloves and miscellaneous possessions. One of her Godmother's had given it to her on the occasion of her confirmation and God knows it has had shamefully little use since then. Janet places the precious parcel between its leaves then carefully wraps the little volume in a liberty print handkerchief that had been a delightful, but ultimately unused, Christmas gift from her Aunty Linda. She closes the drawer and sighs. For some reason, she experiences a sudden thought that she is also somehow closing a chapter of her life. She wonders what the next will bring.

Bethnal Green
18th June 1984

Dear Frank,

I hope this letter finds you well and that you can forgive your old friend for being such a hopeless and irregular correspondent. It is difficult to believe how quickly time passes, and there are never enough hours in the day. And although this is but a poor excuse for my negligence, it must suffice.

Life is going better than ever I could have hoped and I smile when I think back to your wise words about just "getting on with it". As my hero John Lennon once said, Life is indeed what happens when we are busy making other plans.

Janet has transformed the rundown old house we bought into a veritable palace, but more importantly, into a real home. And I do at last feel that I have indeed found my place in the world. Does that sound odd? I suspect you will not think so, as I sometimes think you know me better than I know myself. Looking back, I wonder sometimes how I could ever have deluded myself that the life of a priest was my real calling. And you will laugh out loud when I tell you that I now believe that it was, after all, teaching. And those are words I never dreamt I would say. But again, you seemed to intuit that my gifts lay that way, despite my apprehension. There is something about the joy of engaging the appetite of a young mind that I could never have imagined. All too often the kids I see do not even know that they hunger, even as they starve, and yet you have only to lay a banquet before them, with an invitation they can understand, for them to devour the last morsel with a relish, that only the hungry can truly enjoy. Perhaps this sounds a little florid, but it is the only way I can put it into words.

Yet strangely enough, I do not think I could have understood what it truly means to be an educator without having been involved in the Boxing Club. I have learned more from Jim than I could have done from a PhD in Education. And he has also taught me more about myself than I care to admit.

I guess what I'm trying to get at is that my life at long last feels meaningful, so it does. I still have those moments where I feel in the grip of remorse about what happened with Margaret, but there does not seem any way for me to make it right, so I have learned to just let it go. Last summer, when I attended the Art School annual exhibition again with Janet, I felt myself on high alert, in case there was a trace of her. But the lad who had painted that image the year before was long gone and I realised how foolish I was being. London is such a big place, and he had simply sketched the face of a stranger in a pub. Maybe it was not even hers. All too often we see what we want to see. It is time to move on, my friend.

So now I want to ask a favour!

I am going to ask Janet to marry me. And I want to do it right. Of course, we cannot be married in church, it will have to be a civil ceremony, but I was wondering if you would be willing to perform a blessings service? I think it would mean the world to Jan, and I know it would mean so much to me, but I will of course understand if you do not feel comfortable accepting.

You are of course invited to the wedding, regardless of what you decide. I hope that goes without saying.

Well, I hope to hear all of your news soon? I trust the flock up in Liverpool is keeping you on your toes. I hope to come up and visit over the summer and bring Jan along. I would love you to meet her. You will very much like her, I know. I have promised her a Beatles tour. She might not be such a great fan as I, but even she is excited about the prospect of spending an evening in the famous Cavern Club.

Your ever-devoted friend,
Jack.

Father Frank feels tired. Tired and old. Sometimes the complications of life entrap us like the sticky silken threads of a spider's web; the more we struggle to free ourselves, the more fastly ensnared we become. He re-reads the letter he has received from Jack and sighs. It was a letter that should have gladdened his heart, and had indeed, gladdened his heart before he had given it further thought. But now he finds himself impaled upon the horns of a dilemma. And it is a dilemma that is both personal and moral.

He looks down at the scrap of paper on his desk, next to where he has lain the letter. He scratches his head. It seems so innocuous. A simple three-line address scribbled hastily in ballpoint pen. He picks it up.

"Ah, Margaret," he sighs, "if only you could have remained hidden amongst the flowers of Covent Garden in your Peabody Buildings. You had eluded us for so long. Better not to seek that which you do not really wish to find, I suppose."

But Jack had seemed to need it so. To need some closure, in order to turn over the page to the next chapter of his life. So, Frank had put his feelers out, and although it had taken years, the search had eventually proven fruitful. It can be easy enough to find someone when they are not taking particular trouble to hide and, aside from trying to steer clear of folk from the Old Country, Margaret Doyle had taken no special pains to conceal her identity or whereabouts. It had only been a matter of time.

Frank folds and unfolds the little slip of paper in his fingers. So much time has passed, and Jack seems so settled at last. Frank has a horrible feeling that sharing this information now could well jeopardize the brightness of his friend's future, for there is no telling what course of foolishness Jack might pursue. And it is a future he has fought so hard to win. But if he does not tell him, is he not making himself complicit to a deceit? Not quite a frank lie, perhaps, but an omission of the truth. And it would be a deceit that would have to remain forever between them, a cancer that must eventually erode the very core of their mutual trust.

And what of Margaret Doyle? Is she not owed some reparation? Yet if she has somehow forged a life for herself, could not the unexpected appearance of her lover from the past put *her* new life at risk? It is no uncommon thing to harbour skeletons in the cupboard, but the skeleton in Margaret Doyle's is unusually tiny and unconscionable. If she has closed and firmly locked that particular cupboard door, then it most likely best left that way and Jack has no right to turn up wielding the key.

Frank picks up his tumbler of whiskey and takes a long swig. He closes his fingers around the paper, then crushing it into a tiny ball, lobs it into the waste paper bin next to the fire-place.

Friday 13th July 1984

Peter pours out a couple of glasses of whiskey whilst Maggie soaks in a long hot bath to ease her aching arms and knees. Every inch of her body seems to be in protest, yet Maggie could scarcely feel happier. The night of the final show has arrived. She and rest of the third years have worked all week preparing the fourth floor for the exhibition, whitewashing walls, scraping paint off the parquet floors on hands and knees, then assembling frames and hanging canvases.

Then at lunchtime today, she had been thrilled to discover that she been awarded a first-class degree. She and Peter had shared a bottle of champagne in the Staff bar with anyone who cared to join them. To top it all, after a couple of glasses and a tidal wave of congratulations, Peter had confessed that he had surreptitiously invited a couple of gallery scouts to the private view. There had been a great deal of interest in the photographs he had shown them and he has every reason to believe that Maggie's show will warrant honourable mention in the Evening Standard's critique of this summer's London's Art School graduates.

Peter stands outside the bathroom for a moment listening to the strains of Maggie's soft voice as she half sings, half hums *La ci darem la mano*. Peter smiles. Don Giovanni. It had been the first opera he had taken her. He smiles to himself as he recalls how her face had shone with unalloyed wonderment as she sat in the upper circle of the Coliseum, drinking in the rapturous harmonies of Mozart's greatest masterpiece.

To Peter's great delight, she had become an instant convert and at long last, he has somebody with whom to share his lifelong passion. Wendy had had no time for opera of any description, designating it as bourgeois and narratively deficient. In her view, it went on too long and held no relevance for the twentieth century. Her criticisms may have had their merit but privately Peter suspected that she must be tone-deaf. Indeed, music had hardly seemed to feature in her life at all and he was consigned to listening to his LP collection on headphones or when she was out. As the years of their marriage passed, he had continued to attend one of two new productions a year on his own, but now, he and Maggie scarcely missed a season at The Coliseum. Once in a while he would even splash out and treat them to a performance at The Covent Garden Opera House.

He listens a little longer at the door. Maggie may not be Kiri Te Kanawa but she has a sweet tone and can hold a note. She has an enviable ability to remember a phrase or melody accurately, after only one hearing. He has said it before, *she is quite a woman.*
He makes a perfunctory knock on the door then enters.
"I'm very proud of you, you know," he says sitting on the edge of the bath and handing her the glass.
Maggie beams.
"To butter and whiskey," she proclaims, holding it high.
"No, Maggie. Not tonight," smiles Peter, "tonight we drink to the marvellous Maggie Doyle and her very, very bright future."
Maggie grins and clinks her glass against his.
"Now be off with you, while I make myself beautiful," she jokes.
"You could never be more beautiful to me, my Maggie."
But perhaps he is wrong because ten minutes later, Maggie emerges from her bedroom in the velvet suit she has kept at the back of the wardrobe since January and Peter's jaw all but hits the floor. A vision in green, she seems the embodiment of all the beauty and charm of the Emerald Isle itself. Peter lets out a low whistle and offers his arm.
"This is your night, Maggie," Peter whispers squeezing her hand.

Up on the landing of the fourth floor of the Central building, Yvonne and Kathleen are already waiting for Maggie. They fidget a little nervously, feeling very out of place in the art school setting and conspicuous in their best Sunday frocks, court shoes and patent handbags. Maggie spies them from the landing below and gives a little squeal of excitement then bounds up the stairs two at a time, leaving Peter panting to keep up. She throws her arms around her sister and then Yvonne and hugs them both warmly. The pride glitters in their eyes as Maggie escorts them through the two great glass doors into the painting department, while Peter hurries off to find drinks for them all.

The narrow corridor is already teeming with family and friends invited to the private viewing, and all around is a sea of faces that are proud, or happy, or both. Maggie ushers her little family to her display space, nodding to friends or calling out congratulations on the way through the crowded corridors. At last Yvonne and Kathleen stand in the little space which houses Maggie's final year exhibition. Their mouths drop open in unison.

Seven of Maggie's largest canvases span the longer side of the partition, whilst a collection of smaller studies and life drawing are displayed together on the adjacent wall. Although each canvas is quite different from its neighbour, the effect of the ensemble is one of drawing the viewer into an alternate realm or dimension. Whether that dimension is quite Heaven or Hell, seems ambiguous; it is certainly not Earthly. The images are not quite abstract nor yet purely representational, shifting dreamscapes, which change as different elements capture the eye's focus. At the centre of the seven canvases is the largest work, titled *The Lady of Shalott*. In some ways, it is the most figurative of the works and the easiest to read. Its fractured planes and angles suggest the splintering of reality, as the lady herself appears to crack along with the glass of the mirror that so long held her captive. Anyone feeling uneasy in the presence of such images would not be alone.

Maggie waits patiently for a reaction. Her sister seems lost for words. Maggie wonders if she is simply horrified, but too polite to say as much. Then Kathleen starts to sob, and Yvonne puts her arm around her shoulders and pulls her close. Maggie's face is all concern. *She hopes that Kathleen is not offended or upset, she knows they are a bit full-on...* But

Kathleen takes her best lace handkerchief from her handbag and wiping her nose, shakes her head. *She feels moved beyond what she is able to express. She is no connoisseur of art, indeed, to her shame, she has hardly stepped foot in an Art Gallery since she first arrived in London, yet the images, strange as they are to her eyes, speak to her here - deep inside.* She clasps her hand to her chest then, taking Maggie's hand, presses it to her lips. The sisters embrace. Maggie dabs at her eyes to ensure her mascara is not running. Yvonne is also struggling to hold back the tears, and exchanges a look of pride with Kathleen, that momentarily betrays a closeness they ordinarily take pains to conceal in public.

Peter arrives with his hands full of glasses of wine and hands them around. He sees the look of relief on Maggie's face places his arm around her waist and gives her a congratulatory squeeze. He knows that whilst Maggie is fiercely independent of the judgement of others, the disapprobation or disappointment of her beloved Kathleen would have been a wound indeed.

Soon the little group of four is joined by Roger, who has a surprise guest in tow. Summer! Returned from Jaipur, where she has been helping to set up a women's batik co-operative, she seizes Maggie in a great bear hug, exclaiming that she would not have missed this night for all the world. Their old friend cuts an exotic dash, with her nut-brown skin, brightly batik printed dress and hair that she has left to matt into red dreadlocks. They have scarcely completed their greetings when Tony and Sarah appear to complete The Gang. They all send up little cheer of excitement and more embracing and cheek kissing ensues.

Sarah, in particular, seems positively to glow in the warmth of the reunion and shares the news that she and Tony, only so newly wedded, are to be parents. Maggie's happiness would be complete, had she not caught the fleeting look of sorrow that flashes across Roger's face. But Roger is as generous in his congratulations as any amongst the little group, and if he holds onto Tony's hand a little too long when he seizes it to shake it, then it is only Maggie who notices.

The Gang are effusive in their compliments to Maggie, both on the elegance of her attire and of course, on her show. It is a while since they have seen her work, and here, exhibited together, the effect is quite breath-taking. Roger remarks that it must have something to do with this particular space since it is the very same that he had himself had occupied only two years earlier, and he too was awarded a first, if they recall. Summer cuffs him playfully with a scolding reproach. *Tonight is about Maggie, they need no reminder that he is the star student at the Royal Academy.* But Roger is close to bursting with delight. *He cannot believe it - Maggie, his very own Madonna, the very same Maggie he found in The Princess Louise all those years ago. This definitely calls for a toast.* Roger raises his glass. There will be no prizes for guessing that it involves some form of dairy produce and alcohol!

Dusk is beginning to fall outside. Kath and Vonnie are beginning to wilt ever so slightly and make their apologies. It has all been a little bit more excitement and culture than they are used to. But they promise to return during the week and treat Maggie and Peter to the slap-up celebration dinner they deserve.

Peter suggests that he escort Kathleen and Yvonne to the tube station and gets no argument from them, for he has been a firm favourite with them both since that snowy New Year's Eve. Meanwhile, Maggie needs to hang around to greet visitors and, perhaps more importantly, the gallery scouts, should one make an appearance.

Roger, Summer and the happy couple also make their farewells temporarily, as they want to see the rest of the exhibition and catch up with some old faces. They all agree to meet up in the Louise later. It will be like old times. Still more hugs and kisses are exchanged and then they head off towards the next exhibition space, chattering and laughing. Just as they turn the corner, Roger looks back and winks. Maggie, Peter, Kathleen and Yvonne stand a moment enjoying the sudden moment of quiet.

"Shall we?" says Peter extending his hand towards the doorway.

Maggie, thoughtfully anticipating that her sister would prefer the elevator to the long flights of steps back down to the foyer, suggests as much to Peter and accompanies them all to the furthest end of the corridor, to a little landing where the service lift will take them down to the back entrance.

She presses the button to call the car and they exchange yet more happy embraces. Maggie feels the sparkling wine lightening her head a little and reminds herself she should eat before any serious drinking starts, then waves them off as she draws closed the folding steel and lift-cage doors. She turns back into the painting department and drifts happily along the corridor, wondering if it is possible for there to be a more wonderful night.

Approaching the entrance to her exhibition space she spies Janet, holding a glass of wine and scanning around, presumably for the woman of the hour herself. Maggie draws closer and gives a little wave and notices that she is not on her own. Next to her, with his back turned, a man in a corduroy jacket with silver threaded dark hair is peering closely at the name label, with some concentration. As she calls Janet's name in greeting, he spins around to face her. His features stiffen into a rigid expression of surprise then buckle in dismayed confusion.

"Margaret?"

"Father John!"

The blood rushes from Maggie's cheeks. For a moment, the periphery of her vision darkens and she fears she is going to faint. She wobbles slightly. Janet extends a hand to steady her and looks between each in astonishment. But even as she is framing some question, she notices that Maggie has turned quite white. But it is not Jack that Maggie's eyes are now fixed upon. They are fastened, in nothing short of terror, on a figure some way over his shoulder. Janet turns her head. There, in the middle of Maggie's exhibition space stands a figure in a long black cassock and short black cloak, his waist encircled by the red sash of his office. He seems transfixed by the images before him, but as if unconsciously aware of Maggie's stare, he turns his eyes towards her and fixes his gaze upon her.

Maggie freezes momentarily, then trembles and cowers: a helpless doe caught in the headlamps of some unstoppable juggernaut. Jack is turning now and utters a low blasphemy, and it is as though the sound breaks the spell. Maggie pivots on her high heels and bolts, as fast as it is possible to bolt in such footwear, away down the corridor back towards the lift foyer. The Cardinal stretches out his hand in pursuit. Then, breaking out into a half-trot, he tries to put on some speed whilst attempting to retain his dignity. He does not even register Jack and Janet who stand helplessly by as he puffs past, eyes fixed on Maggie's retreating figure. Still, there is no need for undue haste. She cannot get far. Vecellio, his shadowy underling, the very man who has dogged Maggie's steps for the last three years, is close at hand. He has only to be patient a little while longer.

Janet, feeling completely mystified, seizes Jack's lapel and demands to know what is going on, but Jack has no time for explanations. He thrusts his wine glass into her beseeching hand and hissing at her urgently, not to move on any account, takes after off the Cardinal. Janet, too dumbfounded to argue, stands craning her head after them, struggling to fit the pieces together in her mind.

Maggie is not thinking clearly. She has headed for the lift but is already realising her mistake. Since the little lift had only just now taken Peter and the others down to the bottom, she would be obliged to wait for it to come back up.

It is old and slow at the best of times and seems to take an eternity even when you are not in a hurry. Worse still, it does not come at all if the cage door has not been fully closed. That would be just her luck.

Suddenly, the memory of the final show two summers ago comes back to her. Looking around her she veers off around the corner towards the little broom closet, half-praying that it is not locked. She mutters a little prayer of relief as the door swings open immediately then vanishes inside and up the little staircase to the fire-exit door. Yet, it will not afford her the safety she had hoped. What she has failed to see is the tall dark and impeccably dressed man who hovers, almost out of sight, near the end of the corridor, as though in wait for someone: the same tall dark man who steps forward and exchanges glances with The Cardinal as he comes into sight, then nods towards the cupboard door. Cardinal Salvatore spies the fire-escape sign above the door. He raises an eyebrow, hesitates for just one second, then seizes the door handle and disappears into the closet behind her.

Maggie gains the roof then wonders what on Earth to do. She glances around and then asks herself what on earth could have possessed her to choose such an exit. Breathing heavily, she walks across to the edge of the roof that looks over onto the central hall. The glass dome is brightly lit and she can see the marble floor and pillars of the exhibition hall, half-empty now, as most of the guests have begun to make their way home. At any other time, she might appreciate the enchantment of the scene, but as she swivels around to check whether she has been followed, she can already see the dark form of the cloaked cardinal emerging from the fire escape door. Maggie shudders, her last scrap of self-belief fading like the dying flicker of a spent candle. She turns her face away and screws her eyes shut, wholly unable to face her fate head-on. Yet even now, a tiny part of her notices the deliciousness of the breeze on her face and she is touched by the sheer pleasure of such a simple thing.

If only Maggie's eyes were open, she could see that The Cardinal is walking slowly towards her, his hands held up in a gesture of pacification, his face lit with anxious goodwill. But her eyelids remain firmly shut and she sees only the menacing figure of her imagination. A rush of adrenalin floods her nervous system and Maggie stands statue-like on the edge of the roof her profile etched against the light of the evening sky.

The Cardinal, unaware of the severity of Maggie's shock, softly speaks her full name then crosses himself and kneeling at her feet, reaches for her hand and attempts to press it to his lips. Jack, meanwhile, had seen the Cardinal veer off and into the broom cupboard and is, even now, hard upon his heels. Diving into the closet and up the stairs, he emerges onto the rooftop just in time to see the cardinal sink to his knees and extend his arms to Margaret Doyle, in supplication. Transfixed as he is by the unexpected scene before him, he does notice the dark figure who slips noiselessly through the opening behind him and is lost in the shadows.

Shocked to his core by the Cardinal's attempt to kiss his former lover's hand, Jack strains his ears to catch the soft Italian lilt of The Cardinal's voice as it carries on the wind above the noise of the traffic below. He makes out the phrase;

"Forgive me, Signora, I beg you."

Maggie, however, has neither heard nor heeded the words of this man, the very embodiment of power, she has feared for so long. Unable to comprehend what is occurring, a tremor of panic ripples through her being as she feels the brush of his lips on her fingers. Her only instinct is one of escape. She breaks free of his grasp and lurches blindly back towards the stairs.

Cardinal Salvatore shakes his head in sorrow and turns, still on his knees, imploring her to hear him out. He goes to rise stiffly to his feet but, all at once, stumbles. The heel of his shoe is caught in the hem of his cassock. He loses his balance, cries out. Twisting to try and recover himself, he topples then staggers backwards and sideways against the ankle-high parapet that runs the length of the wall. It is such a little trip, yet the last he will ever make. Hopelessly off-balance, he tumbles and plunges headlong into the night. For a moment he seems to fly; a great dark angel, his short cloak billowing like great black wings. Then there is a crash, the sound of shattering glass and screaming from below.

Some yards away, Jack has caught the fleeing Maggie in his arms and is clasping her tightly to his breast. She has not seen the accident and had been oblivious to the presence of her former lover but is brought to her senses by the screams. She looks into Jack's stricken face with sudden comprehension. Holding on to each other they dart towards the edge of the roof and peer over in dumb horror. The scene below is unholy chaos. People are shouting and running in from the foyer. The black and red figure of the cardinal lies broken and lifeless on the sparkling white marble floor amid the bloodied shards of splintered glass.

Maggie puts her face in her hands. Silent sobs shake her body. Then she becomes silent and strangely still. Jack stands with his arms around her. As fast as his heart is beating, his mind has never been clearer.

There is a sound of shuffling feet and suddenly he realises they are not alone. A tall bearded man in a dark suit stands close to the parapet, just a little way off, surveying the scene below. He shoots a glance towards Jack and Maggie, mutters something in Italian, then turns on his heel and makes towards the fire escape door, where he narrowly avoids toppling a young woman, who lets out a little yelp of surprise, as he clips her shoulder in his haste. The dark man, in no mood for polite apologies this evening, raises a hand

and pushes past her and down the stairs. A handsome ring flashes on his finger. She looks after him in complete amazement. Isn't he the guy she nearly ploughed into a few weeks back? *What on earth is he doing up here?* She frowns with displeasure and, rubbing her upper arm, turns around to survey the scene before her.

Frustrated at being left to stand idly by while some drama seemed to be unfolding elsewhere, Janet had disobeyed Jack's instructions, found the cupboard door ajar and t tow and two together. She has neither seen nor heard the events of the last few seconds and searches around for the Cardinal in confusion, yet there seems to be no sign of him. What she does see, however, is Maggie in Jack's arms. She feels a stab of betrayal. A dimly apprehended and hitherto blurred comprehension clicks suddenly into focus. Why had she not seen it before? A million doubts rush into her mind; Jack's reluctance to commit; his reserve and secrecy; Maggie's luminous beauty and passion for life. Janet must pale in comparison. She should go, leave them to one another. She should have known all along it was too good to be real.

But Jack is even now signalling to her to approach. She makes her way across the roof to them, despite herself.

"Maggie," he breathes, "We must take care of her."

Janet looks again at Maggie and, this time sees the reality. This is not a rival triumphant in the reclaiming of her man, this is a broken and traumatised woman. Her eyes are vacant and unseeing. There is no hint of recognition that Janet is even present. Janet leans to look over the edge of the roof, but Jack waves her back, shaking his head vehemently and suddenly she understands.

"There has been a terrible accident," says Jack in a flat and oddly formal voice. "I need you to help get Maggie home, to our home, not hers, it may not be safe for her, there. I will take care of things here, but we must keep her out of it. I fear she will not cope with any more. Can you do that Janet?"

Janet nods. Jack is placing his trust in her. And she knows enough of Maggie's history to know he is right. She looks with an anxious face at Maggie and places her arm around her shoulders, whispering words of reassurance. Jack goes on ahead and leads them all back down to the fourth floor, scouting ahead to make sure the corridor is clear.

There are already signs of a commotion at the main entrance of the department, as news of the terrible accident makes its way up the great stairway. Students and visitors alike hang over bannisters, shouting and gesturing to those below, and no one pays any attention to the tall dark foreigner who slips out through the little huddles of people and down to the foyer below.

"Is there a back way out?" asks Jack.
Janet gestures towards the elevator just a little further down the way.

"Take a taxi," he says in a clear and measured tone. "I will wait here and deal with the police, for police there must be, to be sure. I will follow you later or ring and let you know what is going on. Just get her out of here and keep her safe, Janet. I owe her that much at least."

"But wait," cries Janet with sudden presence of mind, "What about Peter? She needs him Jack, and he will go out of his mind if she just disappears."

Jack falters. He has no idea of a Peter or what he signifies to Maggie but, seeing the earnestness in Janet's face, he nods in acquiescence.

"Just give me a minute," pants Janet and leaving Maggie with Jack, she hares down the corridor in search of Peter or someone who will know his whereabouts. The first person she bumps into as she rounds the doorway to one of the studios is Roger. He is standing deep in conversation with an extraordinary looking figure with the palest skin and hair she has ever seen. For a moment all she can do is stand and stare. She shakes her head. She cannot allow herself to be distracted. Breathing hard, she waves her hand by way of apology for her interruption and she asks if he has seen Peter. *Well, of course, he has. He is just walking Maggie's sister to the tube station.*

"Please Roger, you must fetch him, Maggie is unwell - I am taking her home with me. We are going down via the back-way. Tell him we will meet him near the entrance to the underground car park. Please, no questions now, just go."

Roger nods, he has not forgotten Janet's kindness to Maggie two years ago or the part he had played in his friend's distress. And he can see how upset Janet is. He makes a thumbs-up sign and sets off towards the main staircase at a run. The tall stranger remains where he is, looking down at Janet with a quizzical expression on his face, his head cocked to one side. Janet smiles at him nervously. To her complete surprise, he places a long white hand on her shoulder and looks earnestly down into her face. He has the most astonishing eyes she has ever seen. She feels the skin on her arms prickle into goosebumps. And then he speaks,

"Take good care of Maggie, Janet Hazelwood. She needs you now, as she has never needed you before."

Janet can find no sensible words of response. She mutters an affirmative then falls silent. Satisfied, Lars removes his hand and steps back. He inclines his head towards the end of the corridor, where Maggie and Jack await her, as if to signal that she is free to go. Janet turns around with a murmur of farewell and races back to the lift foyer.

Who on earth was that? And what the Hell was that about? Never mind, job done. There is no time to think about it now. Peter will be with them soon. There is no one fleeter of foot than the mercurial Roger and no one more devoted to Maggie. He will not fail her.

Behind her, Lars stands for a while longer, then stalks languidly towards the other end of the corridor and the commotion that is sweeping upwards from the bloody scene below.

Janet arrives back at the elevator just as the lift car arrives. She signals to Jack that all is in hand. He pulls open the steel safety cage and folding door then nods. Janet touches Maggie's arm and she shuffles forward into the lift with her, in automaton-like obedience. Janet's eyes meet Jack's as he draws across the outer cage door. She feels a rush of devotion that makes her head swim. She pulls the inner door close, presses the button for the basement, then sees him no more.

Camden Town, Wednesday 18th July

"And then what happened?"
To his irritation, Bernard finds himself uncharacteristically intrigued by the denouement of the plot that Janet is unfolding. Of course, he had heard about the death of The Cardinal in the local T.V news bulletin, who had not? But he had entirely failed to make the link. Then he had received the phone message from Janet, asking for an appointment. He had not expected to see her again, at least not quite so soon, but her voice had been full of urgency on the telephone, and perhaps it was not only curiosity that had twisted his arm.

"Well, we met Peter outside the back entrance and he could see at once that Maggie was in serious trouble. By this time, there were police and an ambulance arriving at the front, and I realised that I could not even give him any real explanation. Maggie has completely withdrawn into herself and barely responded to Peter. To tell the truth, it was all we could do to get her into a taxi. Of course, Peter wanted to take her back to his place; he said being around Stan and

Ollie might help, (they are his cats by the way), but Jack had been very firm about taking her to ours, and besides I needed to be there if he phoned. I can tell you, that was the longest taxi ride I have ever taken. The more I thought about it, the more insane the whole thing seemed. Anyway, when we finally arrived, Peter and I put Maggie to bed in our room; there seemed little point in doing anything else just then, but we left the bedroom door ajar, in case she needed us. We talked about calling a doctor, but we both agreed we were probably the two best people to take care of her for the time being."

Janet lapses into silence. Bernard can see she is gathering herself to continue. He makes some noise of encouragement.

"Of course, there was so much going through my mind, I thought my head would explode. It seemed pretty clear to me that Jack had been involved with Maggie and then I remembered a time, he had begun to tell me about why he had left the church. I recall he mentioned an affair and I think he said something about a child, but I completely over-reacted to the fact he seemed to have told Jim about it first, before me, that is. I felt ashamed of myself enough at the time for my over-reaction, but it was much later I realised I had cut him off in the middle of something very important. I kept waiting for him to bring it up again, but he never did, and I decided that I had to respect that: I guess because I was battling so hard with my insecurity and did not want to force his confidence, and God knows my reaction had been enough to put him off."

Janet falls silent again.

"I remember that well enough." Bernard replies.

"Well, of course, I put two and two together and guessed that Jack had been the father of Maggie's baby. Thinking about it, he had probably been too ashamed to persist with his story, especially given my response. It does make a lot of sense of the way he was, Jack, I mean. But anyway, it seems the whole thing was true. Maggie's child *was* born with wings, and there is little doubt that the Vatican officials would have wanted to take its body away for their investigation, which would have entailed pretty extensive dissection, I imagine. So, Maggie did what she felt she had to do. Jack had gone by the time the baby died, but he had baptised it first. But I am getting ahead of myself.

We waited for hours to hear from Jack. Of course, I thought he would be home, once the ambulance had gone and he had spoken to the police, but then - then he phoned about three o'clock in the morning and said he was at the police station. He wanted to know that Maggie was safe and well, and then he said that he had been charged with manslaughter..." Janet struggles to continue.

"Manslaughter?" Even Bernard could not have anticipated this.

Janet sniffs.

"He told me he had confessed to it straight out. He had followed the Cardinal up onto the roof and there had been an altercation. They had got into a physical struggle, things got out of hand and he had pushed him over the edge in a moment of blind rage. But I didn't believe it was true, not for one moment. He asked me to go and visit him in the morning. He had not even asked for a lawyer. He had used his one phone-call to contact me."

Bernard suddenly understands the urgency of Janet's request to see him.

"Go on...".

"I went to see him first thing in the morning. Peter stayed with Maggie, she had managed to sleep during the night and when she awoke, she was distressed but was at least able to talk to us, though we were careful not to push too hard. She was even concerned about who would be at Peter's to feed Stan and Ollie, but Peter promised to ring a neighbour and ask them to pop around, as they have a spare key. Anyway, I was able to see Jack, as he had been charged so there would be no further interrogation.

This time he told me the truth. I told him outright that I did buy his original story and I suppose he felt he owed me that much. It seems that the Cardinal had come to some sort of conclusion that Maggie's child truly was some kind of genuine miracle and had sought her out to beg her forgiveness and blessings. Maggie, of course, had simply been terrified, as soon as she saw him, and had fled to the roof to get away from the man she had feared for so long.

The Cardinal had pursued her but had tripped and fallen from the roof. Jack had followed close behind him and saw it all. The Cardinal's death was just a terrible accident. By the time I got there, Jack had realised that it was his opportunity to atone for having deserted her in her time of greatest need. He is convinced that Maggie had no other choice but to do what she did. He had abandoned her to her fate, there was no one else there to support her and she could see no other option. He says that he left her purely because of his selfish desire to distance himself from his own transgressions. He is adamant that if he had only had the moral courage to stand by her then things might have worked out very differently."

"I don't quite understand. Atone how?"

"Jack believes that if he had simply claimed it had been an accident, there would have to have been a full inquest and police investigation, which may have resulted in a court case anyway. He truly believes that if it was known that Maggie had been present, the Press attention would have destroyed her, even if she was not under suspicion herself. Apparently, the public feeling against her back in Ireland was so strong, after what happened, that it was deemed a risk for her to return. And even if nobody else knows that Maggie had been there at the time, there is a real risk that a full inquest would bring to light the circumstances that brought The Cardinal to Southampton Row that night, and with it, Maggie's history. Once the press had got wind of it - well you can imagine the field day they would have had with that."

Janet shudders, the very thought of Maggie splashed all over the tabloid newspapers churns her stomach.

"So, he is giving himself up to save her. A kind of sacrifice, I suppose…" continues Janet.

"Is that feasible?"

"I believe so, yes. Since he has admitted to the charge, there is no further need for an investigation, and if he pleads guilty, then there will be no need for a public trial. It will all just follow course; he will appear in court tomorrow to make his plea, then later for sentencing and Maggie's name need never be mentioned.

Jack gave his reasons for arguing with The Cardinal as the festering of the same historic grievances which had led him to leave the church. It had not been personal; he was angry and had simply reacted to The Cardinal as a symbol of the Catholic Church's authority. He didn't go into it, but I suspect he did not have to search very deeply to find a point of contention that would fit the bill. There are plenty of priests of his generation who rail against outdated dogma and the Catholic Church's refusal to address its internal failing. I hardly think a Metropolitan Police Detective would be sufficiently well informed to question his reasons. Besides, there could be no obvious alternative explanation for him pursuing The Cardinal. The two of them had never met before.

In any case, Jack's story is that the Cardinal simply ducked out through the nearest fire exit to avoid a public confrontation. Jack simply followed him as he was not prepared to let him off the hook so easily. It seems a bit contrived, but why should he be making it up? The police are completely unaware that anyone else was on the roof that night. Jack made no mention of Maggie or me, or of the strange guy I saw, the one I had seen a few weeks back. I guess that bit was the gamble but the man seemed awfully anxious to disappear and Jack seemed to have read the situation correctly. But I will come back to that in a moment."

"And how do you feel about this version of the truth?"

"Well, I tried to make him see that it was a lie, but as Jack says, no one will accept the real truth anyway. They want to hear something they can understand. Besides, what is truth, but that which the powerful deem it to be? The Catholic Church deems Maggie's infant to be an abomination, then changes its mind and suddenly it is a genuine miracle. The psychiatrists deem Maggie to have been insane and the world treats her as such. You and I Bernard, we are no better. You see Maggie's so-called psychotic ideation that she gave birth to an angel as some manifestation of some intrapsychic conflict, and I, as a follower of that same doctrine, give credit to that rationalisation. And all this despite the fact the woman is sitting in front of me *telling me her truth. And I can feel how real it is for her.* So, you tell me! When is truth extricable from the narrative of some dominant authority? Whether we choose it or not?"

Janet's chest heaves with passion as she finishes speaking, her eyes blaze with a fearlessness Bernard has not seen before.

"Well, I would think one might have to be a little insane, simply to have done what she did," he offers somewhat meekly.

"Insane or just absolutely desperate, perhaps? Are the two states so very different, I wonder?"

Janet crosses her arms and looks him squarely in the eye.

My God, thinks Bernard, *she is magnificent. This is a woman who has finally come into her own.* And for a moment he feels like Pygmalion admiring his creation. He gives a concessionary grunt.

"And what about Maggie?"

"Maggie? Indeed. When I got back from the police station, I was, as you can imagine, rather upset. Maggie had rallied considerably, with Peter's help. Jack had not wanted me to tell her, but she is not stupid and demanded to know where he was and what was going on. When I explained it to her, she was insistent that she should go and tell the police what had really happened, but she was, I am sorry to say, in no fit state to do anything of the kind. She was still having flashbacks and all her old symptoms had come back. Besides, to be perfectly honest she had no reliable recall of what had actually happened, in any case. I think she may have slipped into a dissociative state at some point. She could certainly give us no clear account of how the Cardinal came to be that close to the edge of the roof, let alone how he had fallen, although I rather suspect that a part of her believes she is responsible. She is pretty unclear as to what went on, or whether Jack was present and has no memory what-so-ever of the tall dark man."

"Yes, and what of him?" Bernard cannot help himself but interrupt.

"Patience, Bernard, I am just coming to that. Well, in the end, Peter agreed he would at least take Maggie to visit Jack, (they had transferred him to Pentonville prison), but Jack refused point-blank to give permission, saying he did not want her name associated with his on any account. And that was that. Anyway, I went to visit Jack myself again yesterday and he told me it was all going to be okay. He had, it seems, had a visit from a Signor Vecellio, a representative of the Vatican, that very morning…"

"The tall dark man?"

"The very same. It turns out that he is a man of considerable authority within the Papal establishment. He knew precisely what had transpired on that rooftop, he was there, but he was more than happy with Jack's version of events. It seems The Vatican has an intense aversion to having its dirty washing laundered in public and is very eager to minimalize the publicity about the whole event, by having any legal proceedings expedited as quickly as possible. Vecellio had already used his position to pull some strings within the mainstream media to keep the whole story as low-profile as possible, although it had obviously not been possible to suppress the initial news report. But you may have noticed there has been no mention of it since then, which does make one think about just how far the Vatican's influence extends. At any rate, Vecellio said that he was authorised to give Jack his personal assurances that, so long as Jack stuck to his version of events, Maggie would never be troubled by him or anyone else from the Holy Roman Church again."

Janet halts to catch her breath. Bernard sighs, unable to decide which is the most shocking part of the story.

"And then?" he asks.

"Well, yes, that is not the last of it. Given Signor Vecellio's visit, Jack assured me that it was safe for Maggie to return to her own home, or to Peter's if she preferred. Maggie agreed to stay at Peter's, she was sorely missing those two little cats but wanted to pick up some clothes and personal things on the way.

They dropped in at her flat and found a large hand-delivered manila envelope waiting for her. It contained the results and report on some DNA testing of some samples which the Cardinal had provided from the Vatican archives.

It was impossible to make sense of the test results themselves, but the report concluded that the DNA in the feathers they had tested exactly matched the DNA in the sample of blood they had managed to extract from the stained bedsheet. At the same time, both sets of DNA were a 50% match for the DNA in a strand of hair, known to have come from Maggie, indicating that both belonged to an offspring of hers. The report went on to say that whilst the DNA in the feathers and blood was almost certainly human, it showed a number of unique markers that could neither be identified nor explained. Do you realise what that means Bernard?"

Bernard shakes his head. He is struggling. He is a man of science, a man of the Enlightenment. He shakes his head.

"Maggie's baby was not a hoax, nor did he have a congenital deformity. He had feathered wings. He was an angel. A bone fide angelic being."

"Hmm - well, I guess there might be another explanation," muses Bernard almost to himself.

"Well, there might be," agreed Janet. "And you know that ordinarily, I am as sceptical as you, but Cardinal Salvatore had come to beg Maggie's forgiveness and he went down on his knees in front of her, almost as if in an attitude of worship. And, according to Signor Vecellio, Miracles were The Cardinal's business."

Both sit in silence.

"I guess there really may be more things in Heaven and Earth," sighs Bernard eventually, "and how is Maggie now?"

Bernard is struck by the concern he feels for a woman he has never met, yet who seems so well known to him.

"She is getting there. Peter is taking her over to France. He is buying a place over there, for them to make into a home. He told me that the other thing waiting at her flat was a couple of messages from local Gallery owners. It seems Maggie made quite an impression, which of course is no surprise to anyone who had seen her work. So, who knows? She has such resilience - and if anyone deserves a happy ending, if you could even really call it that, it is Maggie."

"And what about you, and Jack, now I mean?"

"Well, you know me," with a wistful smile, "always have to go for the unavailable man, and it doesn't get much more unavailable than prison. If Jack has to do this, then I will wait for him and support him and I will be there for him when he is finally released. Jim and I have talked about it for hours. I can get a couple of lodgers in to help pay the mortgage and..."

"Jim?"

"You remember, Jack's best mate..."

"Oh, I remember. I don't recall you two being especially close though."

"Err, no. But - well, I misjudged him, I admit it. I was so jealous at the time, my bloody insecurity again. But this isn't about me; it isn't about Jack leaving me or choosing Maggie over me. It is about something Jack feels he has to do, to be the man he wants to be. I suppose you could even call it a kind of redemption. Wow, I guess I really have come a long way since we first met."

"But what if it does not work out the way Jack plans?"

"It will. I am completely sure of it."

"But how can you be? Where is the evidence that the courts will simply accept his version of events?"

"There isn't any. I have faith, and that is what faith is, isn't it? Certainty in the absence of any proof."

"I never heard you mention faith before."

"That's because I never *had* any before. I guess that is something Jack and Maggie have given me."

"*And me, why don't you come away with me?*" says Bernard, but the words are spoken only in his own head. Instead, he merely says;

"For once, I don't know what to say..."

Janet glances at her watch

"Then perhaps you had better say "time's up!"

She gets up and reaches out to shake his hand.

"Thank you so much for listening. Somehow, I just needed to tell you about it all. My life had seemed so bound up with Maggie's at times, and in the end, it really was."

Bernard nods and watches her leave. He feels suddenly old and tired and his heart feels strangely heavy in his chest. This time he has a feeling she will not be coming back.

Cadenza

Lorenzo Vecellio slips past the Vatican palace guard, almost as one invisible. His unique status affords him a freedom in Vatican City, few outside the highest-ranked Cardinals can boast. He moves around the great halls and corridors of the Vatican Palace as silent and stealthy as the very lynxes to which his masters owe their name. Outside Cardinal Salvatore's office apartments, he checks he is unobserved and lets himself in through the great wooden doors.

An air of dejection hangs around the great library, as though the age-old tomes themselves, temporarily orphaned, mourn their loss in papery silence. Vecellio, in some ways similarly bereft, stands a moment in respectful quietude. There will be a new occupant elected to this office in the fullness of time, but for the moment, he is his own master. It is a freedom he has never before known. It is a freedom he intends to put to good use.

He moves across to the great wooden desk and pauses. He listens out for any footsteps, but all is still. Vecellio looks at the drawers of the desk, then changes his mind and proceeds to the great bookshelf on the wall behind. He reaches up and lifts down a great leather-bound parchment ledger. The book is heavy with the weight of time and history. He carries it over to the desk and opens it where the silken book-marker divides the gilt-edged leaves. To the left, the page is crowded with ordered lines and columns of a hand-scribed inventory. The page on the right remains blank, awaiting further attention. Some of the entries have been drawn through with a single emphatic horizontal line, as though deleted, or like an account that has been settled. Many more, however, remain untouched.

Vecellio runs his finger down the column of the left-hand margin until he finds the entry he seeks. The smoothness of the parchment reminds him that it was once living animal skin. He shudders in offence. Vecellio is a rare thing amongst Italians- a vegetarian. Strange squeamishness in one of his calling, one might think, yet humans are nothing if not complex beings. He chews his lips in deliberation, then taking out his fountain pen scores a line across the page, adding a brief note in the end column, which he ensures is, like the scribble of a man of medicine, perfectly illegible. Content with his handiwork he blots the ink with the blotter from the Cardinal's desk, closes the ledger and returns it to its place on the shelf.

    He listens again. There is no movement in the adjoining rooms or hallways. He takes a skeleton key from his top jacket pocket and tries the lock of the desk's built-in filing cabinet. It readily gives way to his expertise. He opens the large bottom drawer, then cocks an ear. His sharp ears have detected the faint sound of distant footsteps in the ground-floor lobby. He waits until they die away completely, then lifts out a hinged-top wooden box and a manila file. The box bears a stencilled serial number, but no other mark of identity, save for the letters "NC" scrawled in red chalk on one side. Carefully opening the lid, he checks the contents. The samples of down, hair and bloodstained cotton sheeting lie just as the Cardinal had left them. Vecellio opens the file, and draws out the reports and photographs; photographs taken with his very own camera; photographs of the face he knows almost as well as his own by now. For a moment he allows his fingertips to linger over the glossy surface of the photographic paper. He sighs the softest of sighs. Then, gathering the contents of the file back together, he rolls them up, and securing them with a rubber band, places them inside the box on top of the feathers and sheeting. Next, he closes the box, and carefully rubs out the letter "N" with his thumb. Pausing with a soft grunt of satisfaction, he opens the smaller top desk drawer and rummages around until he finds a little stick of red sealing wax.

This time he tiptoes across to the office door, opens it to a crack and peers out into the corridor. He needs to be doubly certain and can take no chances. He is alone. He has picked his time well. He returns to the desk and looks at the box. Slipping his hand inside his double-breasted jacket, he takes out a ring. It is the ring of office worn by his late master. It had been his duty to ensure it was brought back from London and returned to the Holy Father, and he will return it to the Pontiff's private secretary very shortly. But first, he has one final task.

Pulling a cigarette lighter from his trouser pocket, he flicks on the flame and holds up the little stick of wax, watching with a kind of fascination as it softens and melts. Holding the stick above the box, he drips the red wax over the lid and side, then presses the ring into it, embossing the already congealing mass of gluey redness with the Cardinal's seal of authority.

Content with his labour, he returns the ring to his inside pocket, then tucks the box under his arm. Checking that all is as he found it, he returns to the bookcase, compresses a volume of Spinoza's letters and slips behind the hidden door that slides back in the adjoining mahogany wall panelling. The panel closes noiselessly behind him.

Outside in the corridor, a member of the housekeeping staff knocks discreetly on the office door. Receiving no reply, she steps inside. She has been asked to ensure that all is in readiness for the next incumbent. She scans the room, there is little to do. Cardinal Salvatore had been nothing if not neat and orderly. Terrifying, but tidy. She wanders over to the desk. She wrinkles her nose. There is a pungent odour of burning wax. On the desktop lies the little stick of sealing wax. She picks it up. It is still slightly warm and soft. She shakes her head, drops it back into the top drawer and exits the room, humming to herself, without a further thought.

Down in the Vatican vaults, Vecellio makes his way to the archives. Letting himself into its innermost recess, he looks around in wonder at the myriad wooden crates and chests that crowd the left-hand bank of shelves. There are containers of every shape and size, some ancient in appearance, others very new. Then he looks to the other side of him. The shelves here seem oddly bare. Most of the crates on this side seem old and ready to crumble to dust. All, on whatever side, bear the red seal of The Lynxes. Vecellio sighs and chews his lip. He takes the box from under his arm, stands on tip-toe and places it at the back of the top shelf on the right-hand side, almost out of sight.

He steps back and bowing his head, moves his hands over his chest in the sign of the cross. "May God forgive me," he whispers, almost in prayer. Then he pictures Margaret Doyle's lovely face and smiles, and somehow God's forgiveness does not seem so important, after all.

About the Author

Judith S Glover lives in Tasmania with her husband and three cats. She studied Fine Art and Philosophy and worked for many years in the U.K as a psychotherapist.

Also by this author

A Little Book of Tall Short Stories

And find more short stories in progress on Judith S Glover's website:

www.quirky-stories.com

Would you like to read more of Maggie's story?

To be released mid 2021

What cannot be cured: The Continuing Ballad of Maggie Doyle.

Four years have passed. Maggie has found happiness in Provence with Peter, but when tragedy strikes, she will need her friends around her, once more. But where is Roger and what is ailing him? And why is Lars, his lover, building a sculpture of a great pair of wings in Maggie's barn? Maggie may not want to know the answers.

Meanwhile Jack plans his future from prison, whilst Janet struggles with her loneliness. At home, her is lodger spying on her and ruffling some dangerous feathers in the process.

Maggie finds she needs another miracle to make things right, yet miracles bring their own troubles with terrible and unexpected consequences. Friendships will be tested and Love found in unusual places, for *what cannot be cured, must be endured.*